BATTLE SIGHT ZERO

Gerald Seymour

First published in Great Britain in 2019 by Hodder & Stoughton
An Hachette UK company

This paperback edition published in 2019

1

All characters in this publication are fictitious and any resemblance
to real persons, living or dead is purely coincidental.

A CIP catalogue record for this title is available from the British Library

Paperback ISBN 978 1 473 66353 4

Typeset in Plantin Light by Hewer Text UK Ltd, Edinburgh
Printed and bound in Great Britain by Clays Ltd, Elcograf S.p.A.

Hodder & Stoughton policy is to use papers that are natural, renewable and recyclable products and made from wood grown in sustainable forests. The logging and manufacturing processes are expected to conform to the environmental regulations of the country of origin.

Hodder & Stoughton Ltd
Carmelite House
50 Victoria Embankment
London EC4Y 0DZ

www.hodder.co.uk

For Gillian

PROLOGUE

February 1956

Near to the end of a ten-hour shift, his tiredness nagged and his concentration waned, and they kept coming towards him on the conveyer belt. Outside the factory more snow had fallen, another ten centimetres settling on the half-metre already on the ground. He was Josef, from the far south, drafted to the project at Izhevsk. His chance of returning to the warmth of his village overlooking the Black Sea was less than minimal. The heating had failed, although the factory was newly built, and he could not wear thick gloves for the work he did. His fingers were numbed, he needed to piss, and his stomach growled.

His hand was heavy as he reached out to lift it off the slow-moving supply line, and when the belt suddenly stopped, it was jerked up and his fingers had no grip, and it fell. And seemed to shriek.

Martial music had blared from the amplified speakers, a military choir singing the marching songs of the Red Army, to help him and the scores of others on the vast, stinking, echoing factory floor keep their composure and maintain their enthusiasm for their work. Now there was a broadcast from the sergeant who liked to call himself Misha, who told the story again – and again, and again – of how he had led the team that developed the thing that had moved towards Josef on the belt, then had slipped from his grip and fallen. The shriek was the bayonet lug catching the metal rim of Josef's work area. Then there was a clatter as the assault rifle hit the concrete floor by his boots, then a squeal.

Because he was at the end of the line, where assembly of the weapon was completed, Josef was not overlooked. The supervisor in charge of quality control, able, anywhere, to find fault, was lurking close to the area where they fastened the wooden stock to the body of the weapon. Misha's voice droned. Josef, and a thousand other men and women inside the huge factory were supposed to be enthused by the sergeant who had achieved such fame and had performed so valuable a service to the Motherland. Because Josef recognised propaganda, the diet of shit served up to them, he showed little enthusiasm for his work. He would never be recommended for advancement, nor for a transfer to the heat of the coast where his family came from. Home for him was a hastily built four-storey block, one of many erected within walking distance of the factory. They were near to a polluted lake, close to dark pine forests that ringed the complex and were now burdened with snow, and they were under the constant pall of dark smoke that simpered from the chimneys of the foundry where the iron was manufactured for the working parts. It was said that the rifles were revolutionary, a triumph of Soviet engineering, because of the practicality of the sergeant's design: 'complexity is simple, simplicity is difficult'.

After the shriek came the clatter and after the clatter came the squeal. By Josef's left boot lay a splinter of wood from the rifle's stock. It was varnished, barely dry, but it had left a jagged pale strip five centimetres in length, a half-centimetre wide and a little less deep. He bent and reached for the weapon and the torn-off piece of wood.

They had a joke: a woman works in a factory that makes steel-framed beds which are sent to the army, to universities, to hospitals. But she has no bed of her own. The factory operates on three shifts in every 24 hours. She and her fellow workers all sleep on the floor of their homes. Her sister comes to visit from Leningrad. The sister's advice: each day they should steal a piece from the production line, then, eventually, put all the pieces together, and build a bed. She replies they have tried that many times, brought the parts home and assembled them, then discovered that 'instead of having a bed we have an automatic Kalashnikov' . . . Always a grim smile from Josef's friends.

Josef's job was to check the basic mechanism of the weapon, carry out the procedure for arming it which was the equivalent of raising a round into the breech, then pulling the trigger. He had to activate the selection lever that dictated whether the weapon was on 'automatic' or 'semi-automatic', then it would move on down the line to the man who took it from the belt and dropped it, carelessly, into the crate. Forty for each crate. Josef pushed the splinter into the cavity, forced it with his thumb, spat on it to make it stick. He did not think the repair would be seen; it would hold fast as it went with the others into the box for shipment; if it were spotted, the bastard at the end of the line would likely call the supervisor and take pleasure from the reprimand given to Josef.

The sergeant was still talking. He was visiting Factory Number 74 of the Izhevsk Machine Engineering Plant, known to them all as IZMASH – secret, isolated and marked on no maps – because he was credited with designing the rifle. And had been rewarded. Josef and his wife lived humbly. No holidays, no luxuries and a damp apartment although it was only four years old. Mikhail Kalashnikov, or Misha, had been awarded 150,000 roubles four years before, which was precisely thirteen years of salary for Josef. Misha had been allowed to buy the first kitchen refrigerator to reach this outpost of manufacturing, and a vacuum cleaner, so that his wife did not have to risk dirtying her fur coat by sweeping floors. He would have driven to Number 74 that evening in his Pobeda car that would have cost 16,000 roubles to any of the few able to get their name on the waiting list, and he was now a deputy in the Supreme Soviet. Josef flushed with anger, and his heartbeat accelerated with jealousy.

Another one arrived. Armed, checked, trigger depressed. Then the selector moved down, then up, and passed on.

And another.

First it had been fewer than a hundred a day. Then it had been many hundreds. More clouds of choking smoke rose from the nearby chimneys. Now it was near to a thousand for each of the shifts. Over the loudspeakers, Sergeant Mikhail Kalashnikov spoke of his determination to design a rifle that could better defend the Motherland against the Fascist aggressors to the west. And spoke of the privilege of being in a hall, as large as the factory floor, and seeing the inspirational figure of their leader, Josef Stalin. Said that, soon, there would be more workshops, more lines and more belts. Then quiet, and only the throb of the generators and the soft whine of lathes and files and grinders. They were all supposed to applaud when the sergeant graced them with a visit, but on that occasion it was desultory. Josef could have shouted that it was said, at least was *rumoured*, that the design owed much to a considerable team of engineers, and in particular to the German prisoner from the war, Hugo Schmeisser,

And another came. The martial music returned. Josef had no car to take him home, no vacuum cleaner and no refrigerator, but his wife could always put butter and watery milk in a plastic box on the window sill. And another rifle was placed in the crate and the worker at the end of the line turned and shouted that it was now filled.

The top was placed on it, and an empty crate replaced it, fourth filled that day from his line. The top was stamped *7.62 Avtomat Kalashnikova obraztsa 1947 goda*. Josef worked on the belt that brought him the 7.62 Automatic Kalashnikov Model 1947, but had never handled one with an attached and filled magazine, had never armed one of them and raised it to his shoulder and peered down the length of the barrel with the range of it set at Battle Sight Zero, had never pulled the trigger, and probably never would. The filled box was screwed down, fastened tight, levered on to a trolley, and wheeled away. No ceremony, no trumpets, and no celebration yelled over the speakers. He assumed that the splinter of wood from the stock would now be wedged in place and held there by the weight of the weapons stacked above and beside it. It might stay in place until the crate was jemmied open and the rifles allocated to an armoury, or it might detach during its journey. When Josef and his trusted few did not tell jokes, they grunted sour complaints out of the side of their mouth: the Motherland could not produce decent toilets or safe elevators or quality cameras, could not grow wheat or potatoes that would flourish, could not turn out toothpaste without a foul taste, but could make – it was said – a rifle. A brilliant rifle, it was claimed, the best.

He heard the rumble of a door being pushed open and felt the blast of frozen air tunnel through the gap. The box would be lifted by four men and heaved on to a lorry's flatbed. He could do the work required of him if he dreamed, bowed with tiredness, cold. He could perform his tasks and could imagine. He was permitted to imagine because the supervisors and the commissars, always close, listening for subversion, could not read words that he imagined or see what he saw . . . The crate was on the lorry.

Josef imagined . . . The rifle came out from the crate, was stored, then issued to a shivering conscript. An officer, a veteran of the Leningrad siege or the victory at Kursk or the advance into Berlin, would see the damage to the wooden stock and would beat the kid, thrash him for carelessness. And imagined . . . The rifle was buried in permafrost ground, or in sand or in the jungles of the east, or was doused in sea water, and was retrieved and would still operate. Would never degrade or be destroyed, would live for ever, and would kill for ever. And imagined . . . Production increased, the belt going faster until it raced, covered with a squirming oily mess of rifles that were spewed out of a machine that could not be slowed, more and more; great underground bunkers filled to overflowing with them, thousands and tens of thousands and hundreds of thousands, and millions and tens of millions and all the same and all deadly. It was boasted that the simplicity of its design made it a suitable weapon for conscript troops, many with poor education. That children – like the ones at the schools in Izhvesk – would easily learn to handle it, and fire it and kill with it. And imagined . . . Rows of graves stretching further than those at the Piskaryovskoye military cemetery in Leningrad or the Rossoschka military cemetery outside Stalingrad, in the steppes. Stones and posts and mounds of earth and swarms of flies and packs of hunting dogs looking for food. It could be that each year, every year, a quarter of a million people – men and women and children – would lose their lives after being hit by the bullet fired from such a rifle. And imagined . . . the end of the day's work. Not a special day, not exceptional, different from the one before or the one after, when he stood almost at the end of the production line and checked another of them, the AK-47. And imagined . . .

The hooter went. A noise like a beast in pain. Work stopped. Men and women did not finish their tasks, tidy what was in front of them, make good what they had started. The line ground to a halt. Pieces were abandoned, left until the next morning when the factory would again come to life and the music start up. The rifle parts would stay there, untouched. The heating went off and all but skeleton lighting was doused. The trigger, the hammer, the magazine catch, the bayonet lug, the muzzle compensator, the operating rod, and the bolt and firing pin. They would stay where they were all night. The place emptied.

The lorry had gone. Josef walked through the low pall of cigarette smoke that the loaders had left behind them, huddled against the drive of the weather, and imagined his supper: a bit of bacon, with cabbage, and perhaps a glass of weak beer – not as good as Sergeant Mikhail Kalashnikov would enjoy – and the radio, and a magazine that highlighted football. It had seemed important to him that he had dropped a weapon, that it had shrieked – the cry of a whore in pain, he had briefly thought – and a piece of the stock had broken clear. And that particular weapon, with its individual serial number, and the scar on the stock close to where it would nestle on a soldier's cheek, now moved at slow speed on an ice-covered road, out of Josef's life.

I

'You all right, Andy?'

'I'm fine, doing well.'

'Have a good day.'

'Why not?'

A smirk on the face of the security guard at the yard's gate. 'Anything decent at the end of it?'

'Decent enough for what I need.' A smile and a wave, and a little whack on the horn, and Andy manoeuvred the big flatbed out and on to the main drag. He had the radio turned on, not obtrusive, but loud enough to pick up traffic reports for his route.

He set his concentration on the road ahead and the cars and vans and lorries around him and kept up the necessary checks for cyclists. Not a good morning to be shifting close to 40 tonnes in and out of hazards. It had rained in the night, and had been drizzling since he had crawled out of his bed, still dark outside and the only light from the street lamps, outside the bedsit's window. He'd showered, tepid water because the landlord was a creep and exploited his tenants, keeping the temperature low. Glanced at a text that had come on his phone. Grabbed a couple of slices of toast, smeared jam and wolfed them, and sluiced down a mug of instant coffee. He dressed for work: no comfort and no style, needed neither to put a lorry with its load on to the road and guide it across the western outskirts of Manchester. He would end up between Chadderton and Milnrow at a site waiting for him. His wipers worked well and cleaned the windscreen of the filth that came up from the tyres ahead.

He would have appeared to anyone who looked up from their own vehicles – as he sat high in his cab – an ordinary young man.

Difficult to pick out anything in his appearance that made him stand out. Narrow shoulders under his lightweight company anorak, no tattoos on his neck, anyway none that showed above the collar; might have needed a haircut by next week or the one after. He wore a pair of tinted glasses, obstructing his eyes, as he intended.

He drove carefully because – as he would have told the security man at the yard gate – there were some right idiots about at that time in the morning. The lorry cab had been faultlessly clean when he had taken it from the depot, near Oldham, and driven it to the yard where the team had loaded him up with the clean timber A-frames that he would drive to the building site. But, already the doors and hubs of the cab were covered in a layer of wet slime, a skim of dirt.

He told people what they wanted to hear, some of it true and some of it pretend . . . he was good at that. The security guard on the yard gate would have wanted to know. He was fine, he was good, and he'd have a decent enough day. Men, in his experience, liked to know that all was well with the world, and things negative would nag at them and lie heavier in the memory, but if life was liveable then a few quips would easily pass out of the memory chain. He aimed to make the fewest waves . . . and, yes, not a lie, at the end of the day there *was* something 'decent enough for what I need'. A girl. Unseen of course, sitting behind his wheel and steering the beast towards Shaw, in the direction of Milnrow, but a short sharp snap of a smile slid across his mouth. He would meet his girl that evening. He could think of her, not for long and not putting detail on the outlines because there were too many cyclists and motorbikes and general road users around him, and the buses would not give ground unless it were forced on them . . . There had been talk on the radio that it would rain pretty much through the day, then when the light fell the temperature could drop – might even be a sprinkling of snow on the road by the evening. He could look forward to it, seeing the girl, allowed himself only a moment of dreaming, a quick glimpse of her face, and that serious frown she usually wore, and the almond of her eyes, and . . . A supermarket delivery truck came across him and he backed off and gave it space and did not blast his horn or wind down his window and bawl. He liked seeing the girl.

It was one of Andy's qualities that he could compartmentalise what was important in his life. The girl had had a moment, and the man on the yard gate, and the team who had driven the fork-lifts and loaded his flatbed, and so would the men and women on the site out towards Milnrow who were building three-bedroom and two-bedroom houses, and one-bedroom maisonettes. There were one or two individuals who had an understanding of who he was, but more people were awarded the box in which they could sit, stand or stare, and as long as folks were happy to stay inside their compartments, then all was well: which was what Andy attempted to achieve.

School kids were streaming across roads and waving down buses, and a crowd of mostly women was spilling in front of him to get into a bread-making factory before their shifts started and, farther back, the works that made privacy blinds was sucking in its employees, and farther along there would be delays in front of the place that turned out garden furniture. He was Andy Knight. He had been Andy Knight last week, last month and most of last year. It was the name he was currently locked into. He was Andy Knight to his landlord and to the management at the depot, and he was Andy Knight to the girl he'd be meeting at the finish of the working day: later than expected. That had been the text message: *Hi A, looking forward to tonite, but am delayed, Make it 9 at the Hall, Zed xx*. He'd be there. A name was always a problem, the present one and the past one and the one before that. Each name had a history that had to be kept behind a necessary firewall. With anyone he met, he took as much care, exercised the same concentration, as when he was propelling the lorry down the road towards the site.

She was a pleasant girl, and almost pretty. She did not hold his hand when they walked together, but she'd tuck her wrist in his elbow, rather formal, and walked well, with a natural swing. But too often, she wore a frown on her forehead, just below where her hair was dragged back over her scalp. He had known her for three months. She was young and seemed immature, innocent and intelligent, and he was – so the ticked boxes said – older than her, and drove a lorry for a living and wafted building supplies round the city. Chalk and cheese, he thought he might have been the first boyfriend she'd had – if that's what he was, her boyfriend.

He flashed his headlights. A couple of guys in high visibility vests, and with plastic helmets askew on their skulls, were manhandling a makeshift gate aside and then waving him in. A big building site was taking shape in a sea of mud. This was Andy's first load of the day, and there would be three more before he ran short of hours.

'Hi, Andy, how you doing?'

'Doing fine, doing good.'

'Hold-ups getting over here?'

'Piece of cake – thanks, guys.'

It was what people wanted, a bit of cheerfulness; that way he was noticed but quickly forgotten, and the compartments stayed in place and he could remember more easily who he was. And in the evening he would be with the girl. A pretty normal sort of day was ahead, as normal as any.

Most of the night they had taken it in turns to yell at him.

Sometimes they'd started up the chain-saw and revved the engine and brought it close to his face so that he would have seen the power of the racing chain and smelled the stale two-stroke going through its engine – and they'd yelled some more.

The boy on the chair would have seen all the kit they had collected for the session, anything that might be of use in interrogation. Apart from the chain-saw there were pliers with which his nails could have been extracted, a Stanley knife that was not there to slice linoleum, and lengths of wire with clips on them that would have been marketed to jump-start power into any flat battery, and there was a baseball bat. They would have imagined that the boy, faced with such an array of weapons, would have quickly given every indication he wished to speak, tell what truths he knew. The boy was attached with masking tape to a heavy wooden chair.

More tape was wound tightly across his mouth, and he was nominally blindfolded but the material had slipped enough for him to see the implements they had. The place where they held the boy was carefully erected. He was inside a tent of transparent heavy-duty plastic which also covered the flooring. He could not speak so could not have answered any of the yelled questions but he had been told at the start of the questioning that all he had to do was nod, and then the tape covering his lips would have been torn clear.

They had yelled at him, they had started up the chain-saw, had thrust the plug of the cables into a socket, and had smacked the baseball bat into the flooring, but the boy's head had stayed obstinately down, his chin on his chest.

Now, the three of them were uncertain how to go forward. It was past dawn. The traffic beyond the old warehouse was heavy. Rain dripped through a long broken skylight . . . One of them frequently checked his watch as if the passing of time were a lame enough excuse for the failure of his night's work . . . They were certain of his guilt but did not know what target he was launched against nor to whom he reported. The boy was an informer, sent to infiltrate them. They should have handed him over to older men, who'd have claimed greater practical experience, then stood aside and seen their fledgling independence snatched. The boy stank because his bowels had burst and dark stains marked his groin, and earlier in the night steam had risen from his trousers, and they had thought that amusing. But now day had arrived and they were unsure what to do . . . They had a microphone ready, plugged into a tape recorder, and if there was a full confession then the salient parts would be held.

What did he know?

The three stood away from the wall of plastic sheeting and tried rationally to go back over the brief history of the boy as they knew it: where he had come from in Savile Town, who he would have known at school at the big mosque, who his parents would have been friendly with or related to. Since he had pushed himself close to them, where had he been and what opportunity to overhear a call, and who he might have noticed them with, and what did he know of the girl? They argued, were confused, tired enough for logic to fail them, and increasingly frustrated that the boy had failed to submit to the questions.

Perhaps, all three concluded, they had shown too great a degree of squeamishness. Should have taken off limbs with the chain-saw, sliced off fingers with the Stanley knife, and made the clips live on the charger. Of course, once they had what they wished for – the boy's confession – they would kill him. Not a point of debate. Maybe hang him, maybe drown him.

All three were hungry, and all three wanted coffee, and all three knew they needed to sanitise the interrogation area. Too much time already wasted.

One had the knife and another had the pliers and a third dragged at the firing cord on the chain-saw . . . He probably did not know the name of the girl, nor her use, probably did know *their* names and the broad-brush strokes of the conspiracy, probably did know that each of them faced – on the informer's word – a minimum sentence of twenty years.

All three were advancing on the plastic sheeting, and all were yelling their questions and the chain-saw's engine rumbled to life, coughed, then ran smooth. They expected to see him flinch, as he had done previously, and try to flail with his legs and to writhe in the chair, but he did not. His face had achieved the quality of an old candle, without lustre, and the eyes above the drooping blindfold were wide but did not blink, and the head lolled unmoving on the chest where no breath stirred.

One of them called out, 'Fuck . . . fuck, he's dead.'

August 1956

The closed fist of the sergeant's hand, from a short swing, belted the conscript's ear.

It was not a slap, but it was intended to create fear, and humiliation, and pain.

The senior non-commissioned officers of that unit of mechanised infantry rarely failed in their prioritised aims. They needed, constantly, to dominate the youths who were shipped into the ranks – no understanding of discipline – if they were to build companies and battalions and brigades capable of advancing in support of the tanks and through a chaos of smoke and explosions, and the screams of the wounded, and incoming fire. This particular sergeant who had been at the Leningrad battle and also on the final push down the length of the Unter den Linden and the approach to the Reichstag in Berlin, was regarded as a martinet for inflicting hurt.

The conscript crumpled.

They were on a parade ground at a barracks on the outskirts of a town almost at a direct central point in Ukrainian territory. The conscript had never heard of Pervomaisk astride the Pivdennyi Buh river before the train had brought him here from the east, crushed in a stifling cattle-truck, and had dumped him along with hundreds of other teenage soldiers. From the rough concrete of the parade area they would go on to a flat expanse of open field where crops were growing, and there they would simulate warfare, and they were supposed to use live ammunition. In the distance, in front of them, were plumes of smoke from the tanks as their engines started up and belched out fumes. Although the conscript reeled from the ferocity of the blow, he clung to his rifle. They had been taught from the first day of arriving at the barracks and being issued with a personal weapon that they must guard it with their lives, that it was a betrayal of the Motherland to lose it, treason to throw it away in combat, that it must be cherished and safeguarded. Amongst a welter of force-fed information, was the importance of remembering the serial number stamped on to the pressed steel body of the weapon. They could ignore the first three digits but had to recall the next three, 260, and then shout out the final five, 16751. Each was different, but the conscript knew his, what was personal to him. In a sprawled hand, barely legible, he had written his name, as best as he was able, next to that number, had taken the rifle. They had been taught to clean them, to strip and then reassemble them, to load a magazine, fast, into the slot underneath. He had been surprised at how quickly he had mastered these basic skills, and the use of the fore-sight and rear-sight and the elevation that was set for them at a minimum range: what the instructor called Battle Sight Zero. Along with the other youths, the conscript had worked hard on his rifle, had felt a sense of pride that such a piece of complex machinery had been issued to him. They had slapped and stamped through formal drill, and the sergeant had yelled at them. The conscript was in the front rank. With some confidence, as the drill required, he had slapped the rifle's wooden stock with his right hand and done it so that the sound echoed away into the air, had done it smartly, as had scores of others. The sergeant had approached him, then had hit him.

The sliver of wood lay in front of him. He bent towards it, the rifle supporting him so that he did not have to kneel. Had he done so he knew it was likely that he'd have been kicked in the stomach or the chest or the head, by the sergeant's polished boots. He pushed himself upright, then tried to straighten his back. He was accused of an act of vandalism, something that was on the 'fucking edge' of sabotage. He had damaged the rifle given him by the state. It was there to see . . . the piece of wood was five or six centimetres long and there was a raw mark on the stock where it had been. He tried to recall each moment that the rifle had been in his possession since being allocated it in the armoury. He could not remember any moment when he had dropped it, banged it, collided with anything while holding it. Probably it was because the blood had spurted in his face – from embarrassment, from shame, from the blows inflicted on him – that, giving it no thought, the conscript attempted to mitigate his guilt. It was a stammered denial of any guilt.

The sunlight caught the wood on the dull concrete, highlighting the groove from which it had fallen. He heard a tittering around him, alongside and behind. He had done nothing to break the stock of the weapon. The conscript was not yet old enough, experienced in the ways of the army systems, to appreciate that avoiding blame would seldom be successful, but he tried. He had done nothing. His voice was shrill. None of the teenagers who shared the barracks hut with him were prepared to pipe up, in a barely broken voice, that they were 'pretty certain, almost sure' that he had not done the damage, and that the fault must have been in the consignment. Nobody supported him, but he said it: not his fault, but somebody else's.

He was hit again, and harder. He went down. Was hit again, but had time to squirm away as the sergeant's boot was drawn back – and there was an officer's voice in the distance. They were called to attention. He stood, brushed the dirt off the front of his uniform and from his knees. The sergeant strode briskly towards the officer, and the conscript was forgotten. He reached out with his own boot and slashed a kick at the splinter from the stock, and caught it hard enough to break it, then stamped on the two pieces. He spat into the cavity, wiped his tunic sleeve across the wet, and was satisfied that the mark was less obvious. He hated the rifle, designated AK-47, *Avtomat Kalashnikova*, its last five digits of the serial 16751, with the magazine attached to its slot and filled with 7.62 x 39 grain ammunition. Hated it.

They marched off the parade area and into the maize fields and were told to run, and jogged in new attack formations through the sun-blessed crops, and the tanks ahead were beginning to roll forward and there was smoke, and flares arced in the sky, and quite soon the crackle of gunfire surrounded the conscript. He hated his rifle for the beating he had taken from the sergeant, but felt the power of the beast when it thudded against his shoulder, the scar on the stock against his cheek, pricking the skin and making his face bleed.

He charged, as they all did, and felt now that he was indestructible because of the weapon in his fist, hated it, but realised its power, and ran and felt no exhaustion and chased after the tanks. But hated it because of what had been done to him – and had never before felt hatred so strong.

The girl was the last off the train.

She looked around her, scanning for faces that she might recognise, or those of anyone who might indicate they knew her. It was dusk and the rain spat and none of the other passengers getting off at the small station of Dewsbury hung around. The line was the main link between what politicians, local and far away in London, liked to call the 'twin powerhouses of the north' Manchester and Leeds. This halt was east of the Pennine spine of hills and wilderness. Its industries had curled over and died, and anyone anxious for work and a distant promise of prosperity took the train out each morning and came back each evening. The girl was a student, second year Social Sciences at Manchester Metropolitan University. She allowed the platform to clear, the passengers either using the exit on that side of the twin tracks or taking the lift up to the bridge that crossed over to the main part of the station, where she was heading and where there were female toilets. This was her home town; she had come for a fleeting visit to her parents. She had been careful on the train, had seen nobody familiar, was satisfied that she was not recognised on the platform. The train had left, the platform was empty, and the lift returned for her alone. She wore jeans with regulation frayed tears at the knees and with the colour washed out of the thighs, and light-weight trainers, and a sweater hanging loose over a T-shirt and an anorak that enveloped her, and her hair straggled out from under a toggle hat. Slung on one shoulder was a rucksack. In the privacy of the lift, she ran her tongue hard over her lips, worked it hard enough to remove most of the thin trace of lipstick. She was 'Zed' to her boyfriend, Zeinab to her tutors and to her parents, and was in her 23rd year. There was a sort of deal: she came home regularly and, in return, her mother and father, her uncles and aunts and her cousins, did not come over the moorland to Manchester to visit her. They did not and would not know of the new life enveloping her when she was away from the rigid, devout, disciplined life in the quarter of Dewsbury where she had been reared. She went into the toilet, took a cubicle, locked herself inside.

Her jeans and trainers and sweater and T-shirt came off, and she barely took the time to feel the cold: one stifled shiver only. She opened the rucksack, and took out a black *jilbab*, heaved it up over her head, wriggled her arms into it, and felt it slide down over her skin, and the cold seemed to snatch her again. All that she had discarded was screwed up and stuffed into the bottom of the rucksack. The outer door opened. A woman coughed, announcing her arrival. Next on was the *niqab*. She flushed the toilet and checked the floor, hoisted the rucksack, and unlocked the door. A white-skinned woman with bottle-blonde hair and a rolling stomach and tight multi-coloured trousers gave her a look of withering contempt, and the mutual contempt she felt for this sad creature was hidden because only her eyes could be seen through the *niqab*'s eye slit. Even if provoked, the girl would not have risen to a challenge. It had been drilled into her by those who now shaped her life that she should not indulge the temptation to retaliate. She ducked her head, a servile gesture, and left the toilet, walked across the platform, gave her ticket to the machine, and went out into the dark.

She was from the Savile Town district, lived in the shadow of the Merkazi mosque, was a former pupil of the Madni Muslim High School for Girls on Scarborough Street, and her father made a minimal living doing car repairs – increasingly hard with the new electronic functions – and her mother stayed at home and had few relations and fewer friends. Zeinab was their only child, had been pushed by her teachers as a possible university entrant (the school benefited from such an accolade) and others, also, had urged that route on her. She went down the hill into the town and past the Poundland Store and the businesses offering Big Discounts, and the lights blazed to welcome late shoppers.

Near to the bus station, in a shadowed street where the boys usually met her and where there were no elevated cameras, she would wait for them. Always, when she came back to the town and knew they would be in the car and there to meet her, she felt a cold chill on her skin, whatever clothing she wore, not fear but excitement, and she would know that the blood coursed in her veins. She lived a lie, and relished it . . . and later would be back in Manchester and with the boyfriend, and to herself, and soundlessly, she chuckled, the noise from her throat swallowed by the material drawn tight across her face. She was always early; the boys said it was a crime to be late for a meeting they had fixed. She was satisfied with her precautions, what the boys called 'tradecraft'; they lectured her that danger was always close by, that around all of them was extreme threat. She waited.

'Have you done him before?' He had asked her the same question eighteen minutes earlier and fifteen minutes before that.

She gave him the same answer. 'I've not done him before.'

'So, we don't know whether he's a punctual little creature.'

Both were from the North West Counter Terrorist Unit. Both were detective constables and both would have said there were better things to be done at the desk screens where they worked in the city of Manchester than being parked up in a place used by bird-watchers and dog-walkers in daylight, and assorted perverts after dark.

'No, don't know.'

'He's an hour late.'

They were out of the city towards Greenfield, just short of the moor at Saddleworth. Both were well beyond the first flushes of enthusiasm, both would have said that experience had taught them when a rendezvous would not be kept.

'Don't want to labour it, but I can read the time.'

'He's late and I'm not happy sat here.'

They had been half an hour early, and they had sat in the car, kept the engine ticking over and the windows were misted; he had left the car once to head off to a corner to piss, and she had been out twice to steal a cigarette. The CHIS had stood them up. Not that they knew much about him. This particular Covert Human Intelligence Source was newly recruited and not yet bedded down into the system. He should have been at a meeting point the previous evening farther south on the Glossop road where there was a late evening coffee and snack truck, but had not shown and they were tasked for the fall-back option, this car park out by Saddleworth. They had been told that he'd come in an old blue Vauxhall saloon, and they'd waited, had waited some more, and each had risen in their seats when a vehicle had turned into the car park. A guy had come with three plastic bags of stripped off wallpaper that he dumped by a filled bin; another had pulled in and eaten a sandwich and drank from a thermos and then taken ten minutes' doze. Two men together, in the unmarked police car, would have stood out, but the man and the woman would have seemed just like any other couple and there for a few minutes of squeeze on the way home from the office. It went unsaid, but was mutual between them: it was a rotten old life being a 'CHIS' and on the books of NWCTU: Christmas came round rarely and a goody bag was hard to come by, and likely also that the individuals they targeted would not take well to the intrusion. Enough, for these two detectives, to feel a frisson of anxiety for the wellbeing of the source.

'Time to call it?'

'Call it a day, yes. We'll catch the traffic all the way back . . . expect he'll get a serious bollocking whoever sees him next.'

'Yes, a serious one.'

She drove. He reported in . . . Twice an informant had failed to show.

They did it turn and turn about at that time in the afternoon. Their office was in the London district of Vauxhall, not on the river but close to it. The building was off a narrow street and hemmed in by offices and yards. There was the civilisation of one public house and not much else. It was an address that a stranger would have needed exact directions for, or would have had no chance of finding it. Discreet, sensibly located. It had been Gough's duty to slip out to the nearest café, old fashioned and treasured, to collect two beakers of tea, his with sugar but not hers, and excessively large slices – that day – of carrot cake. The cake and the tea were an improvement to what came round on the trolley, and both would have indignantly claimed it was deserved because of the long hours they worked. Most in that office were there early at the start of a day, and would not shrug into coats and go out to face the evening until well after the streets had cleared of the conventional rush-hour. Gough had to do the full rigmarole of his ID at the outer door. Short cuts were not tolerated. Janice who sat there in a cubicle, and Baz who was perched behind her, had known Gough in excess of nineteen years, and had known his assistant – Pegs – for fifteen years, but they showed their ID and would not have taken a liberty ... Not actually ever mentioned, but Gough assumed that Baz wore a jacket every day, warm or cold and sometimes with a cooling fan and often with a two-bar heater, because it would better obscure a shoulder holster and a Glock 9mm. The security was necessary because of their work, all that messy sort of stuff that dealt with agents who needed handling and informants who needed comforting. The work area contained a few of the juniors at a central octagonal table at the centre of the first floor but off to the side were four cubicles with walls of misted glass.

Gough crossed the room, edged around the main table and chairs, was confronted with his own closed door and slopped some of the tea in contorting to open it, and went in, shutting the door with a kick from his heel. He could not have remembered which was his and which was hers but the counter staff had sussed him years back and the beaker with the inked tick would be for Pegs. He was a veteran, never used his rank, but was senior. Had he gone higher, he would have of necessity given up fieldwork, so he had stayed on the plateau. It would see him out, another two years or three ... But the threat was worse, had steadily racheted while he had been in the office off Wyvill Road. Worse now that the kids were drifting back from having their arses kicked in Syria and Iraq, and then there was the home-grown crowd who had not made it abroad and were looking to catch up, climb the ladder fast, do their bit for the cause. Gough would have said, deadpan and serious, that life in an anti-terror environment was only tolerable if there was a generous slice of carrot cake on offer in the late afternoon.

The office was shared with Pegs. She was not a serving policewoman but a civilian enhancer. She did logistics, ran a system, kept Gough and a few others where they needed to be, which was with information pouring out of their skulls and organisation wrapped tight round them. She had a phone wedged against her head, and was belting her keyboard. He would never interrupt when her face was screwed up and the breath came hissing from between her teeth. He put down the tea in front of her and had a small cardboard plate for her portion of carrot cake and the usual plastic knife. He went to his own place and shrugged out of his coat, shook it to get some of the rain off, slung it behind the door, and sat and waited. He would be told when she was good and ready. In Gough's experience very little that came down the phone lines, or that popped up on the screens, slotted into the 'good news' category. Most was right for the pigeon-hole of what he did not want to know, but would have to. He began to nibble at his cake. If it were not for Pegs running his office, and the relationship, then he might well have jacked the job and made things a little warmer with Clare and gone down to the south coast, and hit a golf ball and walked a dog.

She said, 'It's not Armageddon, but it's not nice.'

They called him Tommy when they talked among themselves. Most of the CHIS people had a CHIS name. He was T for Tommy, Tommy Ahmed, and was a new recruit, and had seemed keen, and committed; some were there for the long haul and some were short-term expedient, and it would have been rare indeed for Gough to have said into which box Tommy was squashed.

'What is not nice?' asked Gough, eating his cake.

'Should have been a meeting yesterday, with the locals, but didn't show. Simple enough, then they went for the secondary process, and he didn't show for that either. He's skipped two schedules. No trace on his phone. That's where we are.'

He went on with his cake, and she started hers. Could, of course, be that little Tommy had suffered a puncture, and then another, and in between had switched off his phone, and lost it, or could be something different. They both remarked that the carrot cake was good, and said nothing about an informant gone missing, and where the poor beggar might be, and the implications.

Clean jeans, and a clean shirt, and a brush run over his hair. A glance in the mirror. A grin from Andy Knight. Looked good enough.

He checked his wallet, was satisfied he had sufficient cash, not too much.

It had been a hard day, and the roof spars were all in place on the site, and he was tasked with different deliveries the next morning: pallet loads of concrete building blocks were going across to another quarter of the city. Nothing about his work was particularly varied, day in and day out, but others would have said work was hard enough to find that paid above the minimum, and he never complained or grumbled, in company, but kept the basics of cheerfulness clamped in place.

He looked around him, shrugged. The same as every day and every night since he had moved into the bedsit. It was sparsely furnished: what the landlord would have been able to flog as 'furnished' but without frills. It would have been expected that a tenant would bring with him the keepsakes and mementoes and pictures and ornaments that anyone collected, the debris of life. Andy had not brought such baggage with him, had come only with a sack, and a basic clock radio, and his one book had been a bound street map of the city of Manchester with environs. He had not taken the girlfriend through the front door, and up the staircase that led to the bedsit on the first floor. He had not brought her here, nor had he tried to. The room might have confused her . . . it represented nothing, was as anonymous as a hotel of boxrooms beside a busy rail terminal where men and women did their sleeping, cared not a fig for decoration or anything sparking homeliness. No pictures on the walls, not even a fading print of a Lake District view, or a cheap Lowry reproduction. No fruit bowl in the middle of the table that served for eating meals from or writing out reports at and doing his time sheets. He washed up in a sink that was separate from the basin and small shower cubicle in another corner, and beside the sink there was no towel that might have given a clue of a previous holiday destination. The room seemed to show a conscious effort had been made to eradicate any history of the current occupant. Nothing about the room, to Andy, was strange; all was as intended.

He sat on the bed, hitched his feet up, and stretched himself out. He triggered the alarm on the clock radio, had enough time to sleep, at least a doze. It was a part of Andy Knight's discipline that he took rest when the chance was offered it. He was tired from a long day and had another starting at dawn the next morning. He always reckoned that when he met someone who was outside his immediate circle of confidants – as Zed was – that rest helped to steel his focus.

He had not brought her here. He'd reckoned there had been a few evenings since they had met when her control might have dipped, and she might have come. He had not invited her, had not tugged at her wrist, had not played a trick and told her there was something back in his room that he wanted to show her. He thought that if he had pushed her, gone heavy, then he might have induced her to come through the front door, and held tight on her waist as he'd steered her up the stairs, but he had not tried to.

His eyes were closed. Always he needed to rest, and always he must hold the focus . . .

Car headlights flashed in the darkened street.

Zeinab was sheltered by a shop window overhang. In the last half hour the rain had switched from light drizzle to blustered snowflakes. She was dutiful. She had waited, had not cursed, had controlled her impatience. Some of the snow crusted on her shoulders. The light came on inside the car as a door was opened. She gazed right, left, made certain she was not watched, then hurried with a skipping step across the pavement and into the warmth of the car.

They talked and she listened. There was no apology for having left her to wait for their arrival in the street close to the bus station. She was not expected to contribute, but it was explained to her. The passenger, who was younger, talked most, and the driver chipped in with greater detail. It was what had been decided by the group they were part of: she had been chosen for a defining role. The talk was of fire power, of a strike that would seize the attention of the whole of the country. She heard the two voices;

one was wheezy from a chest cold and the other was shrill with excitement, and neither had a poet's language or a leader's call, but the message was clear. They drove down narrow streets, did not crawl and therefore attract attention, did not push at traffic lights. She had known that a time would come when they would want her, would value her . . . They had crossed the bridge over the Calder river and then up the long hill past Savile Town and at the top they had turned towards the Teaching Centre and then the old factory where blankets had been made when Dewsbury promised high employment and the immigrants had been rushed in from Pakistan and a new life had seemed rose-tinted. The factory was shut, the mines were closed, the quarries went unworked; a sullen anger had replaced the optimism, and the mood had changed. Where was the greatest anger? In the area to which this girl, Zeinab, had been recruited. It was about an attack and about a supply line . . . One voice was interspersed with hacked coughing and the other with brief moments of giggling as if stress were gripping him. The more they talked, the longer, and the farther, the car was driven, and she sensed a growing anxiety among them.

'Why me, why am I chosen for this?'

She was chosen because she was a clean skin.

'There are many who are not monitored. Why me?'

Because of who she was, what she was.

'Who am I, what am I?'

Their breath reeking of the scent of cooking spices, both spat back the answer: she was a woman. So few in the struggle were female. They did not look for women, the detectives in the North West and North East Counter Terrorist Unit. They looked for boys. She was not listed, was not under surveillance . . .

'And that is enough?'

And she had a friend, and the remark was left to hang.

A hesitation. 'I don't know whether he would . . .'

One said she should make him, and the other said that she should manipulate him. They came into the long street where her parents lived, where the small back bedroom was hers. The driver pulled over, and the two men whispered to each other. It was usual for them to contact her, and although she had been given what they called a dead letter drop address, it was to be used in extreme emergency, not as routine. To reach her they used occasional email links from internet shops, or there would be a folded piece of cigarette paper, covered in minute handwriting and fastened with an adhesive into a deep corner of a locker in the Students' Union: two keys, one for her. Street lamps lit a part of the road but they had chosen shadow. She was told to get out. It would be a five-minute walk to her home. She stood and the snow swirled close to her and she struggled to open her umbrella. Both of them were out. One took her arm and propelled her towards the car's rear. She sensed the change in their breathing. She was pushed. A zapper opened the boot, and a dull light came on inside.

She saw the face.

The light pierced the clear plastic that wrapped the head and it reflected back from the pallor of the skin which had no lustre to it, and the eyes stared wide open and the mouth gaped as if the final motion had been a gasp or a cry, and there were marks across the cheeks where sticky tape had been pulled off and a sparse moustache ripped away. Blood had run from the nose and the mouth and had congealed and there was bruising round the eyes. There was a stink, the same as when a dog had done its business on the pavement and she had stepped in it and it was on her shoe. Zeinab was sick. Never in her life had she been sick in a street. There was a neatly trimmed hedge separating a small garden from the pavement, and she vomited into it.

Did she know the face?

She retched phlegm from deep in her throat, and coughed and spat . . . She did not know the face. She was told he was an informer. She repeated that she did not know him. He was a police informer and had started recently to try to get close to the boys, had asked too much and too often, and had been questioned, and had been . . . and had died. He was an informer. She said again that she had not known him, not seen him.

And she was lectured in hissed whispers. She should understand that the death of an informer was inevitable. A betrayer, a traitor. An informer could not extricate himself with untruths. This was how an informer died. She heard them out. She supposed it was a warning. The boot was slammed shut. She was told where she would next see them, what response was expected from her, and for a moment, unexpectedly, the face of the boyfriend, the lorry driver, flickered in her memory. She walked away from them. All she knew of them were their code names: Krait and Scorpion. She heard the car start up, and the lights spun as it turned sharply in the width of the street. She went on down the sloping road and could see a light by the door of her home – her father would have switched it on as a welcome to her. She spat once more and cleared a little more of the taste of vomit from behind her teeth. For a moment she trembled, seemed to feel danger and weakness – spat again, then walked more briskly towards her home. There, nothing was known of her secondary life, with whom she mixed, and what she sought to achieve.

She rang the bell, and the lie Zeinab lived was total. She was brought inside and was hugged and saw the affection in the eyes of her mother and father, and their innocence, and she gave them no sympathy for her deceit. The eyes of the dead boy, wide but dulled, had been the worst of it. It was right that it should have happened to an informer.

A makeshift incinerator reeked of the last fumes of burned plastic. Crab stood at the door, sniffed, waved the beam of his torch. His driver and minder, Gary, held another torch and was a pace behind Crab.

He had been born Oswald Frith . . . He thought, what he could see in the torchlight, that the kids had done a decent enough job with the sanitising of the area. All of the plastic had been taken down, and all of the string lengths that had attached it to the frame untied and removed, and everything off the concrete flooring and that area swilled with bleach . . . Born Oswald Frith, aged twenty, and living in the shadow of the Old Trafford football stadium, and setting up his own minor protection business, just a few shops and a couple of pubs, starting to make a name for himself. He had fallen foul of a bigger man who reckoned to have that area tightly sewn, and had come with an iron angle bar to sort out the intruder on his patch. He'd done six month in hospital while surgeons had put together the bones in his right leg, had eventually been discharged, had limped away from the Wythenshawe wards and had gone to visit the man who had belted him with the bar. With his crab-like walk he had walked into the guy's house . . . The man did not walk again, crab-like or otherwise, and was buried a week later. Oswald Frith, because of his impediment, was from that day known as Crab. No evidence left behind, and the widow had been sensible and not testified, and the business had been seamlessly transferred. Crab liked to joke that, although reared near to Manchester United's stadium, the only season ticket he'd had was to Her Majesty's Prison, Strangeways, and most tended to laugh at his joke. He moved awkwardly and, in the winter, felt bad pain in the injured limb, but never winced and never complained. He was satisfied with what he saw. He liked to work with professional people, could not abide laziness or carelessness. The place, his building, seemed to have been well cleaned. The loaning of it had been facilitated through an old contact between one of his sons and these Asians, and they were friends after a year on the same landing in gaol. First there was an approach, the usual circuitous routes and an offer, and he had not turned his back on it but had dug into his own wad of associates, and had rather liked the taste of what was on offer . . . Then the request, only 48 hours previously, that a bit of floor space was needed. He did not know these new people, the Asians, but the little that had been run by him had seemed effective and planned with thoroughness. He had no complaint. The torch beams flickered over the flooring and up the walls and came down to rest on an old chair, heavy wood – could have been a half century since a joiner had put it together – and there were no stains, no signs of damage. And he liked the way it had been put to him, that these people – the Asians – had a powerful way of dealing with a tout, someone who snitched. He liked it to be robust because that way a message was passed and there'd be fewer volunteers for going up the same road. In the morning they'd have a second check to be certain that any traces were obliterated. The oil drum used as an incinerator still smouldered. Crab hobbled out, and Gary was close to his shoulder . . .

There had been a time in Manchester when the newspapers had referred to him – not by name – as a 'Mister Big' of the criminal underworld, and there had been cheap headlines at the expense of the mystery man, but no longer. He was choosy what he involved himself in, and with whom. Had not been inside prison for seventeen years, had no wish to renew the experience, but a deal had been offered him, and might lead beyond the boundaries of his comfort area. An attractive deal, and a chance to do business with an old friend, one of the best. He had never been into this sort of trade – could do rackets and girls and Class A stuff – never this. But the deal intrigued him. Crab could never resist an attractive deal, and never had been able to . . . and all in place, and all starting to run and the pace of it quickening. Was a sucker for it, a decent deal.

She had seemed withdrawn that evening, not at ease.

Until he had met her, Andy had never been in the company of an Asian girl, and especially one from a conservative Muslim upbringing. What he had learned of Zeinab was that she usually held herself in the shelter of reserve and seldom voiced any opinion remotely provocative, but could also muster up a degree of flirtatiousness. She could raise her eyebrows, pout a little, blink at him, even run a tongue over her lips, and do little quips of joshing with him, as if they understood each other well, and were close. Not often, but sometimes, and the relationship was now in its fourth month, and moved forward at a steady unremarkable pace, and intimacies were becoming more advanced. Neither seemed prepared to go on to a charge, though Andy had begun to think that the time approached when she would make a move, decisive, towards pushing them closer.

Not that evening. Was not going to happen as they shared a pizza in a place round the corner from her Hall of Residence. She was distracted. Not for Andy to pry. If she needed to cry, confess, unveil, he was available. They ate, and sipped cokes because she did not drink alcohol and he could do without, and would be driving in the morning. He thought she realised she was poor company . . . she had been late, the trains were fouled up and the timetable a car crash, and her mother and father unwilling to let her go and having neighbours call round to quiz her on life away as a student. Andy Knight had a good eye for reading people and reckoned her mood reflected more than a late train schedule and parents dragging out a brief visit. They had hardly spoken; he had given a short résumé on his day, trips from the depot to the materials yard, and then to the site where the houses were going up and the roof spars being hoisted off by crane, pretty boring, and where he was headed in the morning, and how many pallets of concrete blocks he'd be shifting. She had the chance, in his long pauses, to contribute, but hadn't. Sometimes they went to the cinema and there had been a couple of dates at small concerts, rhythm and blues, and they did pizzas and anything pasta based, and sometimes they just walked and window-shopped in the city centre. They had a bond, what had brought them together, but each treated it as something in the past. Usually she told him about her classes and what essay she was working on, and it was understood that she was on a university course and he was only a lorry driver. Andy allowed it, didn't set her right. Probably the best times between them were when they tramped the pavements, and sometimes she would nestle her head against his shoulder, and sometimes his arm was close round her waist and holding her there. Once she had been talking about the essay for next week and she had alluded to a problem in the construction of her response, and the solution had seemed clear enough to him but he had stayed quiet, not intruding into that part of her world. Andy Knight merely drove a lorry. Well mannered, yes, polite and correct. Her intellectual equal, no . . . Opposite him, toying with the pizza pieces, she had her head ducked, and seemed irritated when her hair – deep brown, almost black – slipped across her face, and her eyes stayed low. She had no make-up on. How should he respond? Question her or let it slide? Be concerned or be indifferent? He reached out, touched her hand. Normally she'd respond. Take his, squeeze it, then grimace, then lighten. She was burdened, and he recognised it. There would not be an argument. He would not challenge her, not burn boats.

Andy murmured to her, 'Tomorrow, Zed, whatever it is will be better. Always better on another day.'

'If you say so.'

'Yes, tomorrow is always better.'

She tried a ghost smile, made a poor job of it, then reached forward and took his hand, and pushed the fork out of it. Held his hand, fingers entwined. The look on her face was to indicate that she could not share, that he would not understand. A shrug, a tightening of the fingers, a couple of blinks like a mood needed changing. The life was back in her voice.

'What do you do for holidays, Andy?'

He grinned. 'Don't get a chance to think about that, not too much.'

'You have statutory holidays, of course you do.'

'Suppose so.'

'Doing what you do, it builds stress?'

'Just getting a lorry back and forward across town. Plenty have it worse.'

'We all need a holiday.'

'What, Zed, you needing a holiday? Term's another month, isn't it?'

The grip was firmer. He leaned forward, and allowed a finger to run across her lips and the movement dislodged a crumb, or a smear of cheese. A little gesture to loosen her. What she wanted to say was important to her, but he gave no sign of recognising that.

'They'd give you a holiday?'

Andy played dumb. 'Don't know, haven't put in for one.'

'If I asked you.'

'Asked me what?'

'Whether you could take a holiday?'

'I suppose, suppose I could try – but you can't. Term-time, not holidays.'

'I just wanted to know.'

'Whether I can take a holiday? I can find out.'

'Do that.'

'Would depend on what cover they need, for how long, what sort of time-frame.'

'You'd like that? A holiday, us?'

'I would, you and me, I'd like that . . . Should we take your mother along as well?'

She kicked him under the table, and was laughing. First time that evening. He thought that typified his value to her. He doubted anyone else would have made her face crack with an open grin. Then the giggle was in her throat, and she reached into her bag for her purse. Sometimes he paid, sometimes she did. It might have been her turn, might not. She took the bank note out and left it on the table, and stood. A kid came hurrying over, and the gesture was for him to keep the change. She asked it of him again, and he said he would. They stood and heaved on their coats and there was slush on the pavements where the wet snow had failed to get a grip. He always walked her back to the door of the Hall. She held his hand and twice she twisted her head and kissed him on the lips, which was good, encouraging. He thought she had had a bad day but that he'd made it better, softened it. At the door they kissed again. Most of the girls in the Hall, he assumed, did not regard it as a big deal if they led their guy inside and shoved him towards the lift. Andy would not push Zeinab, was happy enough to leave it at a gentle and long kiss in the shadows away to the side of the door, and he sensed she went further than was usual, and that her day had been difficult and had taken her to the edge.

They parted. She said something about her essay and hurried inside. He thought it had been a good evening, useful. At the lift door she turned and would have seen him still standing there, and gave him a little wave, which was the flirty bit. Andy blew a kiss back. The doors closed on her. Perhaps better than a useful evening.

2

A dull old life was a lorry driver's. Andy Knight had done two delivery runs of pallets loaded with concrete blocks, and he had refilled with fuel. He shared his time now between a mug of sugared coffee and a cloth with which he cleaned his mirrors. His phone pinged.

The company he worked for took pride in its appearance. It had a good name locally, and seemed to attract worthwhile contracts. The winter grit and dirt from the roads was hosed off the vehicles each dawn before the fleet went to work. There were no flaws on the paintwork. It was a tradition in the yard that its people were as well turned out as the cabs in which they spent their days. Andy wore laundered overalls and an anorak with the company logo on his chest, and was supposed to have a reasonable haircut, and to be cheerful and helpful towards customers ... not hard for him. To drive for this company was to have work that, putting it with a tinge of exaggeration, a 'guy would kill for'. If they had advertised his position then likely they'd have been deluged with applications. The vacancy had not gone on general release. Word had reached Andy, not his problem to consider the detail of it, that a job was going begging, might be worth applying for, like yesterday and not tomorrow, and he had slapped in his paperwork. At the interview he had not asked how his name might have reached them, and they had seemed uninterested in where he had worked before, but his clean licence was looked at closely, and the chief executive and the fleet manager had taken time to explain how the business ticked, what was expected. It was as if his pedigree was already established, or a guarantee given, and the important bit was when he was taken down from the office and given up to a hard-eyed little runt of a guy with a shaven head, and he had climbed up into a cab. It was the bit that might have mattered most . . . He had driven big lorries before, had always used his driving skill as an employment incentive when he had needed new work. There had been no banter or conversation. A satnav had been switched on for him, and a route marked out, and they were off, dragging a loaded trailer, for two and a half hours. They had gone beyond Ramsbottom, almost into Rawtenstall, and Andy had reckoned he had driven faultlessly, but he'd not been praised. The delivery had been made, prefabricated wall sections for community housing, and they'd taken tea and a sandwich on the site, then the satnav was switched off and he'd had to navigate his own route back. He had pulled into the yard and his escort had jumped out, not a backward glance, and had gone into the office. Must have been a clean bill of health because he'd kicked his heels for fifteen minutes, then been called inside. A secretary had brought in the contract and he had not read it but signed with a flourish . . . Always a difficult moment, and a fraction of a hesitation, long enough to consider who he was that day and month and year. He'd started the next week. Again, his phone chimed.

The remaining drivers, seven or eight of them, pretty much left Andy alone. Not quite suspicious, but wary. Could have been that they had picked up the signs, well telegraphed, that the newcomer was fast tracked in, without explanation. Not hostility, but caution. Most of them went together, with Veronica who ran the office, down to the Black Lion along the road on a Friday evening after the shifts finished and had a drink, not more than two, before heading home. Andy did not. A warm pub, a drink, the end of a week, and chat flowing was when histories were expected, anecdotes, experiences shared. Always an excuse made and he'd go home alone.

He checked his phone. *Hi, Did you run it at them, a break? Hope so. The Hall tonite, usual time xxx.* The slow smile slipped on to his face. That was Zed, the undergraduate studying Social Sciences, and with a string of good exam grades to her name, and not bothering to suggest that he might have something else on his mind that evening, and would pass her up. Taken for granted, but he was only a lorry driver: a sweet boy, fun to be with, and she in debt to him and big time, but not her equal. And the slow smile went wry, and he could remember her kissing the night before, and her enthusiasm. He went on polishing the mirrors until the view in them was without blemish, and he saw them. Saw them quite clearly, both IC4 on the ethnic register, and they made a poor fist of looking casual.

They were joined by the Somali lad who worked in the company canteen where they did the big breakfasts and the lunches, and kept up the supply of tea and coffee. The Somali boy was friendly enough, and seemed to wear a grin most times, and could not have been more helpful in tidying tables. Others said that his history – where he had been, what had happened to him, how he had escaped a civil war – was a terrifying story. The drivers liked him. There were two guys opposite the gate, on the far side of the road. The Somali boy greeted them, and there were hugs, and then conversations, and the boy was shown a phone screen. Might have been a photograph, reasonable assumption. Andy was finishing his mirrors and needn't have gone on but did so because it gave him the chance to stay where he was, face their way and have a purpose for it. The boy made a little gesture, not as anyone else would have noticed. Andy thought he was identified, a rule was run over him. Two guys there, at the gate, and looking to check out a friend – IC1 Caucasian male – of Zeinab, who was categorised as Identity Code IC4 Asian female. A meeting of cultures, young people stepping over a line, and their associates would want to know who he was and do an eyeball on him. He saw the Somali boy almost flinch as if he realised that he had gone too far, like a favour had been called in and pressure applied. The guys stayed watching him as he finished with the mirror. Predictable . . . could have been her cousins, or her neighbours, and there would be anxiety about any relationship that a girl from Dewsbury had formed with a lorry driver in the Manchester suburbs, or could have been other friends of hers, other associates. He thought they might have taken more pictures with their phones, and both stared across the width of the road and through the gate and past the security shed and into the yard . . . and were gone.

She'd kissed well the night before, not with much experience, but fresh, fruity. He replied to the text, said he'd be there when she wanted him. Why? He smiled his private smile, then, satisfied his vehicle was as well maintained as any of them, went to get his next delivery docket from the office.

It was wrapped carefully.

Two men did it. They did not concern themselves with dismantling it, had only detached the magazine. The overall length was a little short of a metre, and the weight of the package would be under five kilogrammes. There would be three magazines, each filled with 25 rounds, near to capacity. Although the two men, working in a warehouse on the southern outskirts of the port of Misrata, on the coast of Libya, had examined the weapon, had noted its age and the poor state of the woodwork, and the discoloration where paint had long since weathered off the metal, they fulfilled their instructions. It was only one weapon, and it came from a store that reached high inside the building's walls. Crates of the AK range, in every state of maintenance, awaiting sale.

They used layers of bubble-wrap plastic sheeting. In many places the weapon, and the magazines which were of the same vintage, had been dropped and chipped, were scraped with coarse scars, almost obliterating the stamped serial number of which only a part was visible – 16751 – but the men would do as they had been told because the alternative was unwelcome. They were dependent on the patronage of a warlord. Because the warlord smiled on them, they could put food on the table where the wives and children fed. If the warlord had thought his instructions were ignored then they might well be shot, and their wives would either starve or perhaps go to prostitution down by the docks. They wrapped it well. Last to slip from their sight was the battered wooden stock. That it had lasted so long, their estimate was 60 years, was extraordinary, and there were notches cut in a line, and one deep groove where grime and rot had set in and weakened it.

Around the bubble-wrap went adhesive tape, metres of it. In English, because they had been told that their native Arabic was not accepted, the younger and better educated of them wrote a single word: 'Tooth'. He knew that a tooth was in the jaw, was used to chew with, but why the package containing a vintage weapon such as the AK-47 should have that written on it he had no idea.

Outside, two pick-ups waited. Neither of the men had actually fired the rifle. It had to be assumed that it would function satisfactorily. Its value might well have been as low as $50. A newer weapon, and the warehouse was heavy with them, might sell in Europe for $350, maybe as much as $500. This one was Russian, almost an original off the production line, almost a piece for a museum – except that in the circumstances of Libya that day there were no functioning museums, and everything of value that had been lodged in them during the times of the fallen dictator, Gadaffi, the dead tyrant, had been stolen. The worst weapons, imitations, were the Chinese copies, but they could be provided in better condition than this old specimen. They did not argue or debate, were thankful to have food on their plates each evening.

The two men, happy with their work, drove the pick-ups down to the dockside area. Going the length of Tripoli Street they navigated the heaps of rubble from destroyed buildings, and the rusting tank carcases, and burned-out cars, and went faster along the stretches where bullet-pocked walls seemed about to topple. An old freighter was tied up, but pungent smoke surged from a stubbed funnel. In the pick-ups were antiquities, also well wrapped, which had come from museums or been chipped from sites farther north. They were loaded by trolley. Last on board was the package containing the weapon, just the one, old and with a history. The Roman and Greek artefacts would stay on deck during the voyage to the west, but the rifle was taken below and stowed under the captain's bunk. It would be gone in an hour.

Neither of the men had an idea of why they had been ordered to choose a worthless relic from the store, nor where it would go, nor why it had importance.

* * *

'I suppose this means it's just about kicking off,' Gough said.

Pegs answered him, 'Usually plays around a bit, nothing much happening, then starts being serious.'

'All seemed rather routine.'

'I doubt you believed that – but certainly beginning to stampede.'

He took a last look at the boy's face. Not pretty. A pathologist would have said to within an hour or two how long little Tommy the Tout had been in the water, but the deterioration was always fast. The eyes had no life and the lips no colour and the arms seemed awkward and barely attached. The main weight of the corpse was in a bed of drooping reeds at the side of the canal. They'd walked past it, Pegs leading and him following and not passing any comment that could have been overheard. The identification came through the North West Counter Terrorist people at their Manchester office, and he'd have been flagged up because of missing two scheduled meetings. Neither Gough nor Pegs would have wanted it broadcast off the rooftops that this guy. Tommy the Tout, was important enough to have brought big players up from London. The operation was at an indeterminate stage, budget not fixed, aims not cemented in, targets vague, and both the visitors thought the least put about was best. It was good of them to have left him in the water for this length of time, and there were crime scene tapes blocking off most of the towpath to the position on the canal, outside of Manchester, now used only by narrow boats and tourists. He nodded, a tiny gesture but one of the detectives picked it up, and it gave permission for them to fish him out.

Gough said, 'You get into a comfort zone. You think you know what you're at, and what's the prospect for the next day and the next week. Start to relax. You don't really know who you're dealing with and what the stakes are, and where it's taking you. Never been any different, but still gives you a jolt.'

'Quite a big jolt, Gough, and one that sends a message.'

'I think I am aware of that, the staying safe bit.'

'This is just a fucking horrible place, Gough.'

Which it was. Farther down from where the people in the frogmen gear were going into the water, was an island of snagged plastic bin bags, and around them were supermarket trolleys. He thought it would have taken some expert navigation from the canal cruiser people to have come through the blockages. Gough had only met little Tommy the Tout the once, no names and no introductions, and in the hour before he'd watched through a one-way mirror as the kid was given his marching orders by the Counter Terrorist detectives. Eager, anxious to please, not what Gough liked to see. He had felt little confidence but had not the clout to get the kid pulled back. They were seldom straightforward . . .

Investigations tended to have various masters, and most times he just hoped they'd not snag each other like crossed over fishing lines – not that there would be much in this polluted waterway for anglers. A heron flew past, languid and ignoring them and moving away from them with a silent wing beat.

'What do you reckon?'

She answered him, 'I reckon we get the fuck out, and the word is it's all narcotics and vendettas.'

He'd leave that to her . . . It might have been wind in the branches above the towpath, and it might have been a glob of water that fell from a dead leaf and landed on his shoulder. Gough was an old stager, had been around too long in the company of sudden death. He flicked irritably at his coat. One good memory, when he had been raw and on the steep learning curve, and the threat was from the Irish and not these home-grown jihadis. His first attachment to the Branch in Belfast, and there had been an 'own goal' call out for a bit of old oak woodland near to Dungannon in the Tyrone rolling country. The device had exploded as the courier carried it from the hide among the trees, down a path and towards his vehicle on the Armagh road. Something had landed on Gough's shoulder and he had flicked at it, and seen it fall to the ground and it still showed a bright pinkish colour. A piece of gristle, or might have been ligament. He'd looked up. Caught among the branches were small body parts. A couple of the local

Branch boys had watched him, looked for a reaction to prove that a newcomer from 'over the water' was soft. He'd ignored it, the bit of meat that landed on him, had given them no satisfaction: it was a long time, a big part of Gough's life, that he had been checking out premature killings. He had not been 'soft' then, but years had rolled, and now he cared more about the people who worked for him, not those they tracked. He was an old warrior, and roughened by the times, and had seen pretty much everything and had all the T-shirts folded away in a wardrobe drawer, had been everywhere that the kids regarded as a battlefield. But he cared more now about his own, owed it to them.

She had no authority. Pegs was a bottle-washer in his office. She had no rank, but instead of status had a personality that was difficult to deny. She was lecturing. 'As you know, offered himself up, but we rated him as a fantasist. Not on our payroll. Best to let it be known, if anything needs shoving into the local news-sheet, he was caught up in a little bit of turf war between druggie groups. Why are we here if he was of no value to us – just happened to be in the area, other business . . . what I've given you would be a good line to follow. Nice to have met you boys.'

He thought she'd bought time. Did not need much of it, more than a week, less than a fortnight, and the pace had picked up. They had come up fast, leaving London before dawn, and some of the way they'd had a bike out in front of them and clearing the way. She'd drive back, and slower. They settled in their seats.

Gough said, 'A death makes it a serious business. He was lucky to have died before they did the heavy work on him. I think we'd have had the alarms by now if he'd known anything, if he talked. I'd put it down to him pushing too fast, gone careless. We're not just talking about pissing off for a weekend and leaving the tomatoes in the greenhouse with no water. If they'll kill then they're close enough to kicking off . . . What do they want, Pegs, want most?'

She'd left the canal behind her. 'Same as what they always want – what makes a big noise, big shout, a big bang. What else?'

October 1956

Upper windows were open and milk bottles cascaded down from them.

They smashed on the upper armour of a tank and on the cobbles of the street. The bottles held no milk but had been filled with clear liquid – petrol fuel – and in the bottles' necks were stuffed rags, already lit. The conscript, holding his rifle across his chest, and petrified, was 30 or 40 metres behind the tank, but his sergeant – leading them – was close. The fuel made spears of orange fire as it scattered with the flying glass shards, and came too fast for a man to avoid. The sergeant was engulfed. The conscript watched, rooted. The NCO, hated by the conscript and many others of this platoon, screamed in pain. None of the young soldiers hurried forward to help him. They would have seen his face and the agony of it, and he would have sucked air down into his lungs and drawn the flames into his throat, deep into his chest tissue, and skin from his face would soon start to peel, and his uniform caught and made him a torch before his legs gave under him. Soon, the spasms became rarer, and in moments the body was still. Another man was on fire in the hatch of the tank and then he was ejected from the turret, chucked out because he blocked the escape of the crew, the gunner and the driver.

An officer, pistol drawn, tried to rally them. They had been told the day before, by women in the crowds, that the bottles filled with petrol and with a lit fuse were known among the Budapest people as 'Molotov Cocktails', named after their own foreign minister in Moscow. The conscript did not understand: yesterday they had fought against the townspeople of a friendly Socialist ally, who should have garlanded them with flowers; instead they had tried to kill them, and brutally. Much that he did not understand: a week before they had set out by train from their barracks in eastern Ukraine and then the commissars had lectured them that there had been an act of aggression from the Fascists of the North Atlantic Treaty nations, and that they would be coming to the help of comrades and friends. He had not yet fired his rifle, the weapon that had the thin chip in the stock, and that carried as its last five digits the serial number of 16751. Nothing had prepared the conscript for the reality of combat. They had formed up at the far end of a long street, and advanced behind three tanks, and had been told that their target was the headquarters of the 'criminal gangs' who had taken refuge close to a cinema. The street had become narrower and the first tank had been disabled, and there was firing from side streets . . . The first tank had most likely suffered engine failure, the second was attacked by a swarming mass of men. The crowd that clambered up on the superstructure had then tipped gasoline through every opening or vent, they could locate. Even against the noise of explosions and the revving of the engine, the conscript could hear the screams of these condemned men. They had practised infantry manoeuvre in support of armour and had been praised for their dedication, and had imagined themselves a formidable army, and had known nothing. It was a harsh lesson confronting them, and they were far from home.

Near to the conscript, a soldier broke ranks and started to run, and was shot by his officer. No warning, no cry for him to stop and retake his place. A raised and aimed pistol, a single shot, and a figure going down and then prone. The conscript had known this boy since their basic training. Had messed together, survived the sergeant together, and joked and drank and been punished together, and the boy was dead, shot by their own officer. A roar of voices broke from a side street on the right of the main boulevard . . . Not élite enemy troops from America or Great Britain, and not from the Nazis in Germany, but men and women in casual clothes, and some were too old to run fast, and the women had their skirts hitched high on their thighs so they could sprint quicker. Their faces were contorted with hatred. They carried firearms, more bottles, and some had butchers' knives, and they came and screamed for blood.

The conscript wavered. To go back he would have to step over or jump across the body of his friend. Going forward, he'd be under the smoke pall from the burning tank. Already the mob was climbing over them. To stay still would be to put himself in the way of the crowd surging towards him. He would go back.

The pistol was aimed at him.

He fired.

It was 248 days since that weapon had moved down a production line, had fallen from the belt and suffered a chipped stock, had been stamped with a serial number, had been shipped out. It had fired 7.62 × 39 grain bullets on target ranges and on exercise, but never been aimed at a man to maim or kill. There would have been a moment when the officer's face flared with astonishment as he realised the intention of the conscript a few metres in front of him. The rifle was at the shoulder of the young man, tight against his shoulder and collar-bone. The sights were set for close range, best for street fighting at 100 metres, the instructor had said, and had called the setting Battle Sight Zero. Beyond the V and the needle was the dun-coloured mass of the officer's tunic, and the pistol aim wobbled then settled, and it was beaten to the punch. The conscript had fired first, and the officer's look of astonishment changed to one of bewilderment, and the body slid as if hit across the upper chest with a pickaxe handle. Bright in the sunlight of that autumn morning, the cartridge case was ejected and it flew in a little arc and then bounced, and rolled among the cobbles. The rifle, the newest version of the AK-47, dropped from the conscript's limp fingers and fell on to the street. The gesture of the conscript who had shot dead his own officer was not recognised by the crowd descending on him. He was to be shot, and stabbed and beaten with clubs and his body would be stripped bare of every item of possible value, and when the army retreated in poor order his body would be left in full view. The rifle, of course, was scooped up, a prize of value.

A small issue. When the rifle landed on the cobble-stones, the stock's weight came down on to the hardened rim of the ejected cartridge case. No rhyme, no reason, just chance. The impact, close to where the splinter had detached, dug out a slight chip in the wooden stock: it might have looked like a gouged tick where the rifle's owner had marked the first kill that the weapon had achieved. A youth had it now.

The youth was an apprentice in a tractor-building factory on the northern outskirts of the Hungarian capital. He fired half a dozen shots at the retreating military, was pleased with himself for taking the necessary moment to go though the trooper's back-pack. He'd found three more filled magazines, which he pocketed. He felt glowing pride.

Farther back along the street, near to the Corvin cinema, the youth, with his new trophy of war and a swagger in his step, came across a furious shoving and heaving knot of men and women, and was drawn to it. Intelligent? Perhaps not. Understandable? Definitely. Some in the crowd had old Sten guns, and others had target rifles, and a few more were equipped with shotguns suitable for killing vermin on the farms ringing Buda-Pest. Because he carried a new weapon of war, the youth was pushed to the front. When the crowd closed around him, behind him, the youth saw hard up against a wall the cowering figure of a man who wore the uniform of the AVH, the security police. The man cringed. The man expected no mercy. The mob ruled. The man uttered no words as if he had realised that to speak was pointless, wasted breath. The youth knew the basics of weapons; everyone who had been to Pioneer camps as a teenager had seen rifles stripped down and reassembled and had been told of the need for vigilance in defence of a Socialist society. The youth was edged forward by the press of the crowd. He could see a notch cut on the stock of the rifle, as if a killing had already been claimed. He shot the security policeman. The crowd around him cheered, and the man was looted before the last shake of his body and the last cough of his breath.

He was photographed. Holding a small Leica camera was a bearded middle-aged man, and on his jacket was a 'Press' sticker and an accreditation for one of the prestigious New York magazines. The youth was not intelligent and struck a pose; behind him, propped against the wall, was the body of the security policeman, violated. And the photographer slipped away. The youth walked proudly towards the cinema, the makeshift command point, anxious to show what he had acquired, and borrowed a pocket knife and made another gouge in the stock, a second tick. And he was confident and held his enemy's weapon as a symbol of his power, and thought himself invincible.

Zeinab toyed with the research needed for an essay, took notes, was far away, and barely noticed the quiet of the library. She had no friends there, none of the other girls slipped alongside her for a quick conversation, or to share a problem.

She was involved at a depth where the sun no longer shone but did not regard herself as ensnared. The two boys had been cousins. Not close cousins, but the blood link had existed. She was a teenager, sixteen years old, and thought herself too tall, too long-legged and awkward, and pained with shyness when she had first met them. They had come with their family from Batley, had moved into Savile Town across the Calder river, and she had been hurrying back from school, lugging her bag full of books, and the car had pulled up alongside her. That was the first time . . . They must have known who she was, or come looking for her, and they had laughed and joked with her, had put her at ease: it had seemed a liberty with the disciplines of life that she had lingered on a pavement and talked with two boys. They had driven away. That was the first time . . . The blood link for her family and theirs came from the Pakistan city of Quetta.

The atmosphere in the library, supposedly where study and learning flourished, seemed of little importance to her. A tutor might recognise that she had struggled with the workload during the last two semesters but was hardly going to risk playing the 'race card', and threaten her with the big boot. She did what she had to, the minimum . . . Other matters concerned her, but failed to frighten her.

Not often, and not regularly, it could have been once a month, or every six weeks, she would be walking back from school, a bright pupil and from whom great things were expected, and a clucking approval from her parents, and the car would ease up beside her, and the window would come down. How was she? How was she doing? Bold talk that rubbished Dewsbury; they laughed at the humbleness of the area that was Savile Town, and how nothing ever happened there . . . The last time she had seen them, these vague cousins, it had been raining and the wind was whipping at the hem of her ankle-length clothing, and the car had stopped and the back door was opened. From behind her veil she had watched their faces, and most of the laughter was lost, and nervousness had played on their faces. She had thought then that she might have been one of the very few who knew that they would be gone within a week, taking a rucksack, and going out from Leeds/Bradford, changing flights anywhere in Europe, then the leg into Turkish territory, and the scramble over the frontier. The older of them, only for a moment, had held her hand, blinked, had done a sort of sheepish goodbye, and the younger had taken the same hand and had brushed his lips across it. Incredible . . . and she was out of the car, and running down the street, through the rain, buffeted by the wind, and had shut herself in her bedroom.

She despised the subject and the words on the pages in front of her had no meaning.

Not quite 'nothing' happened in Dewsbury . . . three of the boys who had gone down on to the underground trains in London had come from Dewsbury. A teenager had been arrested and charged with terror offences, and been convicted. Two more boys had disappeared from Savile Town and one had driven a vehicle at the enemy and then detonated a bomb, and the other was missing, assumed dead. Not nearly 'nothing'. It had been on the local radio. Two boys from that part of Yorkshire were reported killed in the defence of Raqqa, the caliphate city. Their home was raided by police. Zeinab had thought it a cruelty, and without justification, but the street where they had lived had been cordoned, and families evacuated, and their parents taken away, and a bomb team had gone through the house, grotesque in huge kit. She had bridled in anger. They had been gone nearly two years, by then. Would they have left a live explosive device in the home of their mother and father? She had thought the high visibility search was to inflict fear on the community. As if ownership of the street and their homes were was confiscated, taken from them, and they might, all of those who lived there, have been declared 'pariahs', all intimidated and scared and humiliated, and she believed that was the intention. Other homes had been raided, those of the friends of the boys' parents. Not hers. Perhaps because the connection between the families was not proven on the computers, the police detectives did not visit her house and interrogate her parents. She thought often of those boys. Walked home in sunshine and rain and found herself straining to hear the note of that car's engine on the road behind her, and the scrape of the window and the casual way in which she was greeted; almost, still, she could smell the smoke from their cigarettes. No funeral, no repatriated bodies, no confirmation of what had happened to them.

In the Students' Union buildings, across a piazza from where she played at studying, were notice-boards that advertised seminars against radicalism. Kids were urged to report attempts to recruit them to extremism . . . and life had gone on in Savile Town on the south west side of Dewsbury, and the cousins seemed forgotten and were no longer talked of: Zeinab did not forget.

There was a cemetery out of town and across the Calder river. A part of the cemetery was given over to a muslim burial area. A stone wall separated the cemetery from the Heckmondwike Road. Zeinab had taken to going in darkness with a handful of flowers and reaching over the wall and leaving them on the grass. A mowing team came each week and trimmed the grass but she noticed that her flowers, if still in bloom, were always left there . . . It might have been that she was followed, certainly she would have been watched. There were people who looked for recruits, for sympathisers, for activists, for supporters . . . It could have been, before they went on their journey, that the cousins had mentioned her name and that it had been stored in a memory. She left the flowers and would look across the darkness of the cemetery, and she had not forgotten the cousins and an anger had grown in her.

She had been approached. First term at university. She had worn correct dress then, but not the full face veil. Two boys, one materialising on her right and one on her left, engaging her, and using the names of the cousins. Support had been teased from her. Not at one meeting, not at two or three; these boys were patient and respectful, never sought to hurry her. She would launch into monologues of resentment because of the deaths of the boys, and the value of their 'martyrdom', and their bravery . . . step by small step. They were not her friends but were associates, and showed a road ahead. Then, the big step.

No more dressing to advertise her modesty. All consigned to a cupboard in her room in the Hall. Down to second-hand clothing shops, and buying cheap, worn jeans, making the rips in the knees, and loose fitting T-shirts and sweaters and fleece tops, and a toggle hat from which her hair fell. She was no longer the dutiful daughter of her parents. And there was reason for it. Of course, there were spies on the campus. Of course inside the university buildings, watchers scrutinised any person thought to demonstrate faith in 'strikeback' or belief in the armed struggle. She was one of the few and had thrown aside the constraints of her upbringing, another girl hardly worth noticing. The boys had nurtured her, as if there would be, ultimately, at a time of their choosing, a use for her . . .

She had been walking, then was scrambling, now was running . . . the boys, Krait and Scorpion, had shown her the body. She had seen the face. Dead lips and a dead tongue between them and dead eyes above them, and fingers that were splayed out but held nothing, and she understood for the first time the stakes of the hidden world she had joined, understood also what happened to an informer, the lowest of the worst . . . she was running and the wind might have caught her hair, dragged it out behind her, as had happened when she had walked on a moor with him, and the boys had said that there was a purpose to them being together.

Unremarkable, an open-air conversation. 'You are sure about him?'

She was sure.

A young woman huddled against the weather and clutching her pile of books and talking with two young men, unnoticed. 'You could travel in two days or three?'

She would travel when they needed her to.

'He will do it?'

Their question, her answer. He would do what she told him to do.

'You are so sure?'

Not an issue. She was certain of it. He would do as she told him, and she had laughed lightly, had left the boys, had gone in search of a place in the library. She would have liked then to have been able to lean across the stone wall on the Heckmondwike Road, above where she laid her flowers, feel the night cold on her face and tell her cousins what she was tasked to do and imagine them nodding in admiration.

The city of Marseille . . . more than two and a half millennia ago, Greek traders had arrived here from an Ionian town in Turkey, had established a trading post, had quickly discovered a perfect climate for the cultivation of vines and olives. They developed an extraordinary depth of culture, moved inland but also established trading routes by sailing west out into the Atlantic and then south along the coastline of continental Africa. Next to exploit the safe anchorage of the harbour were the Roman colonists. Later, under Julius Caesar, veteran legionaries were awarded plots of land as reward for loyal service. Next to come were the barbarians, Visigoths and Ostrogoths, and after them Arab armies sailing north across the Mediterranean. And then there was chaos and a breakdown in authority and Marseille was overrun by pirates. There were famines and plagues and disasters for centuries until papal power subjugated the unruly territory. Then prosperity, then absolute monarchy, then the construction of two of the finest fortresses in Europe – the Bas-Fort Saint-Nicolas and the Fort Saint-Jean, and the building of cathedrals to the glory of God, and fine public buildings. Marseille became the second city of France, but one that always showed a pithy, bitter, stubborn attitude to any form of subjugation from distant Paris. History, ancient and modern, drips from the civic buildings along with hedonistic streaks of rebellion. A visitor can stroll along bustling boulevards, always staying aware and keeping a firm grip on a bag and the zip fastened on a pocket with a wallet or purse, can visit magnificient museums, can take excursions to a coastline of amazing beauty, can eat well, feel a sense of anarchic freedom, can slip inside the dark quiet beauty of the Cathédrale de la Major and speak a few words of contemplation and feel purged and at peace. Those are a collection of aspects of Marseille.

The marksman had a target in his sights. The rifle was mounted with a telescopic sight and gave him a good, sharp view of the kid. He was entitled to shoot because his target sauntered along the walkway between the apartment towers, north of Marseille, and openly displayed a weapon, a Kalashnikov, and an hour earlier, had blasted shots into the air over a team of undercover detectives who were arresting a small-time dealer, a *charbonneur*. The low-life, peddling hashish, had wriggled free and run. The detectives had done the same, got the hell away, and the marksman had been called out. The marksman was known as Samson.

Samson was the name awarded him by many and tolerated by his commander, Major Valery. The name was abroad in the unit, Groupe d'Intervention de Police Nationale, among those level in rank with him and those recently recruited and far junior. He had chosen a position where he had elevation and could look down into the estate, and he followed the kid. The magnification on the scope was powerful enough for him to check how much of his cigarette was smoked, and how badly his face was affected by a dermatological complaint. There was a bullet in the breech and his safety catch was off, but he had his finger loose against the outside of the trigger guard . . . Samson was also the name given to him by a new generation of *tricoteuses* who would have spotted a single rifle and GIPN sharpshooter and his position behind the bench, and would have recognised the build of his body and the distinctive naval blue of the balaclava that he always wore. He was watched, and with an uncanny and prescient sense of impending drama, women of middle to older age would come out on to the little balconies of their apartments and would wait, would look, would watch for the target the marksman, Samson, had chosen: best if he was unaware, always better entertainment if the target stayed in ignorance.

Below Samson, away to his left, was the sea. It was a cool January day and the wind blew hard from across the mountains to the south, then whisked over the Mediterranean waves, and the washing on the short lines between the buildings billowed and surged. Big cargo ships nudged away from the Marseille docks, and a few trampers lurched in the swell as they came the other way and sought safe anchorage. He was entitled to shoot. His superiors would not have intervened and forbidden him to draw a bead and loose off a round. Police officers going about their work had been obstructed and rounds fired, and that was reason enough for retaliation. It was hard policing in this housing project, La Castellane, and the restraints that would have been required in Lille or Lyons, Orléans or Paris, were not thought obligatory in Marseille's outer suburbs.

The kid was probably high on skunk from Morocco. He meandered and took no care to hide himself, and sometimes the barrel of the Kalashnikov trailed in the dirt. Could have been that the kid had lost his love of life and no longer cared if he was held in the cross-hairs, might have wanted it that way because of the stupefaction of a narcotic. Samson saw a woman advance towards the kid. She was well swaddled against the cold, and slipped twice on the mud. He could just hear her voice. Samson spoke little of the Arabic that was the *pigeon* language in the project. Her words, carried by the wind, were littered with abuse and anger. He'd had his aim on the target for at least four minutes now. At any moment in that time he could have slid a finger inside the guard, adjusted the aim, tightened his view of the chest and made those small but necessary calculations concerning wind strengths coming between the buildings, and fired. He would not have been criticised, certainly not by Major Valery, nor by any of his colleagues in the GIPN team – but he had not. She strode up to him. It was good theatre. Other kids had now formed a horseshoe around the Kalashnikov kid and they would be presented with a decent show, and the *tricoteuses* would be short-changed. She reached him. Samson could not decide whether she was the mother or the grandmother. Whichever, she packed a punch. She hit the kid. While she had belted him, while she stood her ground as he reeled, her insults flowed freely, Then she grabbed him by the ear. The spectators laughed, jeered. The women on the balconies would have looked across the open ground, beyond the feeder road, and almost to the commercial park, and would have checked the bench and the marksman there who wore a balaclava, and would have seen him stand, clear his weapon, turn his back. The woman held the kid's ear and yanked him away and the Kalashnikov was dropped. She had saved his life, if it were a life worth saving. It might have been that the life had less value than the Kalashnikov left in the dirt, and in that housing project its price would not be more than 350 euros. A man came forward, picked up the weapon, was gone.

He walked back to the roadside lay-by where the trucks were parked. It would have been justifiable for him to fire but he had chosen not to. He had been given the name of Samson, taken from that of Charles-Henri Samson, because on separate occasions he had killed three men in the last five years. No other marksman in the GIPN force located in Marseille had killed more than once. Charles-Henri Samson had been first among equals as the official executioner in the years of the Terror, had become a celebrity after supervising the death by guillotine of both King Louis and Queen Marie-Antoinette. He would have said that he never fired for a trophy, only when it was necessary . . . The kid was lucky, except that he'd get a proper hiding from his mother, or grandmother. He emptied his weapon then put the Steyr-Mannlicher SSG – killing range of 600 metres – back into its carrying case . . . Tomorrow would be another day, and he was seldom impatient.

The city of Marseille had recently been reshaped as, post World War Two, an empire collapsed. France needed to find accommodation, and in a hurry, for the white settlers fleeing the colonies of north Africa–Morocco, Tunisia and Algeria – after blood-leaching wars of independence. The city fathers built 'projects' in an arc around the northern suburbs of old Marseille, shoebox apartments in constricted developments, and a time bomb of criminality was born. There had been older and more weathered organised crime gangs, led by such heroes of the city's folklore as Francis 'the Belgian' Vanverberghe or Paul Carbone and François Spirito, and Tony Zimbert and Jacky 'Mad Jacky' Imbert, and Jean-Jé Colonna, and Farid 'the Roaster' Berrahma. Respected and feared, and then gone, swept aside by a new force. The old whites had evacuated the projects, and where they had lived now became a dumping ground for the masses of north African immigrants, those from the Maghreb, who descended – some would have said as a locust swarm – and built a life, and milked the system. Previously, the gangsters had marketed heroin, now the trade switched to the various forms of hashish flooding the housing estates. Some small organisations based around a filthy, daubed stairwell could pull in as much as 50,000 euros each day, many scratched a living at 15,000 euros taken every 24 hours. Turf wars achieved a new state of ruthlessness, and the weapon of choice for settling disputes, real or imagined, had become the AK-47 assault rifle: made in the former Soviet Union, modern Russia, China, Serbia, Bulgaria, Egypt or . . . pretty much anywhere. Sub-editors throughout Europe had fun with headines. *Bodies pile up in gangland Marseille drugs war* and *In the deprived city of Marseille the French national spirit is nowhere to be seen* and *Marseille pupils forced to dodge drug gangs' bullets* and *Marseille: Europe's most dangerous place to be young*.

The estates are near no-go areas for the police, and drug dealing is run with sophisticated and military precision, and life is cheap. A police officer would say that it was difficult to identify the worst of the project estates, but in the top echelon – as feared as any and with justification – he would rate La Castellane, out on the northern road leading to the airport. For that status La Castellane holds a formidable reputation, is awash with hard drugs, with weapons, and with killers.

'Marseille? Sorry, Zed, why do we want to go to Marseille?'

A hesitation, a roll of the eyes, then . . . 'Family business. Something I have to do.'

'Going when?'

'In a couple of days.'

'It's that urgent?'

'Something I have to do.'

They were on a bench in the park near to his depot. She had come out to him, and he was still in his work clothing, the uniform of the haulage driver. The rain had stopped, and snow was not threatening, but there was a cold cut to the wind. A solitary woman walked a toy dog on another path, and ignored them. He'd looked around to see if the boys who had quizzed the Somali from the canteen had showed up, but had not seen them.

'For how long?'

'Two days or three.'

'And we'd fly from Manchester, and . . .'

'No, you would drive. Yes, drive there and drive back.'

He could have said that it would hardly be three days of choice if he were to drive – what would it be, close to 1000 miles each way? – and look at a French resort city off season and walk around a bit. Most times when she spoke to him it was with the confidence that she was a young woman from an intellectual grade higher than himself, but this was difficult for her. Refuse? No. He would show hesitation, gently question what she intended, but would accept. Would do what she asked – as if he were besotted, smitten. She would buy into it because she was an innocent.

'You want me to drive?'

'You drive, you are a good driver.'

'It's a fair question, Zed, would I be going as your friend or as your driver?'

'What does that mean?'

'Do we go so as we are together, sitting in a car most of the time, or because you don't know anyone else who would – for whatever reason – drive you?'

He had pushed her, might as well have given her a punch in the stomach. She pushed herself up off the bench. He thought they were poker players, bluffing, each seeking to exploit the other, neither knowing how far to take it. 'I ask you. If you do not want to, do not. I don't order you. I offer the chance. Don't. If you don't want to, Andy, then don't.'

'What do you know about Marseille, Zed, am I permitted to ask that?'

'Have read a guidebook? No. Have I researched the place? No. But, I have to go.'

'Just, what I heard, it's a tough city.'

'What do you say?'

His heart pounded because success nestled close, within reach, but he played the necessary game and acted hesitant. 'I heard it's a hard city . . . and I don't have the sort of money that . . .'

'You drive, I pay the bills.' She said it decisively, a toss of the head, a small matter.

'The family business? Take much of your time?'

'It would be a chance for us. Not too much time.'

'I'd like that. A few days, you and me, that would be good.'

'You can fix it with your work?'

'Think so . . . and you, you can take the time off, you don't have lectures, a tutorial?'

'Of course, I can.'

'I'll get it sorted in the morning.'

'You and me, just you and me.'

'And the family business won't take too much of your time?'

'My problem, Andy, not your problem.'

Settled. She had a good hold of him and kissed him hard, as she had before, and her tongue went inside his mouth and roved behind his teeth, and she seemed to have enthusiasm for it. Most of the time it was Andy Knight who did the lying, and had told lies that were smaller and lies that were bigger when he was Phil Williams and when he was Norm Clarke. He was paid to lie, not particularly well paid, but adequately. He eased clear.

'If that's what you'd like, Zed. Us, together, down across France and to Marseille and a few days there, and I give you room for your business, the family stuff, and then we head on back. It's a long drive but at this time of year the roads won't be heavy. Brilliant . . . it'll be good.'

Not much light reached them from the edge of the park and the street lamps around a kids' play area. It was enough. He saw that she was smiling. Like a cat with cream, a whole bowl of it. He thought he had done well, struck a good balance.

He had tried to ask what was natural, what he had the right to be told, but not have her on her feet and flouncing away. He put a hand on her arm. She took the side of his head, then pulled off her glove, then her fingers ran down the skin of his throat. Time for her to do the flirt bit. He thought it did not come easy to her. Her other hand was inside his anorak, and wouldn't have been able to get closer because of the raised zip on his company overalls. He gave her a kiss, not passionate, more like a friend. Another kiss that sealed it, and her hand came out from under his anorak. They had both done, Andy Knight reckoned, a plausible job of deceit. He told her that he would get one of the guys at the depot to run the rule over his car to be certain it was right and ready for such a fierce run, and he'd be in the manager's office first thing in the morning to nail down the time off . . . He knew next to nothing of Marseille except that it had deep roots in organised crime, a tough gangster scene that was run by north African ethnic migrants, that it was not a clever place to mess, to play games. He was pleased with how the session on the bench had gone, enough to forget that his backside was cold and wet and his hip joints stiff, and thought he had done the innocent bit as far as was necessary, then had done the guy who was obsessed with her. She was a good-looking girl, pleasant to look at and nearly pleasant to be with, and he wondered how far she would take him . . . He hoped he did not egg it, but thought she'd appreciate hearing it. Not the first time and wouldn't be the last. He thought she was being nurtured for great things, a big moment, and there would be boys round her who pushed her forward, and he didn't think she'd have the savvy for suspicion, not be as clear on risk as the boys behind her.

'I just want to say, Zed, that we may have met up in daft circumstances, but I'm really pleased that I had the chance to meet you, get to know you. Really pleased because you are important. More important than anyone has been.'

3

'Would a young lady be involved?' The boss allowed himself, rare for him, a dry wriggle of a smile.

'Something came up.' Andy Knight wore a poker player's face, part of the game.

'I take it as read, a young lady.'

'And I haven't asked for leave since being here.'

'Pretty little thing, is she?'

'It would just be a week.'

The boss was rolling a pencil across the desk. A trifle of fun, a sort of formal dance being played out. Not as though there was a cat in hell's chance that the request would be denied.

'I've a heavy week in front of us – you did say you might be pushing off in the next couple of days. I heard that right? A pile of deliveries, and all needing a schedule kept, and I'm about to lose one of my drivers. Prepared to say one of my "better" drivers, and the guys left behind – who won't be on a cuddle and kiss – will need to put in some overtime, if that suits at the other end of the chain. And . . .'

'I appreciate it's inconvenient, but was just hoping you could see your way to . . .' Andy shrugged. Gave that near helpless look which seemed to confirm that totty was on offer, too good a chance to pass up and the implication would be that, once, the boss had been young, footloose, not married with three kids, and a dog and a mortgage, and a little villa losing money on one of the Costa del Sol estates.

'I suppose I could.'

'I'd be very grateful.'

'Sure you would, least you could be. Is this – not my business, but I'll ask it anyway – the big one in your life, know what I mean?'

He would not have expected an answer, and would not get one. Would not have it confirmed that a girl was in the melting pot, and would not be told where the love tryst was to be staged. Some, not Andy, would have slipped in a remark about the south of France, a rather adventurous and exhilarating city, and raised an eyebrow, but he gave nothing. He was not aware of what deal had been done, what the link was that had brought him to the depot: the selection process had been vague, and it was a sought-after job. Somewhere down the line there would have been a tap on the shoulder, a nod and a nudge, and there could have been a mason's handshake, small talk over hospitality at a United or City game, could have been a debt called in or a favour begged. It had happened to him twice before when a legend was in the careful process of construction, but behind him and better not remembered. He assumed the boss knew something of where he came from, but would remain far outside the detail loop . . . Tittle-tattle down at the golf club about the contacts he had made and what was required of him, and to whom he gave a helping hand were all to be discouraged. It was all about secrecy, a commodity not to be slack with, and lives would be at stake . . . Top of the list, with a pink ribbon round it, would be Andy Knight's.

'Thank you, really appreciate it.'

'What I asked, Andy: the big love of your life – for real, for ever?'

'Which is what I didn't answer. But thanks.'

He stood. The boss was gazing up at him. The man's mind would have been going at flywheel speed. Who did he have driving for him, what was his purpose, where did he go at night, and what was the danger level? Was it organised crime or national security, or was the boss off the track and understanding nothing? In the past, Andy had found himself applying for work as a delivery driver – the only Brit in a team of Poles and Hungarians and Romanians – and going round Exeter and its satellite villages doing internet shopping deliveries, and enough people had said, after being in contact with him, that Phil Williams was a 'straight up' guy. A pub in Swindon, far end of the Thames valley, had thought it a good idea to offer Norm Clarke the chance of work – basic wages and occasional tips because it was not the sort of establishment where money was flashed. He should live, he had been told, one life at a time. It was good advice, and the life now did not include the months when Williams or Clarke were top of the heap. He smiled. The secretary from the outer office was at the door. She'd have heard every word, Andy's and the boss's, and would be none the wiser, and she'd gossip with the general manager, and the head of finance, and the story would stay rock solid that young Knight, good-looking boy, was off somewhere with his new squeeze. They were decent people, kind to a stranger, welcoming to an intruder, and he'd walk out of the depot the next day or the day after, and likely not come back. It was what happened . . . there, then gone. They'd have a master key and would check his locker and would find it emptied, and no clue as to who he was. It was how it had been in Exeter and how it had been in Swindon . . . and his parents were not inside that loop, and would have been hurt deeply, but it was the way things were done.

Some would always be hurt. Could not be helped. Causing hurt went with the job.

His parents were already hurt . . . they'd not have recognised the name of Andy Knight, nor of Norm Clarke, and would have denied any connection with Phil Williams. His father was a science teacher, in a comprehensive school, and his mother ran the reception desk in a dental practice close to their home on the outskirts of Newbury in Berkshire. They had done well, lived carefully and had managed to make a home close to a cricket ground, pleasant and decent. He was out of their lives and did not go back, didn't claim his bedroom at the back, and they'd not have known why, and would have been bruised, bewildered. Two sisters there, or were when he'd left for the last time, and the best chance was that they'd regard him as wet dog mess for the damage he had done to the family. It could not be different . . . talk had a way of getting into crannies. One way to damage his work would be through his father and mother, and his sisters. The best protection for them was to cut them adrift. The hard thing about it was that he had now become – almost – immune to emotion about family, friends, people who had once seemed important. He had gone, disappeared.

The boss was rewarded with a smile. It would be around the depot within an hour, thanks to the good offices of the secretary and the manager who dealt with the drivers' pool, that Andy was off for a week with a girlfriend. Talk of it would brighten their lives.

'Oh, just one thing . . .'

'What now? Want me to pay for a box of chocolates, or something?'

'Bit of a liberty.'

'One big liberty – what do you want?'

'Can I just have the guys in maintenance run an eye over my motor?'

A nod, and a mock sigh of exasperation. The boss understood a bit, not much but a little. The chances were high that Andy Knight was history as far as this delivery service for builders' sites was concerned. They'd run inquests over what he might have been and where he had come from, and where he had gone, and be left none the wiser, which was how it should be.

Where had his life changed, gone off the straight and the narrow? All down to a rabbit. A rabbit had done the dirty on him . . . a rabbit's hole.

'See you back, Andy. Hope the young lady realises the sacrifices we're making on her behalf.'

'Yes, boss. See you back.'

'My trouble – if I have a trouble – is that I'm fond of a deal.' Crab, with his minder alongside him, walked.

There were times when Crab wanted to talk, not to have a debate and opinions pushed at him that were the opposite of his own instincts, but just to talk and have Gary at his shoulder; the simple pleasure of hearing his own voice. But never at home – they would leave the house and walk the pavements, walk where there would be no microphones – mobile phones, of course, switched off – and they would pass the electric gates of the orthopaedic surgeons and barristers and accountancy partners, and the occasional footballer's pile, and anyone who had a home that had cost the earth and a fair bit more. Walk and talk. Could only be with Gary now that Rosie was gone.

'Life without a deal, sort of empty. Have to have a deal on the run.'

Crab, despite his disability, went at a good speed and threw out his right leg with each stride, then launched his weight on to it, looked as if he might stumble, but always kept his balance. The pavement was treacherous in this weather but he had confidence. If he slipped, Gary was at hand. Rain spattered on his face, ran down his cheeks, distorted the lenses of his dark glasses, and dribbled from his sandy moustache. He had poor teeth, a mess, but they flashed as he talked, and the wind clasped his coat close around him. To go outside to talk was a natural precaution against any of the Manchester crime squads that might have seen him, a veteran, a soft target, worth pursuing.

'It's going to be a trial run, Gary. We see what we like, feel happy with it, then we go forward and into the big time. This occasion we bring only one through, and we do the switch there, and hand it to them there, and it's their job to transport the goodies off French territory and bring it back. It's a joyride. We set it up, Tooth and me, we watch it happen and take our cut. Removed enough for it not to matter if the kids blow themselves out of the water. If they don't, and it's good, then we take the money. Personally, I think it'll work well . . . A girl and a boy coming back from the south of France, all romantic and perhaps a couple of violins scraping, nice-looking fresh kids, in love, clean skins, and the merchandise hidden under the seats. It's good . . . We start with just one and see how it goes. It works, so the next time it's five and that gets through and we look again and this time it'll be ten. Probably about the limit, but by this time some good money is heading our way, and no kickbacks. Have to say, I like it.'

A few years back, he would have walked with Rosie, and they'd have gone up round the golf club. She'd been with him since he had exited Strangeways for the first time, a fiercely loyal confidante. They'd had two sons, both useless and both now banged up, and it was because of the elder that Crab now had the chance of the deal, conversations on the periphery of the exercise yard and then men turning up on Crab's leafy doorstep. They had been polite, had almost scraped their noses on the gravel in respect, had said what they wanted and suggested a price. They had seemed to Crab to be serious men – a touch above ordinary seriousness when they had requested the use of a disused warehouse in Crab's property portfolio, and all left clean and no criticism justified. It was an interesting proposition.

'You're sniffing, Gary. I sense that. Nostrils working overtime. Not our sort of people, that's what you're saying. God, Gary you are an old stick-in-the-mud. I have to go where the opportunity is. How do we make money now? Not payrolls? Not security vans delivering cash? Not going into a jewellers and waving a shotgun around? I have gone into the modern world. Those kids, the keyboards, their little viruses squirming up the tubes, that's getting ahead of the game, and it pays good money and nobody notices us. You have to be ahead of the game And you have to believe in old Crab, Gary, have to . . . I tell you another thing, it'll be good to hook up again with Tooth. Best man there is. Him and me, Tooth and Crab, what a team. Be good to do a deal with Tooth . . . I need it, Gary, need it to stay alive, not bloody vegetate. Look, it's a dry run and we'll watch how it rolls, and from what I see the security is good, or better than good. You worry too much, Gary.'

Four years ago, Rosie had been in her Porsche sports, and might have sunk a couple too many, and the ice had come down fast and she might have been going quicker than was sensible. A beech tree had ended her life: multiple injuries. An occasional girl, when he needed her, was Beth, but she only came at weekends and ironed and cooked and cleaned, and was useful at other duties, but not trusted with the confidences he had previously shared . . . Gary knew Crab's business, lived in an annexe off the main house and – Crab's belief – would die protecting his benefactor. They walked briskly. He was confident of Gary's loyalty.

'And you're still sniffing. Not happy . . . I read your mind, Gary. You don't know them and you don't like them. Not happy that I'm mixing with them. Are they "safe", are they "decent"? Trust me, Gary . . . am I allowed a little laugh? Humour me. Be a funny old day when Crab starts worrying whether the "associates" are "decent". Be a day when I might just laugh too much, even smile big . . . Are they "decent"? They sound right, they take good precautions. They had a kid trying to push in, might have been a tout, and they dealt with it. Dealt quick and dealt clean. I liked it. And, they have this girl who is sharp as a needle, what they say. University. Intelligent, bright, committed. She's a boyfriend who's a dick-head and thinks the sun shines out of her fanny . . . that too vulgar, Gary? Are they enough at arm's length from us? Yes, in my opinion, yes. Lighten up, Gary.'

He'd decided they'd walked far enough; he'd done his talk, it was time to be heading back, and there was racing on the TV that Crab would enjoy. It might be that Gary shared Beth with him, but he wouldn't treat that as a matter to fall out over, as long as it wasn't blatant, was discreet. They passed some kids, pushed them off the pavement, and he heard the giggling because of his uneasy gait, didn't bother him. Good to have a deal in place. He noted that Gary's face was still expressionless.

'Gary, what's eating? Is it because of who we're doing business with? Or is it because of the cargo that we're supplying, they're buying? Any different to heroin, or coke, or girls? I think we made choices too long ago, Gary, to start acting squeamish now. . . .'

He laughed out loud, and wiped the rain off his glasses. Crab always laughed at his own cracks. Late to be worrying about ethics. Hadn't before and wouldn't start now. And he was off the law's radar, sure of it.

The feed had come through from the Counter-Terrorist Command, what they had an eyeball on, and Pegs had grimaced, raised an eyebrow, and Gough had nodded. They'd seen a parked car, two in it, and a languid finger had directed them. They slid into a space, restricted parking for residents, but Pegs was good with intimidation if it came to a spat with a warden: could go high and mighty, could threaten torture and job loss. They watched the door of a convenience store. Pegs had her cigarettes out. Gough grunted. She lit up, using a lighter he'd given her two years back, a clandestine gift. He grunted again.

She said, 'Spit it.'

He cleared his throat, coughed on her fumes, and spat it. 'It'll need Risk Assessment. Need Risk Assessment and a Mission Statement. A bloody nightmare.'

'I can massage it . . . Worse than that, a fucking nightmare.'

Her language was usually fruity and Gough reckoned it the legacy of an independent schooling. Gough said, 'And, what's worse than worse, we need "liaison" down there.'

'I hate nightmares.'

They did their collective moan, competed well with each other. He had a little French and she had some more but not fluent. Language was always a minefield, and French cops rarely spoke English, and if they did they'd not admit it. After the communication matter was the difficulty of breezing in, snapping out a 'want' list, this one would need surveillance and backup, and there would be no clear-cut Assessment and Statement because Gough was in the dark, pitch and black as a January night. She was smoking vigorously and tapping her phone, multi-skilled; a grin from Gough, because he was lucky, desperately so in his opinion, to have her alongside him. He saw her first, nudged Pegs, and ash dropped off her cigarette and landed on her lap, went unnoticed, and she kept texting.

A pretty girl . . . but Gough was supposed to be beyond the age when the curve of hips and bosom and the swing of a stride, and hair flying behind in the wind, was supposed to matter. She had a plastic shopping bag, came out of the store and turned right. One of the guys from the Counter-Terrorist Unit slid out of the car across the street, and started to follow her. He did not need to see her for operational necessity, it was a gratuitous moment. The people doing the tail on her were capable enough. Pegs was edging their car forward: he did not have to preach caution, fret over being noticed; she was as sharp as he was experienced.

He said, 'It's a good plan, I respect it.'

She said, 'Call them short at your peril – nobody suggests they're oafs, talk them down and you'll lose.'

'They're in a car, they're attractive. Where's the threat?'

'And she flashes her boobs, and . . .'

'They're waved through – and he's white, and she's a clean cookie.'

Pegs stared bleakly into Gough's eyes; didn't watch the girl, left that to him. She said, 'A big new ballpark if there's a weapon of choice involved. Worse than a suicide guy's rucksack. A black suit, a busy night in a city centre, pubs and bars full, and the gook walks in with an assault rifle. We are humiliated, we failed. We lose the public's confidence. A Kalashnikov assault rifle, even in an amateur's hands, takes us to a new height of mayhem, on a scale we've not yet had – thank the good Lord. In the court of public opinion we will be torn limb from limb if it reached here on our watch. A gook, black kit head to toe, and a rifle spraying around. That is an horrendous scenario . . . Looks a nice girl.'

'Most of them do, look like nice girls,' Gough said quietly.

She walked briskly along the pavement and Gough reckoned she had little tradecraft. Some of them doing the jihadi bit had a clear and prescient idea of how to avoid foot and vehicle tails. He did not think she had those skills. Most of the ones who did would have learned tradecraft in the top-grade universities offering the course: Her Majesty's Prisons, either on remand or post-conviction. He thought she seemed confident, assured, and he did not sense that danger was on her list. Pegs had pulled out into the traffic and had kept her hazard lights on, which cut down the annoyance of the traffic building behind their vehicle.

Pegs murmured, 'Like butter wouldn't melt in her bloody chops.'

'The immortal words of our fond allies, the Bundesgrenzschutz, in their manuals. "Shoot the women first", always a good idea. Can't read them. Would she know that, Pegs?'

'That she'll be in the cross-hairs? I wouldn't think so, no.'

They were grandstanding, had no useful place there other than to cast an eye on a target. Gough watched her head bob amongst other hurrying pedestrians. He had lost sight of the tail, and the car that followed her. She seemed to walk tall and with a purpose, then turned into a coffee bar. Pegs gave him the quick glance, would have known the answer but it was formal and for him to decide. A nod. She pulled into the fast lane and her hand had gone to the satnav controls and she did the business for London . . . she had looked so damned innocent, but innocence – Gough's creed – was poor defence. The girl had looked pretty, but that wouldn't help her, not in the big boys', and big girls', world. Too much to be getting on with, and all of it French, and all of it a potential disaster zone. Happy days . . . Gough's hand rested on Pegs' thigh, and she drove fast and well, and the pace had quickened, what he loved about his work, and her . . . And the threat loomed big: a gook in a black outfit and the weapon of choice in his hand, and the sound of screaming: what Gough had known all his working life.

September 1958

The digging had taken most of the morning, and tempers had worn thin.

The boy had now been in the custody of the *Allamvedelmi Hatosag* for almost three months. After the uprising and the reoccupation of Buda-Pest by the Soviet military, the local secret police had been given the task of searching out and arresting those who had been principals, and had tried to slide into anonymity. Men had dug several holes in the woodland in their search for the weapon, but he had been a poor guide for them. He barely saw where they dug, with their spades and pickaxes, because the beatings inflicted on him had virtually closed his eyes. They were puffed, the skin around them many-coloured, and cuts and scrapes covered his face, two front teeth were missing, and the gums still bled after a week. He had confessed. In the basement cells after one more session of beatings and kickings, he had admitted shooting the cowering official of state security, then taking away the rifle stolen from the Soviet liberators. Had also admitted using it the next day and the day after in an act of resistance, and then running from the city, going home, taking the Kalashnikov to the woods at his parents' smallholding, and burying it. He had been dragged from his cell that morning and brought here, handcuffed, and had tried to identify the place, two years later, where he had dug. But the boy, through his puffed eyes could barely see a hand in front of him, let alone recognise an unmarked place in the ground.

He had confessed, and gilded the story, and tried to stump up excuses and mitigation, and hoped that, at the trial next week, he would be shown clemency by the court.

Travelling in a closed van, from the prison at Andrassy ut. 60, it had seemed a miracle to him when he had been pitched out near his parents, wooden house. Vaguely and indistinctly he had seen them standing by the porch, and a dog had run forward at the sight of him, but a boot had been aimed at it and it had backed off. He could not see whether his parents disowned him or tried to offer comfort. He knew nothing of the photographer. Did not know that a middle-aged man with a Leica camera was revered in his home city of New York by fellow photo-journalists, and that the picture of the revolutionary and the terrified secret policeman had made a whole magazine page and been widely admired . . . and had been sent by the Hungarian embassy in Washington to Budapest. Painstaking work in the headquarters of the AVH had identified him, and several others. The photographer was a necessary and valued tool in the hands of the counter-revolutionaries.

A spade struck metal.

He had not dug deep. A bare half-metre into the ground, and then had covered it, scattered leaves over the scar in the ground, and dumped manure from the family's pigs, and had beaten that down with the flat of a spade. He supposed his father knew, but it had never been spoken of. The secret policemen had come at dawn, had kicked in the door and found him in his bed . . . The killing of their colleague had been long ago, and he had dared to hope that time had ebbed away, and secrets would not be solved.

He should have gone, as others had, across the border into Austria, and turned his back on his country and on his parents, made a new life, but he had not.

Men were on their hands and knees, staining their trousers and manhandling wet sods of earth, and the rifle was exposed. He stared at it. His focus was on the barrel and the stock; he remembered how it had felt in his hand, its weight, and remembered the kick against his shoulder when he had fired on the thug who writhed on the ground. He had felt a power and a strength that had never been part of him before, that he had never felt since. He had been shown the work of the photographer, but did not recall seeing the man himself. He could see the faces of the men and women who had pressed close around him when he had shot the policeman, and could almost hear the clamour of jeering when the man had wriggled a few more times, hurrying to his death.

One of them took a handful of grass, bundled it together and started to scrub at the metal body of the weapon. The number was called out. Only the last digits . . . 16751 . . . Another man flicked over pages on a clipboard, found what he searched for, and nodded, called that he had the match. A fast exchange – it was confirmed? Confirmed that this was the serial number of a weapon lost by a Soviet soldier in mechanised infantry. The magazine was still attached. Mud was brushed from the casing of the barrel and the selector lever and around the trigger, but some was still deeply embedded in the groove of the wooden stock. He looked for what he had done and saw where he had gouged out a small hole, his own record of killing the secret policeman. Another notch was dug the next day: he had fired on a tank commander in a turret and had claimed the hit, and argued with another boy as to which of them had taken the life: each had cut a mark on his own weapon. A short line, neatly cut, designated the Kalashnikov's killing life.

The weapon was fired. The sound of it echoed among the trees and was heightened by the low ceiling of cloud, then it was made safe, and the magazine was detached. One of them said it was remarkable that the Kalashnikov worked – as it was boasted it would – after close to two years buried amongst the oak's roots where the rain was sucked down. He was led away. His parents held each other but did not move from the porch; the dog had been put inside and he heard it scrabbling with its claws at the other side of the door. Perhaps, for amusement, if the dog had been free and able to bound towards him they'd have shot it. He was not thanked for his help. The rifle went ahead of him, carried with all the due care and attention of an item of near worthless junk.

And he cursed it.

In the gaol, some mornings before dawn, he would hear the procession of boots and the locking and unlocking of doors, and the little whimpering cries of a condemned man, and the rattle on flagstones when a chair was kicked away. He cursed the weapon, thought it damned. They would take him out of his cell, lead him into a yard, hoist the noose over his head, lift him on to a chair, and let him swing. The rifle was carried in front of him and silently, he swore at it. His eyes misted in tears, he could no longer see the oak trees that grew around his home. He had no answer from the dulled and dirt-cased carcase of the rifle.

He'd been working, done two deliveries, and was late for their rendezvous. She looked sourly at the face of her watch, and he tried to explain that he was late for her because of a problem with the number of cement bags that needed dropping off. Might as well have told the moon. She had been there fifteen minutes.

Andy apologised. She had shrugged. Andy told her about the volume of traffic. A deep breath, and her eyes were hard on him. Had he squared it?

He had. He was starting to tell her that they were not too pleased at him swanning off, and that it meant the driver roster was going into a melt, and . . . he had done it, was ready to go. She oozed relief. Was that the reaction of a girl when her boy said he could make a journey all the way to the south of France, a sunshine holiday thrown in. The boss had wanted to know what sort of a trip it would be; he said it lightly and with some irony. She flared. None of their business. Nothing that involved them. He sought to calm her.

Andy said, 'It's all going to be fine. I have the time off from work. It's agreed. I told them I was dead lucky, told them I was going away across France with a super girl, a really pretty one – don't blush, it's the truth – and we had some family business of yours to settle, and I was going to drive. Hey, Zed, I tell you the truth, all the guys are just dead jealous. It's going to happen, and I've fixed for the vehicle, my motor. The mechanics in the depot will go over it tomorrow, tune it up a bit. It's a hell of a drive and won't be the newest lady on the autoroute. They'll get it going and smooth, do a good job.'

It was a good little speech and it satisfied her. She'd leaned across the width of the table and had kissed him on the lips. Not lingering but better than usual. She was good at rationing affection, like it came with coupons: he was rewarded because he had put in place what was demanded of him.

She would see him tomorrow. Where would he be when the car was fixed? He said where he'd be, at the Hall of Residence. She didn't want that. Too public, and too much CCTV with lenses that recorded faces and registration plates. There was a park half a mile away from the Hall. He wanted to know when they would be on the road and going south. Why did he want to know, why?

He sensed she was primed, had a crib sheet of questions to ask and answers she was to get. He was smiling, he was the happy boy, and he thought her tight as a damned bowstring which he had not seen before. He needed to know the time they'd cross the Channel, or travel under it, so that the tickets could be booked. She hesitated.

Zed said, 'Not your problem, Andy. I'll do that. I'll fix that . . . What's the registration? They'll want it for the booking. I can do that.'

'Of course you can. And pay for it? I think I should . . . you want to pay, your shout – I won't argue.'

And did not argue, and would have told anyone who'd asked that, in his view, she would be hard put to buy a ticket for a tram in the city, or to use the automatic vendor for the train going over the Pennines and back home. He told her the make and the year and the colour and the registration and she wrote them carefully on the back of a notepad. He let his hand rest on her wrist . . . so innocent and so vulnerable, and quite pretty, and screwed up, and not knowing how it would be. Join the club, my love, he might have said. He gazed at her, looked earnest, and honest. He'd learn, all in good time, what the family business was, why she needed a simple boy – with a Labrador's devotion – to drive her the length of France and back. Interesting times.

The winds came off the Sahara and climbed above the mountains and gathered force when they came back down to cross the beaches and the fishing villages and reach the western Mediterranean. The freighter was the *Margarethe*. She flew a Dutch flag of convenience, was registered in Rotterdam, but at that point her connections were severed. Her master and navigation officer, along with the engineer, were Egyptian; her deck crew and mess stewards Tunisian. The journey she had set out on was some 900 nautical miles and she rolled and rocked in the swell that the wind stored up, and would make poor time on her journey towards the great bite that formed the coastline of southern France.

The captain was resting in his cabin. He was spread-eagled on the bunk bed awarded him, with a decent mattress and good storage space underneath for his personal baggage. Behind his rucksack and his grip bag was the package. It had been well wrapped up but, from its length and its general shape, though hard edges were disguised by the bubble-wrap, he had a fair idea of what it was: and only one. The looted antiquities that his boat carried, to be sold on the clandestine market to high-value collectors – in secrecy – were of far greater value than one rifle. He had been told that future cargo would be put his way, all of it paid for in the crisp currency of used American dollar bills, if this mission was performed satisfactorily. He had met a fearsome elderly man, of short stature and with a thick and blunt-trimmed grey beard, who had worn dark glasses even though the light on the quayside at Misrata was pitiful. He had thought it in his interests to perform satisfactorily, or at a higher standard, but wished – a little – that the introduction had not been made. The *Margarethe* pitched in the swell, rolling him from one side of his bunk to the other, and they made slow progress. It was extraordinary to him that one rifle was an important piece of cargo.

A tension weighed heavy in the air under the Mediterranean sun.

They all recognised it, including Karym. At nineteen years old, with a haircut that represented the fashion of the day – styled on the scalp and shaved close at the sides – wearing cast-off clothing from the big store in the shopping mall across the valley where his sister worked and had concessions, and with a weak, diseased arm, carrying a lit cigarette – permanent, Karym had good antennae for approaching danger. Not for him, for another.

He sat among the huge quarried rocks that blocked the main entrance to the La Castellane project, making it impossible for cars to get inside and spill out their passengers. Who might have wanted to? The police . . . rivals from other projects. His damaged left arm was the victim of childhood polio. Karym was the younger brother of Hamid, which mattered in the jungle life of the project. His elder brother treated Karym with contempt, insulted and abused him but looked after him. Not to have had such protection, in a place like La Castellane, and to be crippled by a useless arm and unable to fight back would have been fatal. Not to be able to fight, to wield a knife, was weakness, exploitable: Karym had heard stories of the fights between rats, a pair placed in a high-sided galvanised tub, and sticks used to annoy, then goad them into fighting – to the death. Only one rat could survive the combat in front of a raucous crowd of youths in La Castellane, but in its moment of victory it would be clubbed to death, or have a cross-terrier set on it. Karym was protected because his elder brother had power, and exercised it. Karym had no power, no influence, was an impediment and a burden, and his intelligence was seldom asked for.

What hung in the air, like smoke from the oil drums where rubbish was burned when there was no wind, was the knowledge that a dire punishment was about to be visited on a wretch who had allowed arrogance or pills or stupidity to mess with an assault rifle. The rifle was part of the armoury owned by Karym's elder brother. The weapons were not stored in one place, but were kept in various safe houses, watched over by the *nourrices*, the 'nannies', women with no criminal record. A boy who was a braggart, pumped up with the sensation of carrying a loaded Kalashnikov taken from his mother's store, had walked through the project, firing off shots. Hamid had retrieved the rifle. The 'nanny' had led away her son . . . there would be retribution and the imposition of discipline. It was what happened, it was normal. The mother would already have tried to open channels to Karym's brother, perhaps through a schoolmaster, or with an imam, or any figure who had age and status.

With a population of nearly 7000, La Castellane was the work of a celebrated community architect. Once, half a century before, it had been a source of pride, admiration; now, it was known for unemployment, drugs, prostitution, arms trafficking, anything to do with the black economy. Turf wars were fought with the intensity the rats would have used. Newspapers in the Marseille area described it as a 'supermarket' for all things criminal. Three networks controlled the various trades: the 'place de Merou', the 'Tour K', and 'La Jougardelle', but below those feral power bases were individuals who had obtained franchises and paid tithes for the privilege of operating . . . It was the same in all the projects, and one of those, operating out of a stairwell, was under the power of Hamid, brother of Karym. His world was one of gaunt towers peppered with narrow windows and disfigured by satellite dishes, narrow walkways and dense heaps of concrete buildings that strangers would find impossible to navigate. There, his power base, Hamid could turn over some 50,000 euros each day and customers would come from across the region, and some would buy small for their own consumption, and some would buy big and then sell on in German cities, or to the Dutch market, or take the arrangement across the Channel and market it to the British.

Karym, his antennae twitching, watched, waited, as the tension built. Growing in strength, the wind funnelled between the buildings and chivvied rubbish into corners, and the sunlight made stark shadows from the few trees surviving in the open spaces, and the washing flapped on its lines and seemed to cry.

The boy who had taken the Kalashnikov and who had ambled around in the project had not been seen. But his mother had been noticed as she flitted between those whom she believed might influence what would happen to her son. Where was he? Hiding in his room, perhaps smoking as if that were a release from the fear, and unable to flee because there was no world for him outside the project. His family was in La Castellane, every person he knew was there. He could not pitch up in Saint-Barthélemy, or La Paternelle or La Bricarde, and knock on a door and ask for refuge. Could not go to a *gendarmerie* down the road and towards the airport or up by the big school and request food and lodging and protection and offer to name names and . . . The boy would have to hope that his mother came up with something, and would be sitting on his bed and looking from a high window and might see the sea, and the blue between the white caps of the waves, and might see the cleanness of the sky, and might think everything was beyond his reach.

On earphones, Karym listened to music. It was still early in the day. Night was the time that the customers came, parked in the main road, left vehicles with the engines ticking over and hurried through the checks and were directed to the *rabbatteurs* and be sold the goods and hand over the money. The police were not there often. The chances of infiltration were slim – this was an area skilled in the recognition of the 'pigs'. There were informers, occasionally, who had taken the police money – never much – and who lived short and dangerous days. Recently, the police had dressed up two of their men in full-length Arab clothing and had sent them into La Castellane to arrest a *ravitailleur*, a supplier, and their suspect had run, and the crowd had gathered and the police had legged it, scampered for their lives, their robes billowing behind them. The music Karym listened to was from across the sea, from Tunisia where his father lived: never seen, did not write or telephone, never sent money. The music beat in his head. He was one of many who watched the entrance to the project. Later, when darkness came, he would be busy, alert. He had a grievance with the boy who had taken the Kalashnikov rifle stored by his mother. A sharp grievance.

He had never fired one. Had never peered with his right eye down the barrel, locking on the V and the needle, with the setting at Battle Sight Zero. Had never slid his finger inside the guard and wrapped it on the trigger and squeezed until there was the clap of the explosion and the thud of the recoil in his shoulder. Had never done it. Hamid said that his weak arm would not be strong enough to hold and aim and fire . . . But he was an expert on the weapon. Of the one hundred million that were believed to have been manufactured, Karym could name the principal factories where the Russians had produced them and all the other copies had been made: Russia, Poland, Romania, Bulgaria, Hungary, old East Germany, Finland, Serbia . . . knew them all, those and many others. Knew the calibre of the ammunition and the weight of grain that propelled the bullets. Knew the weapon's effective range. Knew the art of stripping one, and reassembling it, could do it blindfolded. But had never fired one in practice or in anger . . . It was a grievance and it festered . . . He could tell the Chinese one from the Egyptian one, and both from the Iraqi one. Knew everything, except how it felt when the impact careered into the shoulder joint. The kid, an idiot, knew more of the Kalashnikov, the AK-47, than Karym did and had fired it – and would face a terrible retribution for taking it from his mother's safekeeping. There was little forgiveness in the project, clemency came rarely to La Castellane, and the boy was a walking dead. Karym heard his music and absorbed the atmosphere around him. His brother had gone to Marseille to meet a man: had not shared the details. He had never seen rats fight but imagined it to be dramatic, but had seen a walking dead, had watched, and knew the smell of it.

The wind blew more fiercely, but could not remove the atmosphere of spectacle and anticipation, and a clock ticked.

* * *

He was in his bedsit with a grip bag on the bed, and a plastic sack.

Andy cleared drawers.

Most of his clothes went into the sack, and a few – what he'd need for a week – were laid more carefully in the grip. Shoes, trousers and overalls, underwear and socks, sweaters and his second anorak, and his sponge bag, and the little bedside clock with the built-in alarm went in to the plastic bag because he would have no need of them down in the south of France. He was meticulous. Each cupboard and drawer was checked, double-checked, and he'd been down on his hands and knees to look under the bed. When he chose to, he could close the door after him and hear the lock in the catch and go down into the hallway and know that nothing of Andy Knight was left behind for a stranger to find ... They'd come looking, too right. Would look, maybe in a fortnight or a month, and curse and swear and damn him, would find nothing. He'd see her tomorrow, after the car had been tuned up, would talk with her and get the schedule: where they were going and when.

Rather basic, how it had started, him and her. Manchester, out to the east of the city centre. He was there.

Three boys. They would have seen a young woman, heading for the Deansgate area where the bright lights were and the big shops and the crowds. Head held high, and no scarf and no robe covering the jeans and the anorak that the guys she's been meeting had wanted her to wear. They'd have expected her to take a bus, but there must have been trouble on the route that night: a coincidence. No bus, so she had walked, and three boys had spotted her. She would have had a handbag held close to her body as protection against a mugger, and she would have had her rucksack strap across a shoulder and she might have been hurrying and nervous or might have been sauntering and digesting what had come from her meeting ... Could have seen the three boys, or not. The road went past a couple of old warehouses, converted in to smart office space but most of the employees would have shut down their screens and gone to the bars in town.

Andy ambling along, a lorry driver, doing deliveries for a company providing materials from a wholesaler to building sites . . . Did not have to be specified what he was doing in that side street, where he had been, where he was going, not a necessary part of the story. But he was there, and saw it unfold.

One in front of her, one alongside and one behind her, hands reaching out for her. She was jostled first, then pushed, and someone would have grabbed the strap of the rucksack and another would have gone for the handle of her bag, and she would have stumbled. Pretty classic mugging technique, and that part of the city had high marks for street crime. A little squeal, then a shout that was strangled down in her throat, as the boy wrestling with the rucksack hit her. Something between a slap and a punch, catching her across the mouth and cutting off the squeal. No one to hear her except for Andy, who happened to be around a hundred yards away up a side street. She went down, but was spirited. A bit less naivete and she would have let go of her rucksack, and with plenty less obduracy, she'd have given up her bag. What was in the bag? Student stuff, some cosmetics, and a purse which would have been near empty because she hadn't been to the bank for weekend spending money. She was clinging to her rucksack and had the bag in front of her and went down on to the dirt and the weeds of the pavement. A boot went in hard, into her ribs, and most of its force was probably deflected by an arm; one of them had bent down and hit her in the face and might have worn a ring because she was cut below the nose and above her top lip. Not much blood but enough to make a mess. Andy was running.

Andy – way back, before he was Andy Knight and before he was Norm Clarke, before Phil Williams, before the intervention of the rabbit – had been a recruit at the Commando Training Centre, down on the south Devon coast and close to the wide mud-flats of the Exe estuary. He knew, long time ago but lessons not forgotten, about intervention. Move in fast, achieve surprise, use maximum and sudden force. All three were bent over her and she was fighting with true bottle, real guts, to protect her possessions, seemed keener on defending them than herself, and their frustration grew, and their violence increased. He was close when he heard the wheeze as air was sucked from her lungs after a knee had been forced down on her chest and he thought her kicking and writhing were losing strength. He reached her: as if the cavalry had turned up, and not much time to play with. He had chucked himself at them. Three against one. Fists, knees, a choice head-butt, and the guys would not have known what had intervened, who had joined the fight, and the surprise was total. No quarter asked, they'd not the wit, and none given because his response was murderous. One rolled away on his side and was facing a wall, and his hands were across his privates and he'd cried like a pony that had hurt a fetlock, and another was stunned and might be concussed and had given up on the struggle. One had her bag, had wrested it off her. She kicked the stunned one, didn't connect with the back of his head but not for want of trying. The handbag was gone, and the guy limped off down the pavement. He'd gone after that guy, had jumped on his back and pressured him down, and there might have been a little cry, 'Easy, mate, easy' or 'Steady down, mate, that enough, that's . . .' He didn't hear it if there was. He had the guy by his hair, then banged his face down, hard enough to split his forehead, maybe loosen some teeth. The guy took off, abandoned the bag.

Andy had carried the bag back. The clasp was still fastened.

She was crying, not self-pitying, but from shock. A couple of cars went by and it was that part of the city where a wise driver would not have stopped to be a Good Samaritan but would instead have checked that his lock button was depressed. She was shivering. Andy held her tight. He knelt beside her and cradled her upper body and head against his chest, might have murmured something comforting.

The one who perhaps had concussion spat clear a tooth, coughed out, 'Fuck you, mate' and went on his way. The one who was against the wall still cried, and still held himself but scrabbled with his fingers against the wall and was able to stand, and looked at Andy – pure malevolence – and shambled away and was sick as he walked, half doubled up, and shouted back, 'See if I don't fucking get you, see if I don't.' He bent to lift her, was prepared to take her weight. She might then have realised that a man, a stranger, had an arm around her waist, and that her head was close to his chin. She'd have felt the warmth of his body. He picked up the tooth, eased a handkerchief out of his pocket, wrapped it, put it in her hand and said something quiet about a 'souvenir'. He told her she had done well, that the guys – all three of them – were in worse health than her. She clung to him, went weepy, and might have realised that she was now safe, that he'd not allow anything else to come close, frighten her, or hurt her.

That was how it had been, how they had met.

They had gone for a coffee. He'd been at the counter and she'd been in the toilets, and had come back, looking almost normal. The battering had been washed off with warm water, but there were dirt stains on her jeans and anorak, and there would be a worsening graze across her nose by the morning, and big discoloration above and below her left eye and the cuts would take a while to heal. He had reached out, across the table, and she'd taken his hand and held it. She had told him a little of herself and where she was lodging, had clung to his hand and he had found it difficult to halt her trembling, and he was her saviour. A week later, he had gone to her Hall of Residence and a porter had called up to her room, and he had handed over a cheap but decent bunch of flowers, and it was likely that no one had ever done that for her before . . . All a few months back.

4

He left an envelope on the bedside table. On the mattress were the sheets and duvet, all neatly folded. In the envelope was a month's rent, and an unsigned note of thanks. He'd be long gone when a phone call was made to the landlord announcing that the room could now be treated as vacant. It was the way Andy Knight, who he was that day, operated. No more checks to be done, and dawn was coming up, and he closed the door quietly behind him. There had been sex in the night on the floor above, discreet and quiet. Later, he'd heard footsteps on the stairs, and no doubt the guy who had that room had seen her to the street door, and she might have had to walk to look for a taxi rank.

Zed had never been in his room. Celibacy, of a sort, went with his job. He could have a girlfriend who was not under investigation, quite separated from the targets, and could do something with her, but it was frowned on and would load him with complications . . . and no queries about what was possible for a guy who was inside the small élite group of Level One Undercovers. Level One was the pick of the bunch and was hedged around with regulation. To have brought Zed here, turned the light low, maybe lit a candle, and started with kissing and slipping the buttons, was just about the most heinous crime he might commit . . . The professional standards body stipulated – no 'perhaps' and no 'maybe' – that it was never acceptable to bed anyone who was targeted. An unequivocal statement, a ban. The journey now was for the two of them: hotels, maybe narrow beds and a warm belly against his flat stomach. He went down the stairs carrying the grip and the plastic sack, and closed the front door quietly, and would have disturbed nobody. He had been through Foundation level, had passed those hurdles as Phil Williams, had been moved on to Advanced stage and had survived as Norm Clarke. He was one of the best, and psychologists queued up to meet him, evaluate him. Analysis said that he was the model product, what they all should strive to be. He was thought to have the personality that inspired trust, seemed incapable of deceit, and had in the past infiltrated a group working to sabotage medical experiments involving animals, had seemed a genuine and committed activist. Had also become integral to a gang bringing in Class A through the ferry port of Plymouth and then flogging the stuff along the M4 motorway corridor, and had been trusted. The ones who found him 'genuine' were still banged up with plenty time to serve, and the ones who had 'trusted' him would not walk freely before their kids were adults. Done, dusted, and behind him.

He went to his car. He drove a VW Polo. The registration said it was eight years old, had about a hundred thousand on the clock, and he'd bought it at auction for close to £3000, and the boys in the depot might fix him some better tyres, do retreads for him. He could not be seen to splash money, and the Polo would get to Marseille and he wouldn't be on a French autoroute hard shoulder with fumes seeping out.

For this operation, codenamed Rag and Bone, there would have been an examination of three principal parts. Did it have Proportionality to the potential threat? Was there Justification in launching it? Could Necessity be lined up with the danger posed by the target? It would have gone, with the pitiful relevant information available, to the Office of Surveillance Commissioners, and the case would have been put with all the emotion of a guy going down to the High Street bank and pleading for a mortgage. A judge would have warbled about 'intrusion' and the sins of 'trawling' but he'd have nodded, signed on the dotted line – then gone to lunch. Then the talent contest . . . Clutching their authorisation, they'd have gone to Specialist Crime and Operations 10. Who was available, who was suitable, who could say what the time parameters might be for Rag and Bone. The chances were that SC&O10 would have had to evaluate the competing bids, and juggle rosters, and decide which of the Level One people was best for what was asked. He had been chosen. Had taken the new name, had gone into the purdah world while a legend of his life was concocted, and the psychologists would have had their say: how to get a white-skinned boy up close and personal with an ethnic sub-continent girl from Savile Town in the depressed little Yorkshire community of Dewsbury. That was how it was done, and he was tasked, and they held him up, the Controller and the Cover Officer, as the best man they could have had . . . and knew so little.

He went to the car.

Some truths were bigger than others. Truths existed around the area of backup. The biggest truth, up for argument but peddled by every controller, said that backup – guns and intervention, the cavalry coming over the hill – was not negotiable and was guaranteed. A pretty story, and wheeled out often enough, and not believed. For Andy Knight in the little VW Polo and about to head off for foreign parts with the girlfriend, Zed, there would be nominal protection but no intervention if he flagged up suspicion. The smallest truth, not talked about, shrugged at: the thought of leaving an Undercover up the creek, no paddle. Wear a wire? Too easy, and any sort of microphone built into a shirt button or a belt, or posing as a pattern in a tie, sent off a signal, as did any sort of bug worn in a shoe's heel. Every shop doing security stuff, sold the hoovering kit that could locate microphones and bugs, and any people who were serious about what they did would sweep a room before they met in it. He would be alone. Better accept it. Somewhere down the road and round the corner would be the cars and a van where the boys would be with the H&Ks and the Glocks, and the fags and the coffee flasks, and a bucket to piss in . . . down the road but too far. Alone and beyond reach. It would take just one slip. Forgetting bugs and microphones, and heading into the territory of the legend, and saying one thing about where he had been to school and then, four months later, contradicting himself, and the school was somewhere else . . . Saying he had a sister one time but not the next . . . Claiming he had met someone a year back and it had not featured on the 'legend' that a hood had been kept on in prison for assault on an officer and had not been released . . . Too many times when mistakes could trip off the tongue, and the firearms too far away. And another truth: people on the other side who were targeted did not take kindly to the thought that a guy they might have liked, believed in, joked with, cuddled, was a fraud. The animal people would likely have laid hands on butchers' cleavers and the druggies would have gone in search of a friend who could rustle up a chain-saw. Zed's people? He doubted they were short of imagination. A mistake would go badly for him, and he was alone, beyond reach.

It was difficult, impossible – however hard the effort he put in – to lose sight of truths.

Andy Knight was where he was – there because of a rabbit, would have been a big bastard because it had dug a big hole, but hadn't the time to curse the rabbit because he was in the traffic and this was the last stage of the journey that was predictable. Nothing else would be. She was a good-looking girl, and could be fun when she lightened up, and he would betray her because that was the job – take it or leave it. Had belief in the job? Did, didn't he? He squeezed his eyes shut, risky when driving but the only way to lose the question, and it was worse in the night when the darkness was around him – worse than bad. When she knew, she would spit at him, curse, hate him, and meantime would kiss him. He drove to the depot.

Krait and Scorpion flanked her. Zed walked in the shopping mall, wide and open, music playing.

She knew the place. Anyone who lived in the city was familiar with it, visited, talked of its good bargains. She knew what the Irish had done to it years ago and how it had been rebuilt. Not that day, but on others, she had seen armed police suddenly materialise out of the crowds, looking at her, into her, past her, then gone. She carried with her the memory of their laden belts of equipment and the weight of the vests covering their chests, and their accessories – worn as easily as a handbag or rucksack or a furled umbrella

– were machine pistols while holstered pistols flapped against their thighs.

The guys with her were those who had first briefed her, who had told her, while she was in Manchester, to bin the traditional garments favoured by her father and mother. They had known those distant cousins . . .

One of them would carry the rifle, not her.

Zeinab could not have picked out either as being more suitable, had no idea who would be more efficient. The crowds were light. It would not be done on a morning such as this, but on a Saturday afternoon, or on the Sunday of a public holiday, or on the last late shopping night before Christmas. She could imagine it . . . Perhaps they would dress in black, the colour favoured by the defenders of Mosul or Raqqa or any collection of concrete block buildings that was an oasis of sorts in the desert sands of Iraq or Syria. Black was the colour of fear, recognised as a signature of the martyrs. So also was the profile of the rifle, with its curved magazine and distinctive fore-sight. She had never seen an AK-47, had never held one, felt its weight. She did not know whether it was easy to lift, whether the shots needed to be fired with the stock at the shoulder . . . She looked into the faces that swam past her. Ordinary people . . . Asians and Africans and swarthy south Europeans. It would not be an opportunity to choose who was innocent and who was guilty. Who lived, who died. Inside the mall the hot air was blown the length of the corridors and she felt sweaty, uncomfortable. Outside it was cold and clean and the wind purged dirt from her skin. Religion, in Zeinab's mind, was a straitjacket that refused flexibility. When the rifle was brought to this floor of the shopping centre, or another in the city, or carried across the Pennines to Leeds – it would be about her sense of freedom. She thought the guys harboured the same motivations. They did not pray at prescribed intervals throughout the day, get out their mats, face towards the estimate of the direction to the places in Saudi Arabia, did not go to the mosques, as far as she knew, even on the designated days. She was in a commercial shopping zone, not in a seminar presided over by a tutor whose attention would likely have been on the curve of her arse and the weight of her boobs . . . nothing about religion. In the seminar, she'd have articulated a view of a degree of liberty, with the weight of white persons' domination off her people's backs. She could imagine the raw, throat-stripping exhilaration as she pushed towards a bank of TVs in a shop and saw the aftermath. Heard sirens, sobbing eye witnesses, screams and hysterical yelled instructions from security, and maybe even heard the double tap of a weapon – then the silence. Would be a place like this . . . She gazed into the faces of the shoppers, the old and the young – some used sticks to balance better and some ran and skidded and chorused their shouts. It would be one of the two guys, or a man she had never met, and perhaps he would leave behind, whichever one it was, a recorded message that shouted defiance. And it could not happen without her. Because she knew it, she walked with a firmer stride and the guys sometimes needed to scurry to keep up with her. It did not have to be said. Zeinab understood . . . and Andy, her besotted lorry driver Her evaluation of him was 'unimportant but useful': nothing more. Attractive? Perhaps. She had been brought here, to be in the corridors, pass the huge brightly lit caverns of goods and displays, in order that she might reflect on the high value of a target. That she was brought here was a mark of the reliance they had on her. She wondered which of the two guys it would be, dismissed the idea of another and wondered if they would feel fear, and . . . round a sharp-angled corner.

Close to a toilet door. Beyond a Bella Italia and close to a Pound Store, two of them. Weapons across their chests, their belts sagging under the burden of handcuffs and gas canisters and ammunition, their trousers floppy and creased, and neither was shaved, and . . . they carried all the paraphernalia of their trade. They might have eyed the guys who walked with her, run the rule over them and lost interest, and both saw her. She would not back off, look demure and shy: she stared back at them, and straightened her back and pushed out her chest, and was rewarded: one smiled at her, the other grinned, and when they moved on down the corridor she was certain they'd have chuckled. 'Right little fucking goer' and 'Bloody come-on eyes, gagging for it'.

She turned to the guys, said she'd seen enough. Could picture how it would be amongst the blood pools and the glass shards and the sliding chaos of the flight, and the islands of those on the floor who could not move. Zeinab did not need to see any more. She left them, a flick of her wrist to indicate they should stay. She felt control, authority. They should stay where they were and wait for her. She knew what she would buy, looked for the display, found what she wanted: like silk, and the right size. Paid, left, rejoined them . . . Needed to see nothing more.

It was about a rifle. One rifle. To start with.

'You will do the close support, I watch. You will be rewarded.'

An old man had done the equivalent in his world of snapping his fingers for attention, and the younger man, like an obedient dog, had come running.

'You take care of it, the transfer. Small business I accept, but it will grow.'

In the world that Tooth occupied, his instructions were rarely ignored, and any idiot who did not accept what was 'requested' of him, would suffer. The reputation of Tooth still counted in Marseille and its environs. The years when he was a familiar figure seated in the cafés on the narrow side-streets off La Canebière, always facing the door, were long gone. Most of his time was now spent in the quality suburbs to the south of the city, at the villa he had built – still regarded as extraordinary that building permission had been granted for construction on that headland – looking out across the Mediterranean and towards craggy islands. He was the last of the Corsican era, as criminologists liked to call it, the big men who had run the drugs scene, and the girls, before the Arabs – savages from north Africa – had elbowed them aside, trampled on them.

'If it is satisfactory, this route and these people, then much will follow. You have my word: my word is the best currency.'

If he looked at himself in the mirror, the large one with the gilt frame in the hallway of the villa – which he never did – he would not have easily understood how it was that a small man, thick bearded but tidy, usually wearing a tartan cap on his greying hair, could create both fear and obedience. But, had he paused before the mirror and examined himself, he'd have been denied the sight of his eyes. Always he wore dark glasses. When he came out of the bathroom in the morning, they went on along with his socks and underpants, and only when he changed into his pyjamas did they come off. His eyes were pale blue, a lighter colour than the sea, and cold, cold as if frozen. The reputation that had lasted into his old age was fearsome, the reason why the younger man had come from the north of Marseille when told to. His name came from the Bible – Exodus 21–24 – an eye for an eye, a tooth for a tooth, and could have been a 'hand' or a 'foot' or a 'burn' or a 'wound', but Tooth was the name that had stayed with him. Anyone who crossed him risked serious reprisal: many teeth had been extracted, without a whiff of anaesthetic, because of stupidity, refusal to acknowledge the obvious. He had been told of this young man by a policeman who he paid well, had gone to visit La Castellane to seek him out. Tooth had walked past the kids who had challenged him, seemed about to threaten an elderly guy, lining up to jostle and challenge an intruder. He had told them to 'go fuck your mothers' had not backed off – never had. The kids had: would have recognised authority. He had not been armed, never carried a weapon, but he was known, and his reputation was alive. Having failed to find the man he wanted he had left the instruction to summon him, then had walked back through the kids and seen that they stayed warily clear of him. Most of those who had gone in the generation before him, the big men of Marseille, were dead – the Belgian, the Roaster, the Big Blond – shot in cafés while enjoying strong coffee, doing deals. He survived because he was discreet.

'It is one weapon. What do you have yourself, of the Kalashnikov, five or six, seven? This is one. We look for a new route. If successful we have the contract to bring many. Not from Serbia, or overland from Spain, but by sea. I believe it an opportunity.'

His best investment had been the filtering of cash into the serious crime squad working from L'Évêché, close to the cathedral, the name all Marseille gave to the headquarters offices of the police. With his back well covered he had been regarded as the Emperor of the 3rd District, his authority total either side of the autoroute from the St Charles railway terminus and almost to the airport. He was an institution in the city, could command tables in any restaurant or at the better hotels.

'Your name was given me. I'd not want trust abused.'

The meeting was in a park off the wide and busy Boulevard Charles Livon. Lawns were enhanced with well-tended beds, and the shrubs would soon be sprouting after the winter pruning. The view across the harbour, down on to the Fort Saint-Jean, was superb, and on this clear and sunny day, with a scouring clean wind, Tooth could see beyond the ferry terminal and container docks as far as the indistinct and hazed image – white buildings crushed close together – of the La Castellane project. They were sitting on a bench and behind them was a statue dedicated to local seamen lost in the Mediterranean. It had a realism in the work that might have created anxiety for any who might be about to sail in gale force conditions: he had no fear, and the work was meaningless to him. He had let the young man park his motorbike, go toward the bench, had checked he was alone, then had joined him. Nothing was challenged, everything was agreed.

'You will put the people in place, do what is necessary. Understand also that if your work is satisfactory you will find you are given access to those in significant positions who can advance you. I think that is very clear. I ask you one question, just one.'

A smile might have slipped across his face. Difficult to ascertain because of the thickness of his beard. 'My question – how do you respond to a man or a boy who cheats on you, who breaks the trust you have shown?'

He was answered. Nodded, seemed satisfied, said how and when the next contact would be made. The younger man was dismissed and started to walk away across the grass, skirting the mothers and nannies who had brought the children out after school and nursery . . . and he was pleased.

The life of a person with the status of Tooth was based on friendships: very few but of a lasting quality. He would be with Crab . . . At home he lived with his long-term mistress, Marie. They had been in a restaurant, Nice, on the Promenade des Anglais, and beside the Plage Beau Rivage. She had played the bitch, complained, irritated, raised her voice. Another couple, same age, were at an adjacent table. Marie had acted out a scene, would not have done anything like it at the villa or would have found herself out on the step with her clothes in a heap at her feet. It was about a bracelet in a jeweller's window that he had not bought her. She had made theatrically for the door. The guy from the other couple, a frown knitted in sympathy but grinning widely, had voiced his opinion, in regional English but Tooth had understood. 'Can't live with them, can't live without them'. He had scowled, then smiled, then let himself go and his laughter had pealed through the restaurant, and he had joined them. The start . . . him and Crab. Together, Tooth and Crab. After half an hour, Marie had come back. He had not welcomed, nor acknowledged her; he had made a new friend. Tooth had a strong nose. He recognised Crab's trade. They would hug, do business, laugh and drink. Make a good profit. They would eat well and talk of old times. They would feel blessed that they, old men, could still broker deals.

Tooth pushed himself up from the bench and the wind lifted his cap. He looked across the fortresses of Marseille and the city's terminals and docks, and saw the indistinct white outline of what they called La Castellane where the new generation came from, some of them . . . He liked what he had been told was the fate of a boy who broke his word, could no longer be trusted. Enjoyed that. He missed business, it hurt him not to trade; he was lost if he could not.

The younger brother, with the damaged arm, remained at the principal entrance to the project.

A couple kissed, sitting on one of the rocks that restricted entry to La Castellane. They made no effort to seek out privacy. Karym knew the boy. Both had been pupils at the huge Lycée Saint Exupéry, both drops-outs, leaving on their sixteenth birthdays. A teacher had told Karym that it did not have to be this way, that he was too bright to walk away from education. The boy had his hand under the girl's coat and she had draped her thighs over his legs, and the kissing was hard: the boy had already fathered a kid, by another girl . . . Karym had no girl. He did not have a pretty girl, a girl with a model's waist, a fat girl or an ugly girl. No girl, not even one with an itch who wanted it each day. In La Castellane, girls looked for a boy who could fight with a knife, who had the patronage of a dealer, was able to act as an enforcer. Any boy who could fight. Not a boy who was crippled, and who only had a scooter because his weakened arm was not strong enough to handle a serious bike . . . He would ride his Peugeot later, when his shift was done, round the nearby streets, go painfully slowly . . . What he wished to own and what he saved for was a Piaggio MP3 Yourban, and one day he would be able to afford it, and hoped his arm would allow him to ride it. The kissing couple did not see him.

The kid's mother came into the project. She walked heavily, like her feet hurt, and her face was puffed where there had been tears. Karym thought she would have been rewarded only with vagueness, had received no promises. No imam or school teacher could guarantee protection for her son, and the *gendarmerie* would not have listened to her because her son was worthless to them and had no barter value . . . The girl had removed the boy's hand from under her clothing and the kissing had stopped and she chewed hard on gum and he lit a cigarette. For a moment the mother's eyes met Karym's, and her anguish welled, but he looked away . . . he had no influence. Karym was without a girl, could not fight, had never fired a Kalashnikov, was worthless. He thought the mother decided the same. She would have known his name, and who was his brother. She trudged past him, went towards her stairwell, and would then climb slowly up the staircase. All the elevators were broken. No one respected him but he was, without grace, protected by his brother. The girl flicked her gum, and the wad hit Karym in the throat, and he turned.

The girl called out. 'When will it happen?'

Karym's head was sunk on his chest. 'Will *what* happen?'

Her boy shouted. 'Where will it be?'

'*What*, or *where*, I don't know.'

'Doesn't he tell you, your brother? Doesn't tell you?'

A crowd had materialised. That was the way of the project. One moment empty walkways and deserted lanes between buildings and under the flapping washing, and the next a crowd gathering and squeezing close to hear better.

'When is the barbecue?'

He did not know, said he did not know.

'But there will be one, a barbecue? Yes . . .?'

He heard someone say that he was 'fucking useless', a 'deformed cripple'. He did not know if there would be a barbecue, what his brother planned. It was usual if a stranger came to the project, or to any of the others where hashish was sold on the north side of Marseille, that the *chouffes*, the look-outs, would hem him in, quiz him, and intimidate. An old man arrived, pushed them aside, told them to go screw their mothers, had asked for his brother. Karym spoke to the man, seen no tremble in his hand, no twitch at his mouth above or below the beard and the moustache. He told him his brother was not there. Karym had been entrusted with the message, spoken quietly, as to when and where he should be across on the far side of the city – where Karym had never been. A name had been given and the man had walked away and when he had reached the outer barricade of big stones he had stopped purposefully, then spat into the ground. Karym had told his brother, and the instruction was obeyed, which had puzzled Karym.

There would be a barbecue, he assumed it. His brother would do a barbecue.

Astride the motorbike, hearing and feeling the power of its engine, Hamid, returned from his meeting.

Checking his mirrors frequently, staying within the speed limits to avoid police attention, he rode his Ducati Monster 821, with a horsepower of 112, towards the *vieux port.* He passed the Irish bars, O'Malley's and O'Neills, but did not know where Ireland was and why its bars were considered important, and went by the McDonalds, and returned to La Castellane. It seemed necessary to get the business of a barbecue done before he was taken on for work by Tooth: he knew the man's reputation . . . knew not to fail, and knew of the potential for rewards.

He wore a helmet; he was anonymous.

The meeting had made him both nervous and elated. Nervous because it was the first time that a legendary member of one of the old gangs had come to seek him out, and much would be expected of him, and he would be watched and bad consequences would follow if his standards were found wanting. Elated because it was remarkable that such a man had travelled all the way to La Castellane, had parked his car, had walked in and ignored the kids who had milled about him, had come to look for only one man, Hamid, which was a mark of his new-found success . . . where might his name have come from? He thought it most likely that a detective, one of the investigators working in the northern suburbs would have been owned by Tooth, would have spoken of him. It was about the future . . . If the future succeeded for him then he would not be riding a Ducati Monster 821, but would be in a Porsche, could be a Ferrari. With successful patronage he would move on from dealing hashish: he saw horizons unlimited and would ditch living in La Castellane. But he loved his bike. The ride was smooth, oozed power.

He turned on to the Boulevard Henri Barnier, did it with a swagger and a howl of his tyres, what was expected.

But, several matters confused him. Why was the packet to be delivered so small? Why was only one item, initially, to be delivered? Why these complicated arrangements for the transfer of a single weapon? He had not interrupted Tooth, not queried him, but he, himself, could have provided six rifles, and ammunition, and at a very acceptable knock-down price. He had been told a man and a woman would come from England to take delivery of just one AK-47. Confusing, but not for him to worry. Time first to arrange a barbecue which was necessary because authority could not be challenged.

'And where's it taking you?'

'Somewhere south of Keele services.'

'Word is there'll be a passenger.'

'Never rely on what you hear.'

Andy could not see the face, nor the shoulders, the head or the back of the mechanic because they were under the VW, but he'd heard the scrapes that meant shit and dirt and filth were being cleaned off cables and joins and from time to time a hand reached out to change kit. It was good of them to have found the time to look over his VW Polo: they were fine guys and he was grateful . . . but would give nothing.

'And the chatter says that it's a week's holiday you're grabbing.'

'Shouldn't listen to chatter, can give you gut ache.'

'What I was told, no one else would have squared it with the boss, no other driver.'

'Something came up.'

He was the newest of the driving team. Normal rules dictated that the last in was the bottom of the food chain, and given the crap work. It was a heavy time of the year and after the Christmas break the sites they supplied were coming up to speed, and the weather didn't matter. He'd joke, sound relaxed . . . but they'd get nothing.

'Boys are wondering how you swung it. One of our old guys, retired last year, he's coming back in as cover.'

'Probably pleased to swap sitting in his greenhouse, watching seeds germinate.'

'What I'm saying, Andy, is you have influence. More than I do, or anyone.'

'I don't suppose any time is ever convenient.'

It was the skill of an Undercover, a Level One, that he would not weaken when talking to one of the good guys, salt of the earth, dependable and the sort you'd always want minding your back. Would give them no more than to a stranger in a pub. Other than when he met the Controller or the Cover Officer, everyone he met was the subject of deceit. There were times – not now, too gentle – when questions were asked and he would act, seem to throw a tantrum. 'What's my past to you, what fucking business is it of yours, how do I know who you are – piss off.' Could do that, or just deflect. Behind everything he was supposed to achieve was the Mission Statement, the Aims and the End Game, and the detail of hour by hour was left to Andy Knight – or to Norm Clarke, or to Phil Williams. It hurt, and the hurting took a toll. Always did, why he had shivered on the bed last night, squeezed his eyes shut, felt weakened.

'And going off with a girl.'

'So they say.'

'For a week.'

'I expect the nation will survive, and the city of Manchester, while I flop around and get pissed up.'

The mechanic came out from underneath. Looked long at Andy, and hard, and was puzzled, didn't hide it, then he ducked his head down into the engine parts. An apprentice kid was whistled over, and was told to sit behind the wheel and do the pedals to turn the engine over. There was plenty more in the workshop that the mechanic could have been at, and plenty that was more useful for an apprentice . . . Andy was not a crusader, not a crime fighter for the glory of altruism, but he was addicted to the adrenaline – not the psychologists. Ordinary folks called it 'buzz'; the challenge of it kept him upright, going forward. A big challenge; bigger than with the animal people and bigger than with the predictable druggies.

'Where's not good enough? It'll not be Morecombe Bay, not Blackpool.'

'And my motor?'

'Motor's fine now, after me sweating on it. Right, Andy, how far's it going?' The eyes pinioned him. A truth at last was to be coughed up. The mechanic wiped his hands on a rag and readied to hear the destination and detail about the 'totty' that was going to be in the passenger seat. Time for a crack, never time for a truth. When he was gone and it was clear he was not returning, then every word he had said would be subject to analysis, and the boss who had given him the time away would be castigated as a dupe. No other way. Never was. 'Hope to die, cross my heart, soul of discretion.'

'Big secret – but I'll let you in.'

'Good boy, where?'

'South of Keele Services.'

The rag hit him in the face. He assumed the matter had come to a head, like a boil stretched by a bag of yellow pus and ready to burst. Most of the animal people were quite honest and very passionate and if he'd stayed alongside them another half year, he might have joined up. And the girl with auburn hair had set sights on him, and another six months would have been a problem. A hell of a mess when it was over and seven or eight ruined lives, and a hell of a lot more beagles getting syringes embedded below their skins. The mechanic and the apprentice had looked after him and put the VW Polo ahead of at least two of the big lorries that were showing grief . . . He thanked them, smiled – did not confide. They'd have loved the story that he was off on his travels, driving down through Europe, and a pretty girl would be alongside and might have a hand on his thigh, and might have felt tired and dropped her head and let it rest on his shoulder with her hair wafting on his cheeks, loved it and fed it round the canteen at the next scheduled meal break. He gave nothing.

November 1969

The cranes at Constanta, along the quayside of the Romanian port, swung the crates high and out, and then lowered them with no particular care on to the freighter's deck.

Twenty crates, each containing 50 weapons, and five more for magazines, and three more for 7.62 × 39mm ammunition; surplus to requirements where they had been. They would no longer clog up space in a Hungarian police warehouse, were being given away. Given, but still with a price.

They had been certified fit for action, had been testified, and with familiar bureaucracy the details of serial numbers, stamped into the metalwork at a factory in remote Izhevsk, were listed on the papers that would accompany the shipment. The particular weapon with a last five-digit identification of 16751 languished, in the ninth crate to be hoisted on board. That AK-47, it had been said in Budapest, was damned. Because it had been buried for so long it had failed to polish up like the other consigned for export, it had no sheen, could not be burnished, and the wooden stock was scarred with two notches and a deep groove. It was at the bottom of the crate and the officer in charge of the storage was pleased to see the back of it. It was a clement day in the Black Sea city, with a light wind, good sunshine and shirtsleeve warmth. The loading was supervised by a member of the Hungarian AVH unit who, when it was complete, would be taken by a Romanian colleague, from the Departamentul Securitatii Statului, to a night club then a brothel because the network of colleagues functioned across international borders. Secrecy was observed. Only nominally were the weapons a gift.

When the last crate was in place, and covered by the principal cargo, Romanian refined auto-fuel, the freighter would sail. Its destination – acceptable between fraternal allies – would be Latakia, the Syrian port on the Mediterranean. Lorries would be waiting there, and local stevedores would first remove the oil drums, then get the crates off and into lorries whose canvas sides would prevent their contents being viewed, and they would drive off with a full-blown military escort of Syrian paratroopers. Why, if they had no value, if they were a gift? Because the thousand assault rifles represented an expression of foreign policy. They would buy approval, cement friendship. Had the cargo been identified, then an Israeli Air Force strike could be expected. It travelled in secrecy.

The gift was only possible because the Hungarians had taken delivery of a newer model of the Kalashnikov, with metal parts milled by machine tools for greater efficiency, not using pressed steel. Only the previous year, Hungarian forces had gone to a state of alert because of an insurrection in neighbouring Czechoslovakia, in which Soviet tanks had been deployed to restore the alliance between Moscow and Prague. More modern weapons were demanded and had been obtained for the secret police. The 'gift' would sail that night, and would thread through the Bosphorus and into the Mediterranean under cover of darkness. It was destined for a Palestinian group, based in a refugee camp in southern Lebanon, and the leaders of the faction were thought to be most at ease with the Kremlin's aims. The price of the gift would be loyalty to Soviet instructions. The weapons, far in advance of what the group already possessed, would be used against Israeli territory when that course was directed, and not before. They were eagerly awaited, would be there within a week. Gratitude would be great, even for a weapon that had no lustre to its body, had a disfigured wooden stock, that looked to be a makeweight and there to ensure numbers were tidily rounded up.

Hawsers loosed, the freighter eased from its berth.

They'd reached London. A clean shirt, and clean knickers, fresh socks and a fresh blouse. Neither had been home.

Gough talked to customers. Pegs had a line into Marseille.

The customer was Counter-Terrorist Command. Clear aims were given to Gough. The dead boy fished out of the water was past history, a warning to others on the price of betrayal, a casualty, and unimportant. The priority, top of the heap, was the conclusion that a piece of kit was to be collected in Marseille, likely to be an automatic weapon with proven killing power, and run back as a test for a new route, one earmarked as ideal for the customer, the *jihadi* group in the north. During its transit, an opportunity was to be manufactured for the weapon to be put in the care of the boffin people and they'd do the insert of the tracker, somewhere in the stock. It would be followed, would see where it ran, and the swoop would net the whole damn lot of them, the conspiracy. It was what a year and more of work had been about, and why the Undercover was in place. The customer was very hopeful and Gough was warned that *SNAFU* was not acceptable. If he had to report that it was a case of Situation Normal All Fouled Up – or 'Fucked' – it would mean that one or more weapons had been introduced to the country, an assault rifle or several, and the consequences were unacceptable. His head would be on the block, and the blade might not be sharp, and decapitation might take a bit of time and cause a bit of hurt. But, of course, the customer was confident in his ability.

Pegs did schoolgirl French. Normally a matter of liaison went through the Europol bureaucracy in Holland, or via the appropriate London-based embassy. She had pleaded lack of time, could not observe protocol. She had been given numbers to call, and a name . . . and it descended, along with her smart school accent, into a matter of trust. At the other end of the line was a police major. She did not want *Direction Générale de la Sécurité Intérieure* which would have dumped her into a spider web of competing camps, did not want their full security surveillance units – wanted only a friendly face and a handful of cops who would sit in a van down the road round the corner and ask no questions and make no suggestions as to how the mission should be handled. Do traffic routes, give local geography knowledge, and leave the rest to her.

She'd launched in French when a call had been answered and the name confirmed. Good enough French . . . a crisp answer in English. A man who sounded in a hurry, and had taken a minimum of his lunch break, who seemed to expect to be regarded as a collaborator, not talked to on a Need To Know basis. He was Alfred Valery. When was she coming? She didn't know. When did she need the backup for an Undercover? She didn't know. She doubted that she would have spilled facts on to his desk to his face; down a telephone line it was impossible. When she did come he would be in his office, and a mobile was given for night hours, and she could call, and Major Valery would see, with his available resources, what was possible. He had finished with, 'We are quite busy here, madame. Much as we look forward to welcoming you, it should be understood that we have pressing matters that involve us.' Call ended. Fuck you, Major. She turned on Gough.

'You know, we don't even have his bloody name. Only know Andy Knight. Know nothing of him. We meet him, no idea whether he is a star performer, or whether he'll crumple. He is what we were given. What did he think of us? Useless bum scratchers? Top of the tree and efficient? Just average, just middling, what they call "premier mediocre". What I'm saying, Gough, would you put your life, happily and with confidence, into our hands? Do we deserve that amount of faith? What do you say?'

Gough said, 'We're what he has. We're where we are and that has to be good enough. Not important, what he thinks of us. We do our best, can't do more.'

She told him how it would be.

'Is that so, Zed?'

'That's how it is, and will be.'

She gave him the envelope, told him that he'd take the ferry out of Plymouth, would be going alone to Roscoff . . . Wasn't a usual route but the ferry company were trying out a winter sailing schedule, but they'd be coming back from Caen into Portsmouth, and he must have looked bewildered. Part of the astonishment was that they'd be going out singly, and part of his surprise was the degree of subterfuge she'd gone for. They were in the same park as before, and it was the same light but driving drizzle as before and they'd both been cold. Should have been in a café and the warm, should have been in the car with the heater on, but she had led and he had followed, and they'd come to the bench. He wondered if her minders watched, had not seen them. Probably the minders were there and watched him a final time, evaluated him: last chance to ditch him. He thought her strained, speaking as if from a rehearsed text.

'How do you go? I don't understand.'

'What is the problem? I fly. You drive.'

'If you can fly, for family business, why involve me?'

'We have a holiday.'

'It's a great holiday, Zed, you and me. Pity we're not together. What do we do, send texts to each other? *Nice where I am. How is the weather with you? Love and kisses – sorry, but imagine them.* That's how it'll be.'

She was flushed, unhappy. It could have been the first time that he had been sharp with her. Proper domestic stuff. A spat. They always said, the instructors that groomed the Undercovers, that a situation should not be entered when the outcome was uncertain. He pushed her . . . He was the guy who had been invited for a naughty week, some nookie was on the cards – a different problem and one to be faced later – and he was supposed to be the obsessed boy who had fallen under her spell, and . . . he heaved her into a corner because that was the reaction expected of him. Could not go docile. He thought her tough, no panic showing, and she might have frowned and her lips might have narrowed, and her eyes blazed. She reckoned she controlled him.

'I cannot get away now when I intended. You drive, I meet you, and we retain our schedule. Accept it. Live with it. You want to argue?'

'Just surprised, just upset.'

She trumped him. Gave credit to her, it was bold. Threw his whine back in his face. 'You don't approve, then you walk away. That's it, Andy, goodbye, good luck, been nice?'

He crumpled, had to. 'It's what you want, Zed. That's good enough.'

Andy had let her know he had worked hard to get the time off, not easy, and let her know that going away with her was important to him because of his feelings for her – admiration, respect, affection, or something more – and he could not fight her, could not take the risk of her marching away, dumping him. He thought it said much of her that she did not apologise, did not excuse herself. She had arrogance, self-belief. More than the animal people and certainly more than the druggies. And her mood apparently changed. Some might have bought it. Not Andy. She kissed him. That was supposed to buy him. She must have thought he came cheap, as a lorry driver would, and a warm kiss was his reward. It was a good kiss and he wondered if it were all play-acting. And the way he responded? Was that also play-acting? A long kiss. Light flashed: her anorak was open, her sweater pulled wide, her T-shirt had slipped down, and the skin on her chest was exposed, and the beam caught the stone on the chain that he had bought for her . . . not exactly, but she'd told him what she'd seen, and how much it was, and he'd given her cash. He did not often see it, and she never flaunted it, didn't use it as an actor's prop. First time in weeks she'd worn it, far as he knew. He saw it, supposed it meant something – something to her, perhaps something to him . . . And she broke, said quietly that work had to be done, an essay, murmured about the risk of being chucked out: first time that excuse had surfaced. She said when she would see him, where.

She was gone. Not a backward glance, not a wave.

He called after her, 'You're looking great, Zed, fantastic.'

She would have heard him but didn't stop, did not turn, went beyond a pool of light, and he lost her. Andy sat on the bench, let the rain patter on him. He needed time to consider and absorb, reflect. He had seen the flash of anger when he had – mildly – challenged her and he remembered when she had had the chance to lash out at the guy on the pavement, unable to defend himself. Vicious . . . how it would be if she learned the truth of an Undercover squirming inside her life. . . .

He had no more business in the city; and the pace had quickened, and the stakes had risen.

5

Out of the suburbs and on to the motorway, Andy Knight drove south.

Not how it was supposed to be. Zed should have been beside him. The radio on quietly, and her dozing and him driving with speed and care, and maybe her head drifting on to his shoulder. As a Level One he was not used to delegating the decision making; circumstances rarely permitted it. There had been control officers when he was down in the west country on the animal business who he had liked and thought conscientious, less so those handling him during the Swindon time, with the druggies, but could not be accused of shirking responsibility. Not then, not now, no one to toss the problem at.

He was separated from her. Object of the exercise was to keep close and keep her sweet, and listen and be trusted – look stupid, absorb. She had broken clear of him. He had needed to decide, straight up, how to respond. No opportunity to talk it over, get a second opinion from the old guy, Gough, and the younger woman, Pegs. Shared decision taking didn't go with the job. She was apart from him, and he had not thought it possible to lambast her for messing with him. He'd tell them all in good time, in London, what had gone wrong with the mission, codename Rag and Bone. But expect no help. He drove, alone, and his morale sagged, and he was supposed to be able to kick 'doubt' out of his path, but she was not with him, which represented failure.

Alongside failure, in his opinion, went error and close behind error was the one that mattered; mistake. Errors could usually be sorted, not so with mistakes which carried a higher level of hazard, usually – in his trade – lethal.

The difficulty with a mistake, which was what they went over again and again to the point of making him want to scream, was the instructors' insistence that most times the Undercover did not recognise it. A slip of the tongue, a confusion over the detail of the legend, something dropped that might refer to a parent, an experience in prison or in school, or where a family holiday had been, or seeing a guy last year – 'good guy, good old boy' – except that he had coughed it two years back, and not realising and no one reacting. Always, the Undercover was the intruder in the group, the last one to join and having to run fast with enthusiasm to catch up, be accepted, and being too helpful and too eager, and nothing too much trouble: they were, of course, the animal people or the druggies or the *jihadis*, dosed to the eyebrows with stories of infiltration. Hard if the mistake was not known, and the Undercover would try to be getting on with life while unaware that the rug could be ripped from under him, any damn moment, that he was watched and listened to, that the way in which he was cut out of sensitive talk was done with skill. If he did not know then there would be no trip to a car park or a motorway hotel or any of the rendezvous points where he could meet his command, the control, and demand out. How would it be . . . They'd ask . . . Was he sure? Certain? Could it not be put off, quitting, for a few more days? So near to pulling off the big haul, such a shame to abort now, don't you think? Big strain, could be wrong in the assessment? They'd say 'Have another drink, Andy – Have a refill there, Norm – Can we top that up, Phil – Wouldn't it be best to sleep on it, not do anything precipitous?' They did not let them walk away without a fight, might even get round to suggesting the Undercover ponder on the resources that had been swallowed by Rag and Bone, and might play the big card about lives on the line, people walking the streets, the great law-abiding unwashed going about their business and deserving, expecting, protection. But there was always a mistake . . . He realised that he had started to meander, had twice changed lanes, twice failed to use the indicator, and there were blue lights behind him. He was in the central lane, and they were coming fast track. That would be the fuck-up, then foul-up, pulled over and a boot-faced policewoman, one of the hard brigade and no ID card to conveniently pull out and wave so that he was sent on his way, was *sir*, a hero from the front line of some bloody war. The car came at speed, and the noise of the siren filled the VW Polo, it would get in front and then do the indicator bit and push him to the slow lane, then to the hard shoulder, and all so bloody inconvenient . . . The mistake he had made was to think vulnerability and so be careless on the road and lane hopping, and concentration down and a civic-minded driver would have been on his mobile and reporting him, and . . . the police, keeping up the pace went past him. He saw the flash of the indicators and ahead was a new Jaguar. It could have been that the cop car with the *feldwebel* in it had a bad thing with Jaguars . . . End of panic, but all about a mistake and what came from a mistake.

He used his mobile, called her. Heard it ring out, needed to speak. Her answer, sharp, querying what he wanted. He did the play-acting, the deception.

'Just wanted to talk.'

'We did, didn't we, a bit ago? We talked.'

'Needed to hear you.'

'What are you saying, Andy?'

'Wanted to hear your voice, just that.'

'Hear my voice, and what should it be saying?'

'Something about our holiday . . . would be good.'

'Telling it to you, Andy, our holiday – together – will be fantastic. I hand in my essay, and we're clear. Our holiday, and it'll be brilliant, and . . .'

'Just good to hear you, where are you?'

'Just coming out of the library.'

'You finished it?'

'You know what they say, Andy – well, perhaps, you don't – they say that an essay is never finished, only abandoned. It's what the tutors say. Not finished, but nearly.'

'It's going to be good when we're there, really good.'

'Course it is, Andy.'

'I'm halfway down.'

'Sorry, what do you mean?'

'I am halfway down the M6, the motorway, the car's going great . . . Zed, you know what, know how it is?'

'What should I know?'

'I am missing you, Zed. Missing you big time.'

'Thank you.'

'Missing you and the feel of you, and hearing you, and us together, and I am on this goddamn motorway, and going away from you. Zed, missing you bad.'

A small voice, and he had to strain to hear it. 'And missing you, Andy, promise.'

'Where are you? Going to have something to eat?'

Zed said, 'Just out of the library. Might grab something at the Kentucky.'

She lied easily. The library at the university was on the other side of the Pennine moorlands. She was in Savile Town, across the Calder river from the main part of Dewsbury. It had been a visit home, and she wore the clothing that her parents imagined she wore each day, every day at Manchester Metropolitan.

A facile question. 'Are you going to stop, have something?'

'Might do, might not.'

'I miss you, Andy.'

And heard his laugh, tinny on the phone speaker. 'God, didn't know if you were going to get round to saying it, Zed.'

'You'll be all right?'

'I'll be fine.'

'It matters to me, you being fine.'

'Look after yourself.'

'I will, and don't work all night.'

'Won't – we'll speak later.'

'Will do – love, Zed, love.'

The call went dead on her. The four-letter word. He had used it. Hadn't before, as if he were too shy of it, or maybe had felt her beyond his reach – race, intellect, education, She hadn't spoken the word, *love*, not to Andy Knight, not to any boy at the university, certainly not to anybody in the Savile Town area. He'd meant it, the call had dripped sincerity. She did not regard it as a complication, more a register of her success in recruiting his emotions: they gave her a car ride out of Marseille with a secreted package and a run through Customs on the way home, and she might have gone for a blouse rather than a T-shirt and left some buttons undone, and the pendant would be on show and nestling in the cleft, and she might have a hand on his shoulder, and the relationship would be on display, open to all-comers to see it and there would be a lift of eyebrows and they'd be waved into a green channel. How far would she go with him . . .? She was walking briskly. Didn't know, could not say. She thought him so easy to deceive, she could almost pity him. Almost . . . She had come to Dewsbury to see her parents. Not necessary to see them, not inside the routine she kept, but because she was going away. Would be with him, close to him, perhaps needing to feed off his ignorance and take strength from him – would sleep with him? Might, might just . . . well, expected to.

What could go wrong? Anything could go wrong. Foreign country, foreign crime group, foreign deceit, foreign police. Could happen, arrested, handcuffs and face down on a pavement, could happen. Or a shout, or running, or a lump hammer blow on her back and the pavement rushing up and weakness spilling, and never heard the sound of the shot. Not that it would but . . . it could. Had been to see her parents. How was it at the university? How was her work? How were her marks? How were her job prospects? Talk, of course, of marriages arranged by parents in their wisdom; nice, dutiful girls married to Pakistani boys in that country of donkey shit and smells and poverty, and a life shut away behind a screen. All that was usual, and she had done her time with them, and had hurried away. She would meet the guys later and they would drive her from the station in Manchester to her Hall of Residence, and alone in her room she would pack. Clean clothes, wash bag, a nightdress – what a bride might have bought for a wedding night.

She could not have said why she had agreed to buy it, his money and his insistence, did not own anything else like it, but felt the slight weight of the pendant on her skin as she marched fiercely along the pavement and towards the main road that led to the bridge and then the train station. She had nothing else like that, had never been given a present of that sort from outside her immediate family. Her confusions seemed to tug tighter. Traffic passed her and her back would have been lit, and she would have seemed the dutiful and obedient daughter of her mother and father . . . If she were taken, handcuffed, and led out through a front door smashed by a ram, her parents would be left to a life of confusion and disgrace. Neighbours would gather and gossip. Her mother would weep and her father curse, and the street would arrive at the front door, what remained of it, to console. It did not matter to her . . . what was important, signally so, was the cheerfulness and the smiles and the laughter, and the determination, of the cousins who had left to fight – as she would, in her way. She crossed the bridge. The super stores were still open, and she turned past the bus station. Then she would walk up the hill, to the station, then take the train to her university city, but after she had been in the lavatories to change her clothing.

Confused, but not frightened. There was no essay to finish. When she was back she would pack her bag, and the new silky nightdress bought on impulse.

The only narcotic known to Tooth was his addiction to varied forms of criminality.

He sat on his terrace, a rug over his legs, and sipped at a fruit juice and looked across at the Ile d'If, the Count of Monte Cristo's gaol, and the gaunt outline of battlements and defensive walls above the fabled dungeons . . . Fruit juice because he no longer drank alcohol: no drugs, no liquor.

Two schedules concerned him. When the *Margarethe* would arrive close enough to the coastline east of Marseille, out at sea but off the Calanques park where the narrow inlets were. A fishing boat would be in place and would take delivery of a package. One at first, but a trade that would grow with success . . . When his friend from the north of England would fly in, when they would be together to laugh and joke and decry the passing of the 'old days', the 'good old days'. He felt rippling pleasure as he lounged on an upholstered bench and the wind off the water tickled in his beard, tilted his inevitable cap . . . Tooth had not retired. Many dreamed of that end to a successful career, but would be disappointed. Those who no longer worked at business, at deals, at trading, however much down in the market place, were dead. They demonstrated weakness, no longer enjoyed protection. It could have been the burden of his age, now in his 72nd year, had he allowed it: he did not, and the proof was the slow limping journey of an old freighter out in the Mediterranean sea, and the imminent flight to Marseille of his friend.

He was a careful man . . . methodical, and with the ability to examine propositions put to him, dissect the risk area, and reject or accept. It was why he did not drink alcohol, certainly why he would never addle his mind with the hashish so readily available in the city. Careful since his youth. Tooth had been the tearaway kid, looked after by his sisters after the early death of his father and while his mother took in laundry, went out to clean, slaved to feed them. He had had no fear, no hesitation in striking back if challenged.

A bright dawn, the first sunlight, the start of a September day, had changed him. An execution before five o'clock. A use for the guillotine in the yard of the Baumettes gaol, not far from where Tooth now lived. A rapist and murderer of a former girlfriend, Hamida Djanboudi, had been taken out of his cell, had been walked across a blanket-covered path, minimising the sound of his footfall, had been taken to the machine after a final *Gitane* and a final half glass of brandy. But every one of the thousand plus prisoners had listened, strained to hear, had noted the dulled impact of the falling blade. Forty-two years before but decisions taken: Tooth would never go back to prison, would never have a brain too confused to weigh options, would always protect his back, move with a snake's caution. Others would run risks, not him, and he had survived, and he smiled to himself in the frail warmth of the sunlight . . . There were many investigators living in good homes in the 8th district who would discreetly duck a cap to him if they passed on the pavement, because he had nurtured their retirement with bribery, had successfully corrupted. It was about trust. He thought he lived in a replica of paradise.

He trusted, strange for him, the young man he had met in the park off the Boulevard Charles Livon; trusted him because he believed in the fate, as described to him without a moment of hesitation, of anyone who broke the bounds of discipline. Tooth did not do it himself, exact punishment, but knew plenty of men who would. Trust, and he did not expect to be proven wrong.

It was done with a formality. Done without noise or drama, done with a protocol. Done with inevitability.

The bell did not work. Hamid, kingpin of that stairwell, a little emperor in the world of trading good-quality hashish from Morocco knocked on the door of the fifth-floor apartment. Not a heavy knock, not one that threatened to remove the door from its hinges. He waited. Behind him, at a distance back along the communal walkway from the stairs were the sightseers, like the tourists who gathered at the quayside of the *vieux port*, who were the strong-arm muscle that he needed as watchers and dealers and couriers, but not required now. His younger brother, Karym, was with them. The mob would not be required, and he carried no weapon.

He was patient. He heard the rustling of feet across the floor beyond the thin wood of the door. A TV played inside. There was a spy hole and he assumed it would be used. A voice called out inside, the mother's. He would have been inspected, his identity confirmed. There would have been time enough for her to lift her phone, call 112 and demand immediate response from the *Police Nationale*, possible. But not a single patrol car would be tasked to go and evaluate a problem. Entry into La Castellane would take planning, commitment, probably the deployment of a hundred officers. She, the mother, would have known that. The stink from the walkway of urine and decayed food and rubbish filtered in his nostrils. He would not be kept waiting long. The mother was a *nourrice*, unemployable at her age, and reliant on the small income he paid her for keeping weapons or cash, or pouches of hashish, safe and hidden. She called out again, quite a firm voice. A bolt was drawn, a chain was loosed, a key was turned. He had not expected he would have to force his way inside. She opened the door. He smiled at her, without warmth, but as if it were correct to acknowledge a woman who he employed, and who had not given him – as far as he knew – cause for complaint. Her face was frosted, and her eyes were wide and she did not blink, did not look away from him. She called again.

The boy appeared, came from a room off the hallway.

There was no gesture to the boy. Nothing said. The mother held her son for a moment, then released him. The boy shook. Some mothers might have clung tight to her son, held him with a desperate strength, cried out so that the whole block knew her agony. Not this mother. She might have thought he was condemned, might have thought that her boy would be beaten, roughed up, then returned. The boy could barely walk. He did not try to run back inside the apartment, take refuge in his bedroom. He came out and stepped, swaying at weak knees, on to the walkway. Then the boy wet himself . . . the door closed behind him. They heard the key being turned and the chain replaced, and the bolt pushed across. Hamid took the boy's ear, easy to reach under his close-cut hair, this was a teenager who had regarded himself as a rising star, who had spent money on his appearance, but now had messed himself. A trail was left behind him and along the walkway. He might have been too terrified to fight, and his step was leaden, and the hold on his ear was merciless. They walked towards the youths.

Hamid knew the boundaries of his power. On this walkway and its stairs, and at the well at the bottom, his authority was total. With the small bearded man, knowing his reputation, he would not have considered taking a liberty: no action, no word, that might offer offence. The group parted. A day before, it was safe to assume, the boy would have been cocky, brimming cheek and mischief, and now his trousers were stained and he left the mark, warm, dribbling, behind him, and his mother would now be slumped at her table, head in hands, alone, convulsed in tears. It would teach the boys who followed them down the stairs, hushed and not daring to be heard, a further lesson in the need for discipline, and they would appreciate the show when it was done. A barbecue was always well attended, was popular among the teenagers who followed a leader, and a leader's money.

They went outside, past the overflowing rubbish bins that the corporation had not collected that week, or the previous one, or the one before, citing 'problems of access'. Likely they were holding out for bonus payments if they came inside La Castellane or any of the other nearby projects. The sun was dropping and darkness would soon envelop the close buildings. His hand now rested loosely on the boy's shoulder. The bladder would have been emptied and the boy was firmly pushed forward if he slowed. With darkness came the customers. With the customers came the banknotes, new and old, frayed or virgin. The project's life relied on the sale of hashish, and scores depended on the patronage of men such as the brother of Karym. All of the *chouffes* and the *rabbatteurs* and the *charbonneurs* and the *nourrices* were paid, had families they supported. The government did not come with hand-out cash, nor the corporation in the *arrondissement*, nor the bureaucracy in the Town Hall on the Quai du Port. All were paid well in excess of the listed poverty line. The project depended on hashish and the quality of the entrepreneurs selling it . . . All of the boys who followed saw themselves as coming figures, had ambition – but kept their distance and none had made eye contact. None would speak up, none would defend. He went to another block. The boy was handed over to new gaolers. An astute move: it meant that the credit for the coming barbecue was spread, meant also that the matter could be put to rest for a few hours, leave him free to start trading when the night descended on the poorly lit buildings.

The boy had gone, a door had closed on him. He whistled, and his young brother – the cripple who was Karym – ran forward. He said what was wanted.

* * *

Karym carried the rifle.

Not obviously, not as the boy had done, not as an idiot would.

It was wrapped in a blanket and tucked under his strong arm. He had been sent by his brother back to Hamid's personal apartment – a palace of modern furniture and drapes and a kitchen like those on TV – and had collected the weapon from under the bed. There had been, he noted, two small hand grenades in a half-open drawer and a pistol was protruding from under the pillow, and was loaded, and on a dressing-table was a can of pepper-spray. In the apartment, Karym shared with his sister there were no weapons. When he had retrieved the rifle from under the bed, he had sat on the mattress and had laid out the pieces of the weapon on the floor at his feet, had done it by touch and had learned its history of origin, then had put it together again, barely looking as the parts went back into place. Karym regretted that he had no friend with whom to share his obsession. Not his sister. Not his mother when she came from Cassis, the town where she lived and worked, and she would scream and rail that her family were vermin because of Hamid's notoriety. If the obsession had involved the fans of the Marseille football team then he could have shared. Not that the kids would go to the Stade Vélodrome to watch Olympique because that was on the far side of the city, away down the Prado road and distant from familiar territory, but there were boys who knew everything about the team, the players, the tactics . . . all tedious to young Karym. The weapon, the AK-47, the design of Mikhail Kalashnikov, was principal in his life. Nothing mattered as much as taking any opportunity to soak up information on the rifle, and to handle one . . . This one was crap. It would have come off the production line of the Zastava factory at Kragujevac in the Serbian state. They called it the Zastava M70, a poorly produced copy of the Kalashnikov. They came to Marseille from the Balkans by road or via a great loop which took them to Spain and then another overland route. Frequently they were intercepted and the hauls were large and the prisons bulged with the couriers . . . but it was, to young Karym, still a Kalashnikov. He walked through the project.

It was said – Karym had read it in a magazine – that there were still six million assault rifles privately owned in the Balkan countries, illegal and hidden, and any family that was suffering hardship would take the rifle to a dealer, haggle over it, get a poor price, sell it. It gave Karym pride to know that the projects of northern Marseille were the principal destination for the trade – other than the terror groups circling Belgium and the French capital, but terror was outside all aspects of Karym's interest and experience . . . and, Zastava made the ammunition. It was a clean weapon, might never have been out of its shipping wrapping, previously stored in a warehouse, then put up for sale like it was a used car, 'one careful owner', then bought by his brother. Maybe his brother had paid $150, or could have been less because the market belonged to the buyers.

Carrying the rifle, the boy who had messed with it – now likely to be trussed and in a bunker below a block – was gone from Karym's mind.

It was the freedom weapon. It was the rifle chosen by men and women who believed in seductive wars of liberation, and it was easily available to them. A child of ten could learn to strip and assemble, could kill with it . . . not Karym, who had the liability of his weakened arm. And had never fired one. They had made, he'd read, one hundred million of them, and he had never fired one, aimed down the V sight and the needle set at Battle Sight Zero, not one of the one hundred million – was worse, far more pain to him than the absence of a girl in his life. His brother waiting for him in the shadows, saw him, emerged.

Kids watched. He thought them the pilot fish that swam close to a shark. If the shark fed, ripped at the flesh of a seal or a swimmer then there was debris in the water, meat or gristle, which they'd scavenge . . . but they'd swim where the power was. If his brother fell then the kids would desert him, as they had deserted the boy taken from his mother. His brother took the weapon.

And was gone. Nothing shared. He was not an actor, only a witness – not a player but part of the audience. He did not complain. He had no affection for his brother, and none was shown him, but each was of use to the other. Karym's brother was a protector, and Karym was a useful courier, errand runner.

Karym took his place again, among the other watchers at the entrance to the project. He sensed a growing anticipation around him because a barbecue was planned, but he did not know when, nor where. When questions were asked of him, he merely shrugged, would not admit ignorance. But the mood was there, around him, like jungle creatures sniffing blood, and the first customers were coming to the checkpoint and would be escorted by boys to the payment and distribution points. Blood, to the boys of the La Castellane project, had a clear and distinctive scent.

The binoculars were passed between them, backwards and forwards.

'What do you read?'

'Read something, cannot say.'

Major Valery held the binoculars, high-powered but with a fine cloth mesh over the lenses so that reflection from street-lights did not flash back off them. He wore black overalls, a black balaclava hid his face, and the belt and pistol holster at his waist were black. It was a place he came to once a week or once a fortnight, and it had been found by his companion. There were few evenings when the Major was home, off the Rue d'Orient, near to the hospitals and the city cemetery, and far from the 15th *arrondissement*, when the offices at L'Évêché emptied. The district of Verduron, the project of La Castellane, was at the heart of his responsibility, but he had many, was worked to the bone. He had come from the northern city of Lille, civilisation, had been transferred to Marseille with promises of fast-track promotion after the corruption scandal involving the Brigade *anti-criminalité*. A section of investigators and their infrastructure had been proven to be on the take, doing it big time, for tens of thousands of euros. He trusted few whom he worked with, but one man in particular was marked out, in the Major's mind, as having uncompromising, granite-hard integrity. They hunted together, were often a pair. He thought his companion could not be bought, therefore had the greatest value, and was a proven killer. He passed the binoculars to the sergeant, to the one they called Samson. A grim name, perhaps appropriate, and neither wanted nor disowned. It was their habit to come to a vantage-point above any of the projects, where a decent view was possible, where a secure hiding place was available.

'Difficult to assess, but a tension.'

'Unusual, more kids hanging on corners, and older people safe in their buildings.'

'A priest spoke of a mother's visit to him, came to him because she believed he would have greater influence than an imam. A boy in trouble, a dealer, whatever – we can do nothing. It is a tough place, toughest for those who have to live there.'

'There is an atmosphere, something builds,' Samson murmured.

It was not necessary for them to be there, beyond the duty call, and neither would have shared the results of their surveillance with others, gave no confidences. The Major was known to have been brought to Marseille to restore a degree of integrity in the Brigade, and the Sergeant's identity had been leaked and he, his blue balaclava, his given name and the marksman's rifle, had become known.

'I had a call – not your concern but I took a call. Very grand, the Metropolitan Police from England, Scotland Yard, a voice that seemed to regard me as a hotel *concierge*, and they have an Undercover coming through: no detail, no explanation, just the suggestion that I make a backup team available. Not through the usual channels, but direct and circumventing them to save time. I come here, look at that place, at La Castellane, at the customers coming for purchase of hashish, all criminal and illegal, and I relax . . . I could have broken the phone, Samson, indeed I could.'

'You told them to go fuck . . .'

'Sort it when they come, time then . . . Samson, what do you see?'

The marksman said that his own quiet time in an evening, while his wife cooked or made clothes, or ironed her uniform for the next day's inner city policing, was to watch the nature films on the TV.

He spoke of hyenas in an African reserve, gathering because a big predator was closing in on a kill, and if the hyenas were alerted then so also would the vultures. They could smell, the hyenas could, Samson said, when a death was imminent, and the vultures watched through every hour of daylight. He thought it was like that, a world of hyenas and vultures and the near-dead, in the project.

A mirthless chuckle from the Major. 'And the kids there are the hyenas, or the vultures?'

Samson said softly, 'Nearly, not quite. The kids enjoy the spectacle of the killing. The hyena kills to eat or to clear the scraps left . . . it is a small difference.'

They would give it another half an hour then leave as quietly and as unseen as they had come, and they would go to their homes across the city, far from here, from the scent of blood. More customers came and business was brisk that evening.

And another difference, the hyenas in there, among the blocks and patrolling the walkways and entrances, were better armed than the men and women of the GIPN, had greater fire-power . . . not a place to go short-handed, without good reason.

October 1970

An open sewer ran past the entrance to the building. Old sacking, still marked with the stencilled initials of UNHCR, hung from nails hammered into the beam that crossed the entrance. It rained on the camp; the good weather of the early autumn had gone. Low cloud covered the hills to the east, towards the Syrian border. The building was home to a family that had once owned a villa and an apple orchard and olive groves near to the town of Acre: but Acre was now inside Israeli territory and this was a family that had fled, wisely or unwisely, 22 years earlier. The family was extended – grandparents, parents, and children. And instead of the fine villa and sweet shaded gardens and a smallholding, they lived in a construction put together with a hammer and a liberal supply of nails.

The shot was fired.

The roof was made from rusted corrugated iron sections, as if they had been found on a rubbish heap and brought specially to this camp for Palestinian refugees. The walls were plywood and nailed to the frames of pallets. Two windows were covered with clear cellophane which was stained, darkened and hard to see through. The roof leaked when it rained, the walls gave no protection against the cold of winter, and in that part of Lebanon there would be snow. The mud in front of the entrance was slippery and clinging. The family possessed little except their memories and stories of the past, and the cooking pots that the women used when the camp authorities issued food supplies. There was no work, they had no income, were dependent on subsistence aid. A gift had come their way a month before, but it did not help to heat or feed the family. The eldest grandson had been accepted into the *fedayeen* group that ran the camp. He was fifteen, conceited, proud that he had been given an AK-47 assault rifle as a mark of his acceptance into the training cadre. Many men in the camp carried weapons. But that day the grandson had left the weapon behind when he had gone for cigarettes.

After the single shot came the scream.

It was a hideous sound, that of an old woman pierced by sudden anguish. The sound split apart the sacking rags at the entrance of the building. Neighbours gathered. Those walking either side of the ditch that ran in the centre of the path, that carried raw waste and stank, hesitated and ducked down or scurried for cover. First out was a kid, a boy, five or six years old, thin and emaciated as were so many children in the camp. He was screaming that he did not know it was loaded, was only showing it . . . and already he had been kicked hard in the back and belted across his face. He ran, bent double in pain, tears on his face. Next came a mother, clutching her youngest daughter, three years old perhaps. The blood already stained her clothing. The small girl's face was unmarked and a sort of peace had settled there, but her chest was ripped open, and her back was punctured. Her only movement came from the mother's violent shaking as if to force back to life some movement of the heart or lungs. Next out, thrusting aside the sacking, was the grandmother. The keening scream came from deep in her throat and she carried the AK-47 rifle by the tip of the barrel, her fist clamped on it just below the fore-sight. She threw it, in a high looping arc. She damned it, in full voice.

On that grey afternoon with low cloud hovering above the jerry-built roofing and the air dirtied by the smoke from internal fires and cooking oil, little was clear, except . . . anyone who watched the rifle's gentle twisting flight would have seen that the stock was scarred with a dark gouge where a wood splinter had long been detached, and there were scratches near to it. The eldest grandson had used the rifle to kill a handful of goats, the feral ones that the herdsman could not control. He had added more notches.

A boy reached up, another teenager grabbed the rifle, tucked it against his chest, and sprinted clear.

The weapon with the serial number's last digits of 16751, now in its fifteenth year, had found a new owner, a new home. A child was dead. The camp was a place of misery but life would soon move on, and a burial would close down a small window of grief.

Beth packed for him.

'How long you going for? If you can't tell me, God's name, how do I know what to put in?'

She had a fair point, gave her that with good grace. It irked Crab to have to tell her that he did not know when he would be leaving for Marseille because he had not yet received the necessary from his good friend, Tooth. Nor did he know how many nights he'd need to be there, not yet told. But he felt, whichever day of the next week he was flying, rare pleasure. Would be with his confidant, his equal . . . That mattered. There were old men in the Manchester area who had fallen on hard times after their last stretch in Strangeways, and they hung around pubs and cheap coffee and breakfast bars, and if they'd seen him, well turned out and looking after himself, he'd either get a beggar's fist on his coat, or a foul rant of jealousy. Hardly any had made it to old age and still had good banks looking after their cash, and intelligent accountants who kept down the tax bill. So few people that he could talk to . . . he'd be on a lounger in the sunshine, a weak gin in his hand, watching ships sail towards the container port – half of them carrying Moroccan or Tunisian or Algerian skunk, and it would be good talk, without envy or acrimony. A simple little deal was in place, and he and his friend were far enough removed from the action to be clean. The money was peanuts, but a deal was a deal, business was business. He'd feel good there, like when he was young and a big player.

'Just enough for three or four days. Quiet stuff, what doesn't stand out. Some of the class stuff, where I'm going.'

'I simply don't think that will be possible.'

'Well, it has to be, that's the way we see it.'

Down the motorway, across the city, into the Vauxhall building but not going upstairs where the offices were. Carrying his grip and the sack, he'd been escorted to an interview room where there were hard chairs, a formica-covered table, a water dispenser, and a fluorescent ceiling light. Andy had stood, now paced. The woman, Pegs, was by the door, leaning against the jamb, but the man, Gough, sat on a chair and nursed a plastic cup.

Andy said, 'Of course it's the best option, but things don't work that way.'

Gough said evenly, 'Not saying it will be piece of cake, but it is what's required.'

'It's the easiest way to foul up.'

'Clever boy like you, always able to find a way.'

Generally the raw edge for running an undercover involved reporting back. It had already been agreed that Andy Knight would not be wired. They were saying that he would be required to call in, use a mobile, each day, each evening, make a schedule and stick to it: he was saying that was a straitjacket and sucked. He was tired and the drive had been hard. Supposed to be a professional lorry driver but it was different squashed down low in a VW Polo, hemmed in by big trucks, the light in his eyes, and unfamiliar with London streets. The atmosphere was bad from the start.

'I call when I can call, how it has to be.'

'We're sliding off the wavelength, Andy. I'm saying what will happen.'

'I am about what is practical and what is wishful. I call when I can . . . is there something else? Can we move on?'

'It is all about contact. The whole thing. We cannot watch you, but there has to be a steady link . . . Can I put it more bluntly?'

'Put what?'

He was tired and hungry had not been offered as much as a sandwich. None of the usual talk about what a hero he was and how well he'd done, and how pleased they were, going well. Not said . . . It was small, should not have been a point of issue. They wanted him tied to a schedule, he declined. They wanted control; he wanted a degree of freedom, to be his own boss, make his own decisions: call when it was possible and not manufacture a moment of opportunity. What could be put bluntly?

'Where we're looking from, Andy, we have this perspective. She's floated off, you've lost her. Separate travel. An arrangement to meet at a car park in the town of Avignon, very pleasant place and with a shortened bridge, and a Pope's palace, but a flimsy rendezvous. Not going well, is it, Andy? Needs tightening up.'

'It's the way things play out, nothing I can do.'

'And it's all vague and all loose. I'm not suggesting, Andy, that you're a cannon broken free and careering around the gun-deck, but she needs reining in. Thought you would have done. You don't just swan off into the sunset. You report and report often, and we act on your reports. What problem do you have with that?'

He hardly knew them. Not a case of them picking him, or him accepting the invitation. They were top of the acquisition list, and he was the guy who was available, and Prunella did the operational transfers for them, those on Level One at Specialist Crime and Operations 10. Was not supposed to like them or dislike them. There had been a stilted conversation and he'd gone off to create his own legend and that had taken months because this was a business not done at Grand Prix speed, and then there had been the 'set-up' on the street, and then four months since he had brought her, Zed, the flowers in her Hall of Residence. Slow and meticulous and careful, as it should be if mistakes were not to creep up on his back. And he was here and walking the width of the room and his temper was rising: he wondered if they had yet done a Risk Assessment . . . the dispute was about something so simple. He had to say, 'Look, guys, I'm hearing you and I guarantee that I will call through – any time day or night – when I can. Top of my priority list. Will call. Each time I go for a leak I will call you.' Could have said it, had not, had blustered and all the body language was resentment, as if something unreasonable were asked of him. The man, Gough, could have smiled, reached out and grabbed his passing sleeve, could have said, 'Your best shot, Andy, is way good enough for me.' Had not, and the woman by the door wore a sour face and twice had glanced at her watch, just one of those sessions that hadn't worked out.

Andy Knight said, voice quiet, 'Always difficult, I'm sure you'll agree, for those who have never done something to put themselves in the place of the guys who eat it, live it, sleep it. If you had done it, you would know that it's the equivalent of running up a Jolly Roger flag, skull and crossbones, signals immediate danger, they say something important and the outsider – not quite trusted, not yet on the real inside track, straightaway needs to go and piss, and if anyone follows him to the lavatory they'll hear his voice whispering, or hear the bloody keys going on his phone . . . my life on the line – not yours – and I call in when I am good, when I am ready, not on a schedule.'

A smile from Gough, probably not intended but patronising. 'Not the time for this. Leave it for when the psychologist does the de-pressurising, get it out of your system then. Don't think we are blind to the strain you exist under. It was an observation that you have lost your target, that we have felt the need to put a surveillance detail on her, the full works, costs a bomb, and done it because she waved you goodbye. Where are we? We are at you meeting her in a bloody car park in Avignon. Except, she calls the shots and that was not in the game plan.'

'It's where we are.'

'Not a good place.'

'It's about Kalashnikovs?'

'Our estimate, what they want most. You to drive one, two, three, what we assume. Different issue if they have Kalashnikovs on the street . . . Another thing for the blunt bit, we have major resources invested in this, have emptied out the piggy bank and gambled on the lady and you up close with her, and being taken into a whole network, and learning of people way up the chain. When we move we cauterise an entire set-up, take them off the street. Not just her, and low-level dross. She takes you there . . . Except, you are not with her, are not close . . . And, I run this shit shower – please, do not forget that. Please, do not.'

The voice had not risen but the speech had slowed as if for emphasis, and Andy saw that the woman grimaced momentarily as if that had been an unexpected speech from Gough, pithy and to the point. All for nothing . . . tired, hungry, nervous, and led inexorably into a spat. Trouble was, clocks were never turned back. Could not start again.

Andy shrugged, nothing else to say. He picked up his grip, left the sack in the corner, might catch up with it sometime, and might not. She gave him a slip of paper, an address. Gough did not look up, did not wish him luck. They did not know his name, where he was from, who had been important in his life: was not sure *he* knew. He left them.

Gough said, 'He's gone native.'

Pegs said, 'He needed a good kicking, you gave him a soft one, should have been harder. Suppose it happens to them all, going native.'

He'd gone, and they'd heard the security guard wish him a good evening, and the outer door had swung shut, and there had been a few footsteps, then quiet.

Gough still sat at the table. 'God, and I sympathise, but there has to be a command structure, and he has to understand it. We employ him, we direct him, we task him. The whole business falls apart if we let him just slide away, outside our direction.'

'I think you gave it him, but only one barrel. Could have been two, should have been.'

Gough remembered what a psychologist had told him, about Undercovers. 'Has to have a high motivation for law enforcement, but that's not enough on its own. More vital is an obsessive personality and a need to win. Must be a winner.' They had missed the last schedule where Andy Knight was supposed to see the psychologist, a routine visit, for an assessment, how he was standing up to the stress levels induced by continuous deceit. Such meetings were supposed to be regular but were often casualties, and no one seemed that concerned when the date had slipped. The psychologist had talked to them about the signs that raised a red flag: pulse rate up, fast and staccato speech, a bit of breathlessness, normally punctual and ordered but running late, anxieties about personal safety, short and uncontrolled temper. Standard stuff. He'd thought the psychologist to be a sensible woman, and she'd talked them through what the Undercover should be. The ability to blend, go unnoticed in a crowd. Not be easy to know, keep a reserve. Won't be noisy in a pub, not an extrovert. Suspicion of those he meets will dominate his character. It had seemed a game, not any longer. Might have been, the sea change in attitude for Gough, when they'd been shown the body in the water and a rather second-rate, or third-level, source had been submerged, marks on the face, still the signs of terror frozen in the eyes. Not a game any longer.

'What's to be done?'

'Nothing,' Pegs answered. 'Nothing to be done.'

A career detective, more than 30 years served and able to claim full pension rights, Gough stayed on for want of making the ultimate decision on his domestic life. He shared a small home of pale London brick with his wife, Clare: polite, separate, parallel lives and no children to complicate, and they did not embarrass each other. He spoke with the remnants of the Scots accent coming from the west, along the winding road from Inverary to Loch Awe. Once he was a renowned thief taker, then had been in the Branch, now was a tracker of *jihadis*, but anonymous, never appeared in open court or stood in the witness box. Pegs was a decade younger, and her former husband was on the road and sold printer inks, and the one daughter lived in the east of the country with a guy who hadn't fathered her two children. Both daughter and current partner she described as 'a waste of space'. What was her fault? Nothing. She'd never accept blame. She was the product of an expensive school in south Oxfordshire, came from money, but had turned her back on it and swore and cursed and drank, and the focus of her life was working alongside Gough. They were both comfortably certain that their physical relationship, stretching beyond work matters, was unknown in the building off Wyvill Road. In fact, it was an open secret, and their efforts at discretion caused amusement. The unremitting burden of anxiety, afflicting both – and many hundreds of others working for the Security Service and the Counter-Terrorist Units – was the hackneyed old adage of needing to be lucky every time, and the opposition needing to be lucky just the once. They worked desperate hours, were afraid to relax their guard because luck might then evade them. He would wear, day in and day out, except in the two months of high summer, heavy corduroy trousers, a lightly checked shirt, with a tie, and a sports jacket, and she would be in a white blouse and a black trouser suit and the minimum of jewellery. His hair had thinned, was grey, and hers was highlighted and worn short. They disagreed on nothing of importance, but he bounced at her and usually she'd claim the final word.

'Should I have said that, him gone "native", was that out of order?'

'He picked a fight, a fight about nothing.'

'Should he be there, Pegs? Or should he be pulled?'

'Can't do that. No . . . no . . . can't.'

'All laid down. Duty of care, pages of it in the manual. Down to us.'

'That is bollocks, Gough. Pull him out, just ridiculous.'

'What I said, duty of care . . . what is my responsibility?'

'That is a heap of shite. Can't go now. He has to see it through. Marseille is a crap place. He has to be there . . . Imagine it. About tea-time, Gough, on a Sunday, leading up to a holiday, and big crowds out, and they start interrupting programmes, and your mobile's gone crazy and mine. Someone will have a snapshot on a phone: in black, carrying a Kalash, lifting it up, calm as you like, and dropping another poor whimpering bastard. They hit lucky and we didn't, and the numbers start stacking up and he'd hardly be into the second magazine, and armed response is stuck in traffic . . . You'd tell them at the inquiry that you had a guy inside them, a Level One, but you pulled him because he seemed to be carrying the pressure poorly, and you reckoned that was your duty of care, seemed a bit flat and grumpy: tell that to them. You'd swing in the fucking wind, Gough. You'd hang and swing, and deserve to.'

'Yes, heard. For the greater good of the greater number. That is where we are?'

'He'll be fine. Have to be – yes? – fine. And have to hang on to the girl. Must.'

Back from Dewsbury, Zeinab was in her Hall of Residence room.

She had seen a boy from her floor in the reception area, and two of the girls in the corridor, and had walked past all three, had spoken to none of them. Inside her room, untidy but bare of personality, she had seen that her desk remained, of course, covered with the notes for the essay she was supposed to be busy with. They played no part in her life . . . nor did her parents, or anything and anyone else in Savile Town across the Calder from Dewsbury – except that it had been the home of her cousins – nor did her tutors. She belonged to none of the student societies, played no sports, and her work suffered which was, to her, irrelevant. Important to Zeinab were the shopping mall in central Manchester, or one of those on the outskirts of Leeds, or in Sheffield. Important, more so, were the two guys who had again met her at the train station and had driven her close to the Residence, then dropped her. She had been told when she would be travelling, and by what route. One had smelled of fast food, and the other of old sweat dried on his body, and she felt no affection for either, but they facilitated her though did not seem to give her respect. Most important to her, Zed, was Andy. The first boy, the only boy, who had sought her out, been a protector, then had come back to her. One bunch of flowers only, and she had treasured them and been to a florist to get a 'potion' to put in the water of the vase that she had been loaned by the housekeeper and had only thrown them out when they had drooped. She could picture in detail, like a film slowed, his rush to help her, and the strength of the blows that he had landed against the three thugs who were after her bag. The violence of the response lived with her . . . and he had gone after the one who had wrested away her bag, had retrieved it. Could recall also the joy she had felt when she had kicked the one against the wall, had hurt her foot but a small price.

Other than what they called themselves, she had no names for the guys who had met her, driven her – who had shown her the body of the potential informer in the boot of the car – and handled her. One was Krait. In the Quetta region, where her family originated from before the migration to Dewsbury, a Krait was a common and highly venomous snake, with a diet of other smaller snakes and mice. The second was Scorpion. Around Quetta there was a trade in the reptile which made it a valued creature – a good and healthy scorpion was worth $50,000 because its venom could be regularly squeezed from its stinger, bottled and sent to European pharmaceutical laboratories, highly prized . . . Her guy, Krait, she thought well capable of devouring his own, and the proof had been in the trunk of the car . . . Her guy, Scorpion, seemed overtly deadly, a killer, but had the greater value through care and skill and an ability to read their mutual enemy. She had been told when they would leave. A text would be sent that night to her tutor, saying she needed more time for her essay; she would not be chased because of fear of ethnic harassment. The bag would be packed, and the sales tag taken off the new nightdress.

Zeinab would sleep a few hours before her alarm woke her . . . He made her laugh, was devoted, was more than useful, the boy she imagined in bed with her, and she held a pillow close, spoke his name in the silence of the room – but most important, Andy Knight was *useful*, otherwise he'd have had no place in her life.

He was booked in a hostel south of the river. The woman in Vauxhall had fixed it. He walked there, went down deserted streets, and only occasionally was lit by vehicle lights. A rucksack was hooked on a shoulder. Once he heard the great chime of a church clock behind him. At the hostel, £20 a night per person, and the place was favoured by European back-packers. He was offered a multiple occupancy room – could have slept with three strangers. Pegs had told him what name to use at the desk. Must have been a longstanding deal that she had with the place. He would be alone in the room. It would have been the type of anonymous doss-house that Specialist Crime and Operations 10 favoured when one of their people surfaced for a debrief, for a night. There were voices but reasonably quiet, respectful of others. He found the room. Three iron beds, folded sheets and a duvet, a picture of the Queen on a wall and nothing else, and a doorway to a shower and toilet which made the room top-dollar.

He dumped his grip.

Flopped on the bed, did not bother to make it. Kicked off his footwear, dragged down his socks, shoved the bedding aside, lay in the darkness.

It was a job. It paid every month and the cash went into an account that was in the name he had been born under, and the workload as Phil Williams and Norm Clarke and Andy Knight had been heavy enough to prevent him from using it. No opportunity to spend outside the make-believe life of legends he constructed. It was a job where the psychologists spoke earnestly of burn-out, but the time to quit was never dangled, not while a mission ran. He lay on his back and stared up at the ceiling and a little light came from outside and split the thin curtains not quite drawn together . . . when the stress mounted, at night, he'd dream of the past. Before the dreaming would be the anxiety, growing, of a mistake made.

He kept his eyes open, had no wish to dream. Saw her face: a strong chin and a powerful jaw and a nose that did not hide, and eyes that could pierce, and the flow of her hair. If he watched her face he would find comfort, and that would calm him, then he would sleep.

If he slept, he would dream.

6

'Phil, would you come in here.' *Always a mistake, going to sleep, failing to stay awake. Memory time, vivid.*

'Yeah, just finishing up.'

'No, Phil. Now, Phil. Not after the fucking washing up.'

The door off the kitchen was open. All the rest were in the communal room in the front of the house, terraced and in an old quarter of the west country town of Plymouth, and by a miracle of fortune the street had avoided the local blitz. Phil had been washing up the plates from their lunch. Most were vegetarians, and the meal was a pizza without meat, but the vegans amongst them had just nibbled salads . . . the lettuce leaves had been rinsed under a cold tap but a spider had hunkered down and survived the sluicing and had ended up on its way into the mouth of one of the girls, then had fallen off the leaf and dropped on to a slice of tomato. Was she going to squash it, kill it, cull the poor bloody spider? No. She had picked it up in a tissue, handled with delicacy, had taken it to the back door, had put the spider into an overgrown flower-bed, and had come back to resume her meal . . . He might have giggled. Not a fun laugh, but something closer to a sneer: the girl was pathetic, didn't everyone see that? He was washing up. There were times in the day when Phil needed to be away from them, have his own space.

One of the guys was in the doorway, and barked at him.

'Leave that. Get in here.'

'Yes, coming, yes.'

Buying time, and drying his hands, and pulling the plug in the sink, and his mind had started to sprint because of the tone. Not a request that he might care to join them when he had finished. A demand. Phil was not the newest to be accepted; there was a blonde girl with big glasses and short hair who had come after him but she'd joined after reaching Plymouth from west of Birmingham where her group had been decimated by arrests. Phil was the last 'outsider' to join them, starting at the bottom with leaflet hand-outs, and manning the table with flyers on the evils and cruelties of animal experiments in laboratories. Not something that could be hurried and he must have been at it a full year – which was a hell of a commitment for SC&O10 before he was let into the house: might have been that the auburn-haired girl fancied him, might have smoothed the way. That was a half year back, but he was one of them in name, not a part of them. The rest, except for the Birmingham girl, were the founding fathers and mothers of the group. Still, some of the guys would stop talking if he came into the room, or would slide papers away. He left the kitchen, went into the communal room. The atmosphere cut. Worse than sneering when a girl took the trouble to save the life of a spider and give it a new home among the weeds in the flower-bed. Some looked at him and some dropped their heads so as not to meet his eyes. Two of the guys were standing and one slipped behind him and had guardianship of the door. There was a rug on the floor, threadbare, the pattern faded, and he was waved to the centre of it. They were still on a high, had been to a kennels two nights before, had let loose a pack of young beagles, the favoured breed for the laboratories, and the little blighters had headed off into the woods. Pointless, ridiculous, and they'd be half starved by now but . . . perhaps better than being close up to a hypodermic. Anyway . . . that was good. Next up was an address in the Portsmouth area where a scientist lived with his family, and he did research in a laboratory and was going to get the full focus of a visit, and they were at the planning stage.

Phil stood in the centre of the room.

Sarcasm. 'Hope this isn't inconvenient, Phil, dragging you off the chores.'

Shrill. 'Just a few things we're not understanding, Phil.'

Hectoring. ''Cos you don't fit, Phil. Don't seem right.'

Cold as ice. 'Some questions, Phil, that need answering.'

The bloody obvious. 'We'd be upset, Phil, if you weren't what you said – were a stooge, a plant. Bad times would follow us getting upset.'

He had a car parked down the road. The car had a clapped-out engine and the requisite three different makes of tyres, and the engine was shit, and put down a smokescreen on any cold morning, and it had a dash cupboard. Deep in the dash, behind an old manual, and stuff about the insurance, was what seemed to be a discarded pocket radio, out of date and out of fashion. It could still do broadcasting, could also do an alarm call. Press two of the buttons for pre-set stations and the signal was sent. State of the art technology. And, a two-mile radius for the pick-up. It would sound out in the Hampton Street police station. They were supposed to come running. The alarm meant curtains for the infiltration, also meant that he – Phil Williams – was in danger of a bad experience. Would they come? How fast? Mob-handed? Didn't really matter because it was in the car, and the car was down the road, and the alarm in the dash had been there since they'd been out to the beagle puppy farm. He always drove. He was the one with the car, was also the one with a job as an Amazon delivery driver. He drove and that way the group were supposed to become dependent on him. The signal would go to Hampton Street and then to a particular annexe office off the CID section, had to be picked up by one of the people – not many of them – who knew there was an Undercover doing the animal group. He did not say anything. Phil tried to look confused, a bit stupid and astonished that they came at him this way, no warning and from the big blue.

'Things that don't fit.'

'Too eager. Always there. Nothing too much trouble.'

'You come in off the street and you're a best friend.'

'You might be a cop, Phil. We can't just put a cop out through the door, Phil.'

'You thought it very funny, Phil, when Bethany saved the spider's life, took care of it. I am telling you flat, Phil, that if the spider had been a cop it would have had each leg pulled off it, then would have gone in the flower-bed – dead.'

Whoever he was, whatever his name, he had left home as a pretty straightforward kid, a bag on his shoulder and Mum and Dad quiet, not making speeches. He had gone, had joined up which was not easy, the failure rate was high. He was a Royal Marine, had done all the stuff. Was in a high state of physical fitness. Could do rope and balance work. Could do speed marching, and speed scrambling over rough ground. Could do assault courses and could do the 30-mile march on Dartmoor with his feet raw and blistered but inside the eight hours and with a pack on his back, and had endurance. Some of the NCOs had suggested he might go for officer training, and a captain had said he should apply for Special Forces. All glamour, and all massaging the ego . . . the rabbit had intervened. It was the rabbit's fault. There were eight of them in the room. There was a bay window at the front and he would have to go through the glass. He heard the quiet click behind him as a key was turned. If he made a run that would be the same as saying, 'Fair and square, well done, guys, bright of you'. Admitted. Like bending over and confessing. They would pummel him first, then it would get to be a frenzy, and he had been gone from the Marines long enough for his strength to have dissipated, and he had the injury from the rabbit's digging, and the aggression was diluted. He had heard them talking about what the future would be for the scientist when they paid the visit, late at night. They'd all be on him, and scratching each other for the chance to punch, kick, bite.

'Great cover, Phil, the job. We don't know where you are, don't see who you meet.'

'No background to you, Phil. Nothing spelled out. Where were you before coming to us, and what other group did you work with? Are we the only ones, a late convert?'

'Spit it, Phil, your version.'

'Good answers, Phil, or it gets bad, and bad hurts.'

He thought the girls would be worst, would do the big damage. He looked for a friend, found none. He did not know whether he had 'cop' written on him in big letters across his forehead.

The questions started. Following fast on each other. Hard to think, register. Pummelling him with questions, and waiting for the slip-up, the mistake. Not knowing how he would make it out.

Lying on the hostel bed, tossing, but asleep and unable to wake.

The guys picked her up.

The one Zeinab knew as Scorpion drove. The one who called himself Krait sat beside him. She had the back seat with her bag.

The text to the tutor had been sent: she had to be away, family business, the essay was delayed; a perfunctory apology, it would be completed when she was back. Dark, a spit of rain: foul and dispiriting. She was not greeted as a friend, nor as an equal. When it was Andy who met her, he'd be out of his car and round the side, seeing her coming towards him across a pavement, and he'd open the door for her and see her settled in, like she was special. Perhaps to them she was not remarkable, not pretty, not able, not a part of the team, just a convenience. To the tutor she was not remarkable. Perhaps he had a kid at home who was crying, who had woken him, and his mood might have been soured by the messages he found on his phone. The tutor was not supposed to have read the feeble excuse until she was well clear and had given her phone to the guys, had it replaced. Not remarkable and not greatly valued.

Dear Zeinab, Regret your essay is delayed and hope the family business is both pressing and soon dealt with. Just a formal thought – if your course work is anything to go by then your interest in that aspect of your degree course is only partial in my estimation. If you are not interested you could always give up your place, not be a version of a 'bed-blocker'. I note your recent offerings to me have been satisfactory at best, poor at worst. Some people, we find, are not well suited to the rigours of university education and move on towards other directions. Enjoy your 'business', and we should talk on your return and when your essay is delivered. Best, Leo (Tutor, Social Sciences, Met Manchester). Like a kick in the teeth, what Andy had done to the attacker on the pavement. She had read it, had not deleted it; had tried to juggle and was failing. They went fast, on an empty road, towards the outskirts of the city.

Was failing to keep up with her work, was increasingly drawn into the world of Krait and Scorpion, spent more time with Andy and the sealing of a relationship on which a plan now depended . . . could not do it, keep the necessary balls in the air. She did not tell them. Three times she had read the message, which seemed a politely phrased call that she should quit, go home to Savile Town, be the little girl who fell short and was not the clever bitch she had thought herself. The guys would have cursed her for removing a brick in the construction of the plan. Her parents would have shouted abuse at her for tarnishing their reputation, first in the family to go to university – first in the street to go to university – and it would have been boasted of at any opportunity. She sat and bottled it. She was drawn in, assumed it was like quicksand. Each step and sinking deeper. Zeinab could remember the heady times when she had first been recruited, in love with the memory of two cousins, dead, could remember every shop window with the careful displays from the last visit to the shopping mall – and the images and the blood – and could recall an old longing to be a part of that army . . . Turning towards her, Krait – whose venom was fatal – eyed her in the light of oncoming traffic, and clicked his tongue for her attention.

'It is about security.'

'Yes.'

'You understand what is the alternative to security?'

'Always I am careful.'

'The alternative?'

'To be arrested.'

'It is not, Zeinab, just to be arrested. It is to sit in a prison cell for ten years or twenty years. I assume the boredom of it is suffocating. You achieve nothing, make nothing change. To be arrested is to have failed, and you are arrested because you have ignored security. Or, Zeinab, you may be dead. If they arrest you, or me, or . . . They will come with guns. They would like to kill you. Who complains if they shoot you? No one complains. Perhaps it is better to be killed than to exist in a cell. If you attack them and are shot then they have to buy your life dearly and the cause is served.

If they shoot you when they arrest you, and say your hand went to a pocket and they feared for their lives, then everything about you is wasted. It matters to us, Zeinab, security. Always you must have suspicion.'

'Yes.'

They hit an outer road, left the city.

Karym watched.

The kid was brought for the barbecue.

A car had been chosen, an old Citroen, with bald tyres and scrapes on the paintwork. The car was owned by a man whose eyesight was failing and who had been told by the clinic that he should no longer drive. The car was in a convenient place, not too near any occupied building. The car was not chosen because it was spare to the old man's needs, but because it suited.

Karym had no role in the barbecue. He had seen several. The first he had witnessed had been when he was fourteen years old. He remembered it clearly: a barbecue in any of the projects was not quickly forgotten, lessons were usually well learned. His brother had organised it as a response to an infringement of discipline. The smell had lingered in Karym's clothes for days. He understood. Everyone in the project understood that discipline was integral in any project, would be enforced. The kid might have thought that he was to be brought out for a public beating, perhaps with an iron angle bar, perhaps with a baseball bat or pickaxe handle. Or he might have thought, possibly hoped, that he was being taken to an area of wasteland to be thrown down among the shit and the weeds and then a pistol fired into his kneecap which would mean hospital for a month and a limp for a lifetime. If he were lucky, Karym thought, then he would not have considered the prospect of a barbecue awaiting him. It was a refinement of his brother that Hamid, himself, did not bring the kid from the building where he had been held most of the night. The job was given to the kid's associates. In La Castellane loyalties switched fast.

Karym imagined the kid's mother sitting on a chair in her kitchen waiting for news of her son and hoping that she would learn before first light of a beating or a pistol shot and hear the cry of an ambulance siren; she would not have considered calling the police, not earlier and not now. With the night's trade over and the project quiet, there was little movement except for the flitting shadows that skirted the buildings, hugged the walls, barely visible, and the kid was led towards the Citroen. A progression made in silence, and the kid cooperated and did not scream and did not fight, did not resist, and might still have hoped. The bad moment would have been when the little procession came to the last corner to be rounded before reaching the car. Quickly, and with expert efficiency by a youth who hoped to take a favoured position in the organisation of Karym's brother, a tightly folded cloth was hooked up over the kid's head, allowed to fall below his nose, pulled taut and past the kid's teeth and into his mouth, gagging him. Round the corner, where the wind buffeted the alleyways of the project, would be the vomit-making stench of spilled gasoline. Now the kid reacted. No baseball bat, no pickaxe handle, no pistol noisily cocked, but the stink of the slopped fuel. A crowd was there – not the old people, but some of the younger women who would have put off their bedtime to come out for the show. They were the ones who knew the colour of the balaclava worn by the policeman who had the name of the executioner of more than two centuries before, and they had elbowed their way to vantage-points, had a clear view. Most of the watchers, joined now by Karym, were the teenagers who had no work other than in the evenings when they supervised aspects of the hashish trade. The smell of the gasoline would have been in the kid's nose.

Closer to the car he began to struggle. Karym's brother was there, at the back, showing no authority, no emotion, and claiming no involvement. It was the life of the project.

Arms trussed behind his back, legs tied at the ankles. A rear door opened. Thrown inside. The window open. He would have fallen on to a seat soaked with fuel. Tried to scream and could not; tried to kick open the door and could not. The kid would have heard the click of a cigarette lighter, would have seen the flame catch at the rag held over the flame, seen it carried close. Then the kid would have cowered as the rag was tossed casually through the window. Unable to shriek, his voice a gurgle, and no one helped him, but many watched.

The car exploded in flames and that was the moment a barbecue, Marseille-style, was lit . . . It was serious punishment but so also was the flaunting of a firearm and the breaking of discipline. Few, at that time, were asleep in La Castellane and the blaze climbed and the acrid smoke soared towards upper windows. When they could no longer see the kid, and his death throes, the crowd dispersed as if reluctant to accept it was finished.

Many slept, not heavily, and some were fortified with alcohol, which dulled awareness, and some were uneasy: none knew what was called the sleep of the good.

In the arms of Marie, her brightly painted nails playing patterns on his back, Tooth snored: he was exhausted from the physicality of their bed play, and had felt slight chest pains but had carried on because he never – from anything – backed off.

Undressed to his underwear and with his wife long gone to bed, the DIGN marksman, Samson, snored in a chair. The television had shown a film of elephant seals in some distant continent, and now displayed a meaningless snowstorm. He loved the world of the wild, its violence and simplicity. In a few hours an alarm would wake him and his wife in the apartment off the Rue Charras in the 7th arrondissement but until then he would sleep deeply, untroubled by conscience pangs.

And the Major – the response that he would make to the English visitors forgotten, expecting him to jump and liable to disappointment – was in his bed, his wife's back against him, and the difficulties of the projects were banished, but his sleep was restless.

Hamid slept. Had not wanted the attention of his mistress, had left the couch for her. He wheezed from phlegm on his chest – he had smoked too often that day – but sleep took him, aided by a dosage of quality whisky. The sights of the evening did not register, he never dreamed, and sleep was a black void for him.

And far away, in the better suburbs of the Manchester area, with the tickets for his flight in the pouch on the dining-room table, and his bag packed, Crab slept. Even the excitement and pleasure of taking up arms again – in a way – or going back to war, being with a comrade and imagining combat, could not stifle his rhythmic grunting.

Pegs slept in the bedroom of the shoebox apartment they rented in the Vauxhall area and close enough to Wyvill Road. But Gough paced and smoked in the living-room, would feel worse than death in the morning, had a surveillance operation – two vehicles – running, and on a table was his mobile . . . He knew the target had left Manchester, knew the tail was in place. The stress factor always built when a Tango was tracked, when the pace quickened . . . but, if the tail maintained contact and the phone did not ring he would hope to sleep in the chair, not disturb Pegs, get a trifle of rest before the start of another day.

In a fast, violent manoeuvre, Scorpion took the car from the centre lane on the southbound motorway route, across the slow lane and into the feeder stretch for the service station. They would do it double-handed.

With a sheet of notepaper against her handbag and a pencil in her fingers, Zeinab did as she had been instructed and noted the registration numbers of vehicles following them out of their lane and into the feeder. Krait, in front of her, had his own sheet of paper, own pencil. Few cars and vans were on the road, and if they were tailed – as Krait had tersely explained in a further lecture on security, what he called 'counter surveillance' and 'going into a choke' – *if* the cop or spook vehicle followed them, they'd have a list of the numbers because halfway down the feeder and before the turns to the Food and Toilets and the Fuel and the Long Distance Parking, they would slow to a crawl. Any vehicles that followed them would have to come off the motorway, track them on the feeder, then avoid passing them. Simple, the way Krait explained it. Zeinab peered into the darkness at the following headlights and screwed her eyes to read and record registrations, then . . . acceleration. They took the exit . . . already she had noticed new precautions; nothing said to her as if at that stage she had not mattered sufficiently for breath to be wasted on her, and Scorpion had gone over the car with a handset, run it along the flanks and the wheel hubs and lain on his back and held it under the chassis. Between themselves they spoke in a Balochi dialect; she understood a little but had never admitted it. Krait had been told by Scorpion that the car was clean, not bugged. What did she have? She had two registration numbers. One was for a Transit van with a plumbing logo on the side, a driver and a passenger – men, and the other was for a saloon car, an old BMW 5 series, a man and a woman in the front and another man behind them; she had noted the BMW's driver had both hands on the wheel, classic pose. They bypassed the facilities, drove fast for the exit.

She started to tell them what she had written down. She was waved to silence, like she was an interruption.

They careered back on to the motorway, and a car in the slow lane flashed them and a horn blasted behind them. They made for the central lane, and almost immediately for the outside, and the needle climbed. She sensed their stress, then abruptly the guys relaxed and their hands came together, like they were kids and it was football, and they made little squeals of excitement.

She was not part of them; they did not include her. What numbers had she written down? Told them, and expected praise. They said nothing, stayed within the speed limit. Scorpion flicked the radio's buttons, found Asian Sound Radio, let it play softly, music. They thought they had done well, thought they had done better than well when they passed the transit crawling in the slow lane, then passed a BMW and she matched its registration and it was crawling too. It was what they had expected, and they were laughing, but she was not part of their celebration.

Phil slept, still dreamed, tossed and sweated.

They were more aggressive. Questions came from behind and in front of him.

Some shouted, others whispered close to his ears.

His hair, sparse and cut short, was held, nails gouging his scalp, and his head was dragged back that he might listen better. Fingers jabbed him, a knee that was small and sharp cannoned into the back of his leg and he nearly toppled. He was beyond bewilderment, astonishment. He tried to answer the questions. Attempted to cling to the legend he and the instructors had put together, sanctioned by his Control.

He felt coherence drifting. Where had he been two years before? What town? What street and what number? What job? Where had he lived two years before, what sort of house? What colour of house, what colour of front door? The girl, Bethany, had her mobile phone and was clocking the keys, waiting for an answer. Describing the house where he said he had lived two years before, and it was the first time that Phil realised that he was slipping, could not sustain the lie. The instructors said how to react: 'Hit back'. The common refrain was to go for the big bastard, for the top man. Louder and louder, the circle round him, and he was digging into the limits of the legend and starting to blurt and he thought his defences were pretty much shredded. Had the instructors ever done it, the work that they lectured on, ever been part of it? Might ask them one day . . . He slapped a hand away from his hair, stood his full height. The big boy in the group was Dominic. Dominic got to shag most of the girls, had them on a roster. Right now, pretty much every night, Dominic was taking Tristana to bed, and making a hell of a noise of it, and Bethany was sulking because she had been stood down. Dominic was the big man . . . it was what the instructors said.

He caught hold of Dominic's chin, got some fingers into his thin beard, heard the howl, pulled again. Phil called it.

'Pretty old one, old as the hills. Like a bad B movie. Blame someone else.'

'What is your shit?'

'Put attention away. Turn it away. Clever, what the police told you?'

He was hit full in the face, but he noticed the chance. Like ice on a thaw, starting slow, but the moment of doubt was laid. It was the same as making a breach in the wire round a defended sangar anywhere in the Middle East, and had to be exploited and fast. The hold on him had slackened and the questions were drying, and his eyes smarted from the blow. He would not hit back, could have put the guy, Dominic, back into the Stone Age. He was jabbering accusations.

'Go out every morning. Say it's for fags . . . Who goes with you? Nobody is with you . . . Don't send anyone to get your fags, have to do it yourself.'

The guy readied for another punch, and Phil would parry it. He kept belting out the accusations. Spittle in each of their faces and voices rising, and the guy seeming to realise that a table had been turned, that the high cards had changed hands.

'Which pigs pay you . . . Hooked up with local CID, or hooked up with Branch . . . When were we last raided? You made this an off-limits safe house, Dommy? Leave it nice and tidy and they don't need to search because it's all given them, word of mouth, that you, Dommy . . . Are you their "chissy", Dominic? Know what a "chissy" is? Course you do. Tell them all what a Covert Human Intelligence Source is . . . tell everybody. You are shit, Dommy. Line me up and protect yourself. You are a fucking snake.'

One more blow was swung. Easy to weave away from it. The current girl was Tristana and the passed over goods was Beth, and they no longer tugged at Phil's hair, nor poked him, nor kneed him, nor had their mouths curled in fury, nor looked to do him harm. What Phil did was to offer a short silent prayer of gratitude to the instructors and what they preached. He had the guy by his shirt front and Dominic had gone limp and the punch was his last effort. He made no effort to defend himself, might have been too shaken to think on his feet.

A little voice: 'You think you are so clever. You pull the big stunt.'

'Do I?'

'Don't fool me.'

'That right?'

'I'll have you, have you bad.'

'Careful how you go.'

'You think you've done well – just get the fuck out.'

Phil gave a final shake of the guy's clothing, dropped him, let him slide into a chair.

Dominic hissed into his face, 'I'm going nowhere – a "chissy", a tout, a plant – I'm watching you. You are scum. Watching you.'

Phil stood his ground, had to. They drifted away, shaken, low voices. A survival, but close run.

And he still slept, could not wake or lose it.

The driver, Scorpion, repeated the procedure, the same manoeuvre. The stretch of motorway had been checked out on the road atlas. Few sections of the motorway had two service stations within a few miles of each other, and accessible on the southern route. A little chuckle from behind the wheel, and time enough for Krait to put his hands, defensively, on the dash, and the brake pedal was stamped on, the briefest use of an indicator light, and they crossed from the fast lane to the centre lane and over the slow lane and into a feeder.

Not expected by Zeinab, neither had bothered to warn her. She was thrown across the seat and her bag took her weight. She might have gasped, might even have sworn, and provoked fuller laugh. Then, a snapped instruction. Paper and pencil. She scrabbled for them and Krait turned round in his seat and grinned. The car slowed as it went up the feeder.

She knew what to do.

Easy enough, nothing interesting came after them. A long-distance haulage lorry with an address in Krakov, and an empty coach, and a tiny Italian car with the back stuffed with plastic bags and bedding. Zeinab did not need to be told . . . In the distance between the two service stations, *they* would not have had time to call up another vehicle, and a slow performance Fiat 500 had not the legs for following them on a motorway. She remembered the plumber's transit and a number for an industrial estate outside

Stafford, and remembered the BMW with two passengers. Neither came through. She said there was nothing. Krait had made the same decision and murmured it to Scorpion, and they did a brief punch of their fists and repeated the tactic from the first service station, but then took a different exit and crossed over the motorway by the bridge and went north.

She didn't ask, but was told.

They would go north for two exits, then come off again, then use cross-country roads. Why? On the motorway and the main arteries there were police cameras for ANPR. Which meant? Automatic Number Plate Recognition. First, they had not been tailed, were not under surveillance. Second, they had thrown the system's computers. Was that good? It was good. Both guys were laughing and punched closed fists, one against the other.

'The transit and the BMW – could they have been?'

'Could, but they would have to have followed into the second – simple.'

The headlights lit narrow roads and spray kicked up from rain puddles and the car shook from pot-hole impacts. Zeinab was a child of the urban sprawl: knew Savile Town across the Calder river, and the big stores round Dewsbury's centre, and the high spires of the churches she had never been into, and the higher minaret of the Markazi Masjid, and knew the fast food places and the narrow streets of the old town, and the Town Hall that had been smartened up by the council, and the bus station and the train station, and the streets of terraced houses. On the train from Dewsbury to Manchester, she sometimes looked at the desolation of the moors through the grime-caked windows but usually she studied. Zeinab had been out of Manchester and up the coast with Andy; they had parked on the dunes walked at low tide miles along damp sand. It had been useful in the association with the boy: showing gratitude for what he had done, his rescue – then a closer intimacy, holding hands and sometimes kissing, and his arm around her back and against her hip, as she had built up to recruiting him; her driver, her cover when coming back into UK with the package stowed in his car. She did not know the countryside or wild coastal places, would have said she thought them hostile, and had seen in the headlights the badger's corpse with its innards splayed where tyres had disembowelled it. Scorpion drove fast and Krait called the turnings which kept them on the minor routes.

Tiredness overwhelmed her, and the motion of the car was so soporific. She dozed.

The phone rang. Eyes still closed, Gough groped for it, could not locate it, flicked it over the table's edge. On his hands and knees, and the call clamouring for him, and starting to swear. She was beside him, had found it, answered it.

'Yes, the office, where else? Of course we are. You on the road, a target on the move, the only place we'd be.'

He thought she had done well. In the upper echelons of counter-terrorism, relationships with colleagues were frowned on: bonking, screwing, shafting, shagging – whether inside office hours or at the end of a day – was regarded as a quick route to a transfer out. He grimaced at her. He was half dressed and she was half naked, her pyjamas sagging open. He took the phone, cleared his throat.

'Gough here.'

And he was told.

And answered, 'No, I am not criticising, nor am I querying the decision.'

Was told some more. He assumed at the other end of the call was a night-duty staffer who would be poorly briefed on the implications of what he relayed.

Gough said, 'So they aborted. Very good. I am sure it was for sound operational reasons. But they aborted.'

The manoeuvres were set out, what the target car had done. He listened.

Gough answered, 'Had to abort, understood. Pulled back in the face of a tactic first used by the Provisionals, no doubt learned from them. To show out is a disaster, accepted . . . just repeat the end line for me, please.'

It was explained. Gough rang off. He had a sombre face, like death had come to the family. Pegs was no longer beside him, and he heard the shower start, and her splashing. He went to the bathroom door, opened it, saw her flesh pinking from the scalding level at which she always set the water.

'Doesn't get much worse, does it? An abort and a back-off, and they do a clever bit – we think – and go up the motorway in the wrong direction, north, then take an exit. Right now there is no ANPR on them. We've lost her. We are blundering, . . . which is worse than worse.'

He threw her the towel. One that they'd nicked from a Travel Lodge or a Holiday Inn, skimpy but adequate. He put on the kettle, would shave and wash after he had made coffee, strong coffee. Always a desperate time when a target was lost and an operation seemed to shudder to a halt, desperate and bad.

June 1971

A post had been sunk in a freshly dug hole that morning. The bone-hard ground at the edge of the camp had needed brute force and a swinging pickaxe to make the hole. The post inserted in it was not exactly vertical, but the best they could do, and the cavity had been filled and the excavated stones stamped down. The post stood alone and behind it was a clear view of gradually rising foothills on which sunlight shimmered. There were few trees and rare patches of shade on the slopes where goats grazed.

Watching the arrival of the firing squad was the intelligence officer of that section of that faction of the umbrella organisation, *Fatah*. They were late, usually were late on any schedule set them. It had been decided that the squad, of half a dozen, should wear uniform for the event. They did not have a common kit so some of the camouflage clothing was American, some was Soviet, and for the younger participants there were trousers and shirts in the dun colour that was close to that of the sand and scrub beyond the camp's perimeter. They marched past the officer. Few had an understanding of drill and how to carry a rifle while moving in step. Some tried to copy those in front, but two had no comprehension and walked easily, briskly, and made no pretence at being part of a disciplined force. An older man, who once would have had a fine carriage, but now was paunchy, and had an exaggerated moustache, called the tempo of the march, and had been in the camp for 22 years, there since the first of the shanty town buildings had gone up. Everyone in the squad carried Kalashnikov rifles, held them across their chests, and strutted. They were formed into a line – at first ragged and then kicked into shape by the drill man – and commands were given as if that would increase their legitimacy. He took a handkerchief from his pocket and waved it towards the gate leading through the wire and into the alleys of the camp. He was ready, they could bring her.

The IO, a good-looking man of Palestinian origin, in his late twenties, and wearing a scruffy uniform that showed he had little interest in military theatre, lit a cigarette. He felt calm, had reason to. The post, by rights, should have been for him. Should have been his arms bound behind it, and the blindfold lying at its base should have been going round his head, masking his eyes. He had deflected attention, and had used what opportunities were presented to shift evidence away from himself and on to the girl. He felt no guilt. He was an asset. Those who controlled him believed that his importance was such that his survival was paramount. He would be protected. He smoked the cigarette casually, while the crowd gathered behind him, and other young men, all armed, held back the spectators. He had believed he had begun to attract attention, and the Internal Security were efficient, and his position as intelligence officer was of value to those who controlled him, and two of the young *fedayeen* had been about to cut the wire and head into the northern territory of Israel when the flares had been fired and they had frozen in the lights, had been cut down by gunfire. If they had been allowed to go farther, the matter could have been explained as an accidental contact with a patrol, but this was obvious betrayal. He had known he would have been the first on whom suspicion fell, except that the girl had, in the hours before the infiltration, been to the city of Tyre, west from Tebnine where the camp was, and it had been easy to insert US dollar notes in her clothing. She had gone by bus, was unwilling to give a reason, then under fierce interrogation had spoken of a boy. Perhaps there was, perhaps not. She was condemned, and the intelligence officer attracted no more attention.

She was brought out, men hemmed around her. She would find no kindness in the last moments of her life. A spy was hated, a traitor was loathed, betrayal was the ultimate crime. He thought she walked well.

She faced the squad. One among them caught the intelligence officer's attention. A boy, sixteen or seventeen years old, trying to stand to attention and with the poorest combination of make-do uniform, a camouflage tunic in sand colours and olive-green trousers that would have looked well in dense vegetation. He carried an old weapon, held it rigidly as if it were the most important possession in his life: no doubt it was. The sun played on the boy's face and accentuated his youth; his cheeks gleamed and the officer realised that he was weeping.

They brought the girl forward. Some of the men had hold of her. Her wrists were tied loosely with cord and her arms hung down by her sides. She was dressed in black, a generous robe that showed none of the lines of her body. Some of her face was visible, but a scarf was tight across her head. She did not blink but looked ahead and around her . . . and gazed straight at him. He offered nothing. He looked through her – should, probably, have been grateful to her for stepping forward, however unwillingly, and taking a place he might have filled, deservedly. She walked past him and his eyes followed her and she would have seen the teenage boy who shed tears, who carried the old rifle with the damaged stock. Any other make of weapon, of that obvious age, was likely to jam. Except . . . that the rifle was the AK-47, an old version but of that pedigree. The intelligence officer wondered if the boy would miss the target.

She was taken to the post.

Her hands were freed, then pulled behind her, the same cord used to tie her wrists to the post. A man bent and picked up the cloth but she shook her head violently and seemed to try to pull away. It was the first moment that he had noted genuine agitation. They did not know what to do. There was talking, shouting, and she yelled that she would not wear the blindfold. The intelligence officer believed that none of them had ever executed a woman, certainly not one so pretty with a blazing anger in her eyes. Had reason to be angry, was innocent, her life was considered less important than his, an asset of importance to the Israeli Defence Force beyond the frontier to the south. They did not want to touch her, handle her, and seemed ashamed and stepped back. She regained composure. A white cloth was roughly fastened with a safety pin to her chest, where they estimated her heart to be. The squad, in line, was twenty paces from her.

The moment of importance and prestige had arrived for the old guy, the one with the moustache, and he yelled a command. There was a scrape as the weapons were armed. Aim was taken. He held out his handkerchief and the squad waited for his signal. A good girl, and pretty, with the bravery of a lioness, and without guilt and giving them – the rabble around her – no satisfaction. The handkerchief was raised.

She was dead. The kid who wept had fired. He broke the drill. He cried and heaved back his trigger. As the handkerchief landed on the dirt there was a ripple from the other rifles but she was already sagging and some might have missed. Not the first shot. The cloth on her chest had a drilled hole in its centre and blood seeped.

The intelligence officer walked away. He assumed another notch would soon be scratched on the wooden stocks. It was predictable that an AK-47, old and without maintenance and likely rarely cleaned, had performed at the top of its power. No surprise to him . . . he lived a dangerous life, on the edge, alone and without support – and another had died in his place – and he was vulnerable, every hour of every day.

The car braked. She was jolted forward, went as far as the seatbelt allowed. They were in the suburbs of a town, residential but with warehouses. Zeinab looked at her watch, saw they were still deep in the night.

'Were we followed?'

Krait said, 'Not now, maybe earlier. If we were, we broke it. It was a good trick we did, and if they were behind us, two cars, they would have noted our professionalism, then backed off. They would have had to.'

Scorpion said, 'I believe we have their respect, they are professional and trained. We have to be. It is important to be good enough to earn respect.'

Krait said, 'Believe nothing, believe nobody, or you will not see Savile Town again . . . The boy who died, he tried too hard, was not believed. They are all around us, watching. They look for weakness: the boy pushed too often. You believe no one who comes with an offer of friendship. Believe no one.'

'We have been deservedly promoted to this dizzy height, where our incompetence is easy to see.'

Pegs had typed it, printed it, stuck it with adhesive to the front of their office door. It might raise a laugh, and any degree of humour would be welcome that day, not that the night cared to go fast. They had carried out an inquest, which wasted time, and irritated. He was alone. She had gone for supplies, for the fortification of morale.

In the inquest, taking the advocate of the devil's role, Gough had remarked that they were guilty of underestimating the qualities of the adversary. Did not understand them, gave too little credit for their tradecraft skills: their opponents were not enrolled in a bloody kindergarten. He thought he might suggest to her that there was space enough on the frosted glass of their door for another slogan to be added under the one explaining Peter's Principle: 'Parkinson's Law is practised inside, is compulsory in an area of bureaucratic free-range thinking.' Or, and they would discuss it, they might follow with the Dunning-Kruger Effect: 'Those with low ability rarely recognise their ineptitude.' The others, who sat at an octagonal table, each with their own computer screen and only low partitions for privacy, might sense that the levity came out of crisis. The target was lost, the Undercover was adrift, and Gough had acknowledged that the skills of adversaries were rarely underestimated and the outcome happy. Too old? Perhaps. Past it, and should be put to grass? Maybe . . . He sat, the responsibility burdening him, and . . . she came back.

Pegs brought with her, from a depot café down the Embankment, two plates of full English, enough sausage and bacon and black pudding, and mushrooms and hash and a sunny side egg, to keep a navvy going through a day. Or should they go for Murphy's, Law. Murphy reckoned that if anything could go wrong then it would. Cutlery and paper napkins and coffee in a beaker.

Gough said, 'Damage done, yes. Trouble with damage is that it takes time to repair. If it's not repaired then . . .'

With a mouth full, and spluttering, she said, 'Then the people we rely on are fucked. People at the sharp end, but that's how it always plays out.'

Still sleeping, deep, but dreaming.

The two cars were pulled off the road. It had been a squeeze but eight of them had come. It was two weeks after the crisis, and Dominic was with them but less a part of them, and the auburn-haired girl had taken over the leadership, was first among equals. Tristana had not been back to the former leader's room, nor had Bethany. There were a few lights on in the house, and they waited for the one in the downstairs hall to be doused, and the one in the bathroom upstairs to come on. The dog, a yappy spaniel, had already been out, and had peed and been called back in. A warm night, no moon and only a few stars.

He could not be a perpetrator and could not be a provocateur. Instructions were clear on the limits of his engagement. Phil was able to commit a criminal act, but not be a principal player, nor be party to any serious injury being handed out. The two cars were side by side in a field gateway and the scientist's house was a hundred yards farther on . . . The hall went dark, and lights had come on upstairs. They'd need a little time to get the clubs out of the car boots, and the paint sprays, and the pepper that they'd squirt at anyone in the family who intervened. Last out would be the battering ram: a considerable investment at £200 and care taken in disguising the purchaser's identity. Bethany was out and Tristana, and the guys with them. The auburn-haired girl had had her hand on his thigh most of the time since they had left Plymouth, had put it there before it was dark, had made her statement and would have been seen. She would expect to be high, like it was a big spliff smoked, by the time they were back and would expect to get what she wanted. After standing up for himself, he had become a more attractive package. Phil Williams knew how it would end, and it would not be with her hand on his thigh, as they made the return journey – all bubbling at the success and the violence meted out to a 'horrible bastard' who put animals in the path of misery.

There were car headlights coming towards them down the lane and another car's lights appeared behind them. Phil had stayed inside his car while the gang cleared the boots of what they needed, and all were caught. The lights, at full power, beamed hard at them and some protected their eyes, and Bethany swore, and the first to realise – of course – was Dominic. Cops poured out of the cars and a van came up behind the lead vehicle. Not the local people, but a specialist team and fearsome in overalls, with Tasers drawn and batons extended.

Very quick. Handcuffs on, and everybody down on their faces. A torch shone full into Phil's face.

'You all right, mate?'

'Fine, yes, I'm good.'

He unfastened his seatbelt and stepped out of the car. The uniforms around him were polite but no praise was given. It might have been that these men and women understood he operated in a world of shadows and of deceit, lived off a diet of lies, might not have liked what he did. He was told that a cop would drive his vehicle, and that a squad car was round the corner and would take him to a safe place. A 'safe place'? Hardly needed it now, but had needed it two weeks back . . . There was enough light on them, on the ground, for him to read their expressions: anger, contempt, shock, loathing.

Dominic said, 'Rot in hell, you bastard. One day, I swear it, I'll fucking find you.'

The girl with the auburn hair said, 'Find you and burn your balls off. You broke our trust. Happy?'

He walked past them. Did not feel good, only numb. Before dawn he would no longer be Phil Williams, like that legend had never existed.

Still slept, and hated the length of the night.

7

He lay on his back, and his breath came in heavy spasms, asleep but suffering.

'What problem, guys?'

'You're it. You're the problem.'

Norm Clarke played it calm. He had been asked into the back room of a club close to the bus station. No music, and the grille down over the bar and the lights low, but a pall of tobacco smoke in the room, and the old gang were there – sitting, watching. Their younger people stood and a couple of the bigger men – likely enhanced with steroids – were behind him. They had the door. The back room's one window was barred, with a steel shutter on the outside. Had all seemed good, and Norm was back in Swindon after a run across country to Bristol. Had come back all innocent: might have thought the sun shone sweetly on him . . . now wondered where he'd made the mistake.

'Not that I know of, don't see myself as a problem.'

'We do, we see you as a problem.'

'That's just a laugh . . . I'm no problem.'

'You're a problem because you don't stack right.'

There was no fast way into a group. Took time. Street corner selling, school gate trading, doing running and lookout for a dealer in Exeter, best part of a year of a life gone, and somebody must have said something about him to one of the boys, up the chain, who handled Class A. They might have taken a long slow look at him, and then small bits and pieces were put in his way, trivial jobs. Opportunities came rarely and were not to be missed. He had offered himself. Could do driving . . . did not say that he had been to prison because that was the fastest and easiest place to do a check on his history. The instructors said that advancement was never to be rushed, had to go with the flow and the tide. A long story, told short, a big flu virus went the rounds, guys dropped like flies hit by an aerosol spray. A supply chain of what came in from Spain on a Brittany Ferry to Plymouth staggered to a stop. Norm was around, people knew of him, talked of him, and nobody had gotten round to running a deep examination of his legend. A packet, a couple of kilos, perhaps less, and a location. It was done. Delivered to satisfaction. But the virus was stubborn and showed little sign of easing, and another run was needed. By the time the antibiotic did a good job on the virus, Norm had made himself useful, seemed – almost – a part of the furniture: he did not ask questions, had never been caught eavesdropping phone calls nor seen flicking through papers in the office. Easy to be with, and every trip he made seemed to get through, no hassle. The way they might have looked at it, 'too good to be true'. Just took one guy to open his mouth and start questioning a newcomer's credentials, and then an examination and more guys chipping in with anomalies, what did not fit, and the starting of a trade in them because no one wanted to be left high and dry and defending a casualty . . . and down the line, somewhere, was a mistake. When it went sour, it was always because of a mistake, and most times the Level One, skilled and trained and alert, never knew it. One of the 'tecs who had briefed him at the start had said of them, 'Not idiots; foul and vicious and no education, but not idiots. Cunning, take the job seriously, don't want to go back to gaol, and they have a sniff of who you are and we have to hope the cavalry and the guns come running and quick. They are hard little shits, our evaluation. Good luck, lad, good luck.' Might be a trawling run, might be because Delia, one of the groupie girls with them, had taken a fancy and put another's snout out of joint, might be because he had fucked up big. Only one of them did the talking. The son of the founding father of the group. Clever little shite. Big glasses and did the accountancy and when the hit came – which it would – then his mobile would do the work of a good prosecutor, would send them all down with the key thrown away.

Didn't hold anyone's gaze, failed to confront at this early stage in the game.

'I'd say talk is cheap. I'd say I am not a problem.'

'A problem is a difficulty, a difficulty is something we care to avoid. A problem that becomes a difficulty is then a danger. We don't want it, a danger to us.'

The father sat at his desk. The boy would have his say. In with them were the principal buyer, the main distributor, who looked furtive and unhappy and who would not have appreciated negative shit being talked, and there was a woman who had a reputation as a hard bitch and who did the contracts and was a law school drop-out, and a couple of enforcers, and two guys behind Norm. The voice of the boy was cold and quiet and dripping, and he'd have fancied himself as a Pacino clone, a poor man's Scarface, and thought he was God's fucking gift to forensic interrogation.

'Is this some sort of therapy session? Don't see where we're going. I do my job, I get paid, I do my job satisfactorily, you all say so. I don't appreciate this shit. Can we move on, what's shifted tomorrow.'

'About your face and about what you wear – Norm, if that's your name.'

'That is bigger shit. "About your face and about what you wear", means what?'

No panic button with him, and no gas in his coat or pepper spray, no knife and firearm. When he was on the way back down to Plymouth or up towards Swindon, he would go off the road halfway along and meet his handler and his control officer, and just seem to be sitting at a table and reading his newspaper, taking time off from eyeing the tits and bums, and his own people would sidle towards him and then sit down, and a full team for surveillance and protection would be deployed. The stresses ran in his mind, and the veins of his face filled with pumped blood, and he was scared: had reason to be. His face? Start with his face . . . the beard was crap, looked recent and was, might have looked designer grown, straggly with no body. And the clothes . . . The mistake could be with the clothes. He lived in a bedsit. The cover was a jobbing gardener. Wore those sort of clothes, and most of these guys were in the smart casual range, but what cost money. Stuff bought with cash. They didn't touch Class A, none of them. If the kid had, the boss's son, he would have been dismembered. He could not play the part of a dope addict with a concave chest and clothes hanging off him like he was a goddamn skeleton, but what Norm Clarke wore were the clothes that went with his gardening work, rejects from a charity shop, and it might have grated in comparison. Where was the mistake? The usual one, the one that did serious harm, was being 'too eager', too ready to do anything required, and it might have been what the boy – thinking himself Pacino/Scarface – had detected. The room was dim, and the smoke misted up around the neon, and nobody had offered Norm a fag, and it had taken a while before he had been able to see around the corners of the room and into the shadow. He saw a petrol-driven chain-saw, a whole big heap of plastic, and the sort of drill that would have a battery's power and was big enough to make a decent Christmas present. Difficult to know how to react, because it was vague and did not demand specifics in his answers, but there was a hatred in the air: this was not the Crown Court and they'd not need sworn and tested evidence . . . it would be about what instinct told them. It happened too fast for him. A blow on the shoulder. Would have been a sign from the boss. Big boys, those behind him, and the steroids did well for their strength. One minute standing and the next disoriented, and the next sinking down and the pain welling and his arms wrenched behind him and cord binding him, and he was trying to duck his head and weave, but they had the hood over him and then he was down and in the black space.

He heard the scrape of a chair across the floor and the rustle as plastic was unwrapped. He was put in the chair.

'What the fuck? Why the hell? What gives with you lot? What is the problem?'

He did not think he was heard and there was no response, but he heard the plastic being spread on the floor around the chair. He felt the piss welling in him . . . the instructors did it well, and the

Marines in 'Resistance to Interrogation', and they had no comprehension of how it was.

And he still slept, hated it, but could not wake.

'You watch him, Zeinab, watch him and closely.'

She was given the passport she would use. She flicked it open, saw the name, looked at the photograph, and with the glasses it was a good enough image – heavy and distinctive spectacles, with clear lenses. Among the pages of the passport were bank notes, euros and sterling. They were a hundred yards from the station and would have been short of the cameras that covered the front entrance. She opened her bag, slid it inside.

Krait, the snake with the venom in its tongue, repeated, 'Watch him, always, and be prepared – you understand?'

Scorpion had turned to face her. 'Be prepared, whatever is necessary.'

She came out of the car then leaned back in to collect her bag. Traffic edged past them, heading for the station. Luton, this time in the morning – close to dawn – was busy with office workers heading for the capital.

'I trust him,' she said.

Scorpion said, 'If you suspect him, you act. What is to "act", you know that?'

'Whatever is "necessary", what you said.'

'You saw the boy in the car?' from Scorpion.

'He made suspicion, enough for us to "act", do what was "necessary",' from Krait.

'You think me weak, I am not.'

From Krait, 'We take a gamble with him.'

'He is infatuated. I think, almost, he loves me. He just wants to be with me. He is what makes our chain strongest.'

From Scorpion, 'The ability of the chain to survive stress is not the strongest link, it is the weakest. The weakest link.'

'He is not that, the weakest.'

'If you doubted him, Zeinab, then . . .'

'I do not.'

She lifted her bag and started to walk. There was no call after her from either of them. She did not know how they had killed the boy who had attracted their suspicion but she had seen the bruises and scrapes on his face and the wild glimmer in his eyes, supposed it was a measure of the pain inflicted, did not know which of them – Krait or Scorpion – had done it. Neither called after her to wish her luck, to give encouragement. Had either of them been in Syria, or escaped in the last hours of the defence of Mosul? She did not know. If she brought back one weapon, she did not know which of them would use it: the one who was spindly and tall, the other who was squat and heavy at the gut and the hips. If she failed them, if it imploded, then they would rot in cells for near to the rest of their adult lives: if she failed badly, so would she . . . She walked and started to see the image. Four young men, twelve years earlier, rucksacks heavy on their backs, strolling towards the open doors of Luton station, and less than two hours of their lives left to be lived, and the bombs they carried primed . . . and their targets were in London where she now headed, and they were from her streets, from among her people. They had shown, on the cameras that watched them, no fear, their hands in their pockets, nothing furtive, simply going about their business. She walked in their footsteps . . . Zeinab had read that the names of the men were forgotten, they had been consigned to statistics . . . walked where they had been. Went boldly.

She was Zeinab, 22 years of age, a student at a prestigious university, from a small house in a Leeds satellite town – once vibrant, now dying, and she took the first steps of the journey taking her to war, but needed first to gather the necessary weapons for combat. She was jostled, pushed, and men and women surged past her for the barriers and the platforms, and they were her enemy, and she floated among them and was a 'clean skin' and went unnoticed. She revelled in her anonymity . . . and hated. She did not – never had – analyse the loathing she felt for the flow of society around her, whether in the mall at Manchester that they had paced out, or at this station near to London . . . It did not matter to her whether those who might be maimed, killed, bereaved, were Christians or Jews or Muslims, not important whether they were old and frail like the woman who sheltered close to a wall, clinging to a walking frame and letting the crush pass her, or whether they were young and ambitious and hopeful like the kids on her corridor in the Hall of Residence. She could not have pointed to a particular slight, or an insult. She had never suffered humiliation because of her faith, her dress, her appearance, her intellect. She was ignored. She detested those, pushing past her, who did not see her, never had and never would – unless she brought back the weapon and it was used.

She queued, bought a ticket. Wondered where he was, and wondered whether she should have boasted to them about her control of Andy Knight – where he was, sweet boy and stupid and loving – but realised she had developed a growing degree of softness for the boy – and spat from her mind talk of suspicion and acting and necessity . . . Zeinab waited on the platform for the next train south, and the start. Did not know where it would take her, how far beyond anything in her experience.

The first light of the day peeped over the rim of the hillside above La Castellane, and feeble shadows were thrown from the blocks and settled on the ground where the rubbish bins had not been emptied and the trees were snapped off and bushes collected garbage and plastic. Few had work that necessitated them rising early to take the 25 bus down the hill and past the old suburbs and the ferry port and into the city of Marseille. Karym's sister was among the few. She would leave the project, cross the road, climb the rough ground and go into the shopping mall across the valley via its empty car park. She said to him that she hated the 'fucking place, everything about it', and he had turned his back on her, then followed her out.

It was Karym's home.

Had once been his father's home until he had packed one suitcase, gone with a promise of sending back money, a lie, and returned to Tunisia. Once was his mother's but she now lived down the coast and worked there and said her children were scum.

Was still the nominal home of Karym's brother, except that Hamid slept in another block where he had an apartment littered with the trappings of his wealth and with complicated gadgetry that he could not make to function unless Karym came, and fiddled with it. He had not slept well. He walked in the alleyways between the buildings, alone. Was disturbed, and fidgeted and scratched his head.

Two sounds had lingered in his mind, neither good or easily dispersed. The mother of the boy had come out on to her balcony, had cried to the moon, to the stars and to the gulls, had made the sound of an animal in pain, and the cry was piercing. A true lament, that seemed to rip at the very heart of her intestines, as if a part of her soul burned. There was a dog that had been hit by a car on the Boulevard Henri Barnier, both legs broken, and it had screamed, and no one could get close to it with a club or an iron bar, and it had been shot with an AK which had released it from its pain, and had also allowed a degree of quiet to settle over La Castellane which made traders happier. Her son had screamed, that was the other sound that had knifed into Karym. The kid had reason to scream; the gag had worked loose and the gasoline would have been in his nostrils and the flaming rag had come close to the open window, then been tossed inside. He had screamed even after the crowd had lost sight of him behind the flames, had screamed until the tank – more fumes than fuel – had exploded and his efforts to kick his way out were curtailed. Two sounds, mother and son, both sharp. It was always that way, cries and screams, each time there was a barbecue in La Castellane. Sometimes Karym thought himself indifferent to the noises, a few times he shrugged them off: it was rare that they slashed at him, as they had that night. He had not been close to the car but it had seemed that the smoke of the burning tyres, and the flesh, had come to rest on his clothing, impregnated it. The smell was worse than the crying or the screaming. He walked in the estate. He would have been observed though he saw nobody except isolated workers hurrying to the project's exits, escaping for the day with a coveted reward of poor wages.

The flames had long died. Wisps of smoke climbed above the scorched car. He went near enough to see the shape of the boy, but could not distinguish the head or the arms or the torso. The barbecue was part of the life of the project, so Karym neither supported it nor criticised it. The barbecue happened, and nothing would stop it, not the noise and not the smell. A new sound intruded. Sirens came from down the hill.

The day was not yet advanced, and the lights of the convoy showed up well. That the police would come, with the fire team, and in force, was built into the schedule his brother had set. They would come to a halt short of the entrance to the project, would then take a coffee and a sandwich or a piece of pie, and they would have announced their intention and then would come in when they were expected. That way, as the choreography played out, there would be no aggravation and the weapons would be left in the safe houses. It was good, Karym thought, to have understandings in place. He turned away from the burned car. No one would talk: in the newspaper, *La Provence*, they called it a wall of silence. No tongues would murmur in the ears of investigators. His brother was safe, Karym was certain. He saw a girl running, late for her bus, and he smiled at her, good-looking bitch and good hips, and she broke her stride to spit in the mud, then went on running. He was the brother of Hamid. He had protection but was without a friend. The police, now forming up at the side of the road, would come in force into the project and would hope to find an idiot or a lunatic or some person of any age with a death wish who would describe the barbecue and tell the name of the organiser; would find no one. Not even the mother . . .

In the world of Karym, in La Castellane, no one spoke to the police, gave them evidence. It would be a crime on the scale of blasphemy.

He went back to the apartment. It was his turn to clean it. Why should he be bothered? He would lie on his unmade bed, and would look at his books, study the *Avtomat Kalashnikova obraztsa 1947 goda*, although he could almost recite by heart, would wait for the day when, in spite of the weakness of his arm, he was allowed to hold one, fire it, blast with it, turn the selector to automatic and loose off a full magazine over a range fit for Battle Sight Zero, close up, and smell the cordite and hear the crash of the firing and the tinkling landing of ejected cartridges . . .

A policeman shouted at him, told him to come closer. He kept on walking.

The Major insisted that the forensic team came with him.

There was an ambulance, unnecessary for the carbonised corpse, close to the burned vehicle, and a plain-sided dark van, and all those who went close wore plastic overshoes as if the chance of preserving evidence was necessary, and had heavy gloves, and masks over their mouths and noses to counter the smell. Samson watched the mass of identical windows, and the flat roofs, and the corners of the walkways through the magnification of his rifle sight, and he had slept well before being called out and was wary. It was sensible to bring the ambulance. It might be that one of them – uniformed, a plain-clothes investigator, the doctor, the prosecutor, a photographer, an imam – would be hit if a kid fired off an assault rifle.

The police presence was now monitored by a network of calls between PayAsYouGo phones and by coded texts, and by the signs of moving hands, fingers at high windows. Samson wore his balaclava, would have been a marked man. He held his rifle ready but did not strike a pose that threatened. A woman, middle-aged and swathed in black clothing, worn loose, had approached and spoken briefly to an officer, had not been permitted near the car, had been questioned and had shaken her head vigorously, then had turned away, had gone. He thought of himself, here, as an intruder . . . the project, this one and all of the others in the half crescent on the north side of Marseille, lived in a differing authority and culture to the rest of the city. Own codes of conduct, own 'judiciary', own penalties for those who broke the singular rules of behaviour. There were many at L'Évêché, who gathered in the corridors of the city's police headquarters and railed against the lack of a big stick to bring the traders into the orbit of the courts . . . But Samson remained relaxed at the divisions of the society. He was no crusader, had no great desire to find targets, zero on them, squeeze the trigger stick of his rifle: when he did he felt no remorse, no pain, was any other man who had finished a shift of his day-job. He assumed he was watched, recognised by the balaclava, and that half a dozen Kalashnikovs were aimed in the general direction of the forensics. The police would not linger. The photographs would be taken, the remnant of the blackened body would be gingerly removed, a school teacher or a social worker would come forward and condemn the barbarism of the perpetrators. The Major was at his side.

'We have an identity.'

'And . . .?'

'Sixteen years old. A juvenile court conviction, wounding with a knife at school, expelled, no qualifications, no employment.'

Samson nodded, could have written it himself. 'And . . .?'

'The woman was his mother. They came for him yesterday. A dispute.'

'And . . .?' Muffled questions through the balaclava and his eyes roved over the windows, and the roofing.

'The mother says that she did not know which group her son worked for. Nor does she know who came for him. Nor the extent of the "crime" of which he was accused . . . What else would she say? She has to live here. We will not offer her full witness protection, guard her for the rest of her life. She is sensible . . . I cannot criticise her. It is the same as the last time, will be the same the next time. Not more than a quarter of an hour.'

He was alone again. He thought of the return of the vehicles to L'Évêché, and the canteen meal that would be served there . . . he saw the mother, very calm, surrounded by a group of older women and the communal grief suppressed, saw a boy with a withered arm who gazed at him from a clear 100 metres away, saw a man leave the project astride a Ducati Monster, saw a flatbed with a crane hoist up the burned car, saw the body driven away, saw the watchers grow bored.

Many weapons would be aimed at him. He doubted any of the kids would have the balls between their legs, sufficient courage, to aim, target him, and fire. He backed away.

The start of another day in his life, few were different. He climbed into the truck and the plated door slammed shut: it was a place where death came easily, where the assault rifle ruled.

September 1972

The boys watched, entranced.

They sat in a building of plywood walls and corrugated iron roofing. Some were sitting on the floor, concrete and covered by old rugs, some had chairs, more stood.

The transmission came from Beirut and the signal in the Tibnine area was poor and interruptions were frequent, but the flickering picture did nothing to lessen their enthusiasm – it welled and they shouted defiance.

The boys, all dressed in the camouflage now generally available to the splinter parties under the vague umbrella of the Palestine Liberation Organisation, had gathered in the ramshackle building when word had spread, a wildfire of fact and rumour, that the *fedayeen* had attacked the Zionist warmonger team in the Olympic Village of Munich. Only those, not many of them, with more than basic educational skills knew where Munich was, but all were loaded with the skills of how to handle, strip, reassemble and fire the AK-47 assault rifles that lay across their knees, or rested on their shoulders. They had been watching ever since the Lebanese state broadcaster had first come on air, two days before, to show flaky pictures of the Village. Each time that a member of the 'brothers' had been shown on the screen – small and set in an elderly wooden frame – they had cheered, raised their weapons above their heads: they had seen members of the team face off the German so-called negotiators. To have fought their way inside a heavily guarded compound, to have broken into the Israeli house, was a triumph. The commentary was at times exuberant, at other times a recital of what had already happened, the novelty fading. It was said, again and again, that a deal would be done and that many Palestinian fighters imprisoned in Israeli gaols would be freed in exchange for the athletes captured by these heroes. They had sat and stood in their places all through that day, and their mothers or sisters had brought them food in the early evening because none would willingly abandon the opportunity to watch the triumph for their people play out. Each one of them was armed. There were many weapons available now to the fighters in this camp. Most were shiny, well painted, clean, without chips or scrapes, and had been nowhere other than on an occasional hill-side where it was safe to fire and on the rare exercises that were organised for them, and they were used for parade ground drills . . . Only one looked as though it might have been retrieved from a rubbish heap, and it stood out because it was so obviously a veteran weapon – tried, perhaps tested, one with its own history – and it was held with a degree of reverence by a slightly built young man who had only recently started to grow the first shadows of a moustache. They had sat there through the first evening, had debated how many prisoners the Zionists would need to clear from their gaols to get back their precious athletes, had calculated the scale of the victory . . . and had watched late at night, had wept, had cursed the deceit and treachery of the German negotiators. Had sat numbed and silent, with lips bitten in anger as the spokesman for the Olympics had told of an ambush, five heroes slaughtered, three brave men captured, an attack of extraordinary amateurishness.

They had gathered the next morning, taken their places. Little to see, but had heard that the bodies of the fallen were to be shipped back to Tripoli, the Libyan capital. They watched the TV and felt glowing pride in the sacrifice of the martyrs. The pictures now came from Libya, where dense crowds filled streets and squares. The hurdles on which the bodies lay, decorated by the host country's flag, or the Palestinian one, were carried above the heads of the teeming mourners. The cameras were high up in buildings and looked down on to the fervour of the masses. They saw devotion, saw the worship that was accorded only to the bravest. At moments, when the camera zoomed on to a particular hurdle and showed the shallow shape of a fighter hidden by a flag, they would dive outside the building and fire off shots into the air.

They would drown out the commentary of the Lebanese broadcaster with their own slogans and yells to denounce the Zionist state, the deceit of the Germans, the treachery of the United States. Their voices would rise to a hoarse frenzy, then they'd return indoors and swelter again in the heat that burned the hillsides round the camp. The transmission closed. All in the room were converts to the message of war and sacrifice. They started to disperse, and one and all would have sworn they would perform in training with more enthusiasm than ever before.

A man waited outside, seemed not to notice the heat. He picked out the boy with the old weapon, beckoned him.

He was asked, curtly, if he were prepared to volunteer for special duties. Immaterial whether he could have refused. He had stammered acceptance. The man who had waited wore old and dirt-stained clothing, fatigues, and his eyes seemed keen but tired and he squinted as if the sunlight of years' exposure on the hillsides had damaged them. No surplus weight ringed his stomach. What was most noticeable about him was the scar that ran from his ear almost to the side of his mouth, bisecting his cheek; the wound had been inexpertly sealed and ran like a ploughed furrow. The boy would have recognised him as a fighting man, and his assessment was well placed. An experienced fighting man . . . Did the boy, when he came for 'special duties', wish for a new weapon, a replacement, one recently off a production line?

The boy grasped his rifle. His knuckles whitened. He held it tightly, proudly. The boy assumed that good words of him had been said or he would not have been approached. A hand reached towards him. The boy loosened his grip. The rifle was examined and a slow smile spread on the older man's face. He looked for its identification. He spoke the last of the numbers, 16751, then laughed, deep and growling from his throat.

Did he know when this weapon was manufactured? The boy did not. He was told. The factory was at the industrial complex of Izhevsk which was in central USSR, a friend of the Palestinian people, and the manufacture was in the year of 1956, and there were more modern versions of the same, better built, milled and not pressed steel, but the boy was adamant. A shrug, a little sadness in the eyes of the older man, but the boy would not have noticed that, nor considered the consequences of 'special duties', and where he would be taken, and what task given him.

He held the weapon proudly and his shoulder was cuffed, and he was told what time in the morning transport would collect him and that he – and his rifle – would be gone from the camp a long time, many months, and he would not be home soon to see his mother . . . The pride bloomed in him, and he was pleased that he had not given up his rifle, which was a part of him, treasured.

Sleeping, dreaming, crystal-sharp recall and unable to wake.

'My nose can see a copper, and hear a copper, and smell a copper. My nose can.'

That was Bazzer who had now taken over from the father and son. Bazzer had thick lenses held in tortoiseshell frames, and one of the side arms was held in place with Elastoplast. His eyesight was grimly impaired but they all accepted that his suspicions were as good as any dog's. When they dealt in skunk, any of the hashish family, he could tell the quality of what was on offer. Also credited to him was an ability to identify chancers and tossers, liars and frauds. They would not have moved against Norm Clarke if Bazzer had not called it.

'I'm saying he's a copper: what my nose tells me.'

He was on the floor. They had dragged him off the chair, pushed it away, and he was down on the plastic sheeting. They had torn off his clothes, had done some slapping and used their toes to nudge him, and questions had been thrown, and they'd tried to catch him on the detail of his legend – what school, how long there, what class, what name his best mate had – where he had lived then, what his dad did, what his mum did . . . Norm Clarke had gone through the background as worked out with his Control who operated out of the headquarters of Avon and Somerset police. Why had he never been picked up, done time? That would have been the killer, where he had been – what landing, what cell block. Easiest thing they could check out. He was the newest member of the group who was not a blood relative or a marriage relative, had come to them off the street and worked, insinuated, wormed and wriggled his way towards a position of trust. High-risk stuff. He thought they were not sure. Bollock naked, supposed to further humiliate, weaken him. Had had to speed up the process of acceptance, and might have pushed too hard. Always there, always ready, nothing too much trouble. Had to be like that, but was the sure route to the mistake . . . always was going to be a mistake. Could not place it . . . They had a chain-saw revving up, and he'd also heard the whine that a power drill made, the sort that DIY people used when screwing up home improvements, and the plastic was cold under his buttocks, and control of his bowels and bladder was difficult.

'I'm saying he is. Take it or leave it, my reckoning. What I'm telling you, what my nose sees, he's a cop.'

The instructors always said that the copper-bottom guarantee was that backup was in position, ready to go. Through twenty-four hours and through seven days a week, the backup was armed, alert, had the fix on his location, would get the call, would come. But he was stark naked and had no wire to record the threats and denunciations, and no wristwatch that could do a code-alarm if the button for the hands was shifted to a certain degree and then . . . didn't matter, didn't have it. The time they were looking at, scratching for evidence of guilt, was a stop he had done on the run back from Plymouth, on the M5 motorway, services near to Taunton, a chat with his Control, a half-hour break, and he had not made the call to say that he was good, had the shipment, was making decent time. They had done their mathematics, and had reckoned he'd be through the Bridgwater junction at a particular time, but he had not checked in. They'd have put a vehicle and a spotter on the bridge and would have looked and waited for him to sail through, middle lane, and not going fast, and would have checked out that he had no tail, and likely would have done the same procedure at the Chippenham exit for the M4 motorway. He had in the bag a consignment worth, street prices, a million and a quarter. His mistake was not to realise the extent of the precautions and therefore the importance of the schedule. Norm Clarke, country and western music loud on the speakers, had come through both checks around a half-hour after he was expected . . . enough to set off the juices of the miserable little bastard who was half-blind, Bazzer.

'I'm saying he is. Get to work on him, he'll tell you.'

Bound at the ankles and at the wrists, but no blindfold and no gag. They had trouble keeping the chain-saw engine going. Started it up, and it should have ticked over, given up a sound as menacing as any in the limited experience of Norm Clarke, but it had coughed each time and then died, and one guy was heaving, grunting, and yanking the cord. The drill was steady enough, no trouble with the power, and the whine getting shriller. No one would stand his corner. None of them would sing his praises . . . the boys supposed to be – 'copper-bottomed' and a guarantee – alert and ready to go, and firearms loaded, were likely in the canteen and queuing for more tea, more cake, more overtime, and were in ignorance. How well would he last? Not difficult. If the goddamn chain-saw came close to his groin, if they brought the drill near to his eyes, either, then it was curtains. Began to see it different – only a few kilos of good-grade hashish, and when one shipment was lifted and one gang taken off the street then the importation chain would be disrupted for a week and fresh faces would be on the plot: the customers would hardly know that there had been an interruption in supply. He was thinking about the sanctity of his testicles and the integrity of his eyesight, and starting to weigh an equation, and his buttocks moved on the plastic and crunched it and the noise of the drill pounded in his ears.

'He's a cop. I'm telling you. Ask him who he met on the route, where he stopped. Ask him . . . I'm Bazzer, I'm never wrong.'

The sounds rang in his ears, and the shouts buffeted him. The chain-saw was up and running, coughing and then going sweet . . . and, with the power drill, was being carried closer . . . Remembered the guy who had been Phil Williams. Bad times then but not as bad as now. He was yelling, screaming, and no one would have heard him in the back annexe of the club. Shouted and hoped, and

Bazzer's voice was the drumbeat in his head. Always because of a mistake. The hood was off his head, like they wanted him to see the saw and the drill.

A cacophony in his mind, but not enough to wake him.

'That shite . . .' Pegs looked away from her screen, glowered towards the door.

Gough grimaced. 'Enough of them, which?'

'Three zero eight, which else? Banker for top of the league in the "shite" stakes.' In Room 308, down the corridor, was the officer – senior rank – who controlled them. He would have thought himself careful, and unkind towards cowboys, and always eager that matters stayed on 'an even keel'. Rarely dished out praise but had a goading, wounding touch in his fingers when on a keyboard. Room 308's occupant was seldom seen, kept himself behind a closed door, dealt in electronic communication. It was not considered sporting to criticise his lack of personal appearance as a third of his face had been removed by a flying length of four-inch builder's nail enclosed in an Improvised Explosive Device detonated in County Tyrone: the operation to patch up the damage had been cursory and the end result not pretty.

'And suggesting what?'

'Suggesting, beauty and value of hindsight, that we have lost little Miss Zeinab, do not have identities and addresses for her boys, that our own asset is out of touch with her, that we have a considered but unproven assessment of what they are looking for in the south of France, and we are under-resourced . . . Our fault, implied, that we did not stand and shout, stamp our fucking feet and demand more. Throw toys out of the pram, scream for another sack of dosh. Should have upgraded the fuss.'

Still not dawn. The heating not yet on. He was at his desk, still wrapped in his winter anorak; she was at her place and cocooned in her overcoat. Nothing eaten, the coffee machine doing only black because she had not bought milk on the way.

Gough said, 'We are a minor investigation, probably down below a figure of one hundred in terms of priority. Lucky to have the boy, Andy or whatever he calls himself, amazing that we were able to lay hands on him. Had I gone in with a request for a three-shift surveillance of her, of her boys, probably fifty in all, that number of bodies on the ground, I'd have been laughed out. A ludicrous suggestion.'

'And there's a sting.'

'Is he already in?'

'Was in ten minutes before us, or stayed the night. The sting in the tail – the one that is impossible to bloody answer. Should you, Gough, have argued for pulling them in?'

'I have nothing to go to court with.'

Pegs said, 'It's a cheap blow, a low one, it's a kick in the privates, but Three Zero Eight has that talent. Only a query. Would we have been better off if they were lifted, maybe a "conspiracy" charge cobbled together? The usual – some lies and some innuendo, and some nods and some winks. We have our backs to the wall.'

Gough's teeth ground together, always did that when stress scratched him. What to say? It was fouled up. The surveillance had been inadequate. The computers would be scrambling to get a match for the registration recognition. Any arrest swoop would have been laughed out of the magistrate's court, if it had reached that far down the line . . . It was what he lived with, the stress of the work and the shortage of trained men and women, and the skill of the damn adversary, and it was never-ending and would last another decade as a minimum, and his ID would have been long shredded before any tide bloody turned. The ray of light in his life, often thought but never spoken of, was that Pegs – hard, brutal, pragmatic and moderately attractive – shared the workload with him.

'We could not have pulled them in.'

'And it is not a time for a blame game . . .' She was hitting the keys. Pegs was the only woman Gough knew who typed with two fingers, fast and with the delicacy of stamped feet. She was responding to Three Zero Eight, and her message would be signed off as Three One Nine. 'And the attendant shortages of support are what we endure every day, week, month . . . which is so boring.

We remain confident of the quality of our boy in the field – are not yet ready to run up a white flag . . .'

She grinned at him. The neon on the ceiling caught the mischief. She might have typed that, might just have been teasing him, was capable of typing it into the reply.

'. . . we hope for better than the apprehension of a few foot soldiers, look for strategists and controllers and leaders, and remain hopeful. France tomorrow, contact already established and cooperation guaranteed, or the day after at the latest. Gough . . . How does that seem?'

Where was she? The girl who appeared so innocent, who believed she had entrapped a boy with whom she could play marionette games, an experienced Undercover, a Level One. Had lost her. Pegs said something about going for milk, and hit her send key. Bad to lose a key player.

The train pulled away from Luton.

Passengers crushed, body to body, against her. Still dark outside. Around Zeinab were phone calls, ring tones and messages from the self-important as to what they wanted done in the office before they arrived. And eating, even a bulging burger, oozing stuff out, and others on sandwiches and some on flaky croissants. Sound in her ears and spilled food on her shoulder, and the warmth of the bodies pressed hard on her hips or her backside. She went to war. She caught the eye of a young man, perhaps her age. Seemed to have a new suit and a new shirt and a new tie that was not secured at the collar and his laptop bag was wedged against her stomach, and he smiled at her, apologetic because it must have seemed obvious that she was unfamiliar with the daily grind into central London. A nice smile, but she did not return it, but stared hard and through him, and saw darkness and street-lights flit past the window. And debated.

The weakest link, or the strongest, in the chain?

She had said he was the strongest. Pictured him. The grin, that seemed impossible to hide or suppress, the laughter that cracked open his mouth, the arms that were strong and muscled and that she sometimes wrapped round her waist, and the hands that were often dirtied from engine oil and calloused and that she allowed to rest on her cheeks, squeeze them, and the tongue that groped hesitantly into her mouth, and the eyes that stared into hers and were strong, uncomplicated, and did not blink. The strongest in the chain, of course. She imagined how it would be for him, coming off the ferry and slotting into the designated lane and approaching the customs check, and he would be in ignorance and would have no fear and would smile at the world around him, and would have an arm around her shoulder, and she'd have put her head under his chin. And she felt now, on the rolling rocking train with the body smells seeping at her, so alone.

The strongest link in the chain, and she had chosen him. Her tongue smeared over her lips. Some of the women around her were pale, with scrubbed cheeks and clean eyelids and had not yet bothered to apply cosmetics, and some were already painted and scented. She wore no makeup, not even a slick of lipstick. She remembered the taste of his mouth . . . She took her phone from her bag. Pay As You Go. Untraceable calls, Krait said. Did not register location nor recipient of a call, Scorpion said. She had to wriggle to manoeuvre the laptop away from her arms, and the young man smiled at her again. It would have been a train like this, same time of day, on which the boys had come with their rucksacks, and she wondered if they had stayed as a group, exchanged words, or were already walking dead.

She needed to speak to him. Herself, *she* might be the weakest link. Among the heat and sweat and in the motion of the train, Zeinab shivered. She pressed the keys.

Sleeping, but a phone ringing. Still clinging to the dream but its focus slipping.

Norm Clarke shouting, 'Check the fucking tyre. Front fucking tyre. New tyre. Check it. Fucking puncture. A puncture, not what that fucking half-eyed cripple says.'

Bawling loud enough to push his voice over the volume of the chain-saw and the motion of it blowing aside the hair above his privates, and his eyes aware of the fine drill bit inserted in the head of the power unit. A moment of hesitation . . . saw that, and the blade wavered and the drill was pulled a yard back.

'Go check the fucking tyre . . . okay, not new, retread, check it. The blind bastard, could he change a tyre in half an hour? All I fucking do for you, and you treat me . . .'

Would have been the fury in his voice that pulled them back. The cough of the saw as it was switched off, and the whine dying, and soft voices, and someone sent to look at his van. His mum – the real mum who did not figure in the life of Phil Williams or Norm Clarke – used to say that it was always sensible to store something for a rainy day. Torrential rain, flooded roads, rivers rising, that sort of day, and there had been a puncture and he'd not mentioned it because it was only a nail gone through and there was a chap he did drops-offs for who ran a used tyre market, and they'd put a new one on, had not seemed a big deal, and it was just enough for a drink, or three, that he'd paid for the tyre. If the saw or the drill had touched him he would have been yelling the phone numbers of SC&O10. They stood back from him. He felt the cold on his body. Cigarettes were lit. Bazzer must have lined up something to say but he was told to shut his mouth. If they were not happy with the tyre then they might take off his testicles and might drill through an eyeball, but most likely they'd just throttle him with a rope or beat his skull in with a bar, then wrap him in the plastic and pick up a couple of decent spades. They'd drive out to Savernake, the forest, fifteen miles away. Pretty much anywhere was good for digging a hole and losing him, and the plastic would keep the smell down and would prevent the foxes digging him up. None of these boys would split on the others: look at the ceiling, mouth a 'no comment', keep doing it. Might not be found, not for months, or years, not before a whole lot of rainy days had spoiled his mum's washing . . . One of their phones was ringing . . . Yes, his van had a new retread tyre, left side, front, passenger.

And the phone kept ringing . . . No one said, not one of them, that they were sorry. The ropes were untied, his hands needed rubbing to restore circulation. He picked up his clothing, dressed without help, shaking, trembling, would take days to overcome the trauma . . . managed it. Lost it . . .

The same room of the same club. Wearing a wire, and not going to be searched, and the loot was being divided for different markets and the cash was being heaped in separate piles for the share-out. The heavy team had come in, bashing down doors, bringing firearms. No handcuffs for Norm Clarke but a warm congratulation. The last word had been from Bazzer, before they'd been led to the wagons.

'I told you, you didn't listen. My nose can see a cop.'

His sleep was broken, his dream over.

Not Phil Williams and not Norm Clarke, but Andy Knight – who might have made a mistake already and might not, but who *would* make a mistake, as clear as day follows night, and had twice evaded the penalty for a mistake. Reached for it while it pealed, lifted it and flicked the button.

'Andy?'

'Me, hi.'

'You good?'

'Better for hearing you – was dreaming, a horrible dream, won't bore you. Thanks for waking me. Really brilliant to hear you. Missing you, Zed. Where are you?'

'Oh, you know, just, just . . . Just that I wanted to hear your voice.'

A few words, nothing special, and the call ended. He understood loneliness, thought she was learning it – and thought about mistakes and where they'd lead. The first light of day came through the window, rose over the roofs and the chimneys.

8

'Say it again . . . Don't recollect the name.'

Andy Knight knew the sergeant, but the sergeant did not know him. He had come off a slow, stopping train running down the coast of the Exe estuary – the station served the Commando Training Centre. Pegs had rung him, suggested that he might do a half-day there on his way to the ferry, and that she'd fix the welcome party. There would not have been much trading in the deal: someone would brief him on the 'weapon of choice' but his cover name would apply and what he did and who he worked for was off limits. He had left his car farther down the line, a couple of stations back, so the registration would not be listed at the barracks.

'I was here, but it's not important.'

'I believe you, but reluctantly. I was told you were one of us and needed a refresher. Don't recall the name we've been given . . . also went on the website, looked up the name. Doesn't tally.'

'Life's rich tapestry, moved on.'

'Which tells me things I needn't know. Right, let's go to work.'

The sergeant, as Andy Knight remembered him, was rarely amused, but managed a dry grin, raised an eyebrow. Who he had with him would likely tease him most of the day. He thought little had changed. The same buildings, some newly painted and some looked tired, and the same mess-rooms and the same cramped parade ground where he had not been the best, nor the worst. He assumed that a mass of the new intake were away out on the moor or up on the common, on exercise or doing ball-crunching cross-country running or were out on 'stealth and survival'. The place had a strange quiet to it.

A quiet and a familiarity, and Andy Knight felt a homecoming.

It was said of the Marine recruits who were shipped in here – raw eighteen- and nineteeen- and twenty-year-olds – that most came from car-crash backgrounds, and domestic circumstances described as 'difficult', and few had ever before been confronted with 'standards' to be reached. The barracks – some of it modern and some of it out of date – became a home for so many. Gave them a sense of family: the first time. He disliked thinking about his previous life, before becoming a Level One, reckoned it an indulgence that endangered him, tried to erase memories, attitudes, from his thoughts. Reflected briefly that his own childhood had not been a motor vehicle accident, that he had been brought up in a distant and dignified and gently loving atmosphere, and they had all been at the front gate of a semi-detached property to wave him off when the taxi had driven him away to the station. What was true was the feeling of belonging, had come at Lympstone. This same sergeant had lectured them, first day or second: 'It's more than just a green beret, it's a state of mind', and: 'First to understand, first to adapt and respond, and first to overcome'. They had taught him those aims, drummed into him the need to be inquisitive and adventurous, and that being 'close to, near to, success, is inadequate'. He had loved it, might have been made for him. When he had left, he had gone into one of the Commandos, had been thought well of, had been a standout for the speciality tasking of a marksman, a sniper, and was thinking with only minimal apprehension of a deployment in the dog-days of the Afghan commitment.

The sergeant walking briskly beside him might not now have the fitness required for the 30-mile trek. Might not be able to stand at the bar in his Mess all night, and down them and walk in a straight line back to his billet, but was the man – Andy would have said – that you would most want watching your back when on patrol in the maize fields of Helmand, or where he was going. A man who would protect you, no fuss and no drama, in any darkened alley, round any bad corner. No one would be at his back in the alleyway with no lighting, and no one would be watching for him round every bad corner. Somewhere, far down the road and sitting on a radio would be some protection but unlikely to be able to preserve his life if he cracked the mould, made the mistake. They came to a doorway, paused at it. There was an old catch-phrase that the Marines' sergeants used to trot out to the kids with 'crusader' tendencies, looking to make a name for themselves in a fire-fight: 'heroes make poor leaders'. He was no hero, neither had Norm Clarke been, and the title did not apply to Phil Williams, nor could he have said that what he had done, where he had been, had changed the situation of the world around him, nor what he would do where he was going. He'd walked reasonably well but the sergeant – gimlet-eyed in the old days and probably still blessed – would have noted the disability, seen the almost, not quite, hidden limp.

'Where I'm to drop you off.'

'Thanks.

'They'll ring me when they're ready to chuck you out.'

'One thing, can I ask one thing?'

'Ask, I'll try.'

Andy did, said what he wanted before leaving them. Funny old thing to ask for. Nobody now watched his back but then he had left the family.

Zeinab stepped off the train, trailed her bag. She walked at a good pace down the length of the platform, across the concourse, had seen the signs for the escalators to the Underground. The boys, all of whom had known Dewsbury, would have walked those steps . . . She had been ten at school and the day barely started, then older kids talking, hushed, fearfully, of explosions in London. Later, at home, her parents had watched the big television, and the boys had been referred to as 'idiots, lunatics, fools' but she had thought that was for her to hear and did not know what had passed for real inside their minds . . . Did they pause at the top of the steps? Did they hug, kiss, shrug under the weight of the rucksacks, mouth a prayer? Or did they just keep walking towards the Underground? It was likely that they had walked past her home, on the same pavement with the cracks and the weeds at her front gate, on their way to the Merkazi . . . Teenagers, five years younger than she was now, who had gone to Syria and had no known graves . . . and they had been her cousins. They were owed her loyalty, and her stomach ached from hunger, and she glanced at her watch, and reckoned she had the time, and went to a fast-food counter.

Humiliated, could not immediately pay for it. Had not enough money in her purse to buy the two buns she had chosen and the *latte*, and her teeth ground in anger. Cash she had been given was in her passport, zipped securely in her bag. People behind were pushing her, trying to buy and still catch their train. Confused and panic fuelling embarassment. She was groping in the pockets of her jeans and finding screwed-up paper handkerchiefs, and her ticket, and there was £3.78 in her purse and she needed £7.08, and she heard behind her a man's voice, accent smart and southern and English: *Oh, for fuck's sake* . . . Then . . . *Take it out of this, please.* A note was on the counter, pushed towards the girl. Zeinab flushed. The till was rung, the coffee was capped, the buns were bagged. Embarassment soared. She was a nuisance, in the way, and the inconvenience could be bought by the man for £7.08, and he was ordering a *croissant* and a regular *cappuccino*. Her package was in front of her, pushed towards her, she stammered gratitude but was ignored . . . she flared.

Anger soared. The feeling was sharp as a nail. She was an obstruction, ethnic, easy to buy out, patronised. It was not about a belief in the caliphate, and not about the Gardens of Paradise. She was third-Class or fourth. A dreary little creature who stood in a queue and did not have enough to pay for what she wanted. She snatched up her bag, turned on her heel and strode away. The two buns and the coffee left behind. She heard it clearly: *Stroppy little cow, that's thanks for you.* And kept walking, had now regained the route of the boys who had all known Dewsbury, and her street.

Fury engulfed her. She had been told what station she was to head for, and by what line. She wondered how long each of the three of them who had taken a train had waited for the lights to spear out of the tunnel and the clanking carriages come to a halt.

They would have had anger, fury, and the fourth – later – would have found his train cancelled and gone up into the fresh summer air and have looked for a crowded bus at that rush-hour time, and she thought him the bravest of all of them . . . She wondered where Andy Knight was, bit her lip, tried to slide him out of her thoughts. She stood on the packed train and it rocked on uneven tracks . . . She would fight them; uttered a single silent prayer that she would have the chance . . . somewhere on this stretch of tunnel one of them had pressed a button, had gone to his God, was at peace. She was not.

Karym's phone went. His brother.

The project was quiet. The few with outside work were gone, some women had left with their shopping bags to spend the money filtered to them through the tentacles of La Castellane's nightly trading – guarding money and weapons and hashish, getting a percentage of the profits from dealing and enforcing which paid well, watching the perimeter of the project which was rewarded less generously. Late morning and a brittle sunshine and the wind scouring the ground and bending the few surviving trees in what had once been proud landscaping. The police and the forensic technicians had pulled out, and the burned car had been hoisted on to a flat-bed and taken away. The smell still hung close to where the fire had been, but that was from the tyres, not the burning flesh. School would soon be finished and the young kids would spill back into the project, and the older ones who still bothered to attend the big *lycée* down the road towards the city. Karym was owed some respect because of the blood-line to his brother: had his brother not owned his stairwell business then Karym, with his weakened arm, would have been a pitiful creature, hounded and bullied. As long as his brother lived, he had protection . . . He would talk to him again, to Hamid, about his wish for them to go together into the hills, where the scrub was dense, and place some bottles and some cans on a rock, and have an AK-47 with two filled magazines, and fire them at Battle Sight Zero range, close enough for him to hit and feel the sucking of pride in his chest, and have his ears ring with the sound of it. He would not beg, would request, and would hope . . . he had no girl or the chance of one, had no rifle or the opportunity to fire one. He would ask his brother.

He answered. Karym was told what his brother wanted. He agreed, of course.

Karym did not ask about a session in the mountains, with the rifle: another occasion. He was told at what time that afternoon he should do the run. It was part of what was regular in Karym's life. Every four or five days, he took the satchel from his brother and rode on his small Peugeot scooter out of the project and along the back roads, not the main highway, to St Exupéry, to a Credit Union branch. He would bank the cash, receive a chit, lodge it, and within a few hours his brother would have transferred it electronically out of that branch and away into the cyber world of lost money. The cash was usually measured in tens of thousands of euros. Sometimes he went alone and sometimes he would have an escort of kids, his age, riding close to him on their scooters . . . about the only time that Karym felt important. It was said that stocks were low in the project, that a new shipment was coming that afternoon. The events of the previous evening were gone from his thoughts, and the smells, and very soon – within hours – the place would await the next bout of theatre, to which the community was addicted.

He wandered and the wind was on his face . . . He saw her. She walked heavily. She carried a shopping bag. He could not see her face because of the shadows thrown by the sunlight. He thought it likely that his brother, through an intermediary – an imam or a school teacher or a social worker – would send her money. Her son's funeral would be the next day and there would be a good attendance from the project, and some flowers. Karym did not think that she would have seen the brilliance of the flames from the torched car or that the smell would have reached her windows. It was the way of the place, and she would accept it . . . A nice morning, and little in his life changed and he did not wish for anything to alter that. He went to buy a cake. There was one area of change that bothered him, was unfamiliar. His brother had been across the city, had ridden his Ducati Monster down to the centre of Marseille and through it and out on the far side; had gone to a meeting with a man of prominence, otherwise would not have bothered, and Karym did not know why. He was unsettled when he did not know the immediate future, even on a pleasant morning.

'Can a woman fire it, shoot with it easily?' Andy Knight's question.

'No problem – should there be?' A corporal's answer.

'The shape of it, the recoil, whatever?'

'A woman can shoot with it, period.'

He was off the main armoury. He had been told that most of the weapons that had been captured on active service had now been shipped out, but the guys who ran the place had managed to squirrel away some prize parts of the original collection, and reasons had been given that satisfied those above, enough to square a circle. At his feet were half a dozen AK-47s from Serb factories and Iraqi-made, an Egyptian version, one from a Chinese factory, and what was laughed at as a museum piece, five decades old from a Soviet era production line and picked up in prime working order from an Afghan fire-fight. He was alone with the corporal, and a Do Not Disturb note was pinned to the outer door. The corporal, long past his retirement date and it would have required a flame-thrower to shift him from this cramped area, was a veteran of most of the recent conflicts where the UK had pitched up.

'I thought I needed to know.'

'Look at the Kurd battles, Mosul and Raqqa. There were women enough on the front parapets, and most had crap AKs from Iraqi stocks, or Syrian, and they were efficient, brave . . . some say they are harder.'

'Explain.'

'What sort of stereotype do you want? All of them . . . "deadlier than the male", or "hell hath no fury", any more? Go into a safe house at four in the morning and the blokes are likely to be sleeping off the booze or still high on hash, not the women: see the woman, shoot her, what they taught us.'

'And the AK is a good weapon for a woman?'

'Good size, good weight, good accuracy at close quarters, for Battle Sight Zero which would be a hundred metres, it's as good as any, better. Does not jam, does not fail to eject, does not require housekeeping, cleaning. Is this a "one trick pony" briefing, just about women using a Kalashnikov? Are you asking me if a woman could have handled an AK attack such as the Paris concert, could do that in any shopping centre? No reason why not. We feel that a woman can certainly be an equal as a sniper, look at the faraway eyes of a target and be happy to take it down: the stereotype explanation would be that a woman can "dehumanise" that target. Have you ever stripped one? The weapon, not . . .'

A low chuckle, but Andy stayed boot-faced.

'No.'

He was taught. The different versions used the same basic parts. The corporal showed him how to take it apart, how to reassemble. Took a full minute the first time, and then around thirty seconds for the second and his hands were a blur of movement as the guts of the beast were extracted and then placed back inside. He was passed the first one and the lights were full on over his head, and he managed it, the strip-down, but hesitated in getting it together the first time round – not the second time. Had an ache in his head from a dream-filled night; had not recharged, had evaded rest. Did it faster the second time . . . The corporal walked away, left him kneeling, surrounded by the weapons, went to the door, threw the switch. Darkness surrounded him but a sliver of light came under the door; he could barely see a hand in front of his face and the rifles were shadows. He was told to do two of them. And did. Sweated on it, took a bit of time, but managed. His fingers felt clumsy, awkward, and he did it by touch. Andy cleared the mechanism and heard the click of metal scraping together. Some would have punched the air, not his way. The light came back on. The colours of the room flooded round him.

'You've cracked that?'

'I think so.'

'You don't need to know the history?'

'Don't think so.'

'A hundred million have been made, same principles but different models, might at a high point have been killing quarter of a million every year.'

'Thank you, no.'

'The weapon of protest and revolution, of the massacre of innocents, of the worst of the bullying thugs of our world, the authority it gives an illiterate kid who can blow away his school teacher, a notion of invulnerability, you won't understand until you have fired it – want a speech?'

'Not on the list.'

'You know what the inventor said, over ninety years old, revered and honoured, the man whose name it carried, what he said?'

'No.'

'Would have preferred to invent a machine that helped farmers, for instance, a lawn mower . . . It's what he thought when close to death.'

'Sounds as if he felt some grief.'

'Had cause. And one word of advice – don't hesitate, shoot the bitch. It's what it's about, I'm assuming. Drop her. No fucking about, do it.'

The corporal rang for the sergeant to pick up the visitor . . . He waited outside. He saw her face and knew the taste of her tongue, and felt her nose nuzzle against his ear, and her fingers at the back of his neck. He saw her down what the corporal had called Battle Sight Zero, and her chest would hide the vital organs that would be aimed at. He saw, also, the worry lines on her forehead and guessed at the stress factors that dominated her, and doubted she could be free of them . . . doubted that he could be. A vehicle arrived and he walked to it. The weapon he had handled, dismantled and put back together had felt good, comfortable.

September 1974

He waited for the dawn.

He held the old rifle tightly, fearful it would slip from his grip and that he would have lost control of it when the moment came.

It would come, the moment.

The boy scratched a notch on the wooden stock of the weapon and closed the blade of his penknife. He knew nothing of its history, where it had been, what lives it had taken since the one he had claimed. The boy was one day short of his eighteenth birthday, in the camp for Palestinian refugees at Tibnine, and was the youngest of the four in the third-floor apartment of the housing block. Also with them, waiting for first light, were the occupant and his wife. One of his friends was in the kitchen where there was a fire escape door; another was in the bedroom which had a view of buildings to the west; and one was in the corridor and behind the main door of the apartment, splintered and with gunshot punctures and with the lock broken. The boy was in their living-room where the windows were already shattered from the first sprays they had fired when bursting inside, and he did guard duty. Two sons had already escaped through the window and had landed three floors below and, screaming for help, had crawled away. The parents had attempted to block the entry, give their kids a better chance of freedom, had pushed a table against the inner door. The boy guarded them, not that it was necessary. The man lay on his back and had taken two or three bullets to the stomach, and moaned sometimes and his eyes were opaque. The old woman's leg was shattered by a bullet that had impacted against her thigh bone. Her life was concentrated in her eyes. Her night-dress was rucked up where she had fallen, much of her stomach above the bloodied wound was exposed, and she cared for nothing other than to show her hatred of him, the boy. Her eyes blazed. She said nothing, did not need to.

The notch on his rifle stock was for the man who had wandered, half-asleep on to the first landing of the building, perhaps going to drive an early bus or a dust cart in Beit Shean, and who had turned to shout a warning up the steps and had been cut down. The boy had fired the last shot that killed him, or perhaps he was already dead. In faint light he had aimed at the nape of the man's neck . . . Truth was, and the boy knew it, they had already failed: they had not achieved their objective. Should have a room full of residents under their control, needed a dozen or more Jews with which to bargain. They had only two elderly people, both grievously injured.

Where the boy sat, hunched down and far from the window, and seeing only the first wisp of light, and against the wall and close to the family's comfortable, worn sofa bed, was the rucksack that held the leaflets and the loudspeaker and the bull-horn and the typed list of demands that should give their captives freedom. A long list containing the names of many fighters held in the Israeli gaols. They should have scattered their leaflets and had not done so; they should have taken more prisoners but had not done so. The commander who had recruited them, trained them, prepared them, had spoken of initial Israeli prevarication, then capitulation and a bus being driven to the door and them all climbing aboard with their chips, like the people won or lost in a card game, and a journey to the border where they would be met by many more buses that brought the brothers from the gaols, and the swap would take place, and a victory would be gained, and cameras from across the world would be there: it was what they had been told.

The boy was not a fool. Since his selection, he'd been lectured on the likely tactics of the enemy's commando force, the *Sayaret Matkal* knew, also of their reputation.

The boy did not wish to die, but he had volunteered and now sat on a cold floor, before the sun was high enough to warm the room through the broken glass. Was it worse to be captured or to die? The boy wondered whether his name would be spoken in the camp at Tibnine, whether he would be hailed as a hero, whether he would be forgotten within a week – replaced by another who believed what the commander said. He knew no answers except that they, the enemy, would come at a time of their own choosing, when the moment suited.

The boy called to his brothers. What was happening? What did they see?

One, from the hall inside the main door, swore at him in response. One, whose sister the boy admired and hoped one day to . . . had a choked voice and was hard to hear, said he saw nothing from the bedroom. One, from the kitchen, with a low-pitched and laconic answer, said that military vehicles had arrived, had parked out of range of their rifles, added that the buildings to the east gave dead ground, and that the sun was rising. The hatred still burned in the mother's face, and the contempt, and the father's groans were softer, less frequent, and blood dribbled from his mouth. The boy had two magazines for the AK-47 taped together so that he could more easily, exchange them. The others' Kalashnikovs were more modern and cleaner, but he would not have been separated from his, and it was a joke amongst the kids on the training courses and often they . . . Never in his life had he heard such a concentration of noise.

A deafening sound of an explosion, and another, and repeated, and the detonations multiplied and seemed to break through the membranes in his ears, and there were flashes that blinded him, then the hammering of firing.

Should he, should he not?

Blinking hard, the boy saw the outline of the head of the mother, was close enough almost to have touched her. It was as if she had ignored the noise and the flashes . . . the same messages were in her eyes and at her mouth: hatred, contempt, and the sneer that said he had failed, was dead. He tried to raise his weapon and it cavorted in his hands and the aim wavered between her head, her husband's and the door, never locked on one. The boy wet himself, felt the warmth of the liquid and swore in frustration at what he perceived to be weakness. His finger was rigid and he could not insert it behind the guard, get it on the trigger, and his tears welled, and the first of them came through the door.

The love of the rifle, serial numbers of ***26016751, had destroyed him. His hands opened. It had broken him. It fell to his lap. The man in the doorway had his weapon up. His last sensation was the weight of the weapon, disowned and unwanted, across his upper thighs . . . another soldier was behind the first. He felt such fear . . . knew nothing more.

He did not know that his body, hit by 27 bullets, almost shredded at that range, would be tossed out through the window and would land among a group of savage settlers, residents in the new estate for immigrants to Israel, and would be hacked at with a meat cleaver and butchers' knives. He would not know that his brothers would follow him and be dismembered, nor know that he would be buried in a hidden grave, nor know that with the reverence of a garbage collector a soldier in the storm team – known in the country's shorthand simply as The Unit – would disarm the Kalashnikov and carry it away, and dump it as a minor trophy in the back of a jeep.

She met two men.

One could be a schoolmaster, with a Pakistani accent, and wore slacks and a sports jacket and his beard was tidily trimmed, and the other might have been a student and his body stank and his clothes were stained and he had the soft and delicate hands of a Somali, and the older man deferred to him. Zeinab had left the station, followed the directions given her, had come to the park. They had been sitting in the cold, on a bench, and she did not know how long they had watched before deciding it was safe to approach. First she was told that she had been monitored since leaving the station and that she was clean, had no tail. She'd said she was hungry and a boy had been sent away and had come back with a pie, vegetable curry, and they had seemed amused by her. She had eaten ravenously. She was passed a bottle of water, broke the seal and drank.

Then business . . . was given her route out, and a folded wad of notes that was bound with an elastic band. She had been about to put it into a side pocket of her coat, but the younger man had taken it from her, had pushed aside the coat at the zip, and his hand was against her breast and he seemed not to notice, and his fingers found an inner pocket. The money went there, and the zip was closed. She produced her new passport and it was examined minutely, had passed the scrutiny and was returned along with the money already given her. She was shown a photograph of Andy Knight. She recognised him, and saw the line of lorries behind him. The picture was stolen. Was she sure?

Zeinab said, 'I am sure. He is besotted with me. He is a driver. He has no politics, only his work and a drink, and being with me.'

And he knew nothing, this driver?

'He is quite simple, not very bright, not educated. It is because of me that he comes, and he drives well. It is a brilliant solution.'

Was she 'fond' of him, and the word rolled on the older man's tongue.

'I quite like him, not more. I use him and . . .'

From the younger one, asked with exaggerated casualness – and she became aware of the hole, poorly patched with a skin graft at the side of his neck and a smaller hole on the other side and presumed him a war veteran – Did she sleep with him, did he screw her?

The blood flushed in her face. 'I do not. No. I have not slept with him.'

From the older man, an examination of a difficulty because it was hard to understand – in these times of loose morality – how she could hold the loyalty of this fellow, the delivery driver, if he did not receive sexual gratification. Did she understand his query?

'Because he is almost in love with me, cannot do enough for me, he respects me. He thinks I am virtuous. I *am* virtuous. He is a good man.'

The younger man peered at her and his face was close to hers and there was a magnetism in the eyes – as there had been in her cousins' – and the grin played on his face as if he were amused, and the question was simplistic: in France, in a hotel, would she fuck him?

'I don't know.' A stammered answer, never been asked such a question before. 'I am not a whore. I don't spread my legs for the cause I follow. I have not . . .'

Not for them to know what she thought, or planned . . . She

should not lose him, not for the sake of preserving unnecessary modesty. She lied to them . . . The younger man's hand rested on her thigh and squeezed hard, as if that were a threat, squeezed until she winced and then slowly relaxed the grip and she could feel – high on her leg – where his fingers had pressed. She should keep him in this state of infatuation, should do what was required. One more thing that they wished to hear her response to, one thing.

'What thing?'

If she had been wrong, if she had chosen the driver without due care, if she harboured a snake, if the man whose photograph they had was tainted, planted, and she learned this in France . . . If learned it in England then he was gone, dealt with swiftly like the cauterising of a wound, if in France and close to the pick-up point, what then?

She said it with defiance. 'I would not be weak. I would spit in his face. I would stamp where I had spat. I would stamp until his face was unrecognisable, until the smile that deceived me was gone, lost forever. I would not hesitate.'

They would have liked what they heard. The older man gripped her hand as if further to strengthen her, and the younger man told her that the monies she carried were for a man who would make indirect contact, and the codeword for him was Tooth . . . And, she was a brave girl, the younger man said, and the older man nodded fervently, and God would go with her. The result of what she did would be heard across the world, would make *kaffirs* shiver in their beds . . . More tickets were given her, and two cheap phones and both had the batteries out, and she gave them hers, and they were gone.

One moment there, the next she sat on the bench alone. She felt pride that she had been chosen. Felt confusion at what had been said to her about her driver, of Andy, and again could taste his tongue and the juices laid in her mouth, and a great cold because of what she had promised, and they'd not know what she had bought in the shopping mall. A spit, a stamp on that face until it was obliterated: it would not happen. Young men escorted her back to the station, formed a distant cordon round her and seemed to confirm her new status.

'It won't last an hour,' Gough said.

'It'll be there in the morning.' Pegs winked. 'Twenty quid on it.'

He did not take her bet, seldom accepted a wager with her. She had her coat on, as he did. Their passports and tickets were in her bag, and their float for this next stage of Rag and Bone. They would not stop at Three Zero Eight's door and seek a brief audience, but would slip away, shadows down a gloomy corridor. The car was waiting . . . She began to stick the sheet of paper on the outside of the door. Fixed it securely, approved, and the door was closed and they had their bags and the key was turned.

It was behind them, their message to the world and the third floor of the building on Wyvill Road.

Advice from this office to a Level One:
A Controller is a man who is always ready, willing and able
To lay down your life for his customer.

Not a backward glance.

Pegs told Gough that the weather forecast for the next several days in Marseille was good: little rain, a powerful *mistral* wind, and a pleasant temperature, and suggested it would be a good trip – forgetting that they had lost their target, were far up a creek and no paddle, and had a lively suspicion that their man was softening, going 'native'.

Gough said, nodding to Security on the front door, 'It had better be a good trip, or they might be mowing the grass and sweeping up the leaves in Vauxhall Park for a well-attended public hanging, you and me and turned off together. I think it'll be that sort of trip – champagne or sackcloth.'

They were on their way, heading for the airport, and Rag and Bone had now climbed beyond serious, and too much of it was out of their hands . . . but nice of her to tell him that the weather forecast was good.

* * *

'I don't think you'll get any rain, Crab, but you should take a coat, be prepared, just in case.'

Beth had packed Crab's bag, some of his smarter clothes and included was a box of fancy chocolates that she had bought in a supermarket, best quality and difficult to know what to take Tooth that was appropriate. He felt alert, bouncy and was cheerful over his breakfast and would get a sandwich at the airport . . . not much money in the deal and some unpleasant people to be dealing with, obscure and remote from him, but business was business and always exciting. The daily costs of life were met by the little gang of geek kids who hacked for him, used an upstairs room in an internet café and were currently milking a hotel chain for credit card details and a firm of Newcastle-based solicitors that had shedloads of client money: decent trading, but not compared with what he and Tooth were currently at . . . enough cash in the bank to tide him over happily, and his sons when they were eventually freed. Beth fussed round him and Gary carried the bag . . . Beth had done a good performance the night before, and likely would be repeating it with Gary once he was gone, not that it mattered. There was a sharp wind on his face as he left his home, and rain might be following along in the afternoon. When would he be back? Not sure, three or four days and not as long as a week . . . he saw it as routine in his life, not as anything particular and special, not as a game changer. Crab had not, in truth, thought it through or given it too thorough an examination, but business was business.

'You'll be careful,' Beth called to him.

Of course he would, always was, but nothing to be careful of. It was an easy run to the airport for a flight to Marseille.

She tried to call him. He did not pick up.

What would Zeinab have said? 'Hi, Andy, how's it going?'

She heard the ring tone. Might have said, if he had answered, 'Just wanted to speak, missing you.' Might have said, 'So alone, want to be with you.' Zeinab let it ring. He was usually good at picking up . . . but he'd not recognised this number. She had said that she would spit in his face, then stamp on it, remove all trace of him, and could hear her own voice saying it, but did not hear him.

'A dog peed on you.'

'Did it?'

The sergeant said, 'Took me a bit of time, but I remembered it. Remembered it while having my lunch, and remembered your name, young 'un. Went into the adjutant's office and checked the records. The name wasn't there. Either my memory was banjaxed or the name was deleted. What I'm not short of is the memory of the dog peeing on you.'

'Did it?'

Always, the instructors preached a lesson of caution concerning a conversation with an older man, a father figure, who had sussed some truths. Tempting to throw in the towel and confide, driven by the loneliness, and say things and believe in the strength of confidences and promises. Should never be done, the instructors said, whatever the temptation and whatever the trust. They were on a common, dull gorse and dead bracken. Andy Knight, or whoever he had been then, had come back to Lympstone, down the hill and against the estuary shore, for a sniper course, had done a stint with 43 Commando and was on the nuke bomb convoys going up from the Thames valley to Scotland, but it had seemed tame, and sniping would be his chosen field. Here was the place to learn it, the dark art. That day was clear enough to him. Each of them had to cross a half-mile of ground while a pair of senior NCOs sat in comfortable canvas chairs and scanned with big-lens binoculars, and the guy who was spotted failed . . . Not 'nearly managed to stay concealed', not 'almost managed it', but failed. Like it was life and death . . . to a Marine who wanted to be a sniper, be in the isolated and feared élite. He had to get within 200 yards of the spotters, and it was a hell of a way to the finish line. The common was shared between Marines and dog walkers and pony riders. The kids on the ponies stayed on well-worn tracks, but the dogs roamed free and went after rabbits. It was a big retriever, handsome chap, that had found him, had lifted a leg, had doused him, then had skipped off to get back to its mistress, and he had not been seen and had not moved. The woman might have known but they were good ladies and would never snitch on the boys in the undergrowth. He had won through, had reached the final point, had passed and would receive his badge, and the dog's urine was in his hair and across the back of his neck, and all of them had had a good laugh.

'God, and how you stank.'

'Did I?'

He knew where he wanted to go. It was weakness that had brought him here, and a bigger weakness that he had allowed the sergeant to drive him to the common. It was bare, featureless, and hostile in winter to the guys on the sniper course, and the NCOs knew – over the years – every gully and every ditch where a man in a ghillie suit could advance. He did not think that Phil Williams or Norm Clarke would have felt the need to come here, but Andy Knight was a different kettle, and might be closer to burn-out, and needed comfort: would find it and something of his past . . . They said that most rabbits failed to survive in the wild for more than a year. The big beggars, dominant males, might do a bit better. He'd always assumed that it was one of them that had wrecked him. This one – probably a Thumper – had dug the hole wider but had also been cunning enough to get a bit of an old tree root lodged across the width of the entrance which would have given cover from a high-flying predator, a buzzard. He had been going fast, his exam already wrapped up, had been crossing ground, and crouched at the waist, and his right leg had gone into the hole and his impetus had moved forward but his boot was trapped. Wrecked ligaments and a cracked bone, a poor first operation in an A&E which had too great a pressure on it and a novice doing the work . . . He'd be all right, of course, would walk pretty well, would run after a fashion but not far, would be grand for normal life: would be a Marine reject. Sad stuff and all that. Life's tough, that sort of epitaph. Told he would be missed but that life moved on, and briefly wished well. The big rabbit had done him, and he had gone to the police and been recruited and had successfully disguised the worst of the injury. Had been bored, had looked for something special, had been told about SC&O10. He found the hole. Could have been home to a fox, might have later on. It was no longer in use and was stuffed with leaves. He stood by it, gazed into it, and something of the dedication was further shed, but Andy Knight was good – as they all were – at shielding real life from the psychologists who cast a rule over them. Who wanted to quit? Nobody did. Who should have quit? Pretty much all of them . . . He shook his head, like he was trying to dislodge an unwelcome fly. He started to walk away.

The sergeant fell in beside him, spoke quietly, like an uncle. 'Rather you than me, young 'un. Don't think I'd manage it.'

'Manage what?'

'Manage being away from this family, I dread that. Living the lie, existing in deceit, not owning a friend. Trying to remember who you are, not who you were. Being alone. I hope to God they protect your back.'

He did not answer.

'Funny old thing. The dog that peed on you was quite young then . . . I was here a couple of weeks ago. The woman's still grand, slower, but fit for her age; the dog's a bit downhill, looked as if arthritis was setting in. Hope we've been of use here, and good luck. Stay safe.'

It would be a short train journey back to his parked car, then an easy run to the ferry.

9

He sat in the car, engine ticking over, and waited for the queue to nudge towards the ferry.

Andy Knight felt the pressure build, heavier than it had on Phil Williams and weightier than on Norm Clarke, could not have directly answered why this time was harder. Would have liked a drink, but had not had one since leaving the common and his conversation with the veteran sergeant who had successfully read him, and he would not have one now. Alcohol did not sit easily with those living the lie. Remembered the bar of the pub up the road from the Newbury over-spill, but had not been there since enrolling into SC&O10 ... He'd assumed that he would be watched into the port and that they would have picked him up approaching the check-in process. They'd have been likely to determine he'd no last minute debrief from controllers, was only a boyfriend with eyes on a long weekend with a girl.

No protection on the boat, of course. No firearm in the car, of course. No baton, no gas and no spray; what he needed to safeguard him was the authenticity of his cover and its ability to withstand scrutiny ... He would have a shit drive ahead of him and would try to sleep as much as possible in a recliner – and not dream. It nagged at Andy that the sergeant had 'pinged' him. He crawled forward, had the radio on, soft music – what the pub might have played. He rarely drank. Some of them in the animal crowd drank alcohol but most could not afford it and anyway preferred to smoke. The people ferrying dope around the southern counties were rarely drunk and had the wit to stay sober, stay alert, watch their bags, had a paranoia for maintaining security. In both lives he had fabricated a medical reason for staying off hooch, something about an allergy that was half concocted and half downloaded from the net. Did another few yards along the ramp, and the lowered bridge was just ahead. In the Marines he had taken his good share of 'bevvies', and in the early police days he had been 'bladdered' when coming off shift like all the other young guys and some of the young girls. The abstinence had come down like a guillotine blade . . . he had never liked to drink in private, alone and solitary, but yearned often enough for the warmth, camaraderie, of the pub up the road from his parents.

That was the Fox and Hounds. The usual cross-section of professionals and tradesmen and loafers with the layabouts. Did a fair cheese sandwich, had a proper log fire, had live music on a Friday. The joy of it was walking inside and not reaching the bar before his name was shouted out and smiles greeted him, and money was on the counter for his first drink of the evening. An old name and no longer used, consigned to a bin. There would be guys there, and the regular bar staff, who might wonder 'what ever happened to . . . .?', and they might see his mother out walking the dog, or might know his father from the school where he taught and ask them 'Haven't seen . . . around, any news?', and trawl for an answer but not get it. His parents knew no more of him than the clientele of the Fox and Hounds. The drinkers would have been puzzled but his parents would have been wounded. Probably thought that some dispute separated them. The best he had said, one Sunday evening some five years ago, had been a caustic explanation, holding no water: he had been called away to 'special duties'. He was off and gone. Through the front door, a slap on his father's back and a peck on his mother's cheek, and no further explanation and all done with a brusque rudeness because that was a better way of severing the link. Then, to the pub and one big round that had drained his wallet, one drink only and heading for the door on a cold night and feeling the frost forming on his face, and turning round, 'See you, guys,' and getting into his car, heading off into darkness. Had never been back and had never phoned his parents. He did not know whether his legends had held so well as Phil and as Norm and as Andy, that no check had ever reached that far, that the cover had stayed strong.

Worst of it was the angst that he'd given his parents, who had done nothing that deserved that treatment . . . not proud, but the job came at a price, a high one. He had heard from the instructors in that long run of preparation that there were a few who tried to – as it was put – 'run with the hare, run with the dogs', and had a wife and children at home, had friends down in the town who seemed to accept that one year he was clean shaven and with a tidy haircut, and the next year he had grown a wispy beard and had greased hair staining his shirt collar. Better to make the clean break, could have been tracked, followed and stalked and seen going in through the bungalow's front door, and then they were at risk, could have been petrol-bombed and could have been beaten. Spared them the risk, and the upset they'd have felt was cheap return for the absence of danger.

He was waved forward, drove slowly into the boat, came close to the loader who brought him the last few inches. He cut the engine. He sat for a moment. Should have felt brighter, livelier, was exhausted.

She walked well, felt confident, important.

She was the little girl from Dewsbury, and she came off the Eurostar and hitched her bag on her shoulder, had her shoulders back and her stride long, and she headed for the Metro. She would need the link to Gare de Lyon. A soldier stared at her, and raised his eyebrow a fraction, then looked away.

A puff of pride filled Zeinab.

There were four in the patrolling group. They threaded through the swarm of passengers on the concourse. They had camouflaged uniforms, and carried lightweight infantry rifles and one had a radio set strapped on his back and it was topped with a wobbling aerial. Their heads, all of them, were close shaven and berets were precariously balanced on their skulls. Their battle helmets were hooked to their belts. The soldier might have been from a north African background, and the texture of his skin was the same as hers. He had caught her eye, made contact, and had thought her worth the gesture of the cocked eyebrow, then had looked away, had resumed scanning the people hurrying about their business, eating, gazing at information boards, keeping children happy. The soldier knew nothing . . . it was the extent of her deception that bred the pride . . . might have been close to arrogance.

It was always said in Dewsbury, whispered among women in the privacy of their homes, that the parents of the children who had volunteered themselves as martyrs – or had taken the long journey through Turkey to enlist in the caliphate forces – did not know. It was the perceived truth that parents, uncles and aunts, family friends, school teachers – and the imams – had no suspicion as to what their kids were learning on the internet, what they intended for their future. She had seen, in streets close to home and under the shadow of the great minaret of the Merkazi, doors that had been broken down at dawn by the police arrest teams. Long after the wagons had gone, taking the teenagers or young men, neighbours, friends and relatives had called to offer solace, sympathy, support, and would have had the same answer – with tedious repetition – that they did not know. The pride, what gave the spring in her step, was because she had deceived her mother and father, the student kids on her landing, her tutor, all of them and had a mask across her face that served her well. The extent of the deception thrilled her, and she found the entrance to the correct Metro line. There had been armed police wandering among the benches and past the shop fronts at the London end of the Eurostar, but the sight of regular soldiers was security taken to a different level . . . she had no idea how it would be. She flashed a ticket and went down an escalator and followed signs.

No idea what it would be like to face troops down the length of a station corridor, or across a concourse at an airport, along the aisles in the shopping centre in Manchester. She imagined that above the noise of screaming shoppers or passengers, would be the shouting of the soldiers. The young one who had raised an appreciative eyebrow at the sight of her, would have had a good voice coming from a strong chest, would have tried to dominate her with its authority. The chance that he – any of them – had ever fired in anger before, shot to kill, was negligible. Nor would she have if it were her, Zeinab from Savile Town who nobody knew of, if she had the Kalashnikov. She sat on a train and it rolled into the darkness of a tunnel. Shouting and screaming around her, and the hammer of her heart and the panting of her breathing, and the finger on the trigger . . . it was that sense of excitement that gripped her. And she was trusted . . . not just by Krait and Scorpion, but the older man and the one with the scars on his neck . . . and she was the enemy that was not recognised.

She remembered how it had been at home. Weeping from her mother, abuse from her father, and doors slammed in their fury, impotent, when she had announced that she would leave home and go to university across the Pennines, and neither had realised that it was part of her march towards this new role, chosen by her, to be a fighter . . . With the weapon in her hand, could she have aimed at that soldier, seen his face, seen his eyes, seen the shake of the barrel's tip, and fired at him? She had no doubt of it.

Liberated . . . in good time for her train to the south . . . free.

'I will treat you, of course, with respect, and listen to your requests, but . . .'

They had been escorted to the second floor of the city's police headquarters, L'Évêché, and might have come from another planet, a different civilisation, from the way their ID and passports had been scanned at the ground-floor reception desk.

'. . . I have a full schedule, and your approach comes outside the correct protocols. I run the affairs, criminal, of the northern sector of France's second city. Am I supposed to end normal duties, and go back to them when you have finished your assignment?'

In the taxi from the airport, Pegs had suggested some initial 'bluster' was predictable, and the man they'd meet would soon soften. She had launched into her schoolgirl French, and made a fair fist. He was a major, and had replied in flawless English, and both she and Gough had ducked their heads in appreciation. So it had started on a poor footing.

She said, 'Any help that we can have would be gratefully received.'

They had been brought up to the office via a creaking elevator and then along gloomy painted corridors; men and women, some in uniform gazed at them as if they were an alien force . . . probably justified. Gough was familiar with French investigators coming to London who received short shrift in terms of welcome, and cooperation with the Italians was rationed more tightly, barely existed for the Germans. The Major was behind a small desk in a spartan office and both of his visitors were perched on hard chairs. There was a family photograph on a wall, him with a wife and a child, another of the Republic's current President, and a map that his eyes had wandered to that showed the northern sector of the city. On his desk were a screen and a keyboard and model cars in the livery of the *carabinieri* and the New York City police, and a toy wagon in the colours of the Guardia Civil. Against a wall was a hatstand that doubled as a coat-hanger, and it was skewed at an angle under the weight of a harness for a shoulder holster, pistol included, and a flak-jacket . . . at Wyvill Road there were no firearms on display, and protective vests were issued from stores in the cramped basement. No coffee offered but Gough thought that was an oversight, not rudeness. By his feet was the duty-free bottle in a plastic bag that he had protected through the journey, and the building's security procedures.

The Major answered her. 'I have delayed a meeting this afternoon to see you. When we have finished I go to that. Then we have the end of the day – I go home. Perhaps tomorrow we can look more fully at the situation confronting you . . . Where are we? You are working on codeword "Rag and Bone", you believe a weapon is to be brought by a new route into this city, you believe also that this is a test run for future shipments. You have an Undercover trailing a female target – except that he and you have lost her. You are confident of regaining contact. It is vague, yes? One weapon, yes? Perhaps only one – or two or three. A very few. A trial, and the hope that if the system is satisfactory more will be ordered, and you are nervous that extremely potent weapons will replace knives on your streets. We know about such firearms, we have that experience, and Marseille is awash with assault rifles . . . But you do not know the contact with whom the female target deals. You don't . . .'

Gough said, never good with words and not crisp, not slick, 'We want to – hope to be able to – have the target and our boy take delivery, then drive it across your country to a ferry port in the north, and our intention is to have people, our people, on the boat who can fix a tracker, a tracking bug, inside the stock – or several, whichever – and we will then follow it. We intend, hope, to uncover – through the bug – a network.'

Pegs said, to the point and brief, 'Getting the bug in represents success for us . . . We have a duty of care.'

'As we do.'

'We must provide protection.'

'And myself also . . . Recently, I had investigators inside one of the housing projects and to get them there, with the possibility of making a significant narcotics arrest, we had those officers, men, dressed in the female style, a *burqa* full veil, but behind them I had a fast response unit, a dozen men from the GIPN. Never more than four hundred metres away, and a limited incursion into that area. But you understand the manpower required to safeguard an officer. You appreciate?'

'I appreciate it.'

'Any trade in weapons involves the senior echelon of a principal crime clan . . . It may be that you do not know our city. We have serious players, they have a reputation for grave cruelty, excessive violence, and they settle disputes in a barbaric way. Last night a boy who had transgressed the rules of his gang was burned alive in a vehicle fire. Horrific . . . Do we have informants who tell us who was responsible, where there is evidence to be gathered? We do not. Not even the kid's mother will talk to us . . . The people your target will need for association, to take delivery, are spare with morality, live in districts known for their barbarity . . . That is where your target may go, and your Undercover, I presume, will not be far behind. I cannot provide the necessary force, open-ended, for you . . . and anywhere in the city, any place, they have the arm's reach to touch. I am sorry but . . .'

'Well, fuck this for a game of dominoes.'

She interrupted. He stopped in mid-flow, and a frown broke on his forehead and he looked across at her as she ducked down below the level of his desk. Gough felt her hand grope at his socks, his shoes, then there was a rustle as her grip caught the plastic bag. She heaved it up.

'Going nowhere,' she said. Round in circles and nowhere.

The plastic bag was slapped down on the table. It had been paid for from the float of petty cash received from the accountant down the corridor and beyond Three Zero Nine. Good quality whisky, ten years old.

She mimicked a formal response: 'Don't want, "I really cannot accept that, it is against our code of ethics to accept gifts in return for favours done. I am sorry, I cannot." Don't want that shit.'

Gough said, 'We are all professionals, all trying to do a bloody difficult job. The old saying, "Better we hang together than hang separately." We did a bit of work, know about you, know why you were transferred down here, know of endemic corruption in the *Brigade anti-criminalité*, know all that. Know how difficult it is, and that it'll all get worse before it gets worse. I understand your position.'

Pegs said, 'It's called Rag and Bone because the target comes from a town that used to be the capital market-place in UK for the rag trade. Great heaps of stained or filthy or discarded rags, a couple of centuries ago – back in history. Where we are today, living in the past, and hemmed in with bloody regulations. Guarding our precious territory . . . Come on, Goughie, getting nowhere and bloody fast.'

Gough said, 'Sorry and all that for wasting your time, Major. Hope your meeting goes well.'

Pegs said, 'We don't intend, not on our watch, if we can possibly help it, to let the bastards win. Have a nice evening, Major, and enjoy the drink.'

The telephone rang and was picked up. Pegs was standing, taking her coat off the back of the chair. The Major listened, impassive. Gough stood, saw the dusk coming fast through the window, and saw also that uniformed men – overalls, vests, firearms, helmets – were running from the building to their vehicles. The phone was put down.

The Major was behind them, had dragged on his harness and holster, then his coat, then his vest, and was pushing Gough to the door and using a free hand to pull Pegs along with him.

Out in the corridor, and more men and women stampeded ahead and behind them. The Major said, 'Whatever is "fuck this for a game of dominoes", I would like to show you how matters play in our city, and maybe where you wish to put your Undercover, and why I am a busy man.'

A smile had broken on his face, and they moved well and Pegs hitched up her skirt higher so that she went faster. Didn't bother with the lift, careered down the stairs. Gough panted but kept up. In the yard, no ceremony, they were pitched into a wagon. No explanation. The sirens started.

Why? Because a gang in Saint-Barthélemey had screwed up. A car had speared from a side turning and come into the traffic flow, scattering a group of scooter riders.

How? The gang had screwed up by losing the cash required for payment of a consignment already delivered. How was it 'lost'? The sum of 120,000 euros, which would meet the necessary payment to a Morocco-based group, had been in the hands of the gang treasurer and he had vanished, was a memory, a fleeting shadow, and might now be in the north of France or anywhere in Germany or might be in the Netherlands where there was a sizable and well-established Somali community. When? Had all happened in the last 72 hours, and the very minimum that the Somalis remaining in Saint-Barthélemey needed – by that evening or dawn the following morning at the very latest – was a clear 100,000. What? The answer, as determined by the Somalis, was to get their hands on that sort of money in that sort of time-frame: not easy, required good planning and good intelligence. Which? It was important they understood, without doubt, which gang of Moroccan suppliers had delivered and was now waiting for payment. They would not be easily fobbed off with a promise of meeting the debt 'as soon as was possible'. The Somalis would be dead. Death would not be easy. Dying would be hard and painful . . . A way out was finding cash, bank notes – credit was not issued to those Somalis – and taken to a rendezvous up beyond Saint-Antoine at a viewpoint in the hills that overlooked the city and the harbour. Had to be there . . . or face war. The Somalis did not have the fire-power to survive such a feud.

The car had skidded to the far side of the road and a back door had opened and one guy out fast, armed with a pistol, and sprinted towards a scooter, a Peugeot that seemed on its last legs, ready for a breakers' yard.

Who else had that amount of money that might be available? Which other group? Not ring-fenced in security, vulnerable? Gossip, rumour, masquerading as intelligence, identified a guy in the neighbouring project of La Castellane who ran a good stair-well, made a decent profit, and moved his takings either himself by powerful motorcycle, or using his crippled brother to take a satchel to a Credit Union. To fight another gang was high risk, but the alternatives for the Somalis were probably harsher. Those escorting the Peugeot, seeing the pistol, fled down the street.

The scooter was on its side and, under it, its full weight pinioning him, was the courier, the strap of a satchel over his shoulder and the bag, bulging with cash, beneath him.

The Somali with the pistol had reached the boy trapped under his Peugeot scooter, the boy did not have the strength in his free arm to shift the machine's weight, to extricate himself and try to make his escape, with the satchel. Down the road the Somali's car waited, the door still open. It was not a part of the northern sector of Marseille, the 14th *arrondissement*, where another motorist would intervene; certainly no pedestrians on the pavement would be so lunatic as to involve themselves.

The boy pinioned to the road was Karym.

It was one of those moments when any individual – young or old, brave or not, heroic or cowardly – was faced with two options and must make a choice. The pistol was waved at him. The satchel was demanded. The Somali stood above him. It was a Somali confronting a Tunisian, no one else's business. Now the pistol was aimed at him. The boy was thin, with a concave chest, brittle legs and skeletal arms, and a gaunt, unhealthy narrow face, no spare flesh and his belt loose at the waist, and no evidence of strength. The options beckoned at him. The Somali might have been five years older than Karym, with a fuller fatter face. Traffic was going round them, hooters blasting, and the sound of the horn of the car parked down the road outside the internet café. No one, no school teacher who had ever had charge of him, had ever accused Karym of stupidity; everyone acknowledged a keen mind that could focus attention on what interested him, like a pistol did. The Somali was shouting and his free hand reached towards Karym and took hold of the strap. Looking into each other's eyes, snarling, full of loathing and defiance. Karym managed to get traction with his feet, but could not lift the bulk of the Peugeot scooter. But he could propel it up and over with the use of his feet.

He pushed and heaved, and could see every stitch in the collar of the Somali's shirt, and the design of his track-suit bottoms and the embossed badge of Real Madrid on his fleece, and the scratches on the barrel of the pistol, and the nails of the fingers clutching it, and the forefinger wrapped on the trigger, inside the guard. He could see all that, and thrust with his legs . . . and could see the face of his brother, and the pride spreading and the praise, and the respect that would come to him in his quarter of La Castellane, and would walk tall . . . he saw all that. The bike rose, then slewed over and wavered, and the Somali dived to get a better grip on the strap, and the Peugeot fell again, and two-stroke fuel was sloshing on the tarmac. The weight of the scooter, well in excess of a hundred kilos, came down on the Somali's ankle, and the snap was as clear as a lightweight gunshot, and the break would have been complete. The protruding bone lifted the track-suit leg, there was blood, and the boy howled.

The car that was to have taken away the Somali, happily clutching the stolen satchel, pulled out and disappeared down the hill. The kids on the scooters who had been given the job of escorting Karym, were close enough to see the pistol, and to hear the scream, and stayed back. The Tunisian and the Somali were entwined. Might have been a couple of kids enjoying an illicit coupling. Arms and legs were spread and locked, and the scooter's bulk crushed them, and the pain must have been too acute for the Somali boy to shout for long. Neither moved. The pistol was steady, its fore-sight lodged in a slim fold of skin on Karym's throat. The street had cleared.

There were no men and women hurrying past on the pavement, and no cars, buses, vans; just the scrape of metal shutters being pulled down, and then silence as radios and TVs were switched off; a crowd watched from both ends of the street, from windows and from darkened doorways. The pain must have come in surges along the Somali's leg, and he would have writhed because he could not contain the agony of the break, and his hand holding the pistol began to shake and the sharp fore-sight gouged deeper into Karym's flesh but he did not dare struggle . . . as if the courage he had mustered to kick over the scooter and pitch it on to the Somali's leg was all that he could manage and his bravery was exhausted.

It was a groan melded with a whisper. 'Call them, the car.'

No response from Karym.

'Call them, I told you, call my brothers.'

Karym looked. It had been a blur of movement when the car had come out of the side street and had ploughed into the little pack of scooters heading down the hill towards the Credit Union branch. They did the same journey three or four times a month; on other occasions it was done by Hamid on his Ducati Monster. Hamid would have assumed that no one from another project would know how he stashed his money, and that no rival group inside La Castellane would have threatened his cash. Karym had seen the car come out, and expected it to brake hard, had expected to give the driver a taste of his tongue and a finger of derision, and it had kept on coming and its fender had nudged his rear wheel . . . They would have to shoot him to get their hands on the satchel. He looked down the street, along the deserted pavement and the empty road. He seemed to remember what model the car had been, what colour, but could not find it.

'Call them. I told you, call them.'

Looked again, and did not see it.

'What I fucking told you, shout for them, wave for them.'

The Somali's face was a few centimetres from Karym's and he thought he struggled to hold back tears, and the pain would have come in rivers. Would have been like the pain felt by the kid in the car, trussed, seeing the flames around him and feeling the scorching heat. Karym thought he tried his best, and pushed his head up for a better view but that motion would have shifted the Somali's leg and made the agony worse. He could not see the car.

'There is no car.'

'Call it.' A gasped voice in his ear.

'Can't. It's not there. Gone. Run out on you.'

The Somali fired the pistol. The bullet would have impacted on the road close to Karym's head, then ricocheted away, and the secondary sound was its impact into metal shutters. A world of silence fell around Karym. The guy still shouted but Karym heard nothing. The face confronting him was contorted, and he was hit with the pistol across the face, but he did not hear what was shouted at him. Spittle frothed at the Somali's mouth as he yelled.

The sound that Karym could hear was faint, distant, but all his life in the La Castellane project he had known the sounds of police sirens. The Somali fired again, towards the noise. Very slightly, Karym moved his head and could see up the street and the cars and vans with blue lights blocking each direction. He held tight to his satchel, to his brother's money.

The *Margarethe* pitched and rolled but made progress.

The captain called for a greater effort from his engineer, reminding him that he had a schedule to keep to. Far out in the Mediterranean sea the visibility was poor and there was a vicious wind from the south causing the *Margarethe* to buck among the white-capped waves. Would the engine take the strain of the speed needed? The engineer was not a man who committed himself lightly. Watching his pounding machine, clinging to a handrail, he gave an answer that he reckoned was unwise, but which was welcome.

'It will be all right. We will be there. Off that coastline west of Marseille. It is not a problem, but it will be a rough ride.'

And spat on the deck, and did not know what was so important in a general cargo that an exact timetable must be met . . . had an idea that contraband would figure in any answer. And it would be good to reach, after the earlier rendezvous in darkness, the harbour of the city, where they were to due spend 36 hours – where there was a good cat-house, Scandinavian kids and clean, near the market and off the Canebière – and then they would sail for Cadiz . . . but the only tight time reckoning was for the following night. Two of the crew were vomiting, would be useless if they came to sail the Biscay. It was good to carry contraband because then bonuses were paid.

They were alone, no other ships' lights in sight, when the captain turned them to the north where the weather would be more challenging, but give them the most direct route to the French coast.

August 1982

'Is this crap one fit for purpose, Shlom?'

'We were asked for five hundred, and that's what you're getting.'

One was from the junior ranks of the Mossad, Shlomo, and the other was from the Agency, Dean. The Israeli and the American were in a hangar of the air force base that was located far out in the sand and at the back end of nowhere, south of Beersheba. Together they were loading wooden crates with Kalashnikov rifles, with empty magazines and filled ammunition boxes. Their work constituted an act of foreign policy and one seen to benefit the governments of both nations. Their supply would tweak the nose of a familiar adversary, a more appropriate analogy might be the lighting of a firework under the ample arse of the Soviet Union. The Israelis were the suppliers, and the weapons had come the previous evening from Defence Force reserve stocks, and the Americans were the purchasers, generous, and they were headed for distant Afghanistan, where a *mujahideen* force was in full-scale combat with the military power deployed by Moscow. The American queried one in particular.

'Looks like it came out of the Ark.'

'We fell back on some creative accounting, but it was test fired.'

'You saying it'll work, do the business?'

'Not pretty – but it performed. It works and it'll kill.'

The great majority of them might never have been used in any life and death fight, might have been chucked away or dropped in the sand as troops, short of food and desperate for water, retreated only to find they faced the barrier of the Suez Canal and had not the kit to cross it. White flags had been hoisted. Most had not a mark on them. One was different, the equivalent, the American thought, of a well-used spade from his parents' garden shed. He imagined they'd have been short of the contracted numbers and had scoured the store for the last few, rubbish, but still able to shoot. And they were required to make a full inventory of the goods.

'What number we got for it? Do you understand why I need to have the serials of each one of these? I mean what crazy mother said we had to list the numbers?'

'Try this – some guy's handwriting is shit – try something, something, something, 260, then 167, then 51. You have it?'

As they went into the opened crate, three already filled, the Israeli sang out the necessary digits and the American wrote them down. This was basic foot soldiers' kit, and already rumours had splayed out that there might in the future be suppliers of sophisticated stuff going in the same direction: ground to air man-portable missiles that would interrupt the safe flights of the attack helicopters that the Soviets flew, but in the meantime it would be assault rifles in the hands of fighters and a message sent that their true friends were the American people . . . A delightful irony that the accusation of collusion was masked by the supply of Soviet-made and designed hardware . . . choice, and amusing.

'Have it. I mean, think what's happening to them, where they're going, and imagine a bean counter in Langley, Virginia, keeping a watch, making sure that our investment is put to proper use. That the only one of the museum pieces?'

'The rest are Egyptian, from the Yom Kippur. There's a bigger stock of them but they're being held back for further shipments. You people want to see the guys getting them are staying onside.'

'I seen them close up – no lie, they are fearsome.'

The television showed them occasionally, but the American had been there. Had been a bag carrier, protection for one of the Agency's senior staffers who was lifted into Afghanistan, not far but over the border, and had made a rallying speech. The American could remember the hard, hairy, tribesmen who had squatted on their haunches and had listened without expression as they were urged to get stuck into a war – a proxy one – and he thought he had recognised men to whom mercy in the field was not considered. Had actually said to the big cheese: 'Thank the good Lord it's not us that's facing that lot and getting them angry, miserable sons of fuckers.' And his senior had responded: 'But that's not going to happen, and they'll do a good job for us.'

'Awesome, bad people to mess with.'

'Enough people have fouled up there. You'd have thought the Soviets would have read history. I'm not weeping tears.'

'They'll survive the journey in?'

'They get a hell of a ride before they start hitting for real. The same with the mortars and machine-guns we had off you.'

The aircraft that the Agency were using had landed at the base a couple of hours earlier, and would now be refuelled and ready for the next leg. A long loop would take it through Saudi air space, and then over Pakistan where it would veer north and cross the southern Afghan border above the mountains of Tora Bora. It would then start a corkscrew descent and come to a pre-designated plateau and flares would guide it and radio signals from guys already on the ground. The crates and medical equipment would be heaved out of the tail of the transport and would flutter down on parachutes.

'The Kalashnikov has a powerful reputation, and earned . .'

'Heh, that old one . . . you see the stock, what's on it?'

'What am I looking at?'

'There's a gouge out of it, look below that, look at those marks . . . Those are kills. This rifle, it's done a bit of heavy lifting. Done its business.'

On the ground, the crates would be split up into lighter loads, put on to the backs of sure-footed, pig-obstinate mules and would go farther north where the mountains were inhospitable to Russian infantry forces, and impassable to heavy armour. The tribesmen would attempt to evade the high-flying helicopters, and along the trail of precipitous paths the weapons would be distributed. The new business would likely involve ambushes of Soviet caravans moving along the narrow, winding roads that linked their base camps.

'Too right, and where it's going it'll do some more.'

The top was fastened on the last crate and the nail hammer sealed it. A fork-lift would carry it out to the aircraft where straps would go round it, and a parachute attached, and if the landfall was good then the kit would be ready to go, do some killing.

'Do you need to answer it?' Menace in the voice.

Hamid said that he did not.

'If you need to answer it, you do that. What you do *not* do is dither with me, listen to what I say, look at your phone, answer what I say, look at your phone. Always your fucking phone. Do I look at my phone?' Tooth had an ability, considerable, to speak softly, as if in conversation and to imply infinite threat.

The texts were jumping on to Hamid's phone screen. The gutless little shites who had ridden with his brother – useless and incompetent – were sending them. Nothing from Karym.

Tooth had summoned him to a small open space overlooking the north side of the harbour, beyond the fortified position of Saint-Nicolas. The garden was named after the Resistance fighter, Missak Manouchian, who had been betrayed, arrested and shot by firing squad with 22 colleagues at a gaol in Paris. His bust was on a plinth. Hamid believed, had no reason to doubt it, that Tooth did very little that was not planned and thought out. The meeting in the garden was not by chance, or convenience. Tooth had explained. The fighter had not been captured because of the skill of the Gestapo officers, but because of treachery, one of his own. Hamid understood. As clear as any lecture, was the message that treachery and betrayal was the greatest crime. A traitor, a betrayer, had nowhere to run, would be hunted down, would die badly. The message was simply put . . . they had then talked about the arrangements to be made.

He had been listening, simultaneously examining the bird droppings on the head of the executed fighter, when his first text had come. The kids with Karym had fled. They had abandoned his brother, had also abandoned the satchel his brother carried, full of cash. To be in the presence of a man of the reputation such as Tooth's was a matter of esteem for Hamid. To have been chosen by Tooth was a step forward in his career that Hamid had not dreamed of, and he was being scolded as his mother might once have done. He would not have taken the soft-spoken criticism from any other man in the city, certainly not from the biggest personality in La Castellane. Tooth was on a higher level.

He shrugged, said vacantly, 'They come the whole time. A message and another message and another and . . . I had a problem.'

'Always better if a problem is shared. You wish to tell me?'

'I have a brother, a kid.'

'You have a brother, and you go to a meeting that is important to you, and you are on your phone which is insulting – and you have a kid brother.'

'He was ambushed, in the fourteenth *arrondissement*.'

'Why was he ambushed?

'He was carrying money. He was knocked off his scooter by a car. He was in the road. The people who ambushed him are Somalis and from Saint Barthélemey. But the scooter fell on one of them, and has broken his leg.'

'And now?'

'My brother is in the road, still has my money. On top of him is a Somali with a pistol but he cannot move. On top of them both is a scooter. The street is blocked by the police. The kid with the pistol is hysterical. Look . . . please . . .'

Hamid showed pictures from his phone. Blurred, indistinct, a mess of legs and arms and what could have been a head, and an empty road and a scooter on its side with one wheel sticking up.

'How much is the money?'

'A hundred thousand euro. It is half a week's trade.'

'Are you more concerned for your brother's life, or for your money?'

He did not answer, did not wish to lie. His arm was punched, surprisingly painful because the fist was bony and angular, and it was meant to hurt.

'It is in place, what will happen, our business . . . I like a man who understands what is a priority – you should hope that your brother survives, and you should do what you can to safeguard your money, and there is me, myself – Tooth. Above all, you delay going to your brother, and you delay concerning yourself with your money because you have to talk with me, you show flattering respect.'

Hamid stood, turned away, and heard a mocking cackle of laughter behind him.

They were left. Ignored, not brought coffee nor bread rolls, nor told what was the plan, not given any real indication as to why they were there.

Pegs shared her peppermints with Gough. She said that she found the situation 'stimulating' and he said – chewing his mint – that it 'set the juices flowing'. They did not complain, nor seek to attract attention.

It was, to Gough, a classic scene . . . The kid who was underneath, spine wedged down on the road, moved every few minutes but only very slightly, and sometimes was shouted at and sometimes received a cuffing from the pistol when he did so. He was alive, seemed unhurt and did not cry out and had taken the wise course of simply staying still and silent and waiting for others to take action. Gough had done sieges before as a young man, standoffs when a hostage taker had a weapon at the head of an unfortunate: Irish sieges and those in London with PIRA men, also a bank situation, and he could fault neither the actions of the police as he saw them, nor those of the youngster at the bottom of the pile. Different position for the youth above him and squashed down because of the weight of the scooter. The youth, with the smooth chocolate skin of a Somali, was suffering. He shouted often and Pegs translated what she understood – the obscenities graphically repeated – and had cause to shout because his track-suit was rucked up on his right leg and the wound was clear to see. If the kid were to be treated as a human being then he needed to chuck away the pistol and get a shot of morphine, and if he needed to be treated as vermin then he needed finishing, the way a motorist would go to his car boot having stopped after hitting a deer or a badger on a country road and extract from the tool-box the heaviest wrench and bash it on the head and end the misery.

Pegs said, 'I'm cold, Goughie, and I'm hungry, and need to piss . . . The kid says that he wants a car out, no police tricks, no prosecution, and he'll let his prisoner go free, wants a guarantee of immunity – or he's going to shoot, kill his prisoner. Sounds as if he might just do that . . . hopefully it won't happen while I'm looking for that piss.'

The scene was easy to monitor because the police had brought up floodlights, taken power from a first-floor apartment, dropped cables from a window, and had made daylight. She'd gone. Gough was wrapped in his thoughts and supposed there was a benefit in being given a front row, stalls view, and he heard a murmur behind him. Started soft and grew. Like the rumble of water on a shingle beach and repetitive but louder as the time advanced. He tried to identify it – then reckoned it was a name. A car door slammed, he heard boots on the tarmac behind him . . . the kid down the road was calling louder and with a shriller voice and the message seemed the same, but he did not have Pegs to interpret. The Major came past him, made no contact, and there was a soft exchange of voices. He had identified the murmur, and thought the name repeated was 'Samson'. He could not comprehend why there was importance in that name, what was signified. Gough didn't care to rubber-neck, but he turned his head with discretion. The murmur was a whisper, was a call, and it spread among the police who manned the cordon, and from the upper windows where the residents hung out to seek a better view down the street, and from those who were kept back on the pavement but would have a garbled view. And Samson . . .

. . . Gough watched him. Boots tied tight in a hurry with the laces out of kilter. Crumpled overalls and a vest that was not fastened close to the body, and a balaclava that was blue, not the uniform black, and he carried a rifle easily as if it were no more important to him than a handbag to a woman. Gough did not have the knowledge to identify the type or its origin, but mounted on it was a telescopic sight. The sound of the kid's shout reached them, and the Major was deep in conversation with the marksman, with Samson. He nodded curtly and he left the Major, and his head twisted and his eyes would have been roving for vantage-points.

Peggy was back at his side. She had ended up in an alley, in darkness, best she could manage and still no food or drink. She cocked her head, listened, heard the screams of the kid with the pistol, told Gough it was about more threats to send his prisoner off to his maker.

She said, 'Beats staying in and watching television. He's something of a celebrity, apparently. Has a list of kills to his name. I asked a plod when I came out of the alley . . . Samson did the head-chopping during the Revolution, was an executioner . . . we're being shown what's real here, Gough, getting the lesson force-fed. So that we know our place. Don't chuck our weight around and expect them to jump.'

They waited. The kid with the pistol made more threats and fired in the air . . . and the lone figure, Samson, had slipped away, not hurrying, had disappeared into dense shadow, and they'd lost him. Would he actually do it, aim the pistol on to his prisoner's forehead, pull the trigger, leave himself without a shield, or would he cop out? The kid would have to gamble, like Gough did. He gambled all the time, and with other lives ... and he wondered how they did, the girl and his Level One, and where they'd reached.

Zeinab slept.

She had a backpacker beside her. He was a New Zealander and had a badge of his country's flag stitched on the upper sleeve of his jacket. Probably her age, within a few months, and wanting to talk, and he had not enjoyed a shower that day, might not have had one for two days or three, and he had offered her water from his bottle. He told her – whether she wanted to hear or not – that he was between Heidelberg and Lyon, and after a few days in the south of France would be going to London, then the north where his family had relations, and ... she declined his water. Was she a frequent traveller, did she know the French rail system, had she been to Germany, or to Athens, or Buda-Pest, Prague, the concentration camp at Auschwitz, did she want something to eat because he was going to the buffet? Did not tell him that far from skitting around Europe she had never been further by train than the one-hour journey from Dewsbury to Manchester, had never been to London before this journey, and had been nervous of negotiating the Metro system in Paris, said none of that. He was built big and overlapped his seat and his elbow was across her armrest, and the carriage was fully booked ... was he an enemy?

They had pulled out from Gare de Lyon. He had gone for food from the buffet, and had seemed moderately hurt that she wanted nothing.

He had the window seat and she had the aisle. She could hardly pretend to be asleep and then be woken to let him ease past her. He might have been walking in a mall when he came to the north of England, buying socks or underpants, and be confronted with a Kalashnikov assault rifle, and neither she, nor Krait nor Scorpion, could stop and eliminate him from the line of fire – big New Zealand boy who was likely a drop-out from a chemistry or geography course at a local college. Everyone, each last one, walking along the aisle of the mall was an enemy. Could not look into their faces, not engage them and make a judgement, shoot straight or aim off. Could not . . . He came back.

She shifted, and the backs of his thighs were close to dropping into her lap, and his arm brushed her chest, and his jeans had slipped and showed the skin of his lower back and the start of cleavage, and he dropped into his seat, and thanked her for showing patience. He had a happy look on his face because he had found a girl to sit with, and one who spoke his language. He presented her with a bar of chocolate, just a gift, and it came with a bovine, silly smile. They were all enemies, had to be. If some were not enemies then she had lost the necessary determination, was a fraud, should not have been chosen – and had betrayed the cousins she had known in Savile Town.

She refused the chocolate. She turned away from him and closed her eyes and pretended to sleep, and he ate from a bread roll of ham and salad, and crumbs fell on her arm, which he clumsily wiped off. The train went south, at speed.

Andy Knight had the seat tilted back, his eyes closed, and the radio was tuned to a European station that played soft jazz, and he nearly slept.

The VW had driven well and he had held a steady but not excessive speed on the A13 route and had sidelined the Rouen turning and kept heading for Paris, then had skirted Versailles and transferred on to the A6 and headed south-west. Gone as far along the Autoroute de Soleil as a service station, Achères-la-Forêt, and had stopped in a far corner of the parking area, had locked his doors, had crashed out. He had thought himself too tired to dream. One of his last thoughts, dozing deeply . . . the VW had been sweet tuned by the mechanics at the depot. Good guys. They'd not get the thanks they deserved because he would not be coming back to work there, drive a lorry, exchange banter with them and crap talk about the football teams, and ask vacuous and insincere questions about their wives, kids, mums and dads, and would no longer be the decent joker who was liked and had his car given a thorough and professional service check . . . But he had left his customers in the lurch when he had done jobbing gardening and landscaping and they'd have been expecting him next week and some of the projects were half-completed, but he had not been there to finish what he had started. Had had a small delivery business, out of a rented van, and people would have been hitting their phones and trying to raise him, and wondering why such and such a pick-up was not made, and were left angry, let down. It was what he did . . . Came into people's lives, used them, and then eased out. Never went back and did a contact with those who had helped him, had sustained in ignorance his cover; there would be no postcard thanking them sent to the guys in the depot garage.

It sort of hurt. But not enough to stop him sleeping, or from thinking about her, and her touch and her taste, and had a rug over himself to keep him warm into the night . . . and he did not know how it would be there, in Marseille, far to the south, and beyond pretty much all of his experience.

10

Andy Knight slept in. Might almost have found a sort of peace.

The hard part of what he did – and Phil and Norm – was in the first stage of the infiltration. This time round was when he had charged down the darkened street and launched at the guys who were dealing out grief to the girl. They had, all three of them, been well briefed and had known not to hurt her but only frighten her, and had known that they'd take a bit of a slapping . . . had been owed an apology, not least the one who had taken her kick in the groin, where it hurt bad and where he might have suffered some real damage . . . and then the next step in turning up at the Hall of Residence. She would have talked to the people who controlled her, and would have told them of this guy – simple and unsophisticated and politically vacuous – who ate from her hand, was a pigeon in a park. It had worked well, the great idea, that she would get him to drive her back from Marseille and the promised reward was a shack-up night or two in a crap hotel, maybe without clean sheets – which was a difficulty. He was out to the world in his car, had the seat tilted back.

The other hard bit, potentially, was what Phil and Norm had endured; suspicion, and violence chucked at them. But Andy Knight was clear of that. The life and death moment was sidestepped. He slept deep. Had he dreamed, which he did not, it would only have been as a witness of the final curtain being drawn. If he were there to see, then he'd be hunkered down in the back of a police wagon and would have a vantage-point through a smoked glass window. It would be messy if it were done at the university, inside the Hall of Residence or on campus or in the Students' Union, and they were more likely to have chosen her home, Savile

Town. Not necessary to break down the door, just a ring of the bell and a middle-aged man opening it and seeing a street filled with uniforms, some with firearms, and a bare word of politeness before they surged past him. She would be taken out fast, handcuffed, and then, after she had been driven away, the search team would arrive. She would not see him. It would be the intention to lift the whole nest of them, all of the cell, and to take back the weapon with the bug embedded into the cleaning kit hole in the stock. She would be in shock and whipped into a custody suite and the questions would come flying before she'd the wit to gaze up at the ceiling and break her silence to demand legal representation. He might see Pegs and Gough one last time, might not. He would slip into Prunella's office and they'd offer him leave, indefinite, but expect to keep a hold on him . . . It would probably be for the last time, but he'd not share his future intentions with her. Was not for ever, was it? Not pensionable employment – fast burn-out with hefty premiums. Prunella would blow him a kiss when he went out through the door with his grip, all that he owned, what he had cleared from the Manchester bedsit, and he would take a train to anywhere or drive to anywhere. 'Anywhere' was a place where he was not known, had never worked. There would be a court case, but not for at least a year, water under the bridge by then, fast flowing.

It mattered where he slept, whether he slept with her. Mattered that the discipline of a serving officer stayed firm. Mattered where he was, her bed with her, or his bed and alone. A psychologist had talked to them once: had grinned, then prefaced his lecture – 'Sleeping with the Enemy' . . . 'When you're on the plot and you start getting close to one of the women there, and she close to you, don't ever think it is about true romance, won't be. It is *need.* You, for all your training, are vulnerable. So is she. It is a way of sharing the burden for both of you. You are both on the edge, nerves frayed to breaking point . . . not love, just something animal. If you can avoid it, then all well and good; if you can't, then don't think any the less of yourself. It'll be, given certain circumstances, difficult to avoid . . .' And he'd shrugged like there was nothing more to say.

But the hard part of it was done, dusted, and the sleep was good and he felt safe: should have realised that was dangerous at worst, foolhardy at best. Stress leeched out of him and the traffic on the Highway to the Sun swept past the service station, and the sun would be high before he woke, went for a wash, took breakfast, hit the road to where they would meet.

Zeinab was awake.

The New Zealand boy had slept, his head had lolled against her shoulder and his first snore had erupted, and she had kicked his ankle – not as hard as when her toecap had hit the thief's privates. Firmly enough for him to grunt and flail with an arm, and take a moment to realise where he was. He had the grace to apologise. She did not have another opportunity to sleep because the boy had called his mother. His mother was on the South Island of New Zealand. He told her where he was, where he had been for the last two days; said that she should not worry about him, that Paris was well protected and those goddamn terrorists were kept far away from the main tourist haunts. He was fine, he was safe. They talked a quarter of an hour and he seemed interested in the rest of his family.

Did she want chewing gum? She did not.

Then called his father; his father was somewhere else but also on South Island. She had no option but listen. She did not sleep.

'What, Dad? The terrorists . . . No, I've had no scares. They have troops and police out, all the public places are guarded, and Germany, I feel very secure . . . was talking to a guy yesterday, French. You want to know what he said? He said they need decapitating, the terrorists do. He said they were vermin – that's the terrorists – they had different governments in the past, but now they've toughened up. And, Dad, you there, Dad? . . . In Germany they reckon they've too many migrants, don't know who they are, and everything had gotten too liberal. Should be stamped on . . . Lyon, Dad, that's where I am going. Good to speak, Dad . . . The baby is okay? You are a bit of an old goat, Dad, don't mind me saying it. Yes, I'm safe, I'm good. They say, Dad, you can smell these people, the terrorists, and see it in their eyes, animal eyes, sort of dead eyes: I met a sociology guy in Berlin. He said that. Oh, Mum sounded good. This guy, Berlin, he said they can't hide. What? You have to go? . . . Night, Dad.'

She might sleep after Lyon, his destination, if her anger allowed it.

Light reflected off an opening window. A street-light caught the angle of the glass on a first floor and almost opposite, across the street, from the overturned scooter and the two intertwined bodies underneath it.

Pegs saw the moment the light hit.

She had been alongside police professionals all her working life. She was also, irrelevant to a woman of 47 years, a disappointment to her parents who had chucked money at her education – wasted. She had arrived in the secretive offices off Wyvill Road by chance: a 'flu virus rampant and desk staff dropping like sprayed flies. An impression had been made, doors had opened, an offer of extended work had become a posting, and within a year she had moved quietly, discreetly, into both Gough's office and his life, had turned her back on Hackney, and a civilian job collating burglaries, knifings. The position was not abused and she had become fiercely loyal, would stay with him until he dropped, was axed, or retired. She had perception, wheelbarrow loads of it – what she called 'simple bloody common sense' – and was blessed with a good eye.

It was the third window onto which light from the street lamp had bounced.

All the time that the boy under the scooter had yelled increasingly dire threats, she had watched the movements of the officer they called Samson. There had been one in London, as she remembered – right place at the right time, or the opposite – who had notched up more kills than any other. It would be interesting to see his work at close hand, had no doubt in her mind that was how it would end. The man had eased down the street and had kept his rifle against his leg so that it would not be obvious, had tried shop doors and found them locked but then had come to a darkened alley between two buildings, barely wide enough for his shoulders, and had disappeared into it. She had seen the first window nudged open, then closed and presumed the alignment could be bettered, and then the second window. The third had opened, left ajar.

Because of her good vision – Gough would not have noticed it and she had not yet alerted him – Pegs had seen the protruding tip of a rifle barrel.

The wound on the leg, where the broken bone had split the skin, would have hurt as bad as Pegs could imagine. She had been through childbirth once, had not enjoyed it nor thought the end product worth the effort, and she had suffered a broken nose – straightened skilfully in Casualty – when mugged in east London, but had not known the sort of pain the kid suffered. He would be irrational, unpredictable, and several times she saw the pistol jerked so hard into the hostage's neck that the head was tripped sideways . . . it would be a matter of judgement. She liked that, the thought of a decision being taken. Where she worked, a pace behind her mentor, Gough, decisions had to be made on the hoof, not with a committee to refer back to . . . A decision would be made here, perhaps already had been. Time to stir Gough? Probably. Away to her right, she could see the Major intent and listening on his phone. She nudged Gough. She did not point, did nothing to attract attention, just spoke quietly in Gough's ear and he nodded when he'd seen the rifle at the slightly opened window.

Gough said, a whisper, 'You wouldn't envy him. The bad boy shoots first, and who cares about him being taken down a second later. The operation fails. The marksman shoots and the bullet does the necessary damage to the bad boy and then hits a hunk of bone and is diverted into the good boy's upper chest. It fails. He cannot be told what is the right time has to make his own judgement, is alone . . . I am thinking, Pegs, of our own man, and we don't share the weight of his burden, cannot: he is equally alone.'

There was another shout, and the voice was hoarse, like it came from deep in the throat, way into the chest, and the pain must have climbed. She told Gough that it seemed like an end-game. That he'd shoot his prisoner and it would be the same as a suicide. No overdose and no rope slung over a garage roof beam, but a cop doing the job.

'It has to be now,' Pegs said. Has to be . . .'

The shot, breaking the screaming insults of the bad boy, cut her off. The report made less noise than she'd have imagined. She looked, not at the target, but at the window. The barrel tip was motionless and protruded no more than a foot from the sill. No emotion, no stress.

And the hit? Hard to tell. The scooter had shifted, was lifted higher. Pegs saw what should have been the head of the target but only half of it and was confused and her hand came up to her mouth. The second head, which had been underneath, was clear to her, and blood spattered, laced with brain tissue. She felt the vomit rising in her throat. She was supposed to be the hard woman, no tears and no fuss, and no visits to the shrinks – and the sight of an agent pulled from a canal, too young and too fresh and too eager to survive, but shoved into harm's way because it had seemed important, had not turned her stomach. There was a violent motion and one body was pushed and then heaved and it flopped aside.

It had been, she assessed, a dramatically good shot. With the rise of the vomit was a great gasp in her throat. She swallowed. Death handed down. Quick and clinical, like an executioner would have done it. One down and one standing. She did not know his name, his significance if any. A feeble young guy and blood loose on his face, and his clothing messed with it. The street was silent, the shouting over.

He moved like a rat. A satchel bounced on his hip. He was bent low, squirming, and had his hands on the scooter and pulled it up. It was a cheap scooter, an old one, what a teenager would have owned while dreaming of something better, faster, something with style. He had been prone on the tarmac for a long time, had moved hardly at all, had had the weight of the other boy on top of him, and the scooter's, and now he went fast – and had had a pistol pushed against his neck. Showed no sign of an ordeal – Pegs thought him a street fighter, and marvelled.

The scooter was upright. A leg went over the saddle bar. The key was still in the ignition slot. A twist of it, a wrench on the handle. And again, and . . . The engine coughed, spat out fumes. A body with only half a head was left behind. The scooter charged the police line and the satchel was thrown back to the extent of the strap, like hair in the wind . . . How should it have been? Should have been police with guns going forward and waving the medics to follow them, and then a priest, and afterwards the whole paraphernalia of care consuming the boy who had been a hostage and close to death and unable to intervene for his own life. The boy should have been wrapped in blankets or in tin foil as if he were a disaster victim and in shock and nurses close and a doctor working on him.

He drove towards the police line and guns were raised but not fired. An opening appeared – a Red Sea moment. He was not stopped and was accelerating into the gap. She supposed a juvenile rat would have fled as fast if it had been freed from the claws of a household cat. The scooter engine was not tuned and the carburettor was in need of cleaning out, and its noise was raucous. It disappeared from her sight. Not like anything she had experienced. All that was left in the street were a pair of feet in trainers and they stuck out under a strip of canvas that now covered the body. The police protected the immediate scene but the road was opening and the first cars were coming through slowly. She knew her motorcycles, they'd been her former husband's delight and fantasy, and when she had tried to please – not often – she had brought home a magazine for fanatics. The rumble of sound was from a Ducati Monster with a helmeted rider who had his visor down.

'What are you thinking?' Gough asked her.

'That I'd expected this would be all marinas and five-star dossers, a place for tacky celebs . . . and maybe we've had a better view of where we are.'

'I think so.'

The Major walked towards them.

The body was carried past. Cigarettes were lit. They seemed to him to be as cold and as hungry and as out of place as refugees.

The Major said, 'It was interesting, no more. A criminal steals from a criminal. The profits from narcotics trafficking are being taken to a bank – I do not know which one – or where. Another group from another area, had lost the money it needed to pay for a shipment already received, they have to steal, find a ready source of cash. I thought it would be interesting for you to see the city into which you plan to plant your Undercover . . . not always a pretty place.'

It was late and he wanted to be home; Simone would have a meal for him to be heated in a microwave, and the children would be asleep, but he would not be returning to the apartment on the Rue d'Orient tonight because the paperwork would not wait until the morning.

'You believe that a new route for the movement of firearms is planned by a terror group in your country. Very possible. So, firearms come into Marseille; they are not brought here by UK nationals, but by local entrepreneurs, gangsters, those beyond the law. They are not legitimate business people involved in simple import/export, they are not spinster aunts who dabble in something of this and something of that, they are not bankers who see an investment turning out a satisfactory profit . . . They are thugs. They know the market-place and where we are vulnerable, how to move around us. Criminal thugs have risen to eminence through violence. No other way to measure them. The higher they have risen, the greater their realisation that violence, its certainty, should determine their actions.'

Within his first six months in Marseille, men had sidled up to him: lawyers, accountants, guys from the Chamber of Commerce, local government officials, had talked in soft voices of the advantageous of mutual cooperation. Coldly, sternly, politely, he had declined the 'advantages' they offered.

'This is a dangerous city. If you manoeuvre an agent that you employ on to these streets, close to the sources of violence, you take a great chance. A chance with your agent's wellbeing . . . but, that will have been evaluated. Of course.'

Most weeks he did the equivalent job of sweeping up the detritus left on the north of the city: bodies carbonised in cars, corpses slumped in cafés with multiple Kalashnikov bullet wounds, cadavers abandoned in the hills above the projects. Few palliatives to the frustration, and few arrests.

'We are stretched very thin. We are under-resourced. You breeze into our city and require a team from the "intervention force" and want them to sit on their backsides and wait around, and be ready to help your agent, and then another team, then another. Three shifts . . . I regret that it cannot be done. You have the right to go to my superiors and request that I am bypassed, and the likelihood is that you would be escorted to the airport. You could contact the Ministry in Paris and they would request a written communication as to your aims, and perhaps you will receive a suggestion that you come back in a couple of months or three.'

He had one weakness, and knew it. His wife would be in bed having prepared his dinner and would have made sure there was a beer in the fridge, and his children would have wanted to talk to him about football or dancing or . . . No other officer from L'Évêché had been invited to his home, had met his family. It was a small measure of security, about all he could do. It was his heel, where he was vulnerable, and he knew it.

'You were fortunate to have contacted me. This is a dangerous city, it is also a corrupt city. There are officers, investigators, who have sold out, and it would be advantageous for any of them to pass your names, your hotels, your mission – what you call Rag and Bone – to interested parties. Myself, I trust very few – Samson, yes, I trust him, would give him my life for safe keeping. Not others.'

He hoped they would appreciate his frankness. Their bags were still in the wagon they had travelled in. He would have the couple dropped at their hotel, then return to work.

'I give you my mobile. You ring that number. Wherever I am, it is with me. We will come. We will be there as quickly as is possible . . . I do not know what you expected, but you should not have travelled here and should not have permitted your man to journey, naked, to Marseille. For one rifle, for a handful of rifles, a trifle. You should withdraw him . . . My phone is the best I can do.'

'You all right?'

'I'm good.'

'It was delivered?'

'It was.'

Karym had washed himself in a fountain in a little square off the main road coming down the hill from the police blockade. It was the evening when the Credit Union stayed open late, when men came to bank their wages – those with work – to save up for the annual pilgrimage to the family in Tunisia or Morocco, or any fucking place that people who lived in La Castellane had come from. He had crouched over the stagnant rainwater in the fountain's bowl and had rinsed his face, had seen the blood stain the water. He had lodged the cash. The girl behind the secure barrier had not queried why a kid with water dripping from his hair, who had wild eyes, filth on his clothing, should bank that sort of sum, but had counted it and had given him a receipt. He had left the building, had sat astride his scooter and had begun to shake. Could feel the pressure of the pistol barrel on his throat, and the warmth of the blood on his face. Stiffness trapped his legs, his hands trembled. He could not have steered the Peugeot scooter. He had heard the growl of the Ducati's approach. His brother had found him.

'I need to ride with you.'

'Is your bike broken?'

A hesitation . . . he had asked often enough for his brother to buy him a new scooter, the Piaggio MP3 Yourban would be the best, with the tilting front wheels . . . he would not have dared to lie to his brother. 'Just that I do not feel well.'

'You ride with me. I'll send kids down for the Peugeot. Good that it is not broken. Okay, we move, we are missing trade.'

He sat behind his brother. The wind scoured his face, where the blood had been. He was not thanked, not congratulated, not praised for his effort in getting clear of the site so that the police did not take possession of the satchel. They went back, fast and noisily, to La Castellane. Only when they were near to the project did his brother slow the bike and tilt his head back so that he could speak, so that Karym could hear him.

'It was Samson who killed the thief. You were lucky. Anyone other than Samson and you, too, would be dead. He is formidable. You do not want, ever again, to be in the sights of Samson's rifle. Never again.'

Karym heard the squeal of laughter, and the engine was gunned and they made an entry back into the estate, like it was just another evening, and trading had already started, and they were late.

'Welcome to my distinguished friend.'

'Greetings, my old cocker.'

'You look grand.'

At the Arrivals gate, hugging him, Tooth laid kisses on each of Crab's cheeks. Not that Crab was tall, but Tooth needed to be up on his toes to do it. Crab did not respond with his lips, but held his friend fervently.

'Don't deserve to be. It's been a journey from hell and back and hell again. Good to be here.'

Many hours late, Crab had arrived. First, the late arrival of the aircraft in Manchester, then the rostered crew being out of hours, then a light flashing when it should not have, then a delay with one passenger's baggage and the need to offload everything in the hold. It had been a litany of disaster. Crab had suffered. He did not read, nor listen to music, did not drink, and the hours had gone slowly, then a storm over central France, then big crosswinds coming off the sea when they were on the final approach and being tossed . . . Tooth would not want to know.

'But you are here.'

'I am here. I cannot imagine anyone and anywhere, Tooth, that I'd prefer to be, to be with . . . On course, our little matter?'

They were walking towards Tooth's car, predictably a Mercedes, and Crab pulled behind him the case that Beth had packed.

A quiet reply, lips barely moving. 'I assume. What I have heard. All sick as dogs in the weather out there, but keeping to the schedule.'

'Like being back in harness, Tooth, waiting for a freighter. Doesn't matter what it's carrying, just that it's coming. Keeps the blood running in those old veins.'

The keys were flashed, the bag went in the boot, and Tooth walked Crab to the front passenger door, then paused and laid a hand on Crab's arm. The lights over the parking area showed a fraction of a frown on Tooth's forehead.

'You said, "*Doesn't matter what it's carrying*", you said that. You have no problem, what it's carrying, no problem?'

'Business is business, Tooth, no problem at all. Bring it on.'

'You echo me, my friend – no problem. I'm not a preacher, I just go where the market is.'

'I think it's going to go very smoothly. What we call a "piece of cake" . . . So good to be back with you, Tooth. It's a good person our customer is sending, well spoken of. Piece of cake, yes.'

The train pulled into the station at Avignon. Zeinab slung her bag on her shoulder. Where it all started, became real.

A few others, half asleep, followed her. She crossed the platform. Had there ever been a chance to turn back? Not now. Turning back was crossing a bridge and going to the far platform and checking the departures and finding the first train heading north, and never going home, where Krait and Scorpion knew her, and never being within reach of the men she had met in the London park, changing her name and changing the whole identity of her life, disappearing. The lights were dimmed inside the station and the magazine stand was shuttered and the fast-food outlet was closed. She went into the night. A police car was facing the main entrance and she saw the glow of cigarettes: the doors did not explode open. A couple of druggie kids were squatting against the outside wall.

She had directions, knew where to go. The main street leading to central Avignon was the Rue de la République, and she had been told that it led to the road and the hotel she was booked into.

Zeinab was shown by the concierge to a first-floor room, minimal furnishing, a double bed and no view, and opened her bag and took out the nightdress . . . it was where it started.

January 1987

A one-legged boy had positioned himself in the cover of a rock, some thirty metres above the road and not more than fifty metres back from it, where the exchange of gunfire would be extreme. He was already, a couple of minutes after the first land-mine had detonated and brought the convoy to a halt, on his third magazine. In spite of the surprise gained by the *mujahideen* when the explosion had halted the soft-top trucks after the armoured vehicles had been allowed through undisturbed, the battle in the killing zone remained undecided. Many of the Soviet troops who had spilled out from the lorries had been killed, or were wounded, but none of them who lived – damaged or not – would surrender. Tales of their fate were legion – to have the penis and testicles rammed down a throat while still alive was not a reason to hoist a white flag. The boy, with some expertise, fired an old AK-47 assault rifle, tried to go only for aimed targets and at that range had the sights at their lowest point, what he had been told was called Battle Sight Zero, a phrase it was said, taken from old British army sergeants, who had fought and been defeated here. He had some hits and had some misses – he was always with this tribal group when they went forward, across the mountains on narrow paths, into defiles, along river-beds, and hunted for convoys . . . and had not long to do the job.

He was, he thought, twelve years old. He could not ask his mother because she had been killed, decapitated in a rocket attack, and could not ask his father because he had been injured, fatally, when a Hind helicopter had turned its awesome firepower on a small caravan of mules. Could not ask his brother who had been shot in the leg and could not be carried and had been finished by his own people. But the brother's weapon had been snatched, taken away, and given to this child, who had one natural leg and one of crudely carved wood.

The boy's left leg stopped just below the knee. The lower leg had been shattered by a personnel mine scattered randomly in a dried watercourse. No chance of proper medical attention, of hospital care, of anaesthetic, and the surgery had been as brutal and as immediate and as successful as that performed on the injured more than a century before – told among the *mujahideen* when camping at night – when the fight was against British occupiers. A wad of leather to bite on. Men showing harsh kindness in holding him down as an older leader hacked with a blunt knife. Fire to seal the wound. A length of dried birch wood had been carved and whittled into the necessary length for a limb, with a place padded by leather and cloth for the stump to nestle in, and straps attached that could be knotted round the fragile child's waist to hold it in place. There were days of heavy marches when the tears ran on the boy's face as he fought to keep up with the speed of advance, but he would not cry out, nor would any man diminish him by helping: there would be blood seeping from the wound after excessive friction, and it would be washed in a stream, and they would go on. The child had his elder brother's rifle. The child slept with it, ate with it beside him, marched with it, and used all his skills and hatred to kill with it.

He had already scratched notches on the stock. Had added more to those cut out by his brother, and further scrapes in the wood would be made that evening after they had retreated from the ambush site, at least three more. They should hurry, do the killing business fast because by now the armoured vehicles, with their radios, surviving the attack, would have called up to the Jalalabad airbase, and the helicopters would soon be in the air, coming as fast as eagles.

Others in the *mujahideen*, fit and strong and lithe, would move their firing positions, never permit the loathed Soviets from fixing their location – which gully they were in, behind which rock, in which crater where a tree's roots had been taken out by the winter gales. The boy did not move. There was a sharp whistle behind him. The older fighters thought of the boy as a talisman of good fortune, were loath to lose him, watched for him and cared for him. It might have been that the noise of gunfire obscured the shrill sound of the whistle, or it might have been that he cared not to hear the summons to fall back. He did not move. He did not know that a corporal of the mechanised infantry battalion had hunkered down in a ditch that carried rainwater off the road and had seen a point of fire, and a small head that peeped around a rock to search for targets. The whistle was louder, fiercer . . . A new magazine was slapped into the underbelly of the old rifle.

It was realised the child was a sure shot. That he detested the Soviet invaders who had taken his family to paradise, would kill at any opportunity, and dreamed of coming close to the wounded and the helpless and having the knife in his hand. He fired, and fired again, and did not hear the whistle, nor the bellow of anger, nor his name called. But might have heard, different to the close-combat thunder, a softer and more gentle sound, but did not yet recognise it as helicopter engines. Like that of a bee homing in on the heart of a flower, there to make the finest honey. The child was not aware of the approach of the gunships, always flown in a pair; not aware of rockets slung on pods and a gunner controlling a machine-gun and a four-barrelled Gatling type weapon: devastating fire-power. The child was caught up in the elation of combat; small hands gripped the rifle, and the stock rested against a small shoulder, and his eyes searched for a target. He stood.

He stood because he no longer had a target, and would not be denied one. The child did not see the corporal in the rainwater ditch, nor the RPG-7 launcher. The weapon carried an effective range of 300 metres, was expected to hit and kill at that distance, but the corporal lined up the sights on the small body of the child who was well inside that area of limitation.

A flash of light and a storm of dust and the projectile hurtled towards him. Too late to turn and duck away behind the shelter of the rock, too late to identify the engines of the hurrying helicopters, and no chance to respond to the calls of an older man.

Debris was hurled in every direction clear of the impact point. A piece of rock the size of a football – not that the child, before losing a leg or after, had ever kicked a football – speared away from the main body of the rock and careered into the child's stomach. He had no protection.

He was swept up. Still breathing, and with ferocious pain in his stomach but not crying out, and with a pallor settling on his cheeks, the child was taken as fast as sandalled feet could go over the rock and stone. The helicopters' engines came closer and the surviving troops put down a barrage of firing, but the tribesmen melted. He was carried to the next valley, and among the stones of the next river-bed, and up a track that only goats and the most sure-footed mule could have managed. His life had passed by the time they rested and no longer heard the sound of the helicopters.

It was done gently, but needed the strength of a grown man. The child's grip was broken, his fingers prised back, and the old rifle was taken from him. It was thought reasonable to assume he had been responsible for two more fatalities, and those notches were cut with a bayonet's point. A brief prayer was said and the body laid under a cairn of stones so that a wolf or a hyena or a fox would not be able to feast off the child, nor a vulture ravage the carcase. The rifle, with its much scarred stock was kept; the tribal group regarded it with pride, would hand it on.

A nondescript freighter ploughed through a gathering swell.

A detective chief inspector and a civilian analyst who was his bag carrier – both from the national Counter Terrorist Command – arrived in the tourist city of Avignon, checked into their hotel, did a reconnoitre walk of what was billed as the rendezvous point for Operation Rag and Bone, and looked for their target, spotted her, checked her clothing, went for lunch.

A major of the Marseille city police laboured over paperwork following an overnight killing, and eyed his mobile that rested on his desk and that rang frequently but not with a panic in the caller's voice.

A marksman from the GIPN spent the day in his apartment, alone because his wife was working, and he watched a succession of wildlife films and dreamed of being there, seeing those creatures of beauty and feral magnificence.

It was a good day, and the sun shone – and two old men lay on recliners with tweed rugs covering them and gazed out to sea, bathed in nostalgia.

New supplies arrived in the projects, including La Castellane, and one boy with a withered arm was, for a few hours, the centre of attention.

The car hammered the last kilometres on the A7 before the turn-off to Avignon.

He parked by the river.

Near dusk and, had it been the season, Andy Knight would not have had a prayer of getting into a car park. But the tourists would not be here for another two months, would start arriving for the Easter holiday. He saw the bridge that stretched out into the river, then seemed to have been snapped off. Everybody knew about the bridge at Avignon. He looked for her, and did not find her.

Somewhere close by would be the two people to whom he reported. He assumed they'd the sense to stay out of sight. There had been an awkward atmosphere last time they had spoken and he sensed their increasing stress that he was easing away from their control. He did not see them – nor did he see her.

The river was wide and high, and occasional tree trunks were washed down in the force of the flow. If she had acquired sufficient tradecraft then she also would be in a vantage-point and would be scanning the parking area, looking for a tail car, and they might have sent foot soldiers who had such skills and they'd be watching him, hawk-eyed. She would have trusted *him*, he thought, not those who directed her. He locked the car and strolled across damp grass towards the river. Behind him were the old city walls. He shivered; the wind came hard up the river and he was jostled by its strength. He thought it natural, after the long drive south from the service station, to stretch and touch his toes and arch his back and roll his neck. He no longer smoked: Phil had, and Norm, and a Marine far back and forgotten, almost . . . and he saw her.

There was an opening in the tower built into the wall across the road from him.

What came fast in his mind was that she was short of tradecraft. Should have spent longer studying him and the area, but she came towards the road, started to quicken, hardly looked for traffic, walked straight across. She looked bloody good. He was trained to see small things . . . she had been to a hairdresser, had her hair cut and it feathered out behind her. He pretended he had not seen her, looked away and saw a tree branch snag on a pillar in the truncated bridge, then work free. Her coat was open and he could see her blouse: scarlet and navy stripes bold for her, as if she was far from Savile Town. He turned back, faced her, feigned surprise. She did a hell of a smile, wide and open and trusting . . . was she acting? Was she just pleased, far from home – and marginally scared – to see him? His arms out, and hers. They locked, her tight against him, and hugged and held each other. And kissed . . . If she acted then she did well. And Andy Knight would not have said what he was going to do about the edict laid down to Level Ones by the commanders of SC&O10 about the development of relationships between officers and targets . . . It was a great kiss. Not a moment for an evaluation of rule books and manuals – might be later, not then.

Nothing to say, just held each other.

11

Andy sat opposite Zeinab.

What had happened in the night was raw, like a fretsaw had hit a sunk nail.

He maintained the minimum of eye contact and she had her head sunk low and stared down at the plate in front of her and ate a *croissant* untidily, let tiny flakes of pastry litter the tablecloth, and more caught on her lips. He had not slept well, had tossed in sleep and while pretending to, had manufactured a steady, soft snore. An apple did for him. Had not peeled it, or quartered it. Had chewed it down to the core, then left the last piece on his plate, and had drunk three cups of coffee. They had come down together from the first floor after he had knocked on her door. She'd opened it and he'd seen that her bag was already packed and zipped shut, and he had led the way down the stairs, had seemed easier than waiting for the elevator. He'd muttered something about whether she had slept well, and she had nodded: a lie. She would have slept as badly as he had. She wore the same blouse as the previous evening. Colourful, happy, supposedly expressing a mood that might not exist. He was neutrally dressed, nothing that stood out and made him instantly recognisable: dark jeans and a grey shirt. How he was trained to be: out of any limelight and not attracting attention.

They had come to the hotel, had checked in, and she had been handed two room keys, and she had looked at him, straight into his eyes, and there had been a boldness to her gaze. Andy had reckoned there would not have been a boy either in Savile Town or at the university who had seen those eyes, and the challenge in them. They had gone up the stairs and dumped their bags. The bed in her room was big enough for two, a tight fit, but he had eased away from her as she dropped her bag on the floor, and said something about the length of the drive, and a headache building, and had shrugged as if his control over tiredness and pain was not great. They had gone out of the hotel, a little place on a side-street off the Rue de la République, 55 euro a single room, or 65 euro for a double. He assumed the booking had been made before she had felt the isolation, and fear, of being far from home, alone, only a pretend boyfriend for company, and two singles would have seemed appropriate then . . . not now, why he had needed to pretend that he slept, affected a slight snore in a gentle rhythm, and had told lies about exhaustion and the ache behind his eyes and the need for a good rest after the drive.

Across the table, picking at a *croissant*, she looked confused, at a loss. Two other couples had come into the breakfast room. One pair spoke in accents of the south of England and the other ones, from the flags sewn on to their windcheater sleeves, came from New South Wales. Both wives would have thought the boy at the corner table looked decent enough, and both husbands would have run their eyes over her and thought her attractive: all four would have sensed the tension between them, and he was mostly looking at the cornice work on the ceiling edge and she was locked on her plate. They had exchanged a meaningless greeting, and something about the forecast being good for a dry day, and a bit of sunshine, and was it not a shame that the wind had a chill in it. Andy had made a smile of sorts, she had responded with a stare, the old one of the rabbit in the headlights, and neither had replied.

An evening meal in a bistro off the main street. He would damn near have killed for a beer but had declined: alcohol and work mixed a sour cocktail. The place was expensive but she had insisted on paying and she'd bought a half-bottle of wine for herself – like she was steeling her courage for later. They had eaten and he'd noted her growing impatience with the slow service, and they had walked back, collected the keys from the desk and gone up the stairs together. It was pretty much as laid down in the bible of SC&O10. He doubted he had made a good enough job of the tiredness from the drive and the headache racking his brain. Bald excuses given . . . she had turned on her heel on the landing, had had difficulty slotting her key in the lock, had finally managed and had – sharp temper – kicked open her door. It had slammed behind her. He had felt lousy, inadequate . . . had seen the anger flash in her eyes and had believed then that he had demeaned himself, sold her short, believed also that she was a picture of prettiness when fury blazed across her face.

He finished his juice, could not manage more coffee. She pushed away her plate, left the *croissant* unfinished, and scraped her chair back. He looked across at her, then reached out and let his fingers rest on her wrist. She stood. Andy watched.

Zeinab – no backward glance – strode out of the breakfast room, went into the lobby area. She had a small notebook in her hand, and was rummaging in a pocket for her mobile. She made a call. He could not hear what she said. Rang off, dialled another number, was briefer. Then came back and stood beside his chair. Her expression had changed, as if business had been done and matters settled. In a clear voice she told the English and the Australians that they would now be heading off to do the tourist bit, see that bridge that was short of a span, and the Papal Palace, and . . . she tapped his shoulder, flicked her head. Time for them to move . . . like a shower had passed, like the sun now shone . . . In the night he had heard her footsteps in the corridor, had reckoned she paused at his door, would have listened. He had done the snore, loud enough for her to hear. She might have been outside his room for half a minute, then she had retreated, and her door had clicked shut, and he stopped the snoring.

'You have a great day,' the English wife said.

They were in the lobby, and she paid the bill for their two rooms.

The Australian husband called after her, 'Have a brilliant time – don't do anything we geriatrics wouldn't do – or couldn't.'

Laughter played behind her. She might have blushed.

They went upstairs, each to their own room. The silky new nightdress was neatly folded on top of her clothes but she ferreted deep in the bag and pulled out the bulging money belt. Zeinab hooked open the waist of her jeans, lifted her blouse and fastened the strap around her waist. She heard the knock on the door, and it was pushed open. She pulled down her blouse, covered the belt, and zipped up her jeans. He carried his rucksack.

She looped her arms round his neck, straightened his head, made him look into her face, then kissed him . . . It had been so cold in the corridor in the night and she had shivered outside his door, only the nightdress covering her, and she had heard the noise from inside, the same as her father made when he slept in the room at home next to hers . . . They talked about it in the Hall of Residence. The girls on her landing gathered in huddles and part of the talk was whispered and part was covered with laughter, and they swapped stories of good times, funny times and horror times. All except her. She was on the periphery, had nothing to contribute. They exchanged detail on size, and how long it lasted, whether he knew what to do or had to be shown, and who put the condom on and who was prescribed the pill, and whether – afterwards – it felt good or was just a sweaty experience and not as satisfactory as a run round a few pavements. Zeinab did not know the answers, and did not join in . . . kissed him, was content that her phone calls were made, her belt in place, the bill paid. She felt him soften, tension dripping away from his muscles, and his eyes lost their stress.

She took his hand and they came down the stairs and his rucksack was hitched on his shoulder and he carried her bag, and the money belt was tight on her skin and cold. She led him towards the outside door and they passed the breakfast room.

The Australian wife called out, 'A really great day, that's what you need.'

The husband said, raucous in his own humour, 'That's the way, guys, best foot forward and no mischief.'

The sunlight caught her face, and she pushed some strands of loose hair back from her forehead. The first call had been good, and she had made her request and heard a little snigger in response, and the second call had been answered. The sunlight was powerful but the wind gusted down the side road and lifted spent, dried leaves against her body . . . Briefly, in the depths of the night, she had believed she had lost control – now had regained it. She held his hand. They walked along the street as the boutiques were opening, and shutters were noisily lifted. Either, or both, of those couples might have been in front of her in a shopping mall in Manchester's Arndale, or a mall anywhere, and she'd not have cared, would have dropped them, had taken back control. She gripped his hand and they went down the street, towards the Palace and the bridge.

What had happened in the night? Nothing had happened . . . It would happen, at the end of the day, tonight, it would happen then.

The freighter, with a schedule to keep, and poor stabilisers, ploughed into the swell, broke through the white crests of the waves, rocked and shook, and seemed at times to hit a wall of water, then staggered and pushed on. The wind that whipped the storm was the *mistral*, and it could rise in intensity to gale force. The captain, rarely off the bridge, was experienced in travelling the routes of the Mediterranean and understood the area south of the French coastline, taking in the islands of Corsica and Sardinia, and crossing as far south as the shores of Libya and Tunisia, some of the most treacherous on any of the world's oceans. The motion was merciless, and no crew member without a specific job was on deck. He talked constantly to the engineer of the need for speed, but also to safeguard the health of the elderly turbines. Radio silence was not broken. There was a connection he could make on the ship-to-shore system, but he was to be paid healthily for keeping to a timetable, and the promise was on the table of further runs and further increments in cash. The cargo that mattered, the one for which the *Margarethe* tossed in the storm, was small, wrapped in greaseproof and tougher protection, and in his cabin. The captain felt he was on trial. If his work prospered then bigger cargoes were promised, and money was talked of that would smooth and speed his progress to retirement . . . maybe a villa on the Italian coast north of Genoa . . . but the cargo had a deadline for delivery. The freighter pitched and sank and was tossed upwards. Away in a haze to the north was the indistinct line of the shore, but offering no shelter. It was a bad wind, the *mistral* had no lovers among the seamen working those waters . . . bad for him and his crew but worse, far worse, for those who'd meet the planned rendezvous at sea. In spite of conditions, the *Margarethe* made good time.

'Are they going to be able to do it?' Crab asked.

'Why not? It's what I pay them for,' Tooth answered.

The wind's pitch had freshened. Even with rugs and thick coats, the force of it was too severe for them to lie out on the recliners kept on the patio. The sea view, impeccable, was diminished behind the plate glass windows. They drank coffee . . . Crab had no sea legs, distrusted the water, might have admitted to having a greater fear of an ocean's depths, in bad weather, than anything else that had confronted him. A pot, with a geranium in it, was caught by a gust and flipped on its side, then careered over the width of the patio. What they could make out of the sea's surface, through the glass that was encrusted with the sand brought across from Africa by the *mistral*, was a mess of white caps. They talked nostalgia, what they were best at. Since neither could verify the stories of the other, it was possible that the anecdotes were either true or a fantastic fiction of fake news. Unimportant, they were old friends, and amused each other.

'We did this job, centre of Manchester, the smart end of the city, cracked a jewellers, and we'd lifted a souped-up BMW saloon for the getaway. Trouble was, coming out with balaclavas still on and carrying pickaxe handles, and all the loot, an off-duty cop was passing – got a description of our wheels. We were tuned into the radio. Nothing followed us, we were clear . . . What happened? Believe it. The retired Head of Finance, pillar of the city bosses, the council, had the same model, same colour. He picked up half a dozen cop cars. Was rammed off the road, and when they'd finished apologising we were long gone . . . Trust me, one of the better ones.'

'My favourite, here in Marseille, when the Ministry targeted me – personally named me in briefings – the premier smack importer of the city. A team was formed to investigate me, a conviction demanded by Paris. In that team, I promise you, each officer was on my payroll. Each one, eight of them. I was then the Sun King of the third *arrondissement*. All of them now live in good properties by the Botanical Gardens and an easy walk to the Prado beaches. It was a comfortable time.'

They competed.

'Not, of course, what it used to be.'

'Used to be respect.'

'We were decent people.'

'My word was my bond.'

'No honesty among the young today.'

'And the way they wave these AKs around, like it's just a toy.'

'We had the best days, Tooth.'

'Lucky to have lived when we did, Crab.'

And another pot was cracked, and Crab told the story about his hacker boys getting through the cyber defences of the city's main supermarket chain, and lodging an order for boxes of food for free delivery, no charge, to a food-bank warehouse. Kept it up for two weeks and then signed off with sincere thanks from 'Robin Hood, Sherwood Mansions, Near Nottingham' . . . It had been eight years ago but he still told it and Tooth would never let him know he had heard it before, word for word, like a fucking gramophone record with a scratch.

Tooth said that he had the best relations with the cops than any of the big men that had gone before him in the city. Their wives knew him and would near curtsey if there were a party and he was introduced, and their teenage kids greeted him with averted eyes, no lip, called him 'Sir', and bankers queued to manage his investments, and the presents that were courier-delivered at Christmas filled a spare bedroom.

'Great days.'

'The best, we were privileged.'

'And you know what I am thankful for, Tooth?'

'What's that, Crab?'

'That I'm not on that fucking water tonight.'

'Like I said, they get paid. They don't like it, then they should have stayed pimping.'

Karym watched his brother go.

Astride the Ducati Monster, the wind making river trails in his hair, Hamid powered away, rode out of the project, swerved between the big rocks across the entrance to La Castellane.

He thought his elder brother gripped by a foul, sullen mood. He did not know the reason, knew only that Hamid was at work on behalf of the old man – clapped out, past it, from yesterday – who had once been called Tooth: now, likely, had none. Too old, fucked up, teeth rotten or fallen out. He did not know why his brother danced to a tune called by this man who should years before have gone to the knacker's yard.

Himself, Karym felt good – better than good. Hard to remember when he had last experienced that degree of elation.

The Ducati was gone. He had been told where he should be the next day, at what hour. That seemed secondary. His brother had snapped the instructions at him, his mouth quivering and his lips narrowed, and his fists on the bike handles had trembled, and the wind had ripped at his leather coat: cost him close to a thousand euros, but his brother still refused to pay for better transport for Karym, nothing as good as the Piaggio MP3 Yourban . . . The cause of his excitement? It was a declaration of war. War was about firearms. Rifles would be issued.

It had been the most intense sensation in his short life, Karym had claimed to his brother. The moment that the kid beside him, holding the weapon at his throat, had been taken down by the marksman. Blood on him, and the kid's piss, and perhaps some brain tissue. An incredible shot, might only have had a quarter of the head to aim at. The shot of a genius – Samson. They said Samson was a killer, an executioner in history . . . a brilliant marksman and he would have liked more than anything, to meet the man, be face to face with him. Not to thank him, but to admire him . . . and it had been the start of the war that would now follow. War was important.

War brought shape and purpose to life in the housing blocks. The kids would be armed, would go to a state of alert . . . For himself there was the prospect that Hamid would give him a Kalashnikov, one for him to have, hold, look after, one for him to *own* . . . Karym had in his room on that high floor of the building he shared with his sister, every book available in the French language on the history and working of the Kalashnikov. He could recite the dates of manufacture for each phase of the weapon's development. He knew which of the liberation movements had been sold the AK – the Klash, the Chopper. He could explain how the version sold to the People's Army of North Vietnam had proved superior to the rifles of the American marines: knew it all. War would be his best chance, for all that his arm was withered, of handling one, having it under his bed and with a magazine loaded, and with the sites set down at the extremity for Battle Sight Zero, close range. Might . . . His brother ignored him if he talked of the AK. His sister would switch on the TV, turn the sound to its loudest, if he spoke of it. None of the kids who existed off Hamid's cash cared about the theory, the culture, of the most amazing weapon ever built. He had no one with whom to share his enthusiasm.

But that was detail. More important was war. He presumed it, war, fascinating and unpredictable, brilliant. He walked across the project towards the van that came each midday to La Castellane and cooked burgers . . . What he should do, Hamid's instruction, and the hour for it, confused him, and where he should be afterwards. But he had not argued, queried – might have been kicked if he had.

Andy led, followed the Avignon tourist signs.

Held her hand and thought her more relaxed than he'd have expected. He could not say how she had lifted the stress off her shoulders. She talked, he listened. It would be a first time . . . Andy had not been with any of the women on the animal rights group, nor with the girls who hung around on the edge of the cannabis courier gang. Two or three times, on the pavement, pedestrians had come either side of them, and they'd been pushed together, and their bodies had touched. They went down to the river, where the coaches ejected their passengers, saw the bridge, then climbed steep steps in a tower, and she'd laughed at the thought of her needing help, but it was windy at the top, and she had a sheen of sweat on her forehead.

'You good?'

'Fine – very good.'

'You deserved the break.'

'Did I, how did I?'

'Getting your essay done, didn't you say you had . . .?'

She flustered. 'I did . . .'

'Go well?'

'Went good, a decent mark, and . . .'

He knew she lied. But then if her mind was on couriering Kalashnikovs, imagining them blasting in a concert arena or at a bus station, then an essay on whatever turgid aspect of her study discipline a lecturer had chosen was unlikely to be top of the heap. But a lie was a lie, and she'd looked away quickly.

And she wondered . . .

. . . wondered about his future.

Should not have done. Not her concern. Just a lorry driver. Pliable and easy to manipulate. Devoted and simple, and without intelligence – and a possibility that he could provide what she might most want.

Her security concerned her. She did not intend to die, not as her cousins had met death, on a battlefield. Had no intention of being locked inside an airless prison cell while her life moved from youth and on towards a middle-aged barren void. There was one girl on the corridor of the Hall of Residence who had a picture in her room of a cottage with white-washed walls and a vista beyond of the sea and of mountains. Zeinab knew little of the sea, could not swim, had only ever walked on a beach with Andy – had never climbed a mountain anywhere, had only recently walked with him on the moor between Leeds and Manchester. The place was remote, reached by a stone track that had grass growing thick in its centre, and the clouds low on the skyline. The girl was an independent school product, dripped private means and would leave university with her loan repaid. Zeinab had been returning a cup of milk loaned her the previous weekend. 'You didn't have to,' she'd been told. She'd stared at the picture: there had been an offhand remark about going there for a couple of weeks in the summer, 'pretty boring, nothing happens, and it rains most of the time'. A place such as that would be a bolt-hole. She wondered if he would come there. Probably she'd only have to tweak his emotions . . . did not know how they would live, feed themselves, have the cash to survive, but they would be hidden . . . after tonight, he would do as she wanted, was sure of it. She had no interest in the history of a bridge left for hundreds of years without being repaired, little more for an abandoned palace – but could imagine the cottage by the seashore, and a log fire, and them together on a rug. She imagined that she might involve herself in an armed struggle just *once* – once only – then retreat to safety. Hidden in remoteness with the lorry driver to protect her, and lead a new life and be far from the hunting pack. Possible? Perhaps, perhaps not . . . not possible for the boys from Savile Town who had gone away to war and were buried in the sand, what was left of their bodies. Not worth thinking of . . . whether she could break away at a time and place of her own choosing, or could not.

Wondered whether he would make that his future: the cottage, the fire burning, the refuge, could not answer. Held tight to his hand.

'Don't quote me . . . they make rather a pleasing couple.'

'You reckon he nobbed her last night?'

Gough did his pained face. Little shocked him, but they had between them a regular act that she would ramp up her language and he would play the offended individual. Almost music hall, something of a variety show that they played out. His expression seemed to say that her tongue gave him personal pain . . . They had done it themselves the previous night. Him 'nobbing' his assistant, though Pegs had done most of the work, what she'd called the 'heavy lifting'. Then sharing a quiet cigarette, and hanging their heads out of the window. Then a few hours of solid sleep. They had woken, refreshed, were showered and breakfasted, were outside the hotel in the street off the Rue de la République in time to see the couple emerge.

'That is disgusting, quite vulgar.'

'Just asking – remember what you said about him, not that long back?'

Their man, the Undercover, had a rucksack slung on a shoulder and carried her bag. She had a hand tucked in the crook of his arm, like they were an item. They had walked to a car park and the rucksack and the bag had gone into the boot of an old VW saloon. She had given him a kiss on the cheek, and had swung her hips and they had set off at a brisk march . . . They would have seemed the stereotypical couple – far from home and crossing a racial divide – and finding each other and exploring a relationship, and she had manufactured a guise of cheerfulness and he seemed smitten . . . They were in the Rocher des Doms gardens. Had circled a spouting ornamental fountain and walked paths bordered by shrubbery. They filtered between a party of schoolchildren and their minders, and a bus load of Chinese tourists, and nothing showed of the truths guiding them: she was testing the security of a potential arms importation route – and he was an agent of the Crown and committed to blocking her ambition, and now they held hands and were young and looked like lovers.

Gough grimaced. 'Never enjoy being quoted back.'

'I'll remind you . . . put your tin helmet back on because it will hurt. Quote, "He's gone native", end quote. I suggested he needed a "good kicking", but you waffled, Gough, did not stand up to him.'

'Did not have a great many options as I remember.'

'Once his hand is in her knickers, then you've lost him.'

'Quite disgusting and not worthy of you, Pegs.'

'You reckon, Gough, he's going to get her in the shrubs, do it there? Horny enough for *al fresco*? I'd say that he's moving offline, and I'd say she's wanting it bad. You were squeamish on reading a riot to him . . . That's where we are. Like it or not, it's where.'

The couple had moved on and were now at a railing, looking down through bare trees, watching the river far below, swollen with winter rain, and the wind sang in the branches. The main flow of the river was at the end of the broken historic bridge. How it had been broken, why it had not been fixed in many centuries, might have confused Gough had he permitted that irrelevance room to breathe. He and Pegs stood back from them. He – their man – continued to hold her hand and she laughed, and he used his free hand to tap decisively at his backside. Gough understood. Their man's palm was across the back pocket of his jeans, and the gesture was clear enough. Pegs, too, had caught it, the signal . . . First bloody indication they had been given that he expected them to be traipsing after him, having him under 'eyeball', and he had not phoned them in the night.

'We drill it into them, not that most of them are listening, but we are bloody emphatic: it is poor tradecraft to shag female targets. The way to erode objectivity . . . Of course he'll shag her. Just hope they both enjoy it.'

'I know what they're told.'

'They are not friends, they are targets.'

'I merely said that they make a pleasing couple. I don't need a damn lecture.'

'Pleasing?'

'It's what I said.'

'They would, wouldn't they? I mean, they come out of the same locker.'

'Meaning – meaning what?'

'So much in common. Made for each other. If it were a dating agency then it would be a brilliant match. In their veins, compatibility . . . it's so obvious, Gough, it's biting your bum. They both lie to survive, both carry a knapsack of deceit. Both trust nobody, both hide themselves away, and are friendless and incapable of affection, trust, to anyone outside their own security bubble. I echo you, "a pleasing couple", and so they bloody should be, but sorry for the speech. You all right? Look a touch peaky.'

Gough bridled. He felt the stress. Neither he nor Pegs was trained up to the standards required for full surveillance tasking. Didn't have to do it, and there were sufficient specialists from Five or the Counter-Terrorist Command to do the usual play-acting – changing clothes, riding fast motorcycles, wandering around with a water board gilet on, just standing in a street and looking around and having a dog lead hanging in the fist. Not their job. A disaster if they showed out and the girl saw them, identified them as a threat. They hung back . . . Then the couple swung. Quick movement, as if she had seen enough of a bridge, useless for hundreds of years, and she gave her boy's hand a sharp tug. They moved quickly and there was nowhere for Gough and Pegs to go, no hole to crawl into. In front of them was a rubbish bin. In Andy Knight's hand was a slip of paper. No eye contact from him, but the girl saw them, allowed a short smile to cross her face. Yes, they made a 'pleasing couple'. And what did he and Pegs look like . . .? Not worth considering. They passed by the rubbish bin. The pieces of paper fluttered from his hand, then was dropped. Pegs talked, would have the first word and the last, quietly in Gough's ear.

'Then you have to line up the consequences . . . if he didn't shag her last night then he will when they get into bed this evening. She'll get a rough ride and enjoy it. Worth a punt down at the bookies' shop, Gough . . . All right, all right, what could you have done? Not much. Could hardly kick him off the agenda.'

Neither Gough nor Pegs responded to the girl's smile. Their man did not look at them. Gough waited until they had passed, then put his hand deep into the bin, felt the paper, clamped on it, brought it up and into the light. The wind caught it, snatched it and it was carried up the path. She went after it, stamped on it, gave it back to him. Her glance described him as a burden to her, then she laughed. He read it: *Do not know where we stay in Marseille this evening. Do not know her schedule. Will make contact when possible*. He told her. She snorted. His was a lifetime of work handling agents, assets, men and women who worked on the perimeter of safety, most often beyond the Golden Hour in which it was hoped rescue or help would reach them if they were corralled in danger. He thought such a man, at the end of his tether, straining it taut, would easily have the impulse to jack it in – if he were not humoured. There was no other game in town. Gough could have bullied. He had seen the girl and noticed the language of their bodies: young peoples', and he was old, tired, and his confidence in ultimate victory was dented, badly.

'Not possible – a pleasing couple, what I said. I've more faith in him than . . . Ever answered, Pegs, the question? What we ask of them, is that too much?'

'Pretty puerile. They do a job, they're volunteers, get well paid, can fiddle their expenses. No need to bleed for them . . . It's bloody closed.'

What was 'bloody closed? The cathedral was closed for lunch. And the café was closed. And the Papal Palace had been abandoned six and a half centuries before – decamped back to Rome and Vatican City – and entry to it was eleven euro each . . . forget it. How would it end? The weapon would be carried home in a VW Polo, would be doctored during the ferry crossing, bugged. It would travel uninterrupted through Customs, then tailed in a huge surveillance operation. It would be delivered to the individuals in this sprouting conspiracy who mattered . . . the guns would go in, armed police, and the network would be for the cage. Arrest warrants in Yorkshire, and later a trial, and the Undercover behind a screen for his evidence. A triumphant drink after sentences were handed down, but unlikely that the star man would show. They rarely appeared for the post-game binge, were never seen again. That was how it would be if he could hold tight to his man . . . could no longer see him. Could no longer get an 'eyeball' on a boy and a girl who walked hand in hand. He lit a cigarette, gasped on it.

Pegs said, 'Sod it, let's go and find some lunch.'

Gough said, 'The Kalashnikov, it's a symbol of their power. They will walk tall if they have weapons with that hitting power.

We are groping in the dark. It's why it's important, on a whole new and lofty level. It matters.'

February 2008

She was widowed. She wore black and a veil covered most of her face, but her eyes were visible: like those of a she-cat caught against a vertical cliff, towering up and over her as predators closed in. They blazed defiance. Her hands were uncovered; one held the emptied magazine of her AK assault rifle, and the other rummaged in the drape of her clothing for the opening that would allow her to reach the two loaded magazines held in webbing against her body. She could not defend herself, could only rely on her eyes to spit anger at the advancing enemy.

At that altitude in the mountains west of Jalalabad, the rain-bearing clouds were low over the crags and valleys and it was an optimum time for that small force of *mujahideen* to confront the patrol of a section of American troops – Marines. Excellent weather conditions, the rain was heavy and on the verge of drifting to sleet, and in the night it would fall as snow. The widow was not tactically trained, had never attended a course run by military instructors, but she had been a member of that tribal group since her father and brother had been killed soon after the Americans had arrived, almost seven years before. A weapon had been given to her. It had belonged to a cousin, also killed, and she had held it – battered, scraped with two rows of notches cut on the wood of the stock, somehow almost invisible – at her wedding in the mountains, aged seventeen, to the son of their leader and principal tactician. She had been with him, when the American helicopters had come around a curve in a valley, the wind blowing away the sound of their engines, the surprise total, and an Apache had strafed the group. She had fired at the beast, hovering, almost contemptuously, long enough to exhaust the magazine and doubted she had achieved even one strike against its armour plate, and when it had gone, banking away, she had realised her husband was dead. Peaceful in death, his face calm, but his stomach and chest had taken machine-gun rounds. They had not taken precautions against pregnancy, but no child had been born: now no one else looked for her hand in the group. She was a fighter and lived with them, ate with them, was the same as each of them except that, when darkness came, she would move a little away from the men, wrap herself in her blanket, and sleep alone and isolated until the morning. And that day, excellent weather for the ambush because the cloud was low enough on the rock-face to prevent the helicopters from flying, the Marines would not have the protection from above on which they seemed, to her, so dependent. At the moment the first shots were fired, and some Americans already down, and the fierce, anguished shouts of those unhurt or only lightly wounded bouncing from the granite walls, they had scattered.

The widow had believed, as the rain whipped into her face and her veil hung sodden across her mouth, that she had identified a particular rock, 25 or 30 metres from her, behind which an enemy had taken refuge. She had blasted an entire magazine at one side of the rock to shift him, then had reloaded with the second magazine already taped to the first, and had fired another thirty shots, but as the weapon clicked feebly, telling her the ammunition was finished, magazine empty, she had realised she had lost him. She was attempting to reload. Perhaps with more instruction she would have been more cautious in how much she had fired with the selector on automatic. She did not know where he was, and it was difficult to get her hand under the fold of the material enveloping her because it hung heavy from the soaking by the rain.

He faced her. He was enormous, wearing a backpack that broadened his shoulders, a helmet that made his head grotesque, kit hanging from a belt at his waist, and more in the pockets of the jacket he wore over his tunic, had a rifle raised, held at his shoulder. His face was black, his cheeks the colour of burned wood from the cooking fires they lit, and a smile played at his mouth and his gums were pink and his teeth brilliantly white, and he almost laughed. Almost laughed and with good cause. He had come from between a cleft of lichen-covered rocks, and when she had been blasting the granite wall he had been behind a stubby thorn tree, hidden by its trunk. Shooting continued below her, above her, and to her right, and she could hear the cries of her own people and the guttural shouts of the Americans. She could not turn and run because the rock behind her was too steep and wet, and the soles or her sandals would not get traction nor her fingers a grip. She could not charge him. She could not hurl the useless Kalashnikov at him and hope at that distance to disable him . . . She spoke her husband's name. Said it quietly, just a murmur, and the wind broke the words that were her husband's name, and then the endearments, almost a prayer . . . She did not know if the black-skinned American would try to capture her – rape her, torture her, shut her in a cage as an exhibit of interest – or would savour a moment of amusement and then shoot her. She went on with the task, seeming impossible, of freeing a filled magazine from the pouch close to her stomach, where his rifle seemed aimed.

She had a clear view of the finger that was inside the trigger guard. Saw it tighten . . . it seemed, peculiarly, as if it would demean the memory of her dead husband if she wriggled and attempted to avoid what was an inevitability. She hoped he saw, through the slit of her veil, wet enough to cling to her cheeks, the hatred she felt for him, and it seemed in his own eyes, down the sight of the rifle, that he had good entertainment from corralling this woman – as if she were a goat about to be herded into a small thorn-fenced compound. The finger squeezed, the grip tightened, and the fun fled and the teeth disappeared and she saw his lips tighten. She had her own magazine free in her hand and snaked it towards the underside of the weapon, what she had been given and what had once been the prized possession of her cousin.

Against the patter of the rain and the wind's murmur, she heard the metal sounds of the jam. They laughed about it around the fire in the evenings, when they ate and before they prayed for the last time, and she was the only woman amongst them, and was watched and was approved of, and older men told stories of the weakness of American equipment. . . . One old fighter had said, chuckling and croaking on the humour of it, that a child could fix a mis-fire on an AK-47, but that an American needed a college eduction to be able to clear out a jammed cartridge in a rifle used by the Marines – and the same story in every war they had launched: Vietnam, Iraq, and now the quagmire among the rocks that was her home country. Big eyes, once laughing, stared at her, and the fingers had left the trigger guard and now tried to eject the bullet, and his expression changed and reflected fear . . . for good reason. She had the magazine lodged in its place. She had slight arms, little flesh on them, but they harboured enough muscle for her to arm the weapon easily. He would have heard the scrape call of metal on metal as the Kalashnikov was again made lethal. He might have thought of home, and of children, of any place far away, and her own finger was on her own trigger. Her sights were set at what they called, those who had taught her to shoot effectively and to handle the weapon, Battle Sight Zero. He would be another scraped gouge on the old wood of the stock, almost ready for the beginning of a third row.

The widow took her time, savoured it, would not have hurried – should have, should have been long gone, the moment the Marine had displayed the jam to her. Should have, but had not. The grenade bounced close to her like a small toy. She was too involved in the process of killing him to have registered its significance. The hatred ruled her.

She fired. He was attempting to squirm away and duck his big body – what she had refused to do, maintaining her dignity – and she fired, and his movements were insufficient to save him. The weapon kicked hard and she needed all her strength to hold it, keep the aim on the dropping body and she barely heard the shout of her commander, and did not register that the grenade had come to rest five metres from her feet.

It detonated. The Marines pulled back. A sergeant had thrown his last grenade towards her before scampering down the slope. She was felled. The Marines picked up the man she had killed. One kicked hard at her body, wasted effort because she was gone.

She would have no grave beside her husband's; her body would be flimsily protected by a cairn of stones. Her weapon would be carried away, but not her. Her weapon had value.

* * *

He sat on his settee and watched a television documentary.

The marksman from the *Groupe d'Intervention Police Nationale* held a mug of coffee and his hand did not shake, showed no signs of tremor. A pile of newspapers was spread on the cushions beside him. He accepted the name given him. To them he was Samson, to himself he was Samson. It was an amusing name, not one shared with his wife though the chances were she would have heard it uttered in the gossip corridors of Headquarters. The name was best known in the projects on the north side of Marseille, where the north African immigrants were housed. In the tower blocks, the women would lean from windows or step out on to the narrow balconies and would watch for him. He did not know how the name had slipped outside the GIPN 'immediate ready' room where they lounged on hard chairs, played cards, drank coffee, shared rumours. The precision of his head shot in the street's darkness would have enhanced an already formidable reputation.

His wife would have known that he had killed again, but he had not spoken of it to her. She would have known from the talk the next morning among colleagues working out of *L'Évêché*. Unlikely that his daughter would have known anything, an accountancy student in Lyon. Probably, if the Major had thought it necessary, a police psychologist could have been allocated to him. The matter had not been broached. No signs of 'combat stress' were apparent: PTSD symptoms were absent. He did not revel in what he had done, ending that young life with a shot of superb expertise, difficult light, the target's head moving every few seconds, the tension building as the target's behaviour grew increasingly erratic. Took no pleasure from it, and would certainly not have boasted of the challenge he had confronted. Nor did he show any sign of regret that the kid was dead, that a family was pitched into mourning. Showed nothing . . . might have filled in another duty roster with a session directing traffic at the junction where La Canobière ran into the Place du Géneral de Gaulle, short of the *vieux port*. In a commercial break in the documentary he had raided the fridge, been grateful his wife had restocked a box with the pastries he enjoyed. The TV programme told the story of a cheetah family from the Tanzanian reserve of Serengeti, the mother's efforts to protect her cubs from predators, and later would cover the break-up of the family as the cubs achieved maturity, had to fend for themselves. Beautifully filmed, stunning vistas.

He was not indifferent to the killing, but was untroubled . . . he had other wildlife films stacked up in the memory of his TV, tigers from central India, jaguars living in the Pantanal of Brazil, bears from beyond the Canadian segment of the Arctic Circle . . . Nor was he much concerned with the boy whose life he had, perhaps, saved. All he remembered of him was that his arm was withered and almost useless, that he had not fainted in the moment after the single shot was fired, that he had wriggled clear of the corpse had righted his cheap old scooter, that he had fled the scene. Had done that with determination and skill, given the weakness of his arm. It would have involved money, involved the conflict zone of rival gangs . . . not his concern. He doubted he would see the boy again.

In an earlier commercial break – tedious adverts for competing banks, cheap furniture, holidays in the sun – he had checked the papers. Always, of course, he wore a balaclava, had done so once the name, Samson's, was attached to him, was abroad in the projects, since the name had given him almost celebrity status. In *La Provence* one picture showed a grainy image of a man walking discreetly between the shadowed doorways of the street, with a rifle against his leg, and the sniper sight clearly visible, but the balaclava hid the face and there was no mention of his name.

He was a figure of mystery, of contradictions, hoped to remain so. He had enjoyed the film about the cheetahs. Now he would go to the café on Rue Charras, rout out his friends, go to play *boule* with them, the secondary pleasure on any free day, except that it would be cold – even in the sunshine – because of the force of the wind. He was relaxed, comfortable. A body in the morgue did not trouble him, and his reputation as an executioner would have brought a shrug to his shoulders, a grimace to his face. It was his job, to shoot at a man if it were necessary, to kill him, do what was asked of him – stay distant, uninvolved.

They sat in the car. Belts were fastened. Andy said how long it would take to drive into central Marseille. The engine turned over.

Seeming casual, he put the question. 'What sort of business is it, for you – there? What you have to do.'

He was deflected. 'Just some family business. You wouldn't be interested. Boring business.'

He drove out of the car park and together they started to scan road signs for the A7 route. They had enjoyed lunch, done window shopping, ate an ice-cream. He didn't follow up the question. The reason for his insertion, gathering clandestine information, was around an hour and a quarter away, and the city he drove towards had a reputation, deserved, for ruthless brutality. He found music on the car's radio, thought it might drown out the thought of fear.

12

Andy drove, Zeinab dozed.

He went steadily, allowed the local drivers – cars and vans and lorries – to power past him. Her head was on his shoulder.

Because her breathing was calm, and her hand was loose on his thigh, he allowed himself a puckered frown. He accepted it, that the problem eating at him was a career breaker. He could imagine, easily, how it would have been for her during the long night hours.

He headed towards the source of the problem, and before her eyes had closed and her breathing slowed, and her fingers had found his upper leg, he had played the part of the friend from home who was infatuated, obsessed, the ready-made chauffeur who asked only vague questions. He thought her too ill-informed on life outside Savile Town to bother to question whether a guy was that simple, that easy to befriend . . . She would have undressed, put on whatever nightclothes she had packed, had waited in her adjoining room for his light knock on her door. She would have imagined that she could open the door, look at him with a fraud's shock, hesitate, let him enter, let him lay his fingers on her arms, then loop them behind her, then kiss her, then move her back towards the bed, then . . . and she had waited. She had come to his door. She had stopped outside it, would have steeled herself and might even have raised her hand, and been about to knock. She would have heard his bogus snoring, volume lifted, would have listened, turned away. He had told her in the evening and across the bistro table how tired he was after the drive south. Once she had cried out as if a nightmare, had slotted into her sleep. Just the once. The problem would not disappear, he would not ignore it.

They had spent the half-way point in the journey in a camp-site, buying coffee and then walking over fields, using a farmer's track. He had held her hand, comfortable and not passionate, and assumed that an equivalent exhaustion plea, as done the previous night would be barged aside. The light had been starting to dip. Cattle grazed on what grass they would find, and the wind whipped them and tugged at her coat and her hair. The track they'd walked had been scoured clear of puddles. Song birds were pitched in the air then blown towards the olive groves beside the cattle pastures. It was beautiful country, small farmhouses, cottages for workers, clumps of poplar trees without foliage and bent sharply, and a few clouds scurrying overhead. He had noticed, could not have helped it, the way that the wind plastered her clothes on the contours of her body. It was a growing problem that infected his mind.

He saw elegant cranes, swooping gulls, and swans that cowered in the shelter of the river-banks, and a solitary heron that patiently fished, and when they had walked their shadows had merged. The scale of the problem ran riot in his mind, and he could not exclude it, and he did not know what the answer would be . . . With the wind buffeting her, Andy Knight – his identity for that day, that week, and for all of the months of the last year – thought she looked brilliant: which was the problem. They left the camp-site.

Marseille loomed below them. When they were within sight of the sea's churning waves, he eased her hand off his leg, gripped the wheel with his right hand and touched her chin, lifted it, and saw the way that her head jerked up. He recognised the stresses burdening her. Like a frightened cat, stiffening, arching her back, wide-eyed and alert, then seeing where she was, and with whom. Below them, away to the south, was the grey concrete ribbon of the airport runway and a passenger jet was on its final descent. He played innocent, gave no sign of recognising the conspiracy. Smiled at her, warm, and the traffic sped past them.

'Glad you did not take a plane, quicker but less fun.'

She stumbled with the start of her reply. 'Yes . . . well . . . yes – always more interesting, don't you think, seeing, absorbing new horizons? Yes, glad.'

The road took them down a long, fast, winding hill. He saw white clusters of tower blocks, built like fortresses to repel strangers. Far in the distance and hazed in the dropping light of the early evening was a massive cathedral with a steep spire. He had never been a tourist, had no interest in it. Sightseeing would have been a dreary waste of his time, and he concentrated on steering a safe line on the road, and of maintaining his cover. The easiest way to screw up, the instructors said, was to relax, to be loose-tongued, to forget the disciplines. She told him they should head for the centre of Marseille, and was plotting a route on her phone screen. He was just a friend, nothing more and nothing less . . . they were near to the sea and the docks, and the night was closing on them – which was the heart of the problem.

Karym sat in the growing darkness and pondered.

What he should have asked of his brother, how his brother might have answered him.

He nibbled on *pitta* bread. No filling inside it. If he had gone back to the apartment, where his sister would be after a day in the shopping mall, there would have been salad in the fridge, but he could not be bothered to walk that far – not just for tomato and cheese and cucumber. He felt good now as the light fell. A girl had come up to him, had settled beside him on the rock that blocked entry to La Castellane, and had brought him the piece of bread. Normally, that girl would not have spoken to him because he had a damaged arm, had no friends, had a brother who dangled him but gave him only crumbs from the table . . . Now he had the status of a minor celebrity after his experience when rivals attacked, most especially because he had saved his brother's cash.

Question. 'What does a big man, a man with reputation, want with you?'

Answer. 'Mind your fucking cheeky tongue.'

'Everyone knows his name . . . In the city no one knows your name. Why do you have to run to him, like a lapdog?'

'You talk too much, you do not know when silence is better.'

A girl had brought Karym a piece of *pitta* bread, would have straddled him willingly now, but not have known how to talk about an AK-47. The wind blew embers off the cigarettes of those around him on the perimeter of the La Castellane project. He sat and ate, then noted that two kids edged close to him, and that the Algerian boy pushed the Tunisian forward, but both were reluctant to come closer. Karym would have liked to possess a deeper voice, would have enjoyed being able to command. He watched them. They seemed eager to speak, but also frightened of him. He finished the *pitta* bread that the girl had given him . . . nobody, ever before, had been nervous of him: nervous of his brother, not of Karym.

'Yes?'

'Did you know . . . ?'

'Know what?'

'. . . who saved you. Who, do you know?'

'How would I?'

'At the place, my cousin was there. He saw that . . .'

Karym interrupted the Tunisian boy. 'Saw what?'

'His cousin saw, saw who fired,' from the Algerian boy.

'A cop fired, just a cop.'

'Which cop, what cop, do you know?'

And he was bored, and he saw the start of chuckles lighting their faces. 'I don't know, I don't care, I don't . . .'

Both spoke together. 'You *should* care, should know which cop you owe your life . . . it was the cop they call Samson . . . the marksman, the executioner, that cop . . . you owe your life, Karym, to Samson . . . what will you do, go to L'Évêché, ask for Samson? Take some flowers for him? Invite him to come and take lunch in La Castellane? Be his friend . . . ? You live because of the cop, Samson.'

The chuckles had become giggles, then their laughter shrilled at him. They ran. He seemed to feel his knees weaken. He stayed sitting, if he had tried to walk away from his perch he was not sure that his legs would support him. He remembered, hot on his skin, the blood of his attacker, and the weight of him when he had kicked the scooter off, had pushed away the body, lifeless from one shot. He had heard that Samson, the killer, had been inside the project a few days before, when his brother had made the barbecue, and had used the big sight on the top of his rifle barrel to scan darkened windows and the rooftops of the blocks, all the time looking for a target; trapped in his nostrils behind the balaclava would have been the sweet and sickly stench given off by the burned body and the gutted car. He spoke to himself, softly, not for anyone else to hear, whispered the words.

'Thank you, thank you, *m'sieur*. I am grateful. Always will be grateful. You are my friend.'

And meant it, a true friend. He would like to talk with the cop, Samson, and show off his knowledge of the Kalashnikov, and . . . He buried the thought. A friend of a cop? Not possible. The wind was sharper, and the overhead cables were braced against it, and sang like a wounded creature. He felt isolated and no longer revelled in his new attention, and wished his brother were there with him.

Hamid shivered, took a step forward, then hesitated.

The voice rasped behind him. 'You queasy, young man? You scared?'

And he would not have dared show his fear – but could not take the second step.

Deep in a narrow inlet that ran between steep and pitch-black cliffs was a tiny village comprising a few holiday homes, and some traditional fishermen's bungalows. It was reached by a rough track that, over centuries, had been gouged out of the cliffs. Four-wheel drive and a steady nerve were needed to reach the hamlet. He had gone down with increasing reluctance, on the Ducati motorcycle. The area of coastline was called Les Calanques. It was most often visited by boat, in high summer, and tourists were ferried under the cliffs and through the islands. It was now the depth of the Marseille winter, and tourists rash enough to contemplate a boat sightseeing tour would have arrived in the *vieux port* in Marseille and found notices on the quayside telling them 'Cancellation, due to bad weather conditions'. He could not delay long in case his fear shouted to the men snuggled clear of the wind in the back of the vehicle. In front of him, as he stood on a rocking pontoon, one confident stride away, was a fishing boat. The boat was the size used by locals who went out with the long lines and brought in lobsters, crabs, and monkfish – the great prize and paid the best rate. It had an open deck behind a wheelhouse. The vehicle's headlights showed a paint-scraped hull. Two men were aboard.

The older one and probably his teenage son, worked at ropes and at pouring fuel into the engine, and they wore boots that gave them a good grip on the wooden deck. They seemed oblivious to the pitch of the boat. Hamid stood on the floating pier leading to the boat. He struggled to stay upright, had twice groped for an imaginary handrail, and each time he had been close to toppling . . . and this was in the shelter of the headlands to his left and his right.

But Hamid had been recruited because he had a reputation for achieving results. A man of power and influence had pursued him. The possibility of big rewards had been dangled in front of him. He was dazzled by the man's name, and the awesome stories of his ruthlessness as an enforcer . . . Hamid had thought he could be plucked from his present status as one of several local leaders in the La Castellane project who had a franchise, permission to sell, on one stairwell. If this man, Tooth, let it be known that he favoured Hamid it was the same as opening the doors of a bank vault. On the pontoon, his legs unresponsive, he tried to find courage. Behind him a vehicle door opened, then shut, and he heard the sound of shoes kicking at the gravel leading to the pontoon. He knew little of the sea, could not swim. Dinning in his ears was the roar of the water chasing the length of the inlet and rolling up the shingle beach, and he heard the clattering of waves on protruding rocks, and in the edge of the headlights' cone was spray bouncing high.

A voice growled. 'Do you want my work or not? Are you shitting your pants, boy? Are you going or staying?'

He breathed deep. There was a spit in the voice behind him. He was pushed. Firmly, but not violently. Enough force for him to stumble that elusive last step, and then a void was under his feet. He was propelled into an emptied space, and then he tripped on the boat's side. He fell forward, cannoned down on to the decking and felt a bruising pain in his left shoulder. The voice now was a cold chuckle. The older man and the boy eyed him for a moment, then they pulled him up. They were still in harbour, still tied to the pontoon, and the boat lifted and fell. He was given a life-jacket: neither the fisherman nor the kid wore one. The engine started up. They headed out towards a wall of darkness, had not reached the open sea before Hamid threw up over the side, what he had taken for his breakfast and the snack for his lunch, and retched until his throat was sore.

The motion was worse. He said a prayer, first time in years. Recited what an imam had taught him – and could not speak and had no idea how the terror could be confronted. They went for a rendezvous with a freighter, to take delivery of cargo.

Tooth watched the navigation lights round a marker buoy.

'A powerful night out there, Tooth,' Crab said when his friend was back in the car, the door closed and the noise of the night shut out. 'A desperate night.'

'The best of nights, my good friend,' Tooth said. 'The customs, the coastal radar, they see nothing. The waves are too high and the boat too low in the water. It is a good place, and time, to receive parcels, packages.'

'He was shitting himself . . . You know, Tooth, when I was a kid there was a guy in gaol who looked, each morning, as if he'd just wet his pants – fear. We still hanged people then, and there was this guy who had bad sweats because a man he'd shot was in hospital and had relapsed, and if he died short of a year after he was hit then it would be murder. Murder then, in this category, was an execution job, rope and a scaffold. He was counting off the days willing the man to live through the next week. He'd taken a turn for the worse . . . What I saw of that Arab of yours, he was shitting and sweating. What'll it be like out there?'

'Don't think about it . . .' A low laugh. 'Nowhere you'd want to be. I put the bar high for him. Either he is a punk or he is someone I can use. You test a man before you trust him.'

'We are going to do well out of this, and even better once the route north is tested, proven. You ever fired one, Tooth?'

'No, wouldn't want to. It's what little bastards do. Losers and failures, and the Baumettes gaol is full of them, and all of them thought shooting with an AK made them a big man and gave them status. Me, I say that firearms are for the ignorant.'

October 2013

Dazzer looked around him. He had survived . . . with little to spare.

Had to hand it to the chopper people. The helicopters had arrived when ammunition was low, when the opposition was beginning to creep forward, little gooks ducking and weaving between the stones of a dried-out watercourse, and inside fifteen minutes they would have been gearing themselves up for the final charge.

He saw bodies, saw a couple of the lorries alight and, rare good fortune, they were loaded with food and general supplies and not the ammunition and ordnance they often carried, and saw an old man who half sat and half crouched and had lost any ability to fight on, and saw the rifle.

Dazzer, operating out of Bagram and doing runs towards the Pass, down beyond Jalalabad, was no longer military. Had been once. Now in his 40s and with a stomach to prove it, along with a shaven head, a few steroid squits livening his complexion, and tattoos over much of his skin, had served with an infantry battalion, then made the sensible choice. The rifle was near the old man but out of his reach. Dazzer was one of the scores who had chucked the Queen's Shilling and gone for the better pay offered by the host of private military contractors who picked up the military load during governments' downsizing of the Afghan quicksand. He had a good eye for such things and reckoned it an old weapon, a collector's piece. He had not shot the old man himself. The two helicopters, Yanks, had done the damage and lifted the possibility of this being Dazzer's final day as part of the 'mortal coil' business. Could have been a bad day for him except that he was a survivor, with the scars and scrapes to prove it, and a couple of times during his Afghan pay days, the medical teams had wondered if it was appropriate with this guy, given the bawdy nature of the ink work on the cheeks of his backside, to call for a priest. They hadn't, no padre had administered last rites. One of the boys, a scouser, had been hit but a medivac bird had taken him out, not that the regular military ever fell over themselves to get PMCs clear of harm's way and into a surgery tent, but the civilians put food on their tables and bedding on their cots, and often enough it was bullets going into their magazines. They waited now for an armoured escort that would push a burned-out lorry, written off, over the edge of the tarmacadam road and into a gully. He reckoned the weapon the old man had dropped would earn him something.

He'd seen him from the start of the attack. Dazzer reckoned the old man had rheumatism, or arthritis, had mobility problems and had gone as far forward as the factor of surprise would permit. From the first exchange of gunfire, Father William had been at the front . . . good name for the guy, Father William, as good as any. Dazzer had kids in a couple of cities in the UK, might have had more he didn't know of, and there were two more that his wife cared for. There had been times at home when he had read his kids – the legit ones and the illegits – bedtime stories, and he reckoned he did a star turn when it was *You are old, Father William, the young man said, And your hair has become very white: And yet you incessantly stand on your head – Do you think at your age it is right?* And he would do the full act beside the bed and read the next two verses upside down, head on the floor, and the kids would howl with laughter . . . Not that he saw them anymore because they were older and didn't need stories, and their mums didn't want him back in their lives. It was a Father William who lay, very small and seeming to be no threat, on the roadside. He'd fired the rifle.

Dazzer had seen him, and it had near knocked his shoulder away. He knew most versions of the AK-47, but did not think, a cursory glance, that he had handled this one before, a vintage piece.

Perhaps Father William had bad legs and perhaps he'd had poor eyesight, and there was a broken pair of spectacles, heavy black frames twisted and snapped, in the dust of the hard shoulder. He had not been a first: a 'first' for Dazzer would have been when a *mujahideen*, old or young, took off and did a runner. This old boy, a good old boy, had not broken the mould. Dazzer dragged on his cigarette and would have murdered for a beer. The convoy leader was trying to hurry the bulldozer, because this was an idiot place to be hanging about. He walked over to the body. Gave Father William a quick glance, and picked up the weapon.

Worth a bit, or more than a bit . . . It wasn't for Dazzer to interfere with the body, but permitted to handle the weapon, make it safe. He thought him 'a good old boy', Father William, because he had approached without being able to duck and weave, too stiff in the joints, and the Kalashnikov stock had been at his shoulder, and he'd only fired aimed shots, but his eyesight must have been heavily impaired if the thickness of the lenses was a judge. Had come on ahead, the mob of skilled fighting men behind him. Dazzer reckoned that the guy had felt it necessary to prove himself, show that he was not a burden. Father William had fired three times at Dazzer and the gun had been wavering and it would have been pure chance if one had hit. He was rakishly thin and his clothes hung on him, like he was a scarecrow, and his beard was loose and tangled, and strands of hair protruded from under his cap. There had been two spare magazines in a pocket: nothing else marked him as an enemy, willing and able if his eyesight had held up or he had been lucky enough to blast Dazzer to oblivion . . . who would have cared if he had? Answers on a postcard . . . He'd tell them about the old boy when they reached their fortified camp, had had a couple of tins each . . . there must be a story about the age of the weapon that Father William had carried.

It looked to be worth money. He'd heard about dictators and the like, those who had milked their own treasuries, lived in grand sprawling palaces, or did well on the narcotics trails, and they'd bought AK-47s that were gold-painted, real gold, like a bloody fashion accessory. But he reckoned there were others who'd be only too happy – if they were a war groupie or wanted a souvenir of their combat days – to have something that looked to have done business at the coalface. Dazzer had been shot at often enough with Kalashnikovs, and had twice suffered wounds that the field medics had patched, and he knew that age meant no loss of effectiveness. The bloody thing would last for ever. It looked to be 50 years old, but Herbie, who he'd meet up with once the road was cleared and they moved on with a reinforced escort, would be at the stay-over camp, and he'd know if it were even older. Dazzer didn't do souvenirs. Some of the drivers and the guys riding shotgun used to collect anything they could pull or chop off a dead fighter, but not him. Didn't do mementoes but did do the sale of anything that looked to have value stamped on it. And, added value was the blood on the stock that leaked into the notches and the bit where a sliver of wood had long been detached, made a tiny puddle there: blood would stain well and would be a talking point for a prospective purchaser.

He picked it up, made it safe, wrapped it tightly inside the folds of an old *khaffiyeh* that he'd used to keep dust and dirt out of his face since 'winning' it for that purpose in Iraq, out of Basra. Two magazines went with the weapon. He was pleased to have his hands on it, and it would fit snug in his armour-plated cab, down under his seat. It was vintage stuff and would fetch a good price, and Herbie would confirm it.

When he drove away, after the bulldozer had cleared the road, he found that his hands were shaking. Did not usually have the trembles after an action, but it was the sight of Father William that had done it, him being pitched without ceremony down into the gully with the wrecked vehicle, while his rifle was well wrapped and well cared for, and under Dazzer's seat. He'd keep it safe until he had the big freedom flight out, then go to his buyer, and it would be a decent earner.

* * *

Zeinab's phone call was done.

Reservations had been made by the London people, those she had met in the park. Naturally they would have been cautious.

She would challenge him. They were into Marseille and she did not speak, let him concentrate on the signs and driving in close, fast traffic. Her hand had tightened on his thigh. As he increased speed, she increased the pressure of her fingers. He had a strong face, she thought, not an artisan's. He drove well. A strong face and calm eyes. Something nagged. A vehicle ahead of him cut between lanes, carved through his road space, and all around them were blaring horns and oaths, but he had stayed cool, swerved, braked and manoeuvred, had driven on . . . why the nagging concern when he was a professional driver and did not swear or flick a finger in the air? He did not wriggle under her hand, did not make eye contact with her. It would be her challenge. The nagging doubt, or confusion, was gone.

They went below ground, down into the car park she had directed him towards, and named the hotel's street.

He zapped the car, saw the lights flash and the locks click home.

He carried the bags.

She had hooked her hand in his arm, and carried a sheet of paper with a photocopied street map . . . she found La Canebière, the main through road in the city. Evening had come and crowds were dense on the pavements. He felt her stiffen and her hand was claw-like on his arm. She had seen the soldiers; he had not. They were a stick of four and the smallest of them had a big combat radio on his back. They had rifles, helmets slung from their webbing belts, wore bulletproof vests. They seemed wary, alert, fingers alongside the trigger guard. The soldiers came past, then were lost in the crowds.

'Why are they here?'

He said, 'Don't know . . . No idea.'

Ignorance was better than the alternative: 'They are here, dear Zed, because this country is awash with north Africans intent on getting to Paradise, lifting a leg over six dozen Paradise-based virgins, and the best way to stop them, limit their effectiveness, is to shoot them, given half a provocation. Double tap to the skull. Shoot one of the beggars in the chest or stomach and he might muster enough reflex to squeeze off any detonator button in his hand – blow the side off his head and he may drop what sets his gear off and the bloody thing might just fail . . . end result, a few shoppers, some school kids out on a big deal evening, might live. It's what the troops are there for.' Shrugged. How would a heavy goods vehicle driver know why troops were on the streets of France's second city?

They crossed the road, on to a shopping street with a reputation, but he thought it cheapskate. She led. They cut away from the main drag and came into a small square where men hosed down the cobbles and others packed away unsold fruit and vegetables and dismantled the tables. Low light, and music and laughter bubbling from a score of fast food places, and cafés, and the shadows were deep. She'd paused under a high neon strip in a bistro's doorway. Checked her map again. She was looking around her, and the wind caught at her hair and her clothing, and shifted rubbish from where the market had been, and saw the hotel's sign. The notice outside said the rate was 95 for a single, and 105 for a double, with shower. They had come down Rue des Récolettes, were now in Cours St Louis. Opposite the front door was an *armurier*, the double windows filled with pistols, rifles, machetes . . . She was watched. Men ogled her, women looked at her with suspicion. They would have seen the texture of her skin, noted that she wore her hair uncovered. She looked hard at him, then led the way to the door. It was his problem . . . He heard the receptionist question her: it was she who had rung in, had changed the booking?

'Yes, that was me,' she said. 'Not two singles but one double, with shower.'

She was told that a card was needed; she rooted in her bag, found her purse, counted euros on to the desk . . . then looked back at him and he saw, clear and defined, the challenge in her eyes. She was given the key, told what floor. And no one there to feed him advice, nor to reiterate the regulations of an Undercover on the payroll of SC&O10, and hardly cared, and followed her up the stairs.

'When I give up, you know what?' Gough had his hands together like a supplicant at Sunday morning worship, and looked across the cotton tablecloth and over the small candle, and his elbows were firmly planted on the table.

'What should I know about?' Pegs replied, curt.

Their order had been taken. They were the only clients and a woman behind the desk left them in peace: seven of eight tables empty, but the woman's first remark to them had been, inevitable, to enquire if they had a reservation. They were near to their hotel, and had wandered along gloomy streets in the old quarter and had found this place.

'I am going to walk out of Wyvill Road, out on to the pavement, and then . . .'

'And then what?'

'I will have shredded my pass, and my jacket will weigh a whole ton less. Ditched the burden that I carry, and . . .'

'Oh, for fuck's sake, Gough. So tedious when you're maudlin.'

'I will take off my coat, chuck it in the air. I'll use that wall beside the pub to get myself upside down. I will handstand my way across the street . . .'

'You'll fall on your face.'

'Why, why will I do it?'

'Asking me, telling me?'

'Trying to tell you . . . Failure, lack of achievement, not enough success. I go out through the door, magic card gone, expenses reference number deleted, and I'm toast. Maudlin? Perhaps. The truth? Yes. Whether on Rag and Bone, we have lined up a good result is no matter. We screw down this kid, and the boys that liaise with her, and we have a few bottles and think we're God Almighty's élite of detectives. Is London safer the next morning? Is Manchester, or Leeds, or bloody Dewsbury? Don't think so. There's a gap on the ground and there are plenty willing and able, to fill it. We are not going to win ... there is no Mission Accomplished day, even on a faraway horizon. What personal sense of esteem can we fool ourselves we deserve to enjoy? We'll go and nothing will have changed. At best what we have done is shove a thumb against the crack in the dyke wall. Just temporary, sticking plaster. There'll be another crack the next day, the next week.'

The woman brought their food. Chicken for her, fish for him. A litre of house red to wash it down.

Gough barely looked at his plate. 'We are so thin on the ground. We're trying to do this job with paupers' money. We have a man on the plot and pitiful resources deployed to protect him. Why? Because there are a hundred operations competing with Rag and Bone, and we are so fortunate that we happened to be around at the right time and laid a hand on our man's shoulder. We have no slack, Pegs.'

'Eat your food, Gough. Enjoy.' She topped up his glass, filled it to the brim.

'I cannot estimate how he will shape up. Don't know where he is. I have a duty of care, am supposed to have, but it's abrogated.'

'Less time worrying about him, Gough, more time worrying for yourself – and worrying about what happens to me. If we lose the package, worse, if we lose our asset, you and I will be so alone. No one will stand our corner, and ...'

She stood. Her plate was less than half cleared. He might have had a few small bites at his chicken. She cleared her glass, gestured for him to empty his. She walked to the counter and put down 100 euros in notes. She picked up the order pad, tore off a couple of sheets, and would fill them in later, do it with left-handed script. She led him out of the door. The wind caught them on the street, narrow and poorly lit, cobblestones rough under their tread.

'Sorry and all that, Gough, but we need to get close up, personal, do it better than we did last night. Or we might as well get on the first plane out. Ditch it. Cannot leave him much more bare-arsed than we've already done ... Agreed, it would be nice to win sometimes.'

He felt crushed, emotion drained, no ambition. They walked arm in arm.

Out in the city centre, by the hospitals and the principal cemetery – on Rue d'Orient – Major Valery prepared for bed. He had a routine. Had followed it since the start of his duty in Marseille after his transfer from the north. He thought that routine as relevant now, or more so than when he had brought his children and his wife here from the city of Lille.

The children were now in bed.

His wife had spent the evening preparing for tomorrow's classes, but was now upstairs, undressed, in bed, reading. First he turned off all the lights on the ground floor. Then he would sit a full fifteen minutes in darkness and would listen to the sounds of the street: then he would check the pictures from the discreetly sited cameras that covered the front and rear of the property. Then he would go upstairs, his pistol in his hand, would change into his pyjama, would go to his side of the bed. The pistol and his mobile phone would be placed on the table, next to the lamp.

He could not have accurately measured the threat to himself – or to those he loved. The Major, of course, was reasonably trained in the art of personal survival. He could shoot straight, could be effective in unarmed combat, could use a baton and strike an enemy's shoulder close to the neck, disable with the intensity of the pain. What he could not do was be present for the school day to protect his wife, now concentrating on her book – nor safeguard his children, one sleeping quietly and one with a hacking winter cough. He assumed a real and clear-cut threat existed. He might not know the names of all those men who sat in the rotten core of the city's commerce and who had reason to hate him. His defiance of their power and influence was fostered in his refusal to accept bribes, arrangements that would benefit him . . . there had been another attempt to suborn him that evening. So blatant. A Mercedes car parked outside L'Évêché, a message sent inside from the outer gate telling him that he would learn something to his advantage if he came out of the building and spoke to the driver. He had come. Through the opened window of the costly black saloon had been offered a tightly wrapped package. It might have contained 20,000 euro, might have been 30,000, might have been a long lens image of his children in the playground, of his wife returning from the weekly shop, bags around her feet as she fished in a pocket for the key. He had seemed to reach for the package, as if accepting it, and it had been released, but he had not grabbed it. It had fallen in the dirt. He had turned, walked away, and the courier would have had to leave his car, walk round it, pick up the padded envelope, return it whence it came. He would have made those enemies angry, and the ones in the Town Hall, and the councillors and those in positions of patronage, and the gangsters when he took them off the street.

He would climb the stairs. He would go to the bed and lay the pistol and the mobile phone beside the lamp. The weapon would be armed, the safety engaged. The bell on the phone would be turned low . . . He barely thought of the English detective team, trying to do a job for which the necessary budget was not available. He turned out the light. He slept lightly. He liked to have the pistol close, and needed to have the phone beside it.

The room was clean. The bed was covered with a white sheet and a floral duvet. A print on the wall showed a view of the *vieux port*. Outside, a radio played New Orleans jazz. A wardrobe covered half of the wall between the door and the bathroom. An easy chair was lodged by the window that looked on to the square below. The curtain was drawn but thin, and the snap of the wind penetrated the open window and fluttered the material. On another wall was an Impressionist's view of Les Calanques, steep white stone cliffs that were brutally sharp and the sea beneath the rocks was gentle. A forgettable room, suitable for those anxious to hurry on with their lives.

A strip of light shone at the bottom of the bathroom door.

They'd had a café supper, meat and salad, ice-cream and coffee.

Andy Knight – a temporary name with a personality easily altered to suit necessities – sat on the bed. Little said at supper and neither of them drinking alcohol. Total inevitability recognised. Not much of a room and a noisy bed which would not inhibit them. He had opened his bag, pondered what to take out, gone for clean socks and a clean shirt, and a wash bag. Had cleaned his teeth, had undressed, was on the bed, naked, waiting . . . she had gone to the bathroom and had carried a nightdress with her.

He supposed the problem was solved. It had not arisen when he had taken on other legends. She'd washed and the plumbing reacted with a gurgling in the pipes. The toilet flushed, then the taps ran again . . . He could tell himself that it was what they both wanted. He saw the stern face of the Detective Chief Inspector, and the contempt at the mouth of the civilian woman, and the hypocrisy was rank because both, so obviously from their body language, did hard humping. Relationships between officers on a team was as frowned upon as sex by an Undercover with a target . . . they were Gough and Pegs. He had no name, had glanced at her passport and seen that she used a phoney one with the actual photograph but a different identity.

He had been an 'action' man, had walked as a volunteer into a 'heart of danger', had been admired, praised for his 'dedication', might have been a combat hero but for the camouflaged hole burrowed out by a buck rabbit on the common above Lympstone, but understood little of women, had never known a long, serious bond, something that might have a future.

The door opened. she switched off the light. She wore the nightdress, and the curves of her body were well shown by it . . . He thought her more nervous than he was.

One problem settled, another rose to take its place.

Would he . . .? Would he turn her in . . .? She sat beside him, then reached across him and the bare skin of her arm brushed his chest. Would he? Probably would. Would she do her double damnedest to kill him if she knew the truth of his loyalties? Probably would . . . They were touching, like young lovers, clinging to the vestiges of innocence: were able to do that because the lies lived strong and well.

Turn her in, shop her, tout on her? What loyalty, after doing it on a noisy bed above the square by the street market in central Marseille, was she owed? Did affection exist? Questions and issues rampaged. Lust or love, or just eating what was piled on the plate and in front of him? The last thing he saw clearly on her face was shyness. Her hand was on the stem of the bedside light and it wriggled to find the switch. It clicked. She was a shadow, barely lit by the lamp in the square, filtering through the curtains.

He would not choose when the arrest squad came for her. He might be there and might not. He could be bundled aside as the guys spilled out of a convoy of cars and covered her with aimed firearms . . . could have been eased away from her and then would see her taken down and weapons a few feet from her head on the flickering image of a video recording. She would be in shock, near to wetting herself, perhaps not realising at that moment that the heavy goods driver she had taken in her arms and . . . in trauma when she did know. Not screaming, but quiet, crushed and huddled. His call. For him to decide. She was close to him, warm against him. Would he turn her in, after this and when the assignment dictated it, betray her – and walk away, and have a beer at the pub and blow a kiss at the girls who pulled the pints, and take time somewhere at the end of a far track where the demons could not travel, nor trouble him, and go back to work with another name and another target and Rag and Bone ditched? Would he? And have a hug and a squeeze from Prunella in the office? Would he consign her to prison, maximum security? She covered his mouth, kissed him . . . Of course he would turn her in. Of course.

13

They were together, warm, damp, holding each other tight, bodies locked.

The bed shouted for something to be done about the springs. Andy had pain in his back from the scratches her nails had made on his skin, open wounds, like he had been whipped.

It was a sacking offence: an appearance before a disciplinary tribunal, a predictable outcome . . . some grave-faced guy or an angry woman chairing the hearing. No sympathy, no talk about 'how difficult it must be for you people, in the circumstances of close proximity, to keep your zipper fastened and your dick hidden away', no leeway for a caution and a rap on the knuckles. Out, gone, dumped on the street.

It had started slowly, as if both were frightened, coming from opposite horizons. He broke each and every regulation laid down by the SC&O10 bosses. Never discussed with Gough and his woman, never defined how the relationship should play out, and studiously ignored once the trigger had come – him meant to be driving her to the south of France. Had he raised it then, an answer might have been, 'If that happens we'll give advice, but not dealing with a hypothetical, better just kick that can down the street until we have to confront it . . . use your judgement.' She drove the old cart and horse through the culture wall of her parents, then of her cause – neither Krait nor Scorpion would have factored it into their decision that she was reliable on the mission as a courier. Had begun with the sensation, both of them, that they tasted forbidden fruit. Her first time? Of course. She could have shouted, that bloody obvious. It had come to that stage, do it or get off the pot, and he was shown that him and her, that bed, was calculated.

Yes, she had gone into a chemist in Avignon and he had stayed outside, had not followed her because she had waved him away, and then she must have bought the small pack of condoms. Could have been 5 euros for that size of pack. They had blundered towards the first start.

Not the first time for Andy, or any of the alternate identities he'd assumed. But not done many times. A girl in Exmouth, down the road from the Lympstone barracks, seemed to have enough of an itch to want it from any recruit needing a trip to adulthood: fast, perfunctory, in the back of a car. A girl in the town where his parents lived, name and address exorcised from his mind, and pretty much everybody of his age knew her. A leaving dance at school, and some of the kids had left bottles, alcohol, under the shrubs closest to the gym hall, and she could barely stand, nor him, and both had confided dread afterwards, no protection. Another girl in the office, used to do the opposite shift to Prunella . . . All in common with one aim: get it, have the T-shirt, forget it . . . he would not forget her, his Zed.

She had started to writhe and him to grunt, and sweat sheened them . . . He had wanted to shout it into each room of each floor of the hotel, then little squeals from her . . . He would go before the hearing, she would be taken into an interview room off the cell block, and she would spill out the detail of the liaison, be encouraged into graphic detail, and the end-game would have her brief declaiming in court, between theatrical questions delivered with a tone of manufactured disgust. He was the man, and older. He was an experienced officer. At best she was ignorant of the criminal conspiracy in which she was involved, at worst she had been encouraged deeper into the plotting, used as a crude Trojan horse. She was a simple girl, without sexual experience, and the seduction was little more than 'entrapment'. Were the undercover officer's superiors responsible for encouraging him to step outside the parameters of his duty? Did he act without authority? A judge would send the jury out, hear submissions, call them back in, refer to irregularities and dismiss the charges, and would write a note of complaint to the Crown Prosecution Service for their handling of

Crown v Zeinab . . . Out on his neck, disgraced. She would walk free but would be despised in her own community, deplored for providing rich pickings for the popular press, dismissed by the university, after spending months locked up. It was that big, for each of them, what they did.

She nibbled at his ear. He sucked and bit at the moist skin of her throat.

The wind fluttered the curtains, and a bin was blown on the square, and noisy gangs of youths were returning through the old part of the city as the clubs closed . . . she screamed. He called out, pushed a last time, accepted that it was an animal instinct that gave him the last strength left to him. A shuddering, an end to a career . . . something so unprofessional that it shocked him. Her hold on him loosened. He subsided, rolled away from underneath her.

What would he say in court? Deny it. A defence fabrication. His word against hers. An experienced officer against a dangerous and motivated terrorist, an easy choice for a jury: there would be files full of evidence of her proven lies. Deny it, wash his hands of her. Where had he slept? 'On the floor, sir.'

Another couple, below, had started up. He chuckled . . . Heard the rhythm of the springs. Had to laugh. She asked him why, little panted gasps breaking up the question. He said it was because of them, they led the way, maybe now half the street would get going, like it was with the Mexican Wave. But they had been the first – and said also what he thought of her . . . Might have meant it.

'Zed, hope you listen to me, hope you believe what I say . . . you are fantastic. You are the best.'

Enough light came into the room for him to see her skin, and the shape of her when he eased back, gazed at her. The bedding had slipped. She did not cover herself, as if he had snatched away any modesty, had given herself. The great almond eyes gazed up at him . . . nothing like this in his life before . . . he could remember how it had been at the start. Him doing the Galahad stuff, riding to the rescue. Handing out a sustained beating to the 'thugs' who had attacked her. All play-acting, and her buying into the sham. The pendant, usually hidden and private only to them, hung from its chain, nestled in the cleft; a small stone that reflected the limited light, and he had charged for it on his expenses sheet, filled in each month, and it had not been queried. 'Cheap at the bloody price – bit skinflint', the woman would have said as she shuffled the paperwork and what few scrawled bills he could include.

She took his hand. Held it softly. Pulled it towards her. Laid it on the hair, gazed at him, gave trust. It was, he might have said if challenged, 'in defence of the state', but his mind stayed silent.

It had been, for Zeinab, a supreme moment.

She did not know how it might have been bettered . . . not if she had followed any pathway laid down for her by her mother and father, and gone from the little house and the little street and taken the PIA flight to Karachi and Islamabad, and the feeder to Quetta. Met the boy who was to be her husband, seen her parents haggle with his parents, endured an arranged match, gone through it, been fucked that night and hard because that was how his brothers and uncles would have urged him to be. 'Dominate, set a tone . . .' Fucked hard, oblivious to how she felt, and no protection. Nor if she had gone with a boy at the university – with drink or without drink – or a boy from her own culture, and him wanting a notch to scratch on a table in his room, or on a bedpost, hurried and fumbled. No chance of it being better if it had been Krait or Scorpion, or either of the men she had met in London, had done it with her in a car, on the backseat and her across whichever of them and pretending to be expert, and it hurting, and it being fast . . . The girls on the corridors of the Hall of Residence spoke of it usually as too quick, coming too soon for the men, not coming at all for them, and sometimes it was a reward they expected for buying dinner, for getting the cinema tickets, for the club entry fee. Like none of those. His hand moved, was gentle, explored again where it had been before. She took off what he wore, replaced it . . . she could not see her precious nightdress, bought to impress, chucked off the bed and on to the floor.

There would be a cottage, hidden away, remote, where sea birds shouted and the sea ripped at the base of the cliffs, and he would be there and a fire's flames would flicker over the skin of her body and his chest, his legs . . . she would need that, to be hidden. When Krait or Scorpion, or whoever it was decided should have the rifle, that responsibility, and walk into the shopping mall, cocked the weapon, aimed it, fired with it, she would need to be far from the place . . . unless it were she who was chosen. And felt his fingers stroke the skin, and tangle nails in the hair, and ease again across her. Already she had been made a woman, was fulfilled. She pushed him back, was above him, and the pendant fell between her breasts. She lowered herself. Was supreme and had power.

Her phone fidgeted on the table at her side of the bed. He did not see it, did not respond as it shook.

It was good again, better than the first time. He was a useful boy, she thought she had chosen him well. They matched the other couple. The two beds made an orchestra. And she hurried him, tried to tire him, pushed for him to be faster, then to explode, then to sag in exhaustion, would need him to sleep. He called out her name, as if that proved his love . . . useful and well chosen, and his expertise growing, and her now – the first night – controlling. Then he would sleep.

As the fishing boat slowed, so the rolling increased and the pitch became – to Hamid – more awful. He had already been sick more times in the last hours than in the whole of his life. First he had been able to get to the side and vomit over it, and allow the spray to blister against his cheeks. Then he'd thrown up on the deck, and the last time his anorak was splattered with thin liquid, all that his stomach still held.

The boy moved cat-like behind his father. He was offloading fenders, putting them over the side of the small craft and then lashing the attached ropes to hooks. Hamid had only in the last few seconds understood why. In spite of the wind and white crests there was only faint cloud out and abroad that night. Traces of milky moonlight and views of star formations, not that Hamid knew one constellation from another. Now a section of the skies had lost those light pricks and there was a high wall close to them. He heard the shouts and, above the crash of waves around him, realised that a cargo ship – no low portholes as there would be on a cruise boat or a roll on/off ferry – was manoeuvring close to them. The captain shouted close to him, above the pitch of the waves, that he was trying to find a location where they might be able to use the sides of the boat as shelter. The wall towered over him, then they struck the hull, just above the waterline, and Hamid was thrown back, tossed away across the deck. He had lost feeling in his shoulder where the impact had been, but was revived by the water on his face. If the fisherman and his son had noted his collapse they showed no sign. The side of the fishing boat thudded against the freighter. Yells from above and responding shouts from the wheelhouse. A hatch opened, level with the soaked roof of the wheelhouse.

A man stood at the hatch, holding a package. Hamid thought him blessed with the nimbleness of an ape. Hamid had imagined that the matter he had been sent on, personal courier to Tooth, would be of great financial importance – many kilos of refined heroin or expertly cut cocaine. The boy came over to Hamid, grinned, then dragged him upright by the straps of the life-jacket. Grinned again, then speared him back across the deck. The package was thrown to him. It must have been taken by the driving wind. In a moment of desperation, Hamid jumped and his hands clasped at air, spray, then caught it, lost it, snatched again, missed. It soared over him, then down, and he lost sight of it as it dropped into the sea and splashed.

Hamid reached the side of the deck, could just – in the frail moonlight – make out the diminishing bubbles of the air trapped in the bag. He screamed. His voice was beaten back by the force of the gale, by the high side of the freighter as the hatchway was dragged shut, by the howl of the fishing boat's engine each time the propeller end climbed high and out of the water. Hamid seemed to see that face . . . as clear an image as if the man, Tooth, stood beside him: flat cap, narrow brim, and under it the tinted glasses, and the wizened face and the thickened beard and the grey of the moustache which had the texture of his father's shaving brush. Saw it, and shivered in front of it, and tried to explain. Not his fault. The fault of a seaman from a freighter, open hatch, perhaps losing his footing in the moment that mattered. Misjudging the distance, too much force; a sudden gust, the package evading him, going into the water. Had anyone who had ever failed him, ever shrugged at Tooth, ever expected him to understand that it was merely an accident, no blame due? If he came back and had failed – had been given an opportunity to succeed by a man of the legendary status of Tooth and had not taken it – then Hamid thought his future slight. He would be cut down on a dark street, perhaps in a week, perhaps a month. He could not have run, hidden, to escape Tooth's anger. The thoughts cavorted in his mind. He looked back . . . he did not think the boy had realised the package – what they had come to collect on this shit night, in this shit weather – had not been caught. Nor his father, who had jerked the wheel and started to swing the rudder.

Hamid saw the package, the air in the bag almost gone, a pale faint shape, now a metre below the surface, and it was lifted in the swell.

He jumped. Had not intended it, nor regretted it. He could not swim. He went in and went under, then was forced back to the surface by the buoyancy of his jacket. The boy had a flashlight on him. At the bottom of the cone of light, where it was feeble and deeper than Hamid's feet, was the package in the plastic bag. It was hard to contort his body, get his legs above his head, and kick, drive with his arms and power himself into the depth of water, to chase after it . . . It was hard, but it would be harder to survive when it was obvious he had failed Tooth . . . It was said of Tooth that in his youth he had always taken back full interest on a slight, chopped off hands or legs merely as retribution for disrespect. This would be worse, an example made . . . A boy in the project had been barbecued for lack of respect and he could remember the thunder of the igniting petrol tank and the blast of the hot air . . . He could not see. He groped right and left and felt the pain in his lungs, and was touched at the waist and snatched, and caught. His fingers clung to it, difficult to hold the slippery surface of plastic. He had no more air. He kicked.

Hamid broke the surface. The flashlight's beam was many metres away. He tried to shout, could manage only a choking cough, and he reckoned the boat was moving away. If he did not cling to the package then he would have to face Tooth, explain, see his life distroyed. He was sure of it, as he drifted farther from rescue, from the torch's reach, and they seemed not to hear him. The weight of the bag increased and he needed more strength to hold on to it.

He thought himself going, did not know how much longer he would be able to last.

Karym eased out from La Castellane on his scooter. There was good trade that night, and taxis brought buyers to the entrance off the Boulevard Henri Barnier, and waited for clients to be taken into the depths of the blocks, to be supplied, and to pay in old notes, emerge and be driven away.

He left the project, and headed off down the road towards the lights of Marseille.

The instructions he had been given had been memorised, had then been burned. Anxious to please his brother, who had shown some small faith in his ability, he left early, gave himself time.

He woke.

He had always slept well, at school, at Lympstone. Before exams he had been dead to the world whether it was in the struggle for school results or getting through the tough examinations for the marksman's rating, and when he had been on the induction course for the police SC&O10 unit. Not now . . . had not slept fully as Phil or Norm or Andy: never lasted a night, was up and dressed, whether a courier driver or a jobbing gardener or driving a heavy goods vehicle, by six or earlier. It meant that a situation could alter without notice. He did not carry a weapon. Nothing he could reach for. His eyes open, he lay rigid, held his breath and listened. He expected to hear her breathing. He had to know where he was, why he was there, with whom. Easy enough to forget 'where' and 'why'. He might have grimaced, because it had been good: she was a new experience in his confused and nameless life. No breathing beside him but he could make out the sounds of the night: occasional vehicles, the grind of an engine that powered, probably a street cleaning truck . . . and still at it on the floor above. Heard all that, did not hear her breathing.

He reached across. His hand did not touch her shoulder, nor her waist, nor the expanse of her back. He groped further. The sheet was folded back on her side. He sat up, alert, and eyed the bathroom door. No light under it . . . in the Marines, with the reconnaissance teams, with the unpredicted – behind the lines and without close support – they called it 'a train wreck' . . . No sound from the bathroom.

And heard her. A few words. She had barely said a word when she had been in his arms, under him or over him, fitting the rubber and . . . had hardly spoken, allowed only short, sharp squeals, not simulated. Recognised her voice, and heard also someone who struggled to put together a sentence in English but tried. He slipped off the bed.

'You want to come, why not? You see the real Marseille. I can do that.'

He saw a slight young man, grubby clothes that were the imitation of something smarter, and saw the acne scars on his face, and saw a scooter beside him and one arm seemed strong and took the weight of the machine, and the other looked weak. The light was full on the boy and his eyes were bright, and he grinned, and reached out with his damaged arm

She hesitated. 'There's a man upstairs, he's sleeping, he's . . .'

She was half dressed, he reckoned. Most of her clothes were still in the empty bathroom. Just wore her jeans and trainers and a T-shirt, and her arms were folded across her chest, as if for warmth, and avoiding the wind that flicked rubbish in her face.

'You have a boy to fuck you? That's good. Will he beat you if you come with me and see where I live, the true experience of Marseille? Will he?'

'No, he will not. He thinks he loves me. I do not have to explain, I . . .'

'But you do have to trust. That's good, trust. You have to trust me, it is necessary. I would like to show you where I live, and show people there that a woman comes to see me, my guest, a beautiful woman – please.'

'Why not? Yes. I have to be back before he wakes.'

'You have made him tired?'

She giggled, the guilty girl and proud of it. Her head was back and she stifled laughter. She swung her leg, was astride the pillion. The boy used his feet to push the scooter across to the far side of the square, then the engine snapped alive, and the last Andy saw of her was through a haze of fumes coming from the exhaust.

He was supposed to be close to her, and again he had failed. He dressed, as she had, jeans and a shirt and trainers, and what they had done together – and what was done above them – had dulled his head, and he felt cursed.

He had been barely conscious when they heaved him out of the sea.

If he had been able to shout, the rescue might have been quicker. He could only croak. It could have been that the fisherman had realised the risk of going back to the harbour without him, leaving his son to rope up the boat and swab the decking of the passenger's vomit, and gone to the parked car and ducked his head in respect to the man who'd have lowered his window – and apologised, and said that there had been a misfortune, an accident, a loss. The loss of the passenger, and the loss of a cargo. Could have been that the search had only continued for so long because the fisherman dreaded that admission. Instead, Hamid received help from the fisherman and his son as he stepped off the boat, on to the rocking pontoon. One on either side of him, taking his weight. They would have carried the packet had he allowed it.

At first Hamid had bobbed in the water, strong enough to stay upright, his head clear and his body lifted by the waves then dropped into troughs. The salt taste had stuck in his throat but he had lost the will to try to hack it out, cough it clear. The great bulk of the freighter had disappeared within moments, but the torchlight search from the fishing boat had been obvious. He'd heard them shout for him: didn't know his name but yelled into the night, into the wind and the waves. And, neither of them had explained about the life-jacket, had told him that it carried both a whistle and a beacon light on straps to be tugged . . . It was fear of the small man with the trimmed beard, Tooth, that kept him alive, as if he believed that he could still be hurt, face retribution, even when dead, drowned, his lungs emptied of air, filled with seawater.

His grip on the package had never loosened.

They had brought him into the boat after sticking a hook, fastened with whipping to a long pole, under the straps of the jacket. The fisherman had brought him to the boat's side, and his son had leaned out and clasped the package, then had tried to free Hamid's hand from the plastic. He had not released his grip, nor had he done so when back in the boat. Water cascaded off him and chilled his skin, and his clothes and shoes were sodden weights. He had not allowed them to break his hold on the plastic bag. They gave him coffee from a flask, then poured brandy from a bottle into the flask and gave him more, and he spluttered as the warmth ran like fire in his throat.

He managed the pontoon, then shook them clear. He walked in a good line towards the car and the headlights came on. If they blinded him he did not show discomfort. The window came down. He heard the gravel voice, and the question.

'It was in the sea?'

'And I went in after it.'

'You dived for it?'

'Before it sank.'

Only then did Hamid free his grip on the bag. Tooth, the great man, was out of the car, at the boot, took the package, then drained off the water, took a towel from the back of the baggage area.

'You went into the water to find the package? Why?'

'For you, it was for you.'

He heard a growl of laughter, then it was translated and the Englishman too, laughed.

'For me? Incredible . . . Perhaps because you knew who I used to be. Get your clothes off. Dry yourself.'

Hamid stood beside the car, hopped from foot to foot, stripped himself bare, and the cold lathered his skin. He rubbed hard with the towel and brought sensations of heat and chill to his body. He put his clothes into the plastic bag that had held the package.

'Will it still work, after that time in the water?'

He sat on the back seat and the heater was turned high. The doors were slammed. The fisherman and his son stood on the end of the pontoon, did not wave but gazed impassively into the headlights.

Through chattering teeth, Hamid answered. 'It will work, as normal. It is an assault rifle. I can feel it, the shape of it, distinctive. It will work as well as the day it was made because it is a Kalashnikov.'

He was so thin she thought she could have snapped him in half. It did not matter how much Karym ate, he never put on weight. His sister was always fussing about her clothes size, sometimes near to tears. At first her hands had not explored him. Because of the way he rode the old scooter, hardly clear of the Saint Charles railway station, and going west, she did. Prompted by him. At first she had tried to sit upright and hold on to the bar at the back of the pillion seat, and she had shrieked twice, once when he swerved past a slow vehicle and the other when he had hit a pothole. Her arms now were around his waist, her fists clenched over the button on his stomach. She held him tight.

Hot breath on the nape of his neck. A strange smell on her body which he did not recognise. No helmet, and he thought her hair would have careered out behind her. The scooter was not a Ducati 821 Monster, did not have the thrust of 112 horsepower: it chugged at up to 65 kilometres an hour, throttle full . . . The girls on the project, up until the time of his new fame, would not have considered riding behind him, enduring the hard seat, going at such pathetic speed. He had been surprised that she had said she would come with him, fancied it a delusion of excitement. He thought she was naked beneath her T-shirt. He gave her a hard ride and her hold over his stomach was tight.

* * *

Zeinab saw the bright lights ahead.

It had been a moment of madness – the second in one evening. Sleeping – for part of the night – with the driver, her dupe boy, was one. Allowing herself the stupidity of swinging a leg over the seat of the kid's scooter was the second . . . And she was exhilarated, allowed the pleasure to ripple in her. Half-dressed, she was caught by the wind that seemed to scour her body, liberated.

Did not need to have gone to bed with Andy Knight. Did not need to have gone into the deserted streets of Marseille on the back of a pathetic underpowered scooter and did not need to have clung to his waist . . . a madness and a freedom. His English was hesitant, accented, but understandable. He twisted his head, with his eyes off the road, shouted at her that the lights were where he lived, and gunned the engine and coaxed minimally more speed from it. They came to a wide entrance that seemed to be defended by heavy stones. Youths came forward.

There were parts of Manchester where she would have been advised not to be when the light fell. She thought this one an equal. Most of the youths wore balaclava masks, or had scarves tied over their faces. She dug her fingernails into the boy's stomach, felt the scrawny flesh below his shirt. She had not known freedom before. Could have called out into the night, at the sporadic street-lights and high blocks, 'Why not?' All of her life, school in Dewsbury, carted to the mosque, disciplined at home – at the university, and under the strictures of academic work and timetables for producing essays and passing exams – with the little group and struggling to be accepted past the prejudice wall of Krait and Scorpion – never free. She held the stomach of the boy, felt feeble muscles cramped in knots. He shouted at the youths, and they backed off, as if disappointed that he had brought home a girl.

He parked. She lifted her leg, swung it over the pillion. Wind blasted her face, her chest and thighs. She was eyed, a stranger, as would any man, or woman, brought late at night into Savile Town. He took her hand. She was older than him, taller than him, stronger than him: he held her hand and she allowed it. He led her up a dried mud path and they passed shrubs, and their shadows were thrown, and a hundred televisions seemed to blast them, then a pool of darkness and then the hallway of a block. She smelt faeces and urine and decayed food. A queue stood here. A man came from a doorway, clutching fifteen or twenty kilos of merchandise, wrapped in newspaper and wedged into a hessian shopping bag. Two kids stood at the doorway – the door was ajar, a voice sounded from inside, and one of them waved forward the man next in line – and each had his face covered and each carried a gun. Both had slender bodies, would have been younger than the boy who had brought her . . . all part of a liberation, the new-found freedom.

He said the elevator did not work. They climbed together. Too many stairs and she had started to pant. He held her hand, helped her. She smelt cooking, she heard arguments, vivid laughter, her breath wheezed. Up three flights, and came to a landing. No paint on the walls, but graffiti in Arabic, different to what she knew of the symbols used in Quetta, in Pakistan, and her hand was freed, and a key was produced, and a door unfastened, and her hand taken again.

A girl sat on a sofa, had washed her hair and had a towel round her head. Had an empty plate beside her, held a can of juice. The TV showed a singer. The boy nodded to her, and she shrugged. What did it matter to her if he came home with a girl? Zeinab supposed she was regarded as a symbol of success, an object to be displayed. She was led across the room and he pushed a door open. His bedroom was lit by a small lamp beside the bed. The bed was unmade. Clothes, unwashed, crumpled, covered half the floor. A TV was on the wall. A poster of a singer, female, a view of a cliff edge in mountains with a village tucked under the escarpment. In a cheap frame was a photo of a middle-aged man and a woman, probably his mother and father. The image that dominated, stopped her dead: an AK-47 rifle . . . she stared hard at it, then looked around and fastened on the bookcase. She read the titles of the books on the top shelf . . . *AK-47 Assault Rifle, the Real weapon of Mass Destruction* and *The Gun, the AK-47 and the Evolution of War* and *AK-47 The Story of a Gun* and *The Gun that Changed the World* . . . The boy had a library, more than 50 volumes and most of them hard-backed and therefore expensive, and lived in a foul tower block that would be raddled with addicts and drug customers, and all he read was about the gun that she had been recruited to courier back to the UK . . . Everything else in the room was disgusting, dirty, nothing was treated with pride except for the book shelves and their contents. And, she should not have come, and she reckoned she would be late returning, and the boy spoke.

'You are looking at them?'

'Should I call you an expert, on the Kalashnikov?'

'Almost, perhaps . . . I read about it, I hope one day to have one. My confession, I have never fired one. My brother will not let me even hold one. He says that only boys ready to die, wanting Paradise, have a Kalashnikov. I can strip one, can clean one, can . . .'

'Why is it so special?'

'You want to know? Have you not come to purchase a supply route for hashish? It is narcotics that you want?'

'Why is it so talked of?'

'Because it makes a man strong, walk with pride, cannot be defeated. The gun of the humble man, a peasant – the best. Both the *fedayeen*, anywhere in the world, fight with the Kalashnikov, and we do. It is the rifle of the citizen, not just the élite troops they employ – it is so special. I can get you one, a few minutes and a boy will come who keeps them for my brother. I can, if you want, and . . .'

'I need to go back to my hotel. Thank you. Thank you again.'

'This is my room – a nice room?'

'A lovely room.'

He had her hand again. He tried to lead her from the room but she gazed at the poster on the wall, at the weapon they said, all of them, was supreme. He tugged . . . down the stairs, he babbled about how nice his room was and what a good apartment he and his sister lived in, and she absorbed the outline of the weapon, soaked herself in its image. They paused in the stairwell, and the queue was still there as another man was called forward, and she brushed against one of the kids and his weapon, and understood. The boy grinned, spoke in a sort of *patois*, was handed the rifle, put it in her hand, let her cradle it, just for a moment, like something new-born in her mind. It was snatched away. She was taken to the scooter and the engine was gunned, and she was driven out into the night. He was grateful to her for coming to his home. She thought herself unique in his life, and that her very presence imported status into his home, unknown before . . . and he treated her with such respect, and brought her to a world of new experience which she drank from eagerly.

She held his waist and the skin was there for her fingers, and she thanked him for letting her touch the rifle, so precious, so cold, so available.

January 2014.

'I'm a fair man, Dazzer, always have been, and trust to God that I always will be.'

Reuven was a fixture now on the corner of the island of Cyprus that was closest to the Sovereign bases operated by the British military. He was well known as a potential conduit for the off-loading of 'souvenirs' illicitly carried home from the Afghan war.

'A fair man who does a fair deal. Not a man who would cheat, defraud. A fighting soldier who looks for a small reward, in cash, after the trauma and desperate stresses of that brutal place.'

The private military contractor, his stint of duty exhausted, had flown to the garrison airfield with a flight full of UK infantry squaddies. It was normal for the PMC boys to be given a free ride home, courtesy of the military, as if a concession was due because the regular forces could not survive in that hostile environment, the hellhole of Helmand, without the support and logistics of the pseudo civilians. Not a pleasant flight to the eastern Mediterranean because the transporter had been bucked by crosswinds, and for all to see were two flag-draped coffins in the cargo sector. The troops were allowed 48 hours in the sunshine to swim, drink, fornicate if they could find a performing harridan, so that they did not get back to Brize Norton and go home to wives and girlfriends and parents while still reeling from the tensions of the conflict zone. It meant that fewer women were beaten up on their return, fewer pubs trashed to ruin . . . two days was the allotted safety valve period. Checks for contraband were minimal on departure from Afghanistan, would be rigorous at the Oxfordshire airfield and few would breach the security screening.

'And honest, quite honest. If you believe you can find a better price from another merchant in such goods then, Dazzer, you should seek him out and trade with him. The price I offer is – quite truthfully – the best I can manage.'

Reuven was from the Baltic coast of Russia but had moved a decade before to Cyprus. Ethnic Jewish, with good English, a voice that was quiet and seemed to mince goodwill: he was the calling point for those who had smuggled out hardware, ammunition, ordnance, and then had been too frightened to risk confrontation with the Customs men at the UK end – merciless bastards. He operated from a bar that was Greek-themed, that served over-priced food, that played incessant Mouskouri or Roussos tracks. His table was deep in shadow. Beside him on the bench was the package that Dazzer had brought him to make a bid for, unwrapped, still seeming to carry the smell of war, of decayed dirt.

'It is the best I can manage. I am not a charity, but I am not a charlatan. I pay what it is possible to pay. I am aware of the limited potential of myself finding a buyer for this item, very limited. We must be realistic, Dazzer, we must consider who might wish to purchase it, and why. I believe that the opportunity for re-sale hardly exists. Be very frank with you, tell you that it is, almost, worthless.'

They drank, lager for Dazzer and mineral water for Reuven . . . The contractor had enthused to himself about the value of the AK-47, and had done the sales pitch of the old man – and Father William was a good name for him – who was a freedom fighter when he should have been a pensioner, not that there was a good system of care for the elderly in up-country Afghanistan. All the time he had talked, Reuven had kept his face as still and unanimated as a poker player's. Dazzer had little fight left in him – and the dreams in his life seldom had happy endings. A shrug, then the look of keen sincerity.

'Do you know, my friend – my good and trusted friend – how many of these weapons, the different variants on them, have been manufactured, how many? How many millions? Tens of millions? Perhaps a hundred million . . . The value is trifling, even for one of this vintage that has been cared for with love, or that has a history of notoriety.'

He knew. Herbie had told him, but had also painted a pretty portrait of some dick-head who would pay a small fortune for the beast, and would have played up a history of fire-fights and pointed out the old scratched notches of those who had died from bullets shot from this AK-47's magazines, but Herbie had been clear in his telling of the scale of the production line. Then a pause, and there must have been eye contact from Reuven to the bar and more sparkling water came and another beer with a decent head on it. Bad news would follow, but would be put with the reasonableness of a guy who knew he held the cards. There was no competition. It was a monopoly and Reuven owned it.

'If you had brought me, Dazzer, the weapon that had been in the bolt-hole with Saddam when the Americans pulled him up into the daylight, and if you had the rifle used in the assassination of the Pharaoh of the Egyptians, Sadat, by the lieutenant – Khalid Islambouli – then I would say to you, again in honesty, that I might manage a more decent return on the item. There is no celebrity attachment to what you bring to me.'

Just another rifle. The beer was good in this bar. Somewhere up at the counter, almost out of sight but able to watch, was Reuven's minder. He'd be jacketed, and his coat would hang loose to disguise the bulge of the Makharov pistol in a shoulder holster. Not that Dazzer was liable to make a scene and shout, maybe throw a punch because the fantasy of good money was now running in the drains. He'd pointed out the bloodstain that darkened the old wood of the stock, and the notches were now harder to distinguish and the place where the sliver had been was harder to see.

'So, and we should not waste the time of busy people such as yourself, such as myself, the best I can offer to you is one hundred American dollars . . . probably I make a loss on that. But we are old friends, men with understanding and men with a relationship . . . a hundred dollars. Will you refuse it, Dazzer, and then attempt to bring the weapon through the Customs investigators at your British airport of entry, and risk ten or fifteen years in a gaol, or take it? Which?'

Nothing to argue with. Not a seller's market, but a buyer's. He thought the rifle would end up in the arms trade equivalent of a car-boot sale. Not dissimilar from those his parents patronised most weekends in the hope of a bit of a bargain, but never finding anything of value. He looked for a last time at the outline of the weapon. It had been with him in his quarters for close on three months and he had played mind-games with where it had been, who had held it, what stories it had . . . he supposed it might as well, now, have been dumped in the dirt and a main battle tank run its tracks over it, squash it, obliterate it. Did it have a future? Not too sure. An ugly looking old thing, not the rifle that anyone – any more – would covet. He nodded acceptance.

'A good choice, a sensible choice. A hundred American dollars does not represent the true value of this rifle. I will be the loser, but will not regret having been honest with an old friend . . . and for you there is sufficient money to go to the bars in Akrotiri, even to Limassol, and you will find that a hundred American dollars goes far, quite far – not as far as buying a woman, but very quite far. A pleasure always to see you, Dazzer, and God speed you home.'

A single note was passed him. Reuven's face seemed to betray a sort of personal pain as if he had merely helped an old and distant friend, had forsworn all his normal commercial instincts. A bit of kindness . . . Dazzer slipped the note into his wallet . . . he would fly the next day, then in the evening would meet some of the guys who had missed on this tour of duty and they'd swap anecdotes and drink miserably. The morning after, Dazzer would be back at the agency that hired him out, and would try to seem spirited and keen and be looking for another mission back to Helmand and the fag-end of the campaign . . . The rifle? Bloody near already forgotten. Out of sight, on the bench, was the rustle of the paper and the wrapping being refastened, then Reuven flicked almost noiselessly with his fingers and his minder came close behind Dazzer, took the parcel and was gone. A last smile from Reuven, a dismissal. Just a piece of junk . . . Dazzer went out into the warm evening air . . . wondered where it would go, who would have it next. He had seen, the final glimpse of it, that the rear-sight was still at an extremity position, perfect for close quarters, almost hand to hand, where the killing grounds were: Battle Sight Zero. An old warrior's piece of kit, but with tales to tell – and no one wanting to hear them or to pay for them. He'd not get a woman for what he was paid, but the rifle would buy him sufficient beer and shorts to knock him into oblivion. Could have dumped it on the road where Father William had died for the trouble he had gone to . . . and sort of missed it.

Pegs had not slept again. She sat in the chair of her room. In the next room down the corridor was Gough. A part of the conspiracy of their relationship, not advertising the 'man and mistress' roles, she made it a point to get back to her room before dawn, get in the bed, rumple the sheets, make the pretence. She thought the time might come, sooner than later, when the brilliance of a spotlight would be aimed at her. Then, powerful forces would seek to show that her attention, and Gough's, had slipped, almost a dereliction. The substance for her gloom was the brief message passed to her via her mobile.

Not a bag of laughs at my end. Sorry and all that. I assume the transfer happens tomorrow, and we head off then if we are to make that ferry, that schedule. I am not inside her loop, don't know where she will collect. Don't know where she is right now, which is not helpful. I saw her in the square outside the hotel – not having a fag but in conversation with a young male, likely north African, and she went away on his scooter. Best you put me under surveillance, and with back-up close by, closer than the Golden Hour. Sleep tight.

More than a year of work put in, a successful bid for the quality resource of an Undercover, and it came to climax, and the target had gone walkabout. Just bloody depressing – a potential cluster-fuck. She had put off waking Gough, now did so. She wore the sort of pyjamas, thick and buttoned to the throat, which would have been respectable in a practising convent, went out, locked her door, knocked on his, waited. The building was quiet, had that night-hour emptiness. Inside, she sat on the end of his bed, let him blink out the tiredness in his eyes, told him and watched him sag, wince as if it were personal. They'd go down together, walk the plank, the sharks congregated underneath, dorsal fins breaking the surface.

She asked, grim, 'That club of yours, they take new members?'

'What club?'

'Where I said you were signed up, a founder member . . . because, Gough, I don't think we're good enough.'

'What's the club?'

'For God's sake, you old goat, what you lectured me on – the Maudlin Club, and I rubbished it. I'm ashamed. I fear for us.'

'We do our best.'

'Not enough – another day, another dollar. See what it chucks up. Dog shit or rose petals but I'll get my application off, Gough, to your club . . . See you.'

He and Tooth were off to bed late. Crab had been told they would rest in and take a bit of leisure on the patio if that bloody wind eased off.

He'd recognised the respect for his long-time friend that the young man had shown when offloaded from the fishing boat. Bloody near drowned rather than admit he'd failed in his job. Good for a senior man to have respect, not to be treated like filth on the uppers of his shoes . . . He'd look forward to the late morning exchange, money for hardware. Would get the old juices flowing, and only the start of the business plan which would make more juice, more money, and keep his hand in.

But he was a long time getting to sleep and the wind stayed fierce, and noisily shook the villa . . . He seemed to be on the pavement, face down, and his wrists were pinioned with plastic stays, and he heard the fucking gun cocked, and around him were screams, shouts, sirens, and the sobbing of those alive, or half dead. He yelled up at the cop for him not to shoot . . . not to do an execution as formal as those done in his youth on the Strangeways scaffold. 'Nothing to do with me. It was just business. I didn't know what . . .' A bit of an untruth, but the best he could do, and he closed his eyes and tried not to see the boot of the cop, or the tip of the barrel, and hear the scrape of the safety going off. '. . . I didn't know what the fucking thing would be used for. I just do business.'

Hard going to sleep that night. Harder to erase the sight of that drowned rat coming off the boat, up the pontoon, carrying the package in the plastic bag.

He pretended sleep.

She had left the room door unlocked, and he had too when he had gone down to use the reception desk phone – left his mobile clean. He lay on his side and saw through narrow lidded eyes that she came in on tiptoe. Floating across the room, soundless, she stripped and dumped the clothes where they had been before.

He wondered what he would be told . . . She came to the bed and eased in beside him. A grunt, a cough, seeming to come alive, and he started up. Her hand touched his shoulder, as if to calm him.

'You all right?' she murmured.

'I'm good, and you?'

'And me, but I could not sleep. I dressed, went out, walked a bit. Just me and the street cleaners, and they were setting out the fruit and vegetable stalls, just walked . . . I didn't disturb you?'

'Not at all . . .'

He thought she lied well. She was snuggled up close and her fingers worked on his chest. He thought she might, probably had, gained a taste for it, like making up for lost time . . . might have said the same of himself. But each were the other's plaything. He could have quizzed her as to where she had been, what she had seen, and might successfully have picked a hole in the lie, proven the untruth: no advantage gained. *I didn't disturb you? ... Not at all.* He had taken the opportunity, back in the room, listened in the quiet, then worked through her bag, found the money belt. Had unzipped it, had counted, found the value of what he was supposed to take to the ferry port and drive home. Big money ... Not anything else. He would have been more skilled than her in the art of covert searching, but he carried nothing that was remotely incriminating. The couple below had started again, getting value for their bed, and their springs sang.

'... and what's today's schedule?'

'Maybe a walk this morning, then my business, then we hit the road.'

'The business – in the city?'

'I'm collected and ...'

'I'll come with you.'

'Not necessary, and you don't have to.'

Their hands were lower, searching and moving with gentleness but increasing pace, and their breathing was faster.

'Not letting you out of my sight. Won't argue with you. I am with you. Too precious to me, Zed, to have you loose here – a difficult city. I am with you. Don't care what you're doing ... heard the old one? "Hear nothing, see nothing, know nothing". That's my promise. I will be there.'

She squirmed under him. Who led? Both did. The dawn was outside the curtained window. The other couple were quiet. Replacing the sounds of the bed springs were the preparations for the day's market, and the first scrapes of metal as the overnight shutters were lifted ... He had busted the rules of the house, SC&O10's, and he let the wonder of it happen, and did not know where he would be when he next slept, or where she would be.

14

He had showered first, flushed away the smells of the night, had dressed casually – not the previous day's clothes, left stubble on his face. Zed had taken her turn in the bathroom and he thought she scrubbed herself hard as if she too wanted to erase what had happened; or perhaps she always did, washed fiercely. He was not proud . . .

Had reason not to be proud. The psychologists who monitored them had a mantra about burn-out which was apparent when the invented legend palled, lost relevance, when the Undercover might cross over and take up the target's cause or criminality, or when the strain of living the lie became overwhelming. He preferred what an old instructor had told him, a woman of almost unique ugliness, never knew her name, and the stories of her verified successes were often rumoured; she had been with him at the start but he'd not seen her for months before being Phil, then acting out Norm, then Andy. She said that the danger, and the time to quit, was when the Undercover knew that he, or she, was 'running on empty'. Had ignored the evidence of the needle drifting down towards the red sector on the gauge, was on a long road, far from any garage marked on the satnav, had gone on too long . . . was, in effect, a danger to colleagues, a pushover to adversaries, was putting himself at risk and the great mass of citizens that should have been better protected. She said that it wasn't brave to hoodwink the team leaders and carry on with symptoms hidden, was not courageous to be in the field and refusing the inevitable . . . shelf-life, she'd said, was finite, might not be long: the Undercover would know it long before it became apparent. Dressed, ready to go, rucksack packed with the little he had brought, he sat on the bed, and thought some more. Thought where they might be, the people who had seemed – once – important to him.

They would not have been up yet, his mum and dad. There was a machine at his father's side of the bed that made their morning cup of tea. If their cat was still alive it would be marching over their duvet, unless it had been run over, or died from an ailment, might be another. There had been a photograph of him in their bedroom, but it might have been binned. Perhaps, in privacy, they wept at the manner of his going, some crap about 'important work and going under the radar and better that we lose sight of each other. I wouldn't do it if it didn't matter'. Some went home to their wives and kids too often, or to their parents, and the addresses were under the bad guys' surveillance, and ended for the innocents in a shambles of late-night evacuations, even new identities. He thought of them . . . thought of girls who he might have known better and had not dared to . . . thought of men, women, who were either hard cases in the narcotics distribution chains, or just hapless and not knowing another way of survival, or who believed in a cause with passion and were intelligent but could mete out violence. Where were they? Cell doors not yet opened on the landings. Banged up and watching breakfast TV, and remembering the shit face they had trusted and who had lived a lie amongst them . . . thought of a girl – soft skin, a defiant jaw, good hips and good breasts and a good brain – and wanting to kill, or help to kill, and was now towelling herself dry: he had kissed the skin and ridden the hips, and his finger had brushed her breasts. She would be a song bird in a small cage, and would spit if she remembered him. And thought of others in the Marines, in the classrooms, in the uniformed police, but all gone. It would all happen in the next several hours.

Usually, at the end, before he'd sidle off to the shadows, disappear, the bosses would give him a cuff on the back, or a brief hug, tell him, 'Well done, mate, you were fucking awesome. Done great, have a rest, then we'll have the next one lined up. Of course we will, because you're a star boy.'

She came out of the bathroom, had left her towel there. Walked past the window where the curtains were open, didn't seem to care – seemed bleak, like her soul was lost, and started to dress . . . And he thought of the pair who ran him. Probably decent people, bags under their eyes, and smacked with lack of sleep. Demands that they justify the budget, and that a file could be closed, and the next one jacked up on the screen. Never-ending, never finished . . . and saw the script on the TV sets that announced 'Breaking News' and later there would be the footage from mobile phones and the sound of the screams and perhaps the gunfire, and the people running with the gurneys to the ambulances bringing in the day's casualties at the Accident and Emergency entrances. They were Gough and Pegs, and would be somewhere outside the hotel door and would try to tail him, and him drop the message, and it was odds-on that he'd not see them again, have no call to and have no wish to. If he failed they failed, and there would not be a psycologist to offer up excuses for them: burn-out and running on empty. Just another day.

She'd pulled on her clothes. Then went back into the bathroom a last time and carried something but he did not see what it was. He would drive north to the channel port where the ferry was docked. They would not fuck that night. After the crossing he would take her wherever she told him, and she'd walk away with a package under her arm, last he'd see of her would be when she rounded a corner . . . wrong, next to last. He would be behind a screen in the court, she would be in a guarded dock . . . He would not sleep with her on the boat but would sit on the deck whether it rained, hailed, whether a gale blew. Out of the bathroom, and seemed thicker round the waist, and . . . Just another day, as easy or difficult as the rest of them. She zipped her bag, set it down beside his. He went round the room carefully and checked the floor, and the cupboard and under the bedside tables. He found the wrapping of one of the condoms, and pocketed it. They would leave nothing, no indication they had been there.

'Some breakfast?'

'Just something small.'

'And you'll tell me the plan, Zed, for the morning and the afternoon.'

'Yes, of course.'

He carried the bag and the rucksack down the stairs.

Hardly any breakfast for either of them.

He stood behind her, and Zeinab paid the bill. He came forward and said they wanted to walk a little on La Canebière before leaving, and asked if their bags could be lodged for an hour. Why not?

Another couple were behind her, and the woman coughed loudly as if to let her know, forcibly, that they needed to hurry. Could have had a room above them, or on the floor below them, and the man let her do the complaining and merely wheezed. Indifferently, they were thanked for their custom, wished a good day, and it was added – an afterthought – that the management looked forward to welcoming them again ... Zeinab had a reservation, made in London, for two single rooms, had exchanged them for a double, should have had a refund on the bill, had pointed to the sum required, but there was a shrug and she was eased sideways by the next check-out. And did not fight it ... it was what Scorpion, or might have been Krait, had said to her. Not to attract attention, not to be looked at, nor noticed ... She took the receipt, stepped away.

She gave it to Andy, was asked if she wanted it, shook her head. She led and he followed.

The early sunshine lit her face. She blinked, then focused. The knives and firearms in the shop window opposite gleamed at her. She was pushed by the flow of people going to, coming from, the open market, and thought how her mother would have been envious of the chance to buy fruit and vegetables of that quality, and how much better it was than Dewsbury's market, and ground her nails into the palms of her hand to block the thought. Her parents, spiritually, were gone from her life. She would go home again for a weekend – if the university kept her – or would have to move back if they did not, but she would no longer be the servant of their beliefs, ideals, all changed when she had been straddled on the pillion and gone to the home of the boy in love with the Kalashnikov assault rifle and when she had been over Andy, almost an idiot but caring for her, and helping him.

Opposite the hotel, across the width of the small square, were a couple – middle-aged and probably British – and the man had a map unfolded and pored over it, and they talked busily and the woman had an opened guidebook. He was half a pace behind her.

She said they had an hour. He seemed remote to her. Merely nodded acceptance. And herself? Uncertain, excited, wanting to share but unable. As if she wrestled with herself . . . arms flailing and hacking with her knees and biting and scratching, and the signs of it suppressed. But above all, superior to the uncertainty, was the excitement. Not about *religion* as taught in the mosques at home, not about the politics of victimhood as dripped from the TV screens after Westminster or Manchester or the bridge over the river in London. About the adrenaline rush of excitement – not about the denunciations of police chiefs and ministers, or even the stories of the deaths of her cousins. More about the worship of the rifle that the young man with the crippled arm had shown her, and his love for it, and his yearning to hold and fire it . . . to have that power. Hold that fucking power . . . an obscenity, and her mother would have near fainted and her father might have taken his belt to her . . . that power. They strolled, like neither of them had a care. Not the cause but the rifle entrapped her: she went willingly because the weapon had won her . . . Zeinab knew little, beyond the basics, of counter-surveillance techniques. She did not look behind her . . . and Andy's free hand held hers. They walked slowly and climbed the gentle hill and she looked in shop windows.

Abruptly, Andy asked her. 'Where is it?'

'Why do you need . . .?'

'I have to plan the route out . . . I'm not an idiot, Zed. What you do, I don't care. If it's illegal, not my problem. To me, you are fantastic, brilliant, incredible. I am privileged to know you. What do you come to Marseille for, what does anyone come to Marseille for? For weed, for nothing else. I have no difficulty with it. Obvious. We get it on board, and we go. Going fast, quitting the place, burning the rubber. It is in your hand and we are gone . . . okay?

That's good? Where do you meet the supplier? I tell you, Zed, I'm not an idiot, and you should trust me.'

She saw only sincerity. She looked into his face and watched the honesty in his eyes and had thought that afterwards, far away, there would be a place, a refuge, remote, and they might be together, safe and hidden – another day.

'I have to be at the Place de la Major, by the cathedral, beside Quai de la Tourette. I take delivery there.'

'And I'm not asking what you want . . . but I'm there, will watch over you. Trust me.'

She would, believed him. In a bookshop they saw a cat comfortably perched on second-hand volumes and the sunshine fell on its face which was calm, content, and without a trace of fear. They climbed and the street widened. And did not look back.

Karym did the tail . . .

He was captivated by her, amazed that she had come in the night to La Castellane, climbed the stairs of the block, visited him, seen his bedroom, showed interest in his collection of Kalashnikov books. Had held his stomach as he had ridden away to the north with her as his pillion, could still feel her shape against his back, and her softness, and remember the strength of her arms, the sharpness of her nails. Without the experience of the money satchel, and the Samson moment, he would not have dared anything as rash as taking her – a stranger, an outsider – to his home. He was a changed man . . .

. . . took the far side of La Canebière and flitted between doorways, lingered when they did. It was what his brother had told him to do. Hamid had returned in the night to the project, had gone to his own apartment where his own girl was. Had called for Karym, kid brother, to come at dawn. Had boasted of his new relationship with the great man, with Tooth. Had told him – like it was a hero's story, not an imbecile's – of going into the water, catching a packet before it sank, had been 35 minutes, at least, in the water, had been congratulated. Then had been taken to a hotel on the south side, and a room provided while he showered, cleaning the cold and the seawater off him, and his clothes returned washed and dried and ironed. The driver, Tooth's, had then driven him back to the quayside and he had ridden away on his bike, and had known his future was secured.

Two hours in his own bed for Karym, and no sleep, just tossing with the memory of her feel against his back and her touch of his stomach, and recalling what he had said of the rifle, and her understanding that he was an expert. What to tell her? Could be how the army of North Vietnam had out-gunned the Americans, their Marines who had the M16, could tell her that, and believed she would be fascinated, interested . . . if they had the time together.

He followed. Any teenager from La Castellane knew how to look for a tail following, and protecting the girl and her friend. He had not seen one, but it was what his brother had ordered him to do, watch for it. He saw shoppers, saw troops in a patrol of four, saw police in a squad car, saw a tourist couple who seemed continuously to argue over their map, saw no tail.

She had agreed to what he suggested.

His conclusion: her courage was failing her . . . easy enough to be with other fanatics and close to what was familiar and to play the good calm kid, and with a basket load of necessary resolve. Their sex would by now be out of the window, back in history . . . It was becoming real, and far from what she knew, and cash was invested in her. Her face had gone sombre. Clear in his mind . . . her brief's accusation of entrapment, and him under oath in the box. Denial. Who to believe? Her flickering eyes and wavering gaze and bowed head in the dock, and his straight ahead look into the jury's eyes. Her blood-lust against his courage. A no-brainer for the judge when he summed up the case . . . He would lie better than she did. A piece of cake – but not proud of it, seldom harboured pride . . . And almost, put vulgar, wet herself, he reckoned, when she'd been far beyond any horizon on La Canebière, lost in thought and had failed to shift out of the path of another four squaddie patrol. Pretty near been spiked by the rifle barrel. Her eyes would have focused on the soldier, the weapon, the webbing and grenades and the flak-jacket: he had simply assumed she'd step aside. She had deep lines on her forehead: he read them as acute anxiety. Held tight to her hand.

And he made her laugh. Gave her arm a jerk. He pointed across the tram tracks to a narrow central park that divided the traffic lanes. The sun was pretty on the trees, tables and chairs were outside cafés, and there was a bandstand for the summer season, and it looked good . . . looked better with the giant shapes of a giraffe and whatever a new-born one was called. They were double life-size at least, had a myriad of meaningless lines painted on the smooth plastic of the bodywork, and it seemed like they had just wandered in off one of the side streets, or out of a bank, or been in a bar, in a café: that's what he said to her. For a moment she had thought him serious, then had burst out laughing. He supposed most of the kids, in the countdown to a suicide attack and wearing the vest, or any of them who drove the kid to the drop-off point and watched him walk away, first paces to Paradise, or who were just the lowest form of foot soldier, would have felt the stress before playing their part. She held tight to him, might have stumbled if he had not been there, then regained composure. He saw them, back on the pavement, bickering, and him with the map and her with the guidebook. Seemed to come steadily closer. It was a good move and he respected it.

The man said, 'Excuse me – you speak English? Please, if you speak English . . .'

He replied, 'I do and am. How can I help?'

And Detective Chief Inspector, Gough, came close to him. He said in a firm voice, 'Bit lost, and the boss over there seems to think we're in one place, and I've a different view on it. Have a look at our map, please.'

Well choreographed. The civilian analyst, Pegs, had parked herself on a bench a few yards away, had then addressed a remark at Zed, something anodyne, but she responded and gave Gough and him space . . . only for a few seconds and not to be laboured. Something like, 'Where will we need to get the Metro to . . .'

The voice tailed. Andy Knight, who he was that week, day, hour, jabbed with his finger on the map and found the Cathedral de la Major down by the waterside, and said softly that the relevant place was Place de la Major and Esplanade de Tourette. Said it would be there in an hour. The pick-up. Would it be open, the big voice boomed, but Andy apologised, did not know, called her and started to walk away. She came to him.

'Where were they looking for?

'Some cathedral.'

'You showed him, knew where it was?'

'They'd been arguing, and there are two cathedrals.'

They walked on. He thought it a cleverly done brush contact, as it had to be, and Gough had done the switch in voice level correctly. Had to have been clever. The boy was easy to recognise. The arm, maybe a polio or maybe botched surgical intervention after a break, hung awkwardly, and it was easy to recognise his weight and shape and the same clothing as the night before under a light in the square below the hotel window. At the top of the hill was a jewellers, and he led her inside, and murmured close to her ear.

'I don't know where you're leading me, Zed, don't want to know. I still say it, you are more special than anyone I have been with before . . .' Not saying much because that field was bloody near empty, but the dose was well poured and had a high sincerity content. And he needed her trust, and her confidence. '. . . Won't take a refusal. Something to remember Marseille by.'

It was 150 euros, a thin gold bracelet of fine links, simple and understated and a private type of gift: it would sail through on his expenses at the end of the assignment. Inside, the manager had seen the pair of them and had tried to lever Zed over towards the windows where the rings were. He paid, fastened it on her wrist, and the light lit the gold chain. And the pendant on her chest shone, markers of his deceit. They went out, and crossed the road and she laughed again at the sign of the monster giraffe and the little one . . . in his mind was the battering of what seemed a drum beat. Something inevitable but he did not know what.

His wife was in uniform, that of the Municipal Police, assigned that day to an area of Marseille that was affluent, for the smart crowd from the blocks lining the Avenue du Prado. She had put on her pistol, and her belt, from which was slung the kit – cuffs, canisters of gas, a baton – and asked him, from the door of the apartment, the familiar question.

'Are you home for supper tonight?'

'Don't know, don't see why not.'

'Anything special – I am just going to schools. Talk about drugs. You?'

'Planning – a buffoon from Paris is coming. A protection screen. We're talking about it.'

'Those people from England, did they . . .?'

'No idea, maybe they went home.'

He was told what to take out of the freezer so that it would have defrosted for their dinner, together or separately. She closed the door after her. He'd have five minutes more with the newspaper, then follow her out, go to his meeting. An interesting day or a dull one. 'Samson', the executioner, had no preference.

'You know something?'

'I know plenty.'

'Heh, you mess with me, Tooth . . . My difficulty, I think more of the past than the future. I am comfortable in the past, but the future confuses me.'

'I tell you, Crab. You talk shit.'

'My past is good. I am a success, respected. I have a big house, men duck their heads to me. I have around me what could be called "the best police force that money can buy", you like that. That's good, yes? As you have, Tooth . . . To get there, some men lost their lives, others have a worse limp than me . . . But, what happens next is a concern to me. What's round the corner.'

They were on the patio. The wind had shifted, coming now more from the south, and the rugs over their knees were already layered with the fine sand that blew in from the Sahara deserts. Tooth's man had brought coffee for them, and biscuits.

'It is big shit that you talk, Crab – did you sleep poorly?'

'A bad sleep, and a bad dream.'

'Do I have to hear why? You playing at a penitent in a confessional?'

'No. The dream is personal. I . . .'

There was shipping on the horizon, heavy enough to ride the storm, and other craft that went in and out of the docks, but precious few fishing boats. He understood the fear that the French gangster, his friend, created. Could see why the Arab had bloody near drowned rather than face him and cough up a story of failure. A hard man, a hard face, and the tinted glasses masked nothing. Himself, he had, mildly put, lost the appetite for it since the dream.

'You have cold feet, Crab. My old friend of many years, a gang boss thought to be fearless, ruthless, and now old and frightened. It is hard to understand you – what was the dream?'

'Personal, mine alone.'

'What was the fucking dream, Crab?'

'I shouldn't have spoken, forget it.'

'I dream sometimes, my old friend, of the first time I killed a man and the first time I had a girl. I tell you, they are not bad dreams. Killed many and screwed many, and none is a nightmare. Spit it, Crab.'

'About what happens . . .'

'A riddle,' he mimicked. 'You say "what happens". It's monkey talk. It means?'

'My problem. I started it. Knew what I was doing, and called you, and you did the graft, put it in place.'

'Good to hear from a valued friend. Of course I helped. You asked and I answered. Tell me – "what happens" – in plain talk.'

'They don't have weapons like that, not where it's going. Not where a flood of them are ending up. It is mayhem, it's death, pain. An automatic rifle takes killing to a different level. Way up. It is something bad, what the dream said.'

Almost a sneer, like their mutual love affair was failing. 'You should take a pill, Crab, and then sleep without a dream.'

'It was just a dream – sorry, Tooth, rude of me – only a dream. First time I killed a guy and first girl I shagged . . . The guy was a dealer, didn't want to clear a debt. He screamed, God, like – I'm told – pigs in an abattoir, a hell of a noise, so much blood. He went into concrete, foundations of new houses. The girl was good, both of us fourteen. I reckon she liked my pants, City – Manchester City pants – better than what was inside them, she said, cheeky little bitch. I've not had many that were better, and she was the first.'

'You all right now? Don't like a friend to be unsure, an old friend.'

'I'm good now, thanks.'

'Don't want an old friend going weak.' Not spoken like a threat, gently said.

'Have to keep telling myself "I just do business", keep saying it. Can we talk about something else, Tooth?'

'Like the second killing or the third, like the second girl or the fourth, fifth, sixth . . .?'

Two hands met, veined and calloused, the stains of sun damage blotching the skin, but each strong, fearsome. And they were laughing. Tooth told him when they would leave to do the bit of 'business'. Crab wanted the exchange done, the transfer completed, himself out of this fucking place. Should never have come, knew it, and kept on laughing because that was expected of him. Two old friends, raddled with age, each clutching the other's hand, and laughing because that might kill his dream. And home by that evening and back where he was safe.

August 2017

The mother of Nico Efthyvoulu had given him the money to buy it. She had gone into her widow's bedroom after he had told her of his chance to purchase a small stake in a new bar that would open near the train station. Tourists visiting Athens, going to the ruins, walking among the Acropolis stones, would never be close, but he had told his mother that there would be good local trade. She had gone to her tin, kept under the bed, long emptied of sweet-tasting biscuits, and returned to him, in the kitchen, with the bank notes. He had smiled, told her it would be a fine investment, promised the money would be returned when profit showed. It was a month short of a year since Nico had been released from the young offenders' institution. His mother was anxious to the point of desperation, that the boy, 21 years old and with gelled hair and smart clothing from the charity stall at the end of their street, should have a legitimate focus in his life.

Hot, almost to stifling point, and near to midday, and the sun scorching the streets, he wore a long coat that was suitable for when the snow came. He watched the bank and steeled himself. He needed the length of the coat to conceal the weapon he had purchased from a man in the quarter of the city behind the harbour . . . and the bastard had tried to screw him. The agreement was for 425 American dollars, cash. He had already lost out on the exchange rate, and then the bastard had insisted that the cost of the rifle would now be $500. What had been promised, what they had shaken hands on – $425 in a wad of old and untraceable notes – was left on the table. Gone from the table was the AK-47 and the loaded magazines that went with the sale . . . Much of that money would be needed for the new dentures required by the bastard, and perhaps some would go to the costs of rewiring his broken chin. Nico had never been gentle, not as a child and not now as an adult, when crossed.

The bank was quiet and had few customers at that time of day. It was a good neighbourhood, and most of the residents would have survived, not with anything to spare, the collapse of the economy. They would have done their banking when the place opened, when it was cool, and they took out their toy dogs. He sweated because of the thickness of the coat.

All that Nico Efthyvoulu had been able to buy was an old weapon. He had been assured, before rearranging the bastard's face that it might have been manufactured years before, proven by the serial number – many numbers but finishing with 16751 – but its reliability was guaranteed. He had gone into the high wilderness north of the E75 ring road, on a foul day when few walkers would have ventured out, had found a discarded can, had fired two shots it. The first had missed but the stone face behind it had shattered. The second had pitched the can over. A good hit, and two were enough to satisfy him. The mess of scratches and gouges on the wood stock were confusing because he did not know the cause of them, or the reason they were there. Until this morning he had kept the weapon in a bedroom cupboard, at the back, the door locked.

He straightened. Some kids, ten years or so younger than himself, were playing football in the centre of the square. He passed them. At the entrance to the bank, he paused, then cranked the lever that controlled the shot selection, went to 'single', took a deep breath and felt the weakness in his knees and the shake in his hands, and hoped his voice could muster authority. He pulled up the knotted dark handkerchief around his neck until it covered the lower half of his face. The doors swung open in front of him.

The kids abandoned the football and watched, waited, eyes popping, mouths gaping.

Inside, in the cool, there was only one other customer, in earnest discussion with a cashier on the far side of a high screen, older with thin grey hair, and a suit but no tie. A girl was counting money at an open till beside her colleague. He tried to shout, sound commanding, and the counter girl looked at him, seemed bewildered, like he was part of a game show on the TV, Saturday night. But, she hit the alarm button, might have been below her counter, might have been a button on the floor. It shocked him, and his reaction was to fire at her. About as dumb as he could get, and there was as yet no cash offered him, stacked notes on the counter and bound in wads with elastic bands. The bell screamed in his ears. He had not hit her because the glass deflected the bullet up over her shoulder and into the wall behind. It should, perhaps, have been newly made glass that was proof against even a high velocity round, but the cut-backs around all sectors of Greece's wrecked economy dictated the glass was sub-standard, there for show and image. He yelled at her again, but had picked out a feisty one. Behind the glass with the spider's web of lines and distortions, she bawled back at him. He fired again, again, each time releasing the trigger and then squeezing another time on it. He had not looked sideways until he made out the other customer's yell for him to chuck it down. Had he heard that . . .?

And turned, and looked into the face. The lower part of the face was almost hidden by the service pistol the man held, arms extended, eyes above the V and the needle sights. It registered. The man yelled his identification, a police officer. Both fired. The pistol was aimed and the rifle was at the hip and loosely pointed in the direction of the idiot, the fool who had had no call to intervene. Nico Efthyvoulu could have wept that it was his luck, his crass fortune, to try to rob a small-time bank, and find himself standing beside a cop. The stock, scarred and marked and ugly, cannoned back and into his hip and spun him, and the fierce, searing pain hit him in the back. He heard the girl behind the counter scream, shrill and hysterical, and heard the impact as the pistol clattered from a loose hand and hit the floor. The man who'd held it sagged at the knees and the first of his blood was falling on the pistol. Fucked up, all fucked up, and the pain ran in rivers down his back.

He turned, staggered, towards the door. As if for a valued customer, the door automatically opened and the warmth of the street buffeted his face. He lurched through, doubted he would get any further. It had killed him, the rifle had destroyed him, and he had lied to his mother to pay for it. He lurched to the bottom step and the kids were in a line on the far side of the street. The pain had lessened in his back and now there was numbness, and weakness. He would not get down the street, would not reach his home in the little wretched Citroen, all he could afford . . . the rifle slipped from his hand. Nothing left for him . . . He saw the kids. They came across the street. In the distance was a siren, faint but coming clearer. He thought the kids came to help him. Wrong again.

The boldest of them scooped up the rifle. They ran. They whooped in excitement, then scampered as if for their lives. They went round the corner, and his eyes misted. If he had had the strength, before the weapon had fallen from his grip on the steps, he would have taken it by the barrel, two hands beyond the curved magazine, and swung it high above his head and smashed it down on the imitation marble steps at the bank's entrance. Would have battered it until the fucking thing broke . . . but Nico Efthyvoulu did not have the strength, saw little, and heard only vaguely, and there was blood in his mouth.

Hamid had lectured his brother. Where to be and when.

He had used his girl's hair-drier to get some of the moisture off the packet. A lousy night was behind him, little sleep, nightmares of drowning, trying to read the big man's remarks, repeated endlessly, and wondering whether he had secured an alliance . . . The package seemed insignificant for the trouble taken, but not for him to query. Funny thing, and not yet settled . . . plenty of talk about what he might do in the following months, what might be put in his path, and the influence that Tooth's reputation carried, and good contracts . . . Not agreed was what his payment would be, and when the big bucks would begin to roll his way. Had not drawn the lines before, joined up the flag points. Had trusted. No figures to chew on. All about the future, what *might* happen. Options? Could hardly write it all down, then threaten to reveal all to the guys in L'Évêché because the chance was high that Tooth owned half of them, would be told, would send some boys out either to cut him up with half of a Kalashnikov magazine or – worse – put him in a car, do a barbecue on him. Did not know an option. A fast thought: easy to run a small-time distribution and sales business out of a stairwell at the bottom floor of Block K, difficult to run with a man such as Tooth, but too late to be thinking it now. Another thing to consider, Tooth had never touched the package, did not open it, examine it . . . and the fisherman might have been a nephew or might have been in obligation. Hamid thought he was out on a branch, his weight starting to bend it, make it whine and creak. He used tape to fasten the package against his chest and underneath his heavy leather jacket, and he'd wear his biker's helmet with the dark visor.

It would take a long time for him to forget the feeling of agony in his lungs as the air disappeared and the pressure grew, while he had scrabbled to get a grip on the package – and he had not been paid, was on a promise. And his brother had brought a girl, a small-bit courier, to the apartment where he lived with their sister, and said he had talked to her about the history and power, and effectiveness of the AK-47 weapon, the Klash, and been talked about . . . What a fucking fool, would need some discipline and some sorting . . . Much on Hamid's mind as he came out of the project on his Ducati 821 Monster, and took the Boulevard Henri Barnier down towards the main drag that led to the city centre . . . and why they were doing the business in the open, not in the recesses of a café he did not know, no bastard had told him.

He might ask about money, might just, when he was there, had Tooth close to him. Might . . . Felt the package hard against his chest.

Pegs said, 'We're not going to get close again.'

Gough said, 'Little chummy is like a shadow nailed to them.'

'Have to go on what we have.'

'Anything else and we show out – we'll seem like the unwanted bloody relative who keeps pressing for invitations.'

'I'll do it.'

They had exhausted the tourist bit. No way was there justification in again approaching the 'love bird' pair who had and started to come down the hill of La Canobiere, and Pegs had spotted the flash on the Tango's wrist, gold on pale tinted skin, when the pair had come out of the jeweller's door. 'Gone native, definite, and humped her all night', Pegs had said. 'The loose cannon, difficult and dangerous to rein in, and the little guy is the tail to verify they are clean. Can't go near him,' Gough had said. She had her mobile out, and he was back studying the map, and the couple were 150 yards behind, but coming on briskly. She dialled the number given her and punched out the text, sent it. It was about back-up, what their regulations listed as a duty of care. She shrugged, done.

Gough said, 'Then best that we go find ringside seats.'

The Major's phone fidgeted.

Never one to give deference to authority, Samson reached across, took the phone, checked the message. His boss was on his feet at a lectern at the front of the briefing room, using a stick to highlight the proposed route the Paris visitor might take, and where there were interfaces of potential danger . . . He had, himself, been on duty on the morning that a police chief in the city had done a reconnoitre around the roads and locations that the Prime Minister of France, then Manuel Valls – February 2015 – would travel on in the afternoon. Included in the itinerary was the La Castellane project, where he'd visit a centre for ill-educated potential juvenile offenders, on to which money had cascaded. As the police chief's cavalcade had approached the housing estate, a minimum of six Kalashnikov rifles had opened fire . . . the message sent, 'Don't fuck with us' or 'Strangers not welcome'. Done with a directness . . . they had gone in at midday with overwhelming force, and in the afternoon the Prime Minister had been rushed from one handshake session to another. Then the circus in the afternoon had pulled out, and the place had sunk back to its obscurity, and to its usual trading. It was a lesson, and one learned . . . He was in full flow.

The marksman stood. His chair scraped. He held up a single finger. There was a growled ripple of annoyance that a uniformed man of low rank in the GIPN should interrupt an important meeting. The single finger told his superior, the Major, that he should wrap up in one minute. He did.

Samson said, 'The English have bleated for help.'

The Major said, 'Then they shall have it, perhaps with a lullaby sung by a nanny.'

He was told where the meeting place would be.

In the car, powering away to the armoury where his gear was, Samson remarked, 'Open air, wide spaces, well chosen ground. Many approach routes and many exits by vehicle or on foot. Easy visibility and the chance to identify a reaction force. A location I respect, might have chosen it.'

The Major said, 'And I cannot call up a bus load of your colleagues and hope for a degree of covert observation. But, I had exhausted even my own interest, so you have my gratitude for your intervention.'

They headed for the armoury. Not to have gone there would have been dereliction. Without a rifle, Samson was the same as the great strong man of the Bible after his head of hair had been cropped, or after the famed executioner had lost the support of his *tricoteuse*. Small arms were of no importance to him. They went fast but could not use the siren to clear their way, only the flashing lights.

'What do you feel, Major?'

'I feel for those English. It has seemed too simple, without crisis. I think they may not have recognised where they are . . . they will learn.'

'I have to believe, Zed, that I will come out of this in good order. You understand, I do this for you.'

She might not have heard him. Her eyes roved round her. She stood and he was at the wheel of the VW. His mind was straightened, the dilemma answered. He could see the shape of her, and the wind tugging at the cleanness of her hair, and the clothing that hid little of her, and the defiance of her chin and boldness of her eyes: knew what he would do. She spotted the boy.

The boy came on an old scooter. He saw it more clearly in the bright sunlight than in the poorly lit square, past midnight. Not the transport of any person of importance, no status about the Peugeot runabout. A kid's toy . . . and he wondered how far beyond her depth as a sympathiser with the cause, a *jihadi* courier, she now was. The kid seemed to ogle her, like she was a trophy. Not a social worker, Andy Knight – who he was that day – shut his mind to her problems, and to the sight of her. The kid came towards her, running the bike slower, letting the engine idle under him, and pointed to the pillion.

Again he shouted, 'You stay with me, Zed. With me.'

The sun caught the bracelet of gold chain that he had bought her an hour before. He would have sworn that she would have obeyed him, muttered an explanation to the kid, walked back to the car. Wrong . . . she smiled at him. She gave him the wide rare smile, one saved for the grand occasions, the one that had seduced him, and beckoned with her finger, and her leg was lifted, and was swung. She was on the pillion. The Peugeot pulled away.

She played with him. He could see that her arms were round the kid's waist and already her fingers moved on the thin fabric of his T-shirt. His cheap market-stall anorak flew as he accelerated and her head was on his shoulder and her chest hard against his back. Traffic flowed around them and fumes zapped from the exhaust.

He followed as best he could. He thought she teased him Could not lose him, do without him: he was her ride home, but she mocked him. Twice she turned to check he was still in sight, and then had spoken to the kid, and the little beggar had pulled away sharply from lights, and let the exhaust trail out behind. He could not lose her, and followed . . . a good game, but not a game that would play far. Down to the end of La Canebière, and a hard turn to his right, and he broke across the traffic flow and drivers had to brake, hit horns and swore ferociously.

He followed, did not yet know how and where it would end.

15

A dangerous, white-knuckle drive. Before signing up for SC&O10, he had been on speed courses, up to 130mph, sometimes faster. It had been intended that a man 'behind the lines' would be able to wriggle from trouble when it seemed about to surround him, break an umbilical. Harder to follow a stuttering scooter that weaved through three lanes of traffic. He could stay back, or risk losing the kid and Zed. He'd sensed she revelled in this new atmosphere of a heady freedom, and he, himself, was responsible. Had loved her, flattered her, and she seemed to him to walk taller, high on the water, more confident than he'd ever seen her. Like an action film, a chase, what the squaddies watched on daytime TV, and he lost them twice and regained them twice. He drove well – needed to tell himself that he drove well because no one else was around to speak up for him. They came to a tunnel entrance and he was boxed on the inside, and three lanes had become two, and he was blocked from moving into the outside and passing the dawdlers. If he lost her, then . . . Traffic soared past him on the faster lane. They spilled out from the tunnel.

He burst from the darkness, blinking in the sudden power of the sunshine, and could see each speck on the windscreen, then the traffic filtered. He'd chosen the wrong lane and had to barge back into the slow flow. The Peugeot was parked across the pavement, with other bikes and small scooters. He went on past it, had no option because a tanker was up close behind him. She had untangled herself from holding the kid round the waist, and he saw her laugh and the smile came and for a moment the kid had hold of her arm. She took it away from him, not snatched it, but as a gentle rebuke, like she was telling him there was business in hand.

The mirror was his friend. There was one parking space and he realised another car was behind him and was laying claims for the bay . . . and a finger was up and the bellowing was directed at him, first muffled and through the glass, then louder when the window was lowered. If he needed it he should not back off. The usual trick, one of the first they had been taught. He fished his wallet out of his hip pocket, held it up, like it contained ID. It did not. Exhaustion came over him now, hit him in waves. Not her, she seemed fit, well flushed, rather lovely. She looked round for him, and the kid seemed starstruck. It was Andy Knight's work: he had transformed her personality, given it room to breathe. The guy in the car gave up, must have thought he faced an investigator, casual clothing not washed or ironed, unshaven and a beaten-up car: the appearance of a cop, plain clothes.

Always the crisis came on quick. He was trapped now and would sweat it out, no choice. Could not be closer to her . . . to the right was a cathedral. In the Marines, in the UK police, and in the SC&O10 gang, he had had no requirement for any form of church architecture, ancient or modern. He did not know the age or the style of this one. It was huge, but one side of it had problems, scaffolding scrambling up the stonework. Further round the bay was a dock area where a warship was tied up, then a stretch of sea that led away from the old harbour. There were islands out in the bay beyond an esplanade and a plaza which was scattered with concrete benches. Next along was an historic castle and he didn't know its name or its date, or care. Then a café and restaurant doors and a big gym. He assumed it was where she had directed him. He locked the car, walked to a low wall and sat astride it, the car behind him but close enough.

It was his intention they'd get the hell out. Hoped she'd shift herself, be on the road, have taken the fast run for the autoroute and north . . . and wondered how big the package would be, what she was buying. He didn't think he stood out, reckoned he blended well.

She turned, scanned for him, saw him – was learning, did not wave at him.

Pegs was dragging him. Gough slowed her. She said he was a fucking disgrace. He said that it was one of the finest cathedrals he had ever had the pleasure to be in, awesome carving, space and beauty that were humbling.

'You could have screwed the whole thing, messing about in there.'

'You see one of those places, dear lady, once in a bloody lifetime, and four minutes and free entry are worth confronting your impatience. If you did not know, it is near Gothic, that's the design, parts of it are nine centuries old, and the cupola is . . .'

She snapped across him, 'And we were bloody nearly late this morning because of your insistence – don't think I'll protect you if the inquest heats up. And another thing . . .'

'Socks smelling again, are they? What else in this litany of recrimination?'

'We came from our hotel. He'd told us when to be there, but you insisted we were late.'

'For a damn good reason. What did I want, half a minute to be there, to soak it, have that experience. For God's sake it was Napoleon Bonaparte's lodging house we were in front of. Is that not reputable history, where he lived, a colonel in artillery, the great man, here and standing in that window which was above us? Am I not allowed that? God's truth, Pegs, you can be a Grade A nagger . . . I doubt I'll ever be back here. He could have been there, looking out, pondering the changes he'd inflict on Europe . . . and the cathedral is astonishing, a triumph of architecture. Can you not see . . .?'

'Someone has to look after you, just that I drew the chopped-off straw.'

He looked at her. He frowned and the pseudo load of anger slipped from his face. 'Thank you, appreciated. Move on.'

They sat in front of a café, and the wind was full on them, and she might start soon to shiver. They'd a poor view of the sea and the island out in the bay with the big castle on it, and more history and more romance he told her, where Dumas incarcerated the Count of Monte Cristo, but had a seriously good view of the open space in front of them.

'Do you have her?'

'I have.'

They were in deep shadow from an awning above the café table, would be hard to see, harder to identify. He wondered where those bloody laconic local police were. She did a snapshot photo of her and Gough on her mobile, sent it to them. Sat low in their seats, just another elderly couple. Looked left and saw their man, sitting on a wall and trailing his feet, a picture of bored innocence, and looked across the square and had a fine view of the girl, and the Arab kid with her. He thought it was slotting well, dropping into place.

He asked, 'If you had to choose, Pegs, either to walk the nave in the cathedral or look up the wall where Napoleon was, and at his window, which would you take?'

She said, fondness writ large, 'For fuck's sake, Gough, shut up. It's where we either break open the fizzy stuff, or a year's work and resources go under. And soon.'

They were both locked on the girl, Zeinab something, the Tango, the Rag and Bone target, were in a good place, the best seats.

Zeinab stepped out and Karym loped beside her.

Cafés and bars and shopping outlets were on two sides of the plaza, and it was dominated by the cathedral – what Krait would have called a Crusader place, what Scorpion would have called a *Khaffur* place. On a third side was the sea, on the fourth was the great fortress, and it would have been a defence against the *jihadis* of that day, centuries before . . . It was about commitment, why she walked tall, with a good stride, enough for the boy to need to hurry to keep alongside her.

He said, 'What I learn of you, you have interest in the Klash. I can tell you everything you need to know.'

More than she needed to know, left unsaid. Had done nothing in her short life to warrant fame, to have her name spoken on the radio, to have her home identified and neighbours and strangers gathering outside it because she had lived there. Perhaps had reached the stage, and recognised it, where she craved attention, wanted the soft-focus pictures of herself with the weapon in silhouette. Not in love with the Book, had never been a good student, was not one of the kids in classrooms whose heads moved in metronomic rhythm as they recited. Wanted fame as the skinny models had; with the weapon she would have found a catwalk, and flashbulbs. And fighters in the shrinking defended areas of Syria, where her cousins had been, in the last ghetto, the last block of broken buildings, would hear on texts, news bulletins on their phones as the batteries faded, of what she had done. Would know they were not alone . . . And the kid talked.

'And can tell you that US troops loathed their M-16 rifle in their Vietnam War. Too many times, in wet heat and in mud and with heavy rain, it jammed, could not fire and was useless but the AK of the North Vietnamese was superior. Senior officers were told but ignored it. It was a scandal. It is good that you are interested.'

The boy touched her hand when he spoke, for emphasis, and perhaps as a small show of nervous admiration – or attraction.

'And the Americans fighting in the Iraqi city of Fallujah preferred to take a dead *jihadi's* AK, his Klash, rather than have their own more complicated rifle. They want to go "spray and pray" which is ideal with the Russian rifle but that is not what the M-16 is made for. Very interesting, yes? The AK has killed more soldiers, more civilians, than any weapon in the history of small arms. I am pleased so much that you are interested.'

They were in the centre of the square. He had stopped to sit on a concrete bench. The wind blistered her. They would have seemed another boy, another girl. She hitched up her coat and her hands were under it, and then she loosened her belt and let her jeans drop two, three, inches at the waist, and wriggled and manoeuvred her hands. She pulled the money belt clear. Then dragged up her jeans and fastened the belt, pushed down the hem of her coat, and sat beside him. She did not know from where, but assumed she was now watched, every motion and movement.

The boy said cheerfully, 'When you go to war and have a Kalash then you are invincible. You understand? You believe you are supreme. You cannot be defeated, it is the citizen's rifle . . .'

She opened the belt's pouch and stared down at the close-packed bank notes. To her, the girl from Savile Town, living on a meagre allowance from a state grant, it was the greatest sum of money she had ever seen. When she went to a cash machine it was exceptional for her to take out more than twenty pounds. She put her hand on his, as if to silence him, and smiled sweetly.

Karym thought her eyes quite beautiful. He had been about to begin telling her of Mikhail Kalashnikov's life, how it was that the man credited with the rifle's design had achieved such prominence, and . . . he stared at her. When she had lifted her clothing he had seen her skin. To win that smile there was nothing he would refuse, and his chin shook, and he waited to be told what was wanted of him.

'I need your experience.'

'Of course.'

'Your knowledge.'

'If I can answer.'

'You have Kalashnikov rifles in that estate, where you took me?'

'In that project, in all the projects, there are Kalash rifles.'

'Old ones and new ones?'

'Quite old, quite new – from Russia and from Libya and from Serbia, from Iraq, from China – nearly they are the same. Yes?'

'You could buy one here, "quite old, quite new", you could?'

He shivered. Even in the bright sunshine the wind was keen, off the sea, and cut the thin clothing he wore. He snivelled, had no handkerchief. Sniffled again, and shivered, but had no handkerchief to clean his nose.

'I could, if my brother agreed.'

'If your brother refused such permission?'

'I would not have it – you have to understand that my brother is a noted man. We have a discipline. If my brother agrees, then anything is possible.'

'I understand. What would be the price of a rifle, not old and not new?'

'It could be to make an alliance and then very cheap. It could be a quick deal, or a weapon with a history which an owner needs to get clear from. Could have come from Serbia which is more expensive, could have come with cocaine from the Spanish ports and driven here.'

'What is the price?'

'An average . . .'

He looked at the clouds hurrying across the sky, and the white crests on the waves around the islands, and the spray on the rocks, and he shrugged and his hands gestured the difficulty of answering a question with so many parts of it uncertain.

'. . . Your estimate?'

'Three hundred euro. That would be top, without ammunition. For the settling of a debt, my brother would accept three hundred.'

'Only three hundred, not more?'

He remembered the denomination of the notes in the belt. They would buy the delivery of a small parcel in order to test the security of the route and for a down payment on a second, larger, delivery, what his brother had told him, and had chuckled. Her breath caught in her throat, and her fingers clenched as if anger started to burn . . . She would have thought . . . All crooks. Thieves and liars. Deceivers and dishonourable . . . She and her people were ripped off, conned, asked to hand over double or treble what the merchandise was worth, and took no risk, but cheated. But, nothing she could do. The deal had been agreed far away, by Tooth and other men of importance. Her cheeks had flushed. Which made her prettier, and she snorted.

Karym snivelled again. She took a paper handkerchief from her bag, passed it to him. He filled it noisily, and stood and went to the next bench where there was a rubbish bin where a wasp was circling, and looked around. Karym saw Tooth and another man, also old, and a hundred metres away and out of the wind and pretending to read newspapers, and saw his brother and gave no sign of recognition, and saw the boy who drove her, who sat on a wall and gazed at the sea and had the wind full on his face, and he waited for a signal. It was business. If she did not understand 'business' then she was an innocent. Any man or woman who was an innocent in 'business', would fail: in the project, to be an 'innocent' was to be at risk. Quiet had fallen. Some kids were listlessly riding skateboards, and others played football, tried to manage the back hammer kick, but without enthusiasm. He saw his brother go between two café parasols and was lit by the sun.

Hamid sweated.

Must keep his coat buttoned, must keep the package hidden.

The procedure demanded by the old man, with the villa on the headland and still clinging to power, was against all Hamid's instincts. Himself . . . a café with the blinds drawn and a back room, and the customer at the same disadvantage as any purchaser of hashish who came to La Castellane. And deployed around the café would have been a score of his kids, some armed and all wary, with their mobiles cocked, or women with whistles; and the investigators easily spotted because they would only come to the project with huge fire-power in reserve. How he would have done it, but not his decision.

He was a small player, a facilitator. Like a tart who yearned to be in a big man's bed. He grinned – the 'tart' who shared his home was Latvian, pale-skinned, natural blonde, said little, cooked decently, was well built enough to be a symbol of his success, and might even ride with him if he soared in stature, or might be dropped for something better, more attractive . . . one step at a time. He circled the wide paved area, and looked around him. He saw locals with their children, cyclists and the skateboard kids, and a tourist group following a raised parasol and heading for the cathedral, and saw an old couple, foreign, who had a guidebook and an opened map . . . He saw his brother, and saw the girl, and his gaze lingered on her, and she sat upright, looked straight ahead, and the kid was babbling in her ear – would be the usual shit about the Russian-made rifle or its imitators, and he needed to get the business done and then be back in La Castellane before the evening because he had new stock in, and regular bulk customers were forewarned, and he wanted time to prepare for successful trading. The girl said nothing, seemed to look far out to sea, where the wind whipped the waves. He hated the fucking sea. He would never get into a small boat again. Had not managed to choke out the taste of the fucking sea. Nothing that he saw disturbed him. He came to that darkened corner where a big, tossing, bending umbrella denied light to the table beneath. He sat with them. He opened his coat, took out a Swiss knife, slashed the strapping, freed the package, still wrapped as it had been when lobbed from the hatch in the freighter's hull towards the fishing boat and his outstretched hands.

'You are satisfied, my young friend?'

The man beside Tooth, same age but heavier built, without the extreme menace but seeming by his shifting eyes to be more devious, ignored Hamid. Like he did not want to be there, would prefer to be anywhere than here.

'I am. It is clean.'

'On your head be it . . .' And the remark was repeated, after translation, in English, and both were laughing, grimly . . . And when might he expect to be paid for what he had done, near drowned, when might that happen? It did not seem the best moment, the right moment, for the questions to be asked. '. . . on your head. So, do it.'

He had the package in his hand, and started, slowly, and not wishing to hurry, be noticed, to walk.

Tooth said, 'I like an open space, I like the unpredictable, I like to be where they could not have anticipated and there is no chance of a bug.'

'Me too,' said Crab.

But, in Crab's case, it would be an 'open place' somewhere else. He had initiated the question of the deal, had made the proposition. Wished, fervently, that he had not. It had a bad taste, had a smell like the rotting seaweed close to the quay where they had parked the car and spent half the night waiting for the bloody package; brought from the fishing boat by a near-drowned rat who had then wanted to tell his horror story, get his hero-fucking-gram, and he had been cut off as if he'd had a chainsaw at his knees, not acknowledged. Wanted to be back in his home, smart leafy Cheshire, where nothing stank, and maybe taking flowers to Rosie's grave, and maybe discussing what Gary would cook him for supper . . . a bad taste and a bad smell, and the value of an old friendship, and the resurrection of old stories often told seemed to have done its time, become surplus. But he smiled weakly, and thought about the flight, and a gin on the way and Gary at the airport.

Tooth said, 'The kid, that's the motherfucker's brother. Looks handicapped. They'll come together and they'll swap. You know her?'

'Don't, just know her contacts. She's nothing, does as she's told.'

'Good-looking girl. Holds herself well. She came with the kid and . . .'

'Rode on the scooter with him.'

'Don't fucking interrupt me, Crab, don't . . .'

Done coldly, like Crab was just a junior associate, never like that before. Not spoken to as if he were an equal. And momentarily bit his lip, to stop himself from snapping back. No one in Cheshire, nor the stretch of Manchester where he was known, would have silenced him that abruptly.

'. . . and just after she came, the VW parked up, the Polo, and the driver is now perched on the wall. Looks spare – what's he there for?'

'It's her boyfriend. He's taking her home.'

'You know him, Crab?'

'Only know he's a lorry driver. What I hear, she has him wrapped around her finger. Do anything for her. Just a lorry driver.'

'But you don't know him.'

'There's others that have checked him – not me. They get the rifle, we get our stuff. They go. No, I don't know him. Fuck sake, Tooth, what's eating you?'

No reply. He thought Tooth's head was very still. It did not move as if he followed the progress of the girl and the Arab kid, nor of the 'rat' who had the package – bubble-wrap and masking tape – held loose by in his hand. Tooth's gaze was locked, watching the guy who sat on the wall, swinging his feet. Crab reckoned he'd a pain in his stomach, and felt the cold damp at the back of his neck, and decided he should never have involved himself in the smuggling of a weapon, and it seemed that time stood motionless, and heard a rifle fire, and screaming, like the dream . . . Had seemed 'a nice little earner', shifting a weapon and more to come.

September 2018

Two men were deep in conversation at a café hidden away in a side street near to the principal entry gates for the Port of Piraeus. Seedy, needing paint on the walls and new vinyl on the floor, team photos of the perennial Greek champions, Olympiakos, in frames that had lost their lustre after years of nicotine had floated up from tables and enveloped the glass, a place of casual service, where strangers would not feel welcome. They worked to establish a price for the item on offer. On one side of the table, a plastic cloth covering its surface, was the vendor: a former civil servant from the Agriculture Ministry who had lost his job, and most of his income, when he had been fired under the imposed austerity programme. Opposite him was a merchant seaman, a navigating officer, whose regular route in a Greek-flagged fertiliser carrier was between Piraeus and the Somalian port of Mogadishu, beyond the Red Sea, into the western edge of the Indian Ocean – pirate seas.

'They are hard times for me.'

'Hard times for all of us.'

'The bank will not lend me money any longer. I have no opportunity to work.'

'But it is old.'

'The family now live on hand-outs, food-banks, charities.'

'I sympathise, sincerely. But it is an ancient weapon.'

'It is indeed old, but it functions. With it are two filled magazines. I think two or three rounds were discharged. One was inside the bank, one killed an off-duty policeman, who was in the middle of a transaction and intervened. He fired one shot . . . God forbid that circumstances make it necessary for you to use it . . . Not much ammunition, but dealers do bullets for twenty cents each: was on the internet. I have to sell it, but at a sensible price.'

The rifle was inside a canvas bag wedged between the one-time public employee's shoes. Cracked and scuffed and without polish, they were evidence of the poverty consuming his family. He had shown this solitary customer the state it was in, and had explained, truthfully.

'It was my son. He had it for a year. He is supposed to clean his own bedroom. It was under his bed, against a wall. My wife never saw it, nor my sisters, nor me. He picked it up when the gunman fell, and ran with it, hid it . . .'

'Three fifty American dollars. The best price.'

'He was frightened, my boy, and did not know how to dispose of it, anxiety festered in him. Imagine, a boy who is eleven years old and sleeping above a killing machine, with blood soaked into it. It was when we had, three days, only bread to eat, only tap water, and he took me and showed it to me.'

'Three fifty, my bottom.'

'God forbid those bastards come after you, but they are down below and getting a grappling hook on the rails, and you will have more than a pressure hose. You can shoot . . .'

'Three fifty, all I am prepared to pay.'

The seaman had started to scrape his chair back, and he finished his coffee ostentatiously, made a theatrical show of it. The 'take it or leave it' moment.

'Four hundred – help me . . .'

'But it is from another age. It looks uncared for, unwanted, at the end of usefulness. But it has history and the cuts on the wood would be the victims of it, and done in different styles which tells me it has been to many places, had a multitude of owners. I am a man of the sea, been through many ports, sailed many vessels and some were luxury and more had first-class quarters for crew, and some were freighters and trampers and carried filth, rubbish, bottom of the heap . . . Listen to me. Each time we docked we would go ashore and seek out the cat-houses, girls. Always now I imagine such a history given a whore. Fresh, firm flesh when the girl starts out, with a prettiness and an eagerness to learn her trade, and might be in London or in Marseille or hoping to get to Berlin and do the main avenues and have her own roof, and she begins to sag and the lines appear and she is not worth the great capitals' business and might have reached Naples, or Vienna. More lines and more kilos at the waist and it will be Belgrade, or our city here, even Beirut, and her value is tumbling but still she knows how to please but the men are rougher, less concerned about anything other than a fast performance, then getting drunk. Now she is at the end of the line. The whore has come to Baghdad or to Damascus, even to Karachi, and she wears more make-up, puts it on with a shovel, and keeps her mouth closed so her teeth cannot be seen. Her teats drop far down her chest, and she cannot get enough hair dye. I tell you, friend, I will meet the whore in Mogadishu. I will, out of sentiment, pay her what she asks, and hope she does not leave me with a complaint and embarrassment. A man with her should close his eyes, not be concerned when the undersheet was last changed, do it and be hardly undressed, and go back to the hotel and scrub well. It is a sad tale of decline . . . I don't think that the whore, when she can no longer find business in Mogadishu, has anywhere else to go. It is the end. How does it happen, the end, I do not know, but that is the whore's progress. You offer me an old whore.'

'How much will you pay?'

'What you ask, four hundred American dollars – more than it is worth. I tell you the price in Europe is four hundred, and in

Somalia it is also that figure, and if I travel to parts of Sudan it could be as little as eighty-five dollars, for the whore whose legs are almost emaciated with mosquito bites but can still work.'

'Thank you, bless you.'

'Four hundred dollars, and the bag to take it away in.'

They shook hands across the table.

The new owner carried it out into the sunshine, held the bag easily, showed his pass at the guarded gate, and hurried to where his ship was berthed, and it was enveloped in a haze of dust as the fertiliser was tipped into the holds. In the morning it would start a fresh journey, through the Canal and out into open seas, heading for the Somali port.

Samson carried the bag, canvas and unmarked, by the strap, let it swing by his knees, not obvious. The boss was behind him. There were others from the GIPN but shut away in a van and round a corner, out of sight. He took a seat at a table next to the English couple, and Major Valery was alongside. He'd have felt naked without the rifle that banged against his leg. The bag was heavy, had his vest in it, and his balaclava, and the rifle with the telescopic sight fitted – set at Battle Sight Zero, the usual killing distance – and some smoke grenades and flash-and-bang . . . The meeting had been dull enough to send him to sleep, or musing and far away with images of cheetahs and jaguars in his mind. He was alert now, in good shape. A sharp glance from the Major towards the English police officials, a bare flick of an eyebrow for recognition . . . He recognised the kid who walked with the girl, strolling and her with a money belt in her hand, the ties trailing. Approaching them was a slightly older man, north African, who carried a package, long and hard and heavy. Samson had enough experience to recognise the shape of a Kalashnikov assault rifle . . . He was wondering if the kid had burned all the clothing that was bloodstained from the single shot and the head of his target breaking apart, or if the kid had no replacements and had put his gear through three washings. He might have a useless arm but had shown enough guts to get up and go, fire his scooter's engine, and there'd have been something tasty in the bag the kid would not give up. The Major murmured in his ear that the older guy was a dealer in La Castellane, small-time punk. Two targets of interest to watch, and coming closer, and no orders given him, and no understanding yet of what was required of him.

Andy Knight, living with his current name, not Phil and not Norm, and not what he had once been, watched it play out. Thought it had a certain staged quality, but only recognised by him and the very few others privy to the entertainment . . . would not have been noted by the kids who played football, or the skateboarders, or the lovers on benches or the tourists drinking expensive coffees. He saw it, understood.

The girl, his Zed, moved well, and seemed to show confidence, ought to walk well because she was heading in the direction of a life-changing outcome. Something haughty in her stride, and he wondered how close she was to landing on an island of arrogance. Watching her in his role as an undercover, he had not sensed her control waver after she had been spread-eagled on a pavement and him half over her, protecting her and she had been for a few brief seconds helpless and vulnerable. Had not lasted beyond the riposte. Up on her feet and belting one of the boys from the police station who acted out the extras' roles. Vicious reaction . . . And she had dangled the confidence in the face of the lorry driver, had chosen him, patronised him, then had permitted the short experience in their bed before hammering off on the pillion in the night . . . and her life was now at a crossroads. It was predictable which choice she would make: the one that changed her life. Without hesitation she walked ahead.

As he saw it, the man approaching her was streetwise, wary, and glanced around him as he carried the roughly wrapped package. But would only have attracted the notice of a trained officer. They came steadily together . . . the kid sometimes skipped to stay alongside her.

It could have been one of those Cold War scenarios. The spy swap choreography. Their man coming one way across the 'kill zone', or our man on the centre line of a road bridge and heading towards a welcome committee, and seeming all so desperately normal. She had the money belt, and that would go one way and the package would go the other – and unwrapped, maybe smeared with gun oil, its contents would then be destined for a shopping mall or one of those clusters of streets where the bars were close together and the restaurants and the pubs, and mayhem, and then more to follow . . . Except, of course, that the trafficking of the package was monitored and would be managed, and the weapon made harmless in transit, and all would go well and there would be a silver lining to the thundercloud, and a happy ending which left good guys and good girls whooping in happiness. The Undercover knew about cluster-fucks, and cock-ups and failures of coordination, and the right hand and the left hand not acknowledging each other and the law in police covert operations which stated 'If something can go wrong, it will go wrong . . .' which was why what she did was life-changing.

They were close. Normally, in the spy swaps, the pawns in the game came level and did not pause but kept on going. No nod no raised eyebrow, no 'Sorry mate, but I have to tell you the food is bloody awful over there, I wouldn't go where you are heading, not for love and not for money.' He watched a deviance in the laws of quality swaps. He stopped and she did. A quick movement of her fingers and it was more than 100 metres away, but he reckoned she flicked back the zipper on the pouch, and he would have seen the bank notes, and the kid was earnest and close in talk – and the package went to the kid first. He held it, then took out a short-bladed knife and slashed the tape and the bubble-wrap and was pulling away the covering. Had made a small hole, enough for an inspection. He thought that Zed knew nothing about the difference between a deactivated Kalashnikov and one that was all-singing, all-dancing, ready to go . . . an ethnic Pakistani girl and two north African boys gathering for conversation in multi-cultural and multi-ethnic Marseille, nothing more natural. He looked around him and could see the shapes of two men sitting in heavy shadow near to the spot where he had first noticed the guy who brought the package, and saw the people from Wyvill Road, and . . . the hand grasped the money belt. She held the package. The kid tried to take it off her, might have thought it too heavy for her to carry. No bloody way, she pushed him clear and turned, and . . .

He heard the shout. A gruff voice of protest, and of anger. A shout that echoed across the open space of the plaza, and a few heads turned. He saw a man standing at the far extremity of the space, small and bearded, wearing tinted glasses.

'He's a cop.'

Tooth shouted in his own language. Was on his feet. Shouted it again, in Crab's language.

'A cop. He's a cop.'

But his voice would not have reached the cathedral's doors and would not have been beaten back from the walls of the Fort Saint-Jean. He was pointing. To be engaged in business, to be dealing, and to be under police surveillance, was about as great a crime, in the life of Tooth, the legend in organised crime in the *arrondissements* of the northern sector of Marseille. A capital crime, good enough to wheel out the disused cobwebbed guillotine last used in the yard of the Baumettes gaol, was to be so careless as to bring a cop to the party. He was gesticulating, in a fury, and he pointed across the plaza and towards the wall on which a man sat, swinging his legs loosely, and behind him was a small car parked in limited space, then the road tunnel that linked the two sides of the *vieux port*. And the man stopped swinging his legs and froze on the wall, then stood. Tooth did not stay to see the end of it. Scurrying for an exit point, heading for his car, and his long-time friend, Crab, came after him.

Tooth snarled after him, 'You brought a cop. My eyes smell a cop, my nose sees a cop. You did not see it, smell it? Imbecile. He is watching, observing. His eyes track – that's a cop. He sits in the sun, is alert, sees everything. It is surveillance. You bring this down on me – idiot.'

Tooth ran as best he could, and Crab hobbled after him and tears wet his face.

* * *

She had heard what was shouted, and heard the curse from the boy, Karym. She had seen the pointing arm and had swivelled on her heel, had looked where the arm and the finger directed, had seen Andy straighten, stand, agape . . . Karym had hold of her arm. She clung to the package. She wanted to shout out, 'No, no, that is not a policeman, it's Andy. He's a driver. He drives a lorry. He is nobody. He does what I say. He . . .' Wanted to and could not, and was dragged. She saw the man who had brought the package carrying the belt away, the straps streaming behind him, and he was running as if his life depended on the speed his legs could take him. And she saw the couple from the street, from La Canebière, who had had trouble reading their map and finding the place in their guidebook, and who Andy had helped. Shouted nothing back, allowed herself to be pulled away from the centre of the space.

A chance to stop? Pause a moment? Consider? What actually is best for me? How should I react? Am I supposed to believe the guy who I have known for months, who I fucked last night – who glories in me, who is nothing but a truck driver – is a policeman? Have I been duped? Betrayed? Who says so? Who . . .? Did not have time to scratch her head, frown, think. Her stride slackened and his fist, clamped on her wrist, tightened and then jerked her away. She saw him, Andy Knight – lover or defender or traitor? – and he stood and he watched, and his posture had changed. No longer round-shouldered, nor slouched, as if a role had altered his shape. No linger, nor loiter. She was tugged. The boy was shorter than her and might have been a clear stone lighter. The money had gone. The man who had shouted had disappeared. The couple she had seen at the top of La Canebière – where Andy had made her laugh and had showed her the painted street sculptures of the giraffes – had now come forward from a café, and were with two men, and one of them carried a drooping bag.

Karym did not exhort her to come with him, said nothing, dragged her. She was not asked. They were at the scooter. He wrenched her. What alternative? None that she knew of. She hitched her leg over the Peugeot's pillion seat. The engine coughed.

Dark fumes spilled from the exhaust behind her and the wind took them into her nose. They careered out into the traffic, and she had her arms around his waist, and the package wedged on her lap.

He had not said where he was taking her, nor asked what was best for her.

He followed, felt calm.

Tucked in behind two cars, each loaded with families and going steadily, it was not hard for Andy to slip into a good position to tail. He could not be obvious nor was it likely that he would lose the scooter. He had slept with her that night – as if it were from both of them a final calling card – and he saw already that he was history in her mind. She held tight to the boy's waist, was close to his back and her head was against the boy's shoulder. To what purpose he followed her, he was uncertain. To have evaluated his situation he would have needed perhaps a half-minute of quiet, an opportunity to reflect. Did not have that luxury: never did in his work . . . he was tasked to be up close to her, so he went after her.

The scooter could weave but Andy relied on the cars ahead to push through gaps, and the distance between them stayed constant. He saw signs on a main road that headed towards Avignon, but the boy rode past them and took a diversion on to narrow streets and they now were filling because it was the middle of the day and the traffic was increasing, and following them was becoming harder, and he'd have less help from those in front. Then he was alone. No vehicle was between them. She did not look back, and the boy had no mirror.

He would follow to the end, expected to and wanted to.

16

Not knowing where they led him, he went after them, could see the billow of her hair and the closeness of their bodies, and when the kid took a corner sharply, and banked, he had a brief sight of the package clamped against her stomach . . . and already it had all failed.

The plan had been to allow the single weapon, product of a test run, to enter British territory and to be bugged and tailed, then for a wide-scale arrest swoop, and a network rounded up. To achieve that, Zed should have done the swap and walked away with that lofty haughtiness that he had helped establish as hers by right, should have given the boy a light kiss on the cheek, the big thrill of his day, and should have settled into the Polo and put the package on the floor, and he'd have pulled away from the kerb, and headed for the road out, taken the Avignon signs and the autoroute. Straight sailing from there. Except it had not happened, and now would not – all screwed up.

He was denounced.

Across the open square, he had seen the figure rise from a low chair in the shadows and gesticulate, identify him as he sat on the wall, claim him as a 'cop'. An old man had done it. Could not have been his clothing, his hair or his cheeks, all unkempt but acceptable for a civilian. He could not think that anything he had done would have alerted a guy sitting a minimum of a hundred yards from him. There had been a cry in French, then English; he wore a cap and tinted glasses and had a neatly trimmed snow-white beard. The instructors always preached that old lags, veteran villains, had the knack of spotting an officer, however good the cover. And the scene in front of him had disintegrated fast . . . the money had gone – she might have tried to get to him, to the car, but the kid was shouting in her ear, would have been telling her that she had produced the cop, her fault, her responsibility, and had dragged her away. He wondered if she had tears in her eyes. Wondered if she could see, or if her eyes had misted over . . . It had failed, had shown out, and he didn't know how. What was life afterwards? He followed her: assumed if he followed far enough and fast enough that a moment would come when they'd confront each other. She would spit, he would tell her that it was a lie, he was not a police officer. She would rant. He would claim innocence and deny deceit. But he was unarmed, and she clasped against her stomach an assault rifle. She'd not know how to use it. But the boy would. He thought, in bitterness, that the kid would know, and all his friends, and all of his brothers, how to arm an AK-47, and shoot with it, would have learned all that about a week after being weaned off his mother's milk, and all the rest of them . . . but he followed.

The kid rode the scooter well. His top speed was good enough for the narrow streets, and for other traffic. The bigger problem was for Andy Knight, bogus lover and treacherous friend, and a serving police officer under the direction of SC&O10, to hold the link. Behind him was a faint rumble, like a gathering storm was closing on them. Back to that 'life afterwards' . . . why had he followed them? Had no idea, except that it was his 'duty', big word and unsure of its meaning . . . What did he hope to achieve by following them? Not in Andy Knight's lowly pay grade to make such decisions, had been told to stay close, and would . . . and what came 'afterwards'? An internal inquiry, evidence given, and a reference to the Official Secrets Act, closed sessions, and he'd be walking out of the door, and a flunkey would demand his ID and would slot it into the shredder. Found wanting, surplus to requirements . . . nobody wanted to jostle shoulders with failure. He kept on following. Could have taken the next sign for the autoroute, going north, maybe overtaking her first and giving her a cheery wave, then stamping his foot, and getting the hell out and leaving it to others to sort out the debacle.

The noise was louder. A big bike. There had been a time in his life, before the legend of Andy was cobbled together, and before Norm had shown up, and before Phil had been created, when he'd have gone on bent knee for a chance to ride that sort of machine. Maybe take it out on the Welsh mountains, around the National Park, do a loop that would take in Mallwyd and almost to Dolgellau and down to Corris Uchaf and with the summit of Waen-oer on one side and that of Cader Idris on the other, then to Machynlleth where his parents, the real ones, had had a caravan on a site, might still have, go east towards Cwm-Llinau and finish the circle . . . Because he had failed, it was possible for him to consider the old life, which otherwise was denied. Brilliant to be on that sort of bike, which had been an ambition all through the Marines days, and the uniformed police slog before his transfer into the new existence of living the lie. A Ducati came past him, hovering left and right of the white line in the middle of the road. Seemed to ooze power. He recognised the rider, the leather jacket. The Ducati, the 811 model, was cleaned and the metal parts shone and the paintwork was without blemish. He knew it as the Ducati Monster. It would be a symbol of power where the rider came from. It came level with the Peugeot scooter that was chugging up the long hill.

An arm came off the Ducati controls. Snaked out, reached across, the fist clenched. First there was a punch on the kid's shoulder. The scooter rocked but the kid held firm and he might have heard the pillion scream and bury her head lower on the kid's back and hold ever tighter, and the scooter skidded but the kid held it upright. One punch on the shoulder and one cuff on the back of the head. The scooter held its speed. The hand went lower, was at the package, tried to rip it clear. He saw Zed's foot. It came out, paused, took a bearing, then kicked sharply at the back of the leg of the Ducati man. Where the muscle was. The guy needed both hands for control. Might have had the briefest hold of the package. The two riders screamed abuse at each other. Then the Ducati accelerated past. A siren sounded a long way back. Zed was tearing at her parcel's packaging, bubble-wrap and tape, must have lifted a knife off the kid carrying her, and dropping the wrapping, ditching it as a toy for the wind to play with.

Andy saw the barrel of a rifle as the packaging was stripped off.

Zeinab slashed with the blade. More of the bubble-wrap came loose.

The boy, she knew him now as Karym, had needed both hands on the scooter's steering. In his hesitant English, he'd told her which pocket on his coat he'd find the knife, and she'd opened the blade. If the fist that had punched Karym had groped into her lap and tried to seize the package, had come again, she'd have stabbed it.

The packaging flew away behind her. The bike in front had slowed. She had the rifle, and a magazine slotted into its guts, and another was under her T-shirt, and into the waist of her jeans. The motorbike made one more dart after them, and she saw the anger on the face of the rider; he was revving the engine and cutting his speed, and the hand snatched for the rifle. She stabbed, made a poor job of using the blade, managed only a nick on the hand but enough to draw blood. The bike swung away; one-handed control was hard, and the pain would have been big and blood ran from a small but deep wound. Words yelled between the brothers, him furious and Karym defiant, and the bike – two hands in place – sloped away, went in front, left them for dead.

Karym shouted at her, 'It is yours, it is what you bought . . . I thought it would be skunk of Moroccan black. I thought it was that, not a Kalash . . . why go to such trouble for a Kalash? Why involve my brother and Tooth in this deal? Is that all you wanted, a Kalash? You make my brother angry, I saw his blood. He has a Ducati 821 Monster, and I have a little Peugeot, which says what he thinks of me. You have anywhere to go?'

'If my friend is a policeman, I have nowhere to go.'

'I can hide you.'

'Is it possible there is a mistake?'

'That your boy is not a policeman? The one I saw you with this morning, not a policeman? A mistake? I do not think so . . . the one who identified him is an old legend of Marseille, a big man with a reputation. He would know a cop . . . it is the face, the look in the eye, it is the style of the body, the posture. Old people, they know . . . old gang leaders know better than anyone. Possibly a mistake, but . . .'

'What should we do?'

Karym did not know, could not answer.

The rifle was hidden between them, and the magazine gouged into his back. She had closed the knife, had dropped it back in his pocket. He could hide her, a possibility. Hide her until darkness then take her out of La Castellane, and bring her to . . . where? Could take her to the ferry port and put her on a boat to – to anywhere. Could take her to Saint Charles railway station and buy a ticket for her to – to anywhere. Or go to the airport, or one of the little fishing harbours along the coast and towards the Spanish frontier and see if there were people who would take her to – to anywhere. The siren came closer, screaming. If they were followed, then it was clear to him, that police had been at the plaza, had watched the exchange – confirmed what old Tooth had claimed, that her boy, her driver, was a cop.

What to do? He did not know.

Who to ask? Karym knew no one who could make a decision fast other than his brother, who would now feel the pain of the cut in his hand, and have to get the wound bandaged, and would feel vicious anger towards her. Did not know what to do, did not know who to ask. He felt the tremors in her body, and the weapon seemed to shiver in her grip which made the pain where it trapped his flesh more acute. They went on up the hill. He understood that the previous buried tensions with his brother were now in the open air and clear to view, and rejoiced in it – like he had crawled from the cover of deep shadow. He could not twist sufficiently to see behind him, gauge how far away the source of the siren was. He would not have admitted his fear, certainly not to her, but imagined himself as one of the myriad of small puppy dogs that roamed the project, and when a stone was thrown at them, they'd slink away, look for the safety of a home – under a bush or behind a building, or the corner of a stairwell. In the distance was the large flat landscape of buildings that formed the commercial shopping centre. On the far side of the road was La Castellane. If he could get there before the sirens caught up with him, he would feel a certain safety.

'I will protect you, Zeinab.'

'Thank you.'

'I admire you and I respect you.' Her arms were around his waist. She was different from every other young woman in the project, and so brave – so innocent. No woman of her age in La Castellane retained even a pinch of innocence.

'Thank you again.'

'I will hide you.'

'Yes, I thank you.'

'If you are seen, Zeinab, with the rifle, they will kill you. Samson will.'

'I do not need to know, Karym, what will happen to me.'

'They shoot to kill, Zeinab, it does not matter to them if they kill us.'

'What the fuck do we do?' she shouted in his ear.

'Did you think it would be easy?' he yelled back. 'Here, for us, it is never easy.'

'Who is Samson . . .?'

'Hope, Zeinab, that you do not learn who is Samson.'

The Major drove. Samson, beside him, used a monocular with a steady hand. The English pair were sitting behind them in the vehicle with four uniforms.

Samson said, 'She has a rifle, I can see it. She has a Kalashnikov. It was in the wrapping. We should block them before they get into the rat-house.'

'Get it deployed,' he was told.

And he did.

The Englishman said quietly, almost diffidently, 'We'd like her taken. She'll be a treasure trove.'

The Englishwoman snapped at him, 'For heaven's sake, Gough, she's on the loose with a lethal weapon, and has to be stopped – just leave it.'

It was called up, would be in place, and there were squad cars coming from the east and west, and another from the north, and all would carry the necessary gear.

The Major asked, not looking back, 'The Volkswagen, the Polo, that is your man?'

'Afraid it is,' he was answered.

They drove at the speed of the scooter, but were out in the middle of the road and nothing could pass them. The Major had created a gap in the traffic. The scooter was isolated and weighed down by its passenger and cargo, was alone in its space; perfect for what they intended . . . except for the one car that had stayed at constant speed and at a constant distance behind the fugitives.

It was flicked out.

The road ahead was empty. On the pavements crowds gathered, mostly immigrants from the *Maghreb* but some from central Africa; very few in this district had parents born in France. They would hear the sirens and there was a good feeling that soon another performance would be laid before them, perhaps as exciting as when the executioner, Samson, had come and shot a man, one bullet and taking out the skull.

It slithered snake-like across the road. A second was ready for use on the far side. The police called them 'stingers'. The Tyre Deflation Devices covered half the road's width with close-set spikes, and officers reckoned from experience they could stop any vehicle, shred the tyres and bring it to a halt. Armed police crouched in doorways on either side and could hear the sirens but not yet the erratic engine of the small Peugeot scooter. The intention was that the snakes – one already in the road and the other held back until the target was close – would halt the pair well short of their La Castellane refuge. The instructions called for the arrest of the couple, particularly the female. They had with them, it was said, an automatic rifle but were without experience of using such a powerful weapon . . . And a car followed them, a male driver, and that person should be kept out of the arrest area, should be prevented from entering the *cordon sanitaire*. Many eyes watched, and many ears listened for the approach of the prey, and guns were cocked. In that *arrondissement* a spectacle was always eagerly welcomed.

'What the bloody hell do I do now?' Crab hissed.

'Use your feet, and walk,' was his answer.

They were at a set of lights. The sign by the church said this was the Rue Beauvau. It was near the quayside for the *vieux port*, near McDonald's and an Irish pub, near the marina where the yachts and launches were moored, but nowhere near the airport. And a further answer . . . Tooth had reached across him, unlocked the passenger door and pushed it open, flicked the hold on the seat belt, and propelled Crab out, and he had stumbled on the pavement, scattering pedestrians . . . And another answer, as Tooth twisted round to the back seat, picked up his one-time friend's bag, and threw it out. It careered into Crab's legs.

'How was I to know?'

'You come to me, you fat old fool, with your little idea, and want to play a big man again, and you are now senile and incompetent, and you have brought a cop with you. A cop travels along with you . . . "How was I to know?" . . . You come here, you feed off my hospitality, you threaten my way of life. How, why? Because you have not taken care. You can walk to the airport.'

'Nobody speaks to me, not that way, no one does.'

'Go back where you came from, use your feet to get there. I am not your chauffeur.'

Long years of joshing, laughing, doing deals, telling stories, sharing bad times, were erased, like a sheet of paper held over a flame. About as great a crime as existed in the world of either Tooth or of Crab was to have such slack security that a stranger, an Undercover, could infiltrate a group and threaten both livelihood and liberty. A damning accusation and one never before levelled at Crab . . . Of course, never apologise, keep contrition off the table. Fight back, only way to maintain respect – respect for himself.

He had a fist on the bag's strap, and swung it. There were metal studs on its base, roughened through wear. The bag scraped the bodywork of the Mercedes car, polished and pristine, and he had the pleasure in seeing Tooth's rage, control almost lost . . . but not enough for him.

He dropped the bag and plunged back into the car. Sought to get his hands on Tooth's throat, but had no hold, and came away only with a clutch of hair from the chin of Tooth's beard. Then he stepped back, kicked the door hard enough for it to slam, and watched the car pull away.

What he had done was unforgivable . . . he had seen the young man sitting on the wall, kicking his heels, and had noted the guy's roving eyes, their scanning, apparently relaxed but alert . . . and all so convenient. The little girl with a 'stupid' boyfriend, obsessed with her, and happy to drive her halfway across Europe and be ignorant of the conspiracy . . . The guys his sons had met on their wing at Strangeways, who'd used the old warehouse, had failed to do the checks. He was in hock to people he did not know, who had aims he did not understand, and his premises had been given over to a session of pain, interrogation, agony, all the way to death . . . He might be subject to investigation by the crime squad at Manchester, and might be of interest to the North West Counter Terrorist crowd: a bad outlook, and he could not see it improving. Down to him . . . but he had stood his corner well, and the accusation of being a bloody idiot had come late, after a stonily silent drive.

And his leg hurt, usually did when he was stressed. He went towards the main drag, and hoped to find a taxi, and hoped to get on a plane . . . and had not been fucking paid, not been handed his share of commission on the deal. All for one bloody gun.

October 2018

'I have no need of it . . .' the navigation officer said.

His friend was an Alexandrian and worked in the harbour-master's office of that Egyptian port on the Mediterranean coast. 'What need of it could I have?'

'They are uncertain times, times of revolution and of instability and . . .'

'And times when the possession of such an item is sufficient for a military court to order the hanging of a man. You want me to take it off your hands, yes?'

The navigation officer grimaced because that was the truth. 'We are heading for the Canal, we are due to sail the length of the Red Sea, and then into waters where there is a threat of piracy.'

'I know that.'

'We are approaching Alexandria and the captain is informed that the owners have declared insolvency, and we should return to our home port. If we are lucky, there we may be paid off. But we are Greeks, and used to the imposition of disappointment, and more possible is that we go down the gangway to be abandoned without pension rights, anything. I cannot take it back to Greek territory. I could throw it overboard. Or could make it available to a friend.'

'It is functional?'

'I assume so. I was told it was. I believe that the Kalashnikov has a longer life than me, than you, otherwise why would they have manufactured a hundred million of them . . . If you were a fish, my friend, I would say you are nibbling.'

Both laughed, but without humour. The navigation officer had made the offer of a gift to this official from the harbourmaster's office because the man was of the Christian faith. Many were in Alexandria . . . they lived, as he knew well, in a state of siege, their churches were bombed by zealots, and their children were abused and their wives friendless outside their own small community, and the police seldom answered emergency calls when they were threatened. Not quite a time of lynch mobs seeking out those worshippers, but it would come. He had thought this individual would welcome the chance to have the weapon, hidden away, only to be considered if the mob were on the stairs or had brought flaming torches and gasoline to the front door. A last stand when his family and himself faced death by fire or by stabbing and chopping with butchers' axes, might be an attractive alternative.

First nibbled, then taken into the mouth.

'It would be the noose and the gallows.'

'Whatever you want. It is intended as a gesture of friendship.'

The navigation officer, in the days since they had left their home port, and had gone into the Black Sea for a topping-up of cargo, had many times, late at night and alone in his cabin, taken the weapon out of its protective wrapping. He had held it, then had learned one piece at a time to dismantle it, then reassemble it. He had cleared the magazine, had filled it again. He had learned what he could from the internet about its history and culture, of the freedom struggle that the weapon enjoyed. Set in the metalwork was the identity of the rifle, and he knew by heart, often silently recited its last digits, *16751*, and had wondered at the heritage that an individual rifle, a killing machine, carried. Had not fired it, not stood on the deck in darkness and nestled the stock against his shoulder and aimed at a fisherman's buoy, but had held it in the firing position inside the privacy of his cabin. The scratches on the stock, which tickled the skin of his jaw when he aimed, were of particular interest. Easy to assume that different owners had made those marks and that if their code could be deciphered then the history would be clear. They were gouges, or notches, or crude marks made from a blunt blade or the tip of a screwdriver. Young men, college students, lucky enough to bed a girl, might leave a small memento on the bed post: young men, soldiers or activists, might remember a killing by marking the wooden stock. It had fascinated him. It would be, he reflected, similar to a child abandoning a prized toy, but he could not contemplate, now that the ship was recalled and the owners bust, having Customs men go over it as they docked for the last time – not a hanging offence but the probability of a lengthy gaol term.

Enough . . . 'Do you want it, or not want it? Will you take it or does it go in the sea?'

He would take it. A farewell to a friend. Never used but valued. He would add nothing to the marks made on the wooden stock but hoped it might be of help, or merely comfort, to a friend. He looked for a last time at the body of it, where so little paint had survived the years. It was wrapped again, then would go into the official's bag – where his laptop was and his waterproof clothing, and a change of shoes. They hugged, kissed each other on the cheek, and his friend – he noticed – shook, almost trembled, had gone quiet, and his breath was fast but erratic. He thought the reason was the fear that the weapon, unused, could create.

Over the boy's shoulder, Zeinab saw the silver line across the rough stained greyness of the road's surface. They went towards it with all the speed that the scooter was capable of. The line she saw went only to the middle of the street, and he was steering towards the end of its bright length: the sun caught it, made it pretty.

Two police vehicles were parked up, doors open on the street side. She saw the crowd and seemed to hear also, louder than the siren behind them, a dull timpani from spectators on the pavement behind the police vehicles, when they saw the scooter and Karym and herself breast the top of the slope and then accelerating. And noted the guns . . . registered two handguns, pistols, and a small machine-gun. The guns were held by three men and a woman, all drab blue in the uniform of the Marseille force, what she had seen when walking with Andy . . . and it hurt to remember him and recall his voice, to think of him. She had no idea where they were going, what she would do. Helpless, in the hands of the kid, somewhere she did not know – lost.

'It's a shit old world', the kids at the Hall of Residence would have said. 'Can't make an omelette without breaking eggs', her tutor would have said. There were pictures on the TV of long-distance races through streets, full- and half-marathons, and always there were parts of the nominated course where the crowd was sparse but they were vigorous in their support for a struggling and isolated runner, and clapped and sometimes whistled to show empathy . . . like now. There was applause, there were yells, that she took as encouragement, and Karym took a hand off the steering bar and clenched a puny fist, shook it, as if he were a freedom fighter and they were his followers. It was what she thought. She had realised that the siren noise stayed constant, that the vehicles did not close on them. There was a car behind them but it was not easy for her to turn, see it clearly . . . and some on the pavements saw the rifle and yelled louder and made the gesture of aiming and firing and their laughter cascaded on her. They gave her their applause because she had the rifle, was invulnerable, strong; but she knew nothing. She liked the sound of their clapping and cheering, and held the rifle so it was better seen, and felt the power in her arms, and its weight seemed as nothing.

He veered across the street. The police stiffened, and she thought they aimed. The swerve that Karym made would have confused them, made their target harder to follow. She understood: he rode the scooter beyond the silver line. A woman stepped out of a shop doorway, 25, 30 yards away. She wore police uniform. Karym saw the pistol lodged in a holster. She had auburn hair with highlights, and was powerful at the hips and shoulders, and she carried a thick silver coil, like a big resting eel – and threw it. Nowhere for Karym to go. The road was blocked, The unravelling coil shivered on the street surface, rocked and bobbed and was almost still when he drove over it.

He had said nothing, gave her no warning. She sensed the sudden quiet, heard the squeal of the tyres, and the tight, small explosions as they burst, and the ripping sound where they were torn. The momentum of the scooter reeled under her.

The scooter skidded, slewed across the road, was past the silver line, and she had seen the teeth bared as the tyres shredded. Karym struggled to hold it, and seemed to swear in a language she didn't know. She clung to the rifle with one hand; the other was around his waist, gripping the material of his T-shirt and feeling the little knots of his muscles. They went down and she felt the heat as sparks were thrown up.

She held the rifle. The knees and thighs of her jeans, right leg, ripped. The skin beneath was stripped. She hung on to him, clung on to the rifle. They headed for a street rubbish bin, filled to overflowing, seemed endless getting there, but reached it and the scooter took most of the impact, and Karym took some more. She felt little, until the shot was fired.

They had hit the bin.

Her thumb would have shifted the lever, taken it off safety and on to single shot mode, when her body careered into the bin. A finger would have gone into the space behind the trigger guard and caught the lever, not squeezed it, but yanked on it. A bullet was fired. It would have hit a lamppost, then ricocheted into the road, then struck the surface and maybe gone on, as a flat stone would if flipped on to smooth water, and flew down the street, until breaking a window.

The effect of the shot, fired involuntarily, was as good an outcome as there might have been. Three policemen and a policewoman taking cover, either flat on the pavements and not aiming, and the policewoman who had thrown out the tyre shredder was on her haunches in the shop doorway. She could not have said whether it was she who pulled him up, whether it was Karym who tugged her arm and dragged her upright. No sports races, running for a tape, were permitted at the school she'd attended in Savile Town. Never ran in Manchester. No cause to, no reason to run. She did now, learned how, but never released her grip on the rifle.

Karym was bent low, ducked and weaved and scampered. He took her with him. Nothing said . . . She had fired the Kalashnikov, had seen policemen, policewomen, cower, had known the strength of it when the kick came, and thought it the proudest moment in her life. She did not look behind her, just ran and tried to match Karym, did not see who followed her. She was panting, her chest heaving. There was a drumming of feet, and still the siren, then a rippling, chanting applause.

It was not his business, beyond his remit.

Another of those bloody instructors would have said, 'Something to remember: you do not get caught up in events that are beyond the remit. You stay focused and remain inside the tramlines of your assignment. Anything else and you drift away, go far into the shadows. What is paramount to remember is that personal feelings have no place in the governing of your reactions. Hold on to that and you'll be fine. Ignore that and you will finish up at the wrong end of shit-creek . . . It's simple, and keep things that way – simple.' He was out of the car, left the door open and the engine running, and his rucksack and her bag were in the boot.

He wondered why the police had not fired on them. They did not run fast but would have made difficult targets because the boy had the wit to move with a low gravity centre, and to duck and to zigzag, and the girl, Zed, followed his lead and was pulled after him. She clutched the rifle, and a second magazine bulged from her hip pocket. Perhaps they had been ordered not to fire, perhaps no one in authority had told them anything and had abandoned them to 'use your own initiative, boys, girls, and we're all behind you', the big cop-out anthem.

Nobody told him what he should do, and nobody was there for him to ask. He started to jog up the street. He could recall the good times with the girl and the bad times. He went faster, lengthened his stride.

Behind him, the sirens had been silenced. Ahead of them, astride the slope of a hill, was a housing estate, close-set windows, grey-white walls pocked with satellite dishes, blue sky and bright sunshine and a lapping wind that blew the washing suspended from balcony wires. That would be their goal, their place of safety. An old slogan was in his mind, what an officer would have lectured them at Lympstone, what they searched for among recruits – *First to understand, first to adapt and respond, and first to overcome*, and the officer might just have nodded approval. His advantage, to be exploited, was that the police where the stingers had been thrown, were all looking up the road. He went over the silver lines, hopped over the spikes. There was a perfunctory yell but he ignored it, ran easily. The two of them, in front of him, both limping and in obvious pain, went close to the spectators.

He ran past the scooter, the tyres gone, the tank leaking fuel, dumped in the centre of the street, and useless; he had seen it in the square below the hotel window, and the street-light had shown him the pride with which the boy had climbed on to it and gunned the engine and waved for her to sit behind him, settle on the pillion. He was noticed. A policeman stood up from his crouching position and attempted to block him, jabbered in a language that neither Andy Knight, nor Phil nor Norm, would have been familiar with, and then he was waved aside and grabbed at the anorak and shaken clear, and squeaked something which was ignored, but he did not shoot.

He heard far behind him a woman's bellowing voice. 'You fucking idiot, come back here.'

Then a plaintive voice, her superior's. 'Friend, this is not a good idea. Don't go any farther.'

'She's not your business, not now the whole thing is wrecked.'

'I really do urge you to turn around.'

The boy and Zed were gone from sight. The crowd on the pavement had engulfed them, one moment he could see them, their heads bobbing, and the next a mess of shoulders and backs made a screen around them. They were inside a clamour of noise. The mob had claimed them . . . Like a great caterpillar, the crowd seemed to wriggle up the hill. He caught a glimpse of the tip of the barrel of the assault rifle, and he imagined her thrill at being among people so loving, so admiring; she would have felt herself a fighter and cherished.

Behind him, the couple that he knew as Gough and Pegs, a team suckled on police culture, had managed to run – or hustle – and had closed on him, had stepped over the tyre shredder, were past the scooter. The voices were faint.

She bawled, 'Gone native, have you? You're finished. You're nothing, you're history.'

He called, 'You are in the way of an arrest operation. Do not go any farther.'

He looked over his shoulder. Gough had indeed run and now leaned against a lamppost and heaved as he sucked air into his lungs. Pegs, who used cheerful building site obscenities, now stood in the road with her back bent and might well be vomiting on her shoes. Walking briskly, at the head of a small phalanx of uniforms, was a plain clothes officer, suit and tie, straight-backed, and in his fist was a pistol, carried easily . . . half a pace back from him was a man with a balaclava masking his face, carrying what he recognised as a Steyr sniper's rifle, the SSG 69, what an élite marksman would have chosen, a weapon of quality and with reputation. He started running again. He heard the name murmured, like the rustle of dead leaves hurried by a wind: Samson. The voices were from the people who had lined the pavements down the hill, where the stingers had been used.

He followed the crowd who escorted the boy and Zed, made ground on them.

Chaos, it seemed.

More sirens and more vehicles arriving, and the road blocked, and in the middle of the lights and the confusion was the Volkswagen Polo with the driver's door hanging open. Municipal police on site, and with their own command chain, and Major Valery seeking to confirm primacy. Kids gathering, bricks in their hands. A thunder of vehicle horns because a busy road was blocked and the tailbacks grew. A crowd jeering, except when one particular man passed. And a caterpillar of people, wriggling along, carried two fugitives to an entry road into the La Castellane project . . . rumour running riot, some claimed to have seen a foreign girl, ethnic Asian, carrying an aged Kalashnikov, and reports said she had already fired at the police, but there was no blood on the street or the pavement, only an abandoned scooter.

And the street filled, and mobiles summoned more people to come, and the word was passed that the executioner himself was there . . .

Gough said, 'Little for us to be proud of.'

Pegs said, 'In the big scheme, we are small beer.'

They stood apart. Order was being restored. The marksman had slipped away. The Major was in a tight knot of officers and seemed to be laying down terms and conditions for the next phase. Obvious to all that both of them had attempted to call back their man, and had been ignored. Gough had called it 'a Nelson moment', and Pegs had described it as 'bloody near as makes no difference to mutiny'. And she had retrieved from the depths of her handbag an ancient leather-coated hip-flask, swigged, wiped her sleeve on her mouth, passed it to him, but he shook his head.

He said, 'I suppose among the many operations, different grades of danger, running at this moment, what makes us different, is that we have the usually reliable component on our side, an Undercover. That presence has made us envied, attracts jealousy, and we look to have been inadequate in using it.'

She said, 'And every time a suicider detonates and takes fatalities with him, the folk alongside us – some we know and some we don't – will shiver, get the cramps, guard their backs, against the accusation that they fucked up, it was on their watch. Could be us, we could be the ones sneaking out the back door, no leaving bash, while the TV shows the carnage. We're not a bag of laughs, Gough. Not flavour of the day.'

Far ahead of them now walked the man with the sniper rifle, at his own pace, heading for the distant blocks towards which the girl, principal target for Rag and Bone, had gone. Pegs and Gough were ignored, were outside the equations.

At the entrance, youths formed a line. He took her, and the watchers parted.

She held tightly to the rifle but did not know which posture to assume. He had tried, a minute or so earlier, to remove it from her. She did not permit it. So, instead, he had fiddled with a lever at the side, had depressed it, told her it was now safe. Dead eyes greeted them, and she did not know whether they had the support of the young people or were to be treated with hostility. They went as quickly as their bruised, grazed legs would take them, and her elbows were raw, and her jeans torn. At the entrance to the block where he had taken her in the small hours, parked in the shade of the building was a powerful bike, a big one and a big man's . . . and she remembered. It had come past them, the rider had tried to snatch her weapon. She had kicked full force, the first injury of the day had been her bruised toes. Youths guarded the stairs. Space was made for them, but no encouragement given . . . Did Karym expect a hero's return? If so, would be disappointed.

Andy Knight, the lorry driver who was a straight sort of guy, and did not threaten, had a way of getting where he'd no right to be. He had never been Phil, did not recognise Norm, but also had once been in the Royal Marines, and identified by a service number.

Something distant but an experience to feed off. Older men told stories. Liked the ones that featured bluff, getting where they were not welcome, and having the style to seem to belong. He came to the line of youths. Remembered all he had been told. Out on manoeuvres on the moor and a weathered, gnarled company sergeant major would give them the benefit of his reminiscences, good stuff and the recruits were spellbound. The best were about bluff.

Eyes peered at him, muscles flexed, he saw the light catch the steel-sharpened surface of a knife blade, saw a hand go down and pick up a bottle that had been left on one of the big rocks. They had no weight to their bodies, were small and sinewy and their clothes hung loose on them. Most wore sports kit, designer jogging suits, and designer trainers, and he doubted that any had ever competed on a track. The hairstyles were exotic, most with the sides and above their ears shaved, as the boy's was. The eyes had a deadness to them as if joy rarely visited. He thought the 'trade' employed them all. He walked towards the line, to the centre of it; the youth on the right of where he was aiming to go through them held the bottle, and it would be the work of a moment to break the glass, create jagged edges. The one to the left held the knife, showed the blade.

A firm voice, English. He walked up to them. Something about it being a 'good afternoon', and something more about 'just following my friends', and winding up with 'excuse me please'. The line split, a parting of the sea. It might happen once, and would not happen again. He was against them, body to body, and he reached out to a youth in front of him and seemed to roll his eyes at the boy's appearance, and he fastened the buttons on the youth's shirt and tutted in disapproval at the kid's appearance, and he was through. Others were laughing at the one who had been gently reprimanded . . . There was a corporal, a weapons instructor, and the story was a party piece: a small convoy in some distant snow-bound corner of Bosnia, on a glistening icy road and the road block was Serbian and all half-cut with *slivovicz* high-proof stuff, and tempers frayed and some weapons cocked. The corporal had stepped down from the Land Rover and had lined them up with the acumen of any well-practised drill NCO, had tongue-lashed them for their dress and bearing, had had them on basics, attention and at ease and weapon handling, had inspected them, had drunk a toast to them, and they had gone through with the aid lorries they escorted. Just happened once, and he'd used the 'once', and was through – and had his hand shaken for his trouble. The motorcycle was there.

It had passed him at speed. He had seen the girl, Zed, resist the attempt to snatch the rifle, and he had seen the same man on the plaza. He went inside, was engulfed in darkness, the fierce sunlight lost. Shadows around him, then guttural voices, and one figure had swaggered close to him. Questions thrown at him. He stood his ground, waited, allowed his sight to settle. It would be bluff, another strong dose of it, had to be. He knew well enough the story of the Beirut negotiator who had gone back to the city one time too many and had believed that his status and bearing gave him protection, had walked tall and had seen his mission as clear-cut: winning the release of hostages trapped by the civil war, held as pawns in abysmal conditions. And the bluff was called and a gun pulled on the negotiator and his arms pinioned, and he'd rot for years in a primitive cell with those he'd tried to free . . . A sergeant in the sniper training section had told a story of a plain clothes soldier, masquerading as a journalist, alone in the Creggan estate of Londonderry, and a crowd of Provo supporters round his car and shouts and anger, and no help in sight. The joker had managed to get out of the car, and fingers poked him and fists grabbed at his clothing, and he had seen his saviour: an Irish setter, a big, rangy and adorable dog with feathered auburn hair, had wandered by, oblivious of the tension. Down on his knees, and the animal immediately warming to him, and tickling under its chin, and where was the owner? A man pushing to the front, hostility lining his forehead, and the soldier asking questions about diet, and what exercise it needed, and how his coat was so beautifully kept and how hard they were to train, and him being everybody's friend – and able to get the fuck out. Likely, afterwards, the dog took a heavy kicking when they realised the trick performed on them. A kid, might have been fourteen years old, had a sub machine-gun. It was an Ingram, a MAC-10, obsolete and out of production, a spray close quarters weapon, short barrel, range around 50 metres for doing damage . . . he ignored all the other weapons, made himself the kid's friend. Quick action, and left them confused and had it in his hand and the kid hardly knowing how else to respond. Pitifully poor light, and the big chance taken, and he started to strip it, take it apart, lay the pieces out. Had never done it before. And put it together, and took the magazine out, and cleared it, and was smiling wide enough for all to see in the grim light. He slotted the magazine back in place, and handed it back. Had never done it, and he'd used hand speeds that a magician would have prided himself on. Had given it back. Then had held up his open hand, ready for a high five, and been awarded one from the kid, then from the others.

He pointed to the big bike outside, the Ducati, then indicated the stairs. The kid would lead him. He was their friend, best friend. They guarded the door behind which the goods were stored, where the customers came. They would kill and regard it as less significant than eating a breakfast. All done with bluff, and fast, and never to be repeated. The rancid smell of the stairs was alive in his nostrils. The kid scampered up the stairs.

He followed . . . and tried to consider what he would do when he reached the right apartment, and why he was there. And how it would be.

17

'You betrayed me, bedded me and betrayed me.'

He was against the wall beside the door, in a corridor, and his hands were high above his head.

'You tricked me, deceived me.'

The rifle was held one-handed. She used it as an actor's prop, and jabbed at him with the barrel tip, and the weapon's selector lever was lodged on 'single shot', and her finger was on the trigger guard, and he believed that she had no idea how simple it was for a bullet to be fired if the weapon was waved around like a damn magician's wand.

'I thought you were my friend. I . . .'

He doubted that the kids behind him, a little cluster of them on the stairs, with their medley of firearms, would have understood a word said in a foreign language with the accents of sub-continent and Yorkshire, but the sight of the veteran rifle, and its prominent fore-sight wobbling between ceiling and floor, via his knees and his stomach and his chest and his forehead meant big entertainment. They did little whoops of giggling as her voice rose steadily in pitch, and she grew close to hysteria.

'. . . I thought I could trust you, thought I could believe what you said to me. All the sweet words and no meaning in any of them. You bastard . . .'

The kids had climbed the stairs behind him. The smell was unchanged, the air fetid with decay, the graffiti depressing, and the lights sporadic, and there were only small windows, like gun slits, for the sunshine to come through, and he had rapped the door. Not a hesitant knock. As if it were a demand. A girl had let him into the hall area where he was hit with a barrage of game show music and canned applause and the scream of a compère. Quite a pretty girl except that her face was scarred by indifference and tiredness: she had opened the door, eyed him briefly, then seemed to reflect that he was not her business, no one she should be involved with, and she went back inside and slumped on a settee and was again engrossed in the television. She'd called once, then again, then had bawled, then had regarded her business as done, obligation finished.

'You are a liar, a bastard liar.'

The boy had come first, then had yelled over his shoulder and she'd emerged. Might have been weeping, or might just have had reddened eyes from the sprint away from the scooter. She looked, not that it mattered, quite simply terrific. Always did, his opinion and from the scantiest of knowledge . . . a woman in a temper and losing it, with her chin out and upper lip trembling, a flush in the cheeks and shoulders thrown back, and spitting accusations – that sort of woman always, he reckoned, was a sensation. She had the rifle. He'd lifted his arms, gone to surrender posture. He started to move forward. Not in a hurry, taking it easy, and like any fair to middling boxer, he rode the verbal blows and showed no sign of being hurt by them; but had not started to counter punch, just came on inside.

'I should kill you, what you deserve, and hurt you.'

Would she? He doubted it. Dangerous to be certain of his opinion because the Kalashnikov was two, three yards from him and had an effective killing range of 200, 300 yards, and she had spittle at the side of her mouth. He did not answer her, but came along the narrow corridor where paint was needed and he eased past rubbish sacks, and they both backed off in front of him. He was allowed into a bedroom, would have been the boy's, and realised she now had a soul mate, and could talk endlessly to the boy about the Kalashnikov series and its copycat versions. He saw the books. All the time that he moved he kept his hands high. The bed was not made, there was food – a rice and sauce meal half consumed – on a plate. Biker magazines carpeted the floor, and on top was one with a photo on the cover that showed the Piaggio

MP3 Yourban, and at an angle that demonstrated the tilting front wheels, and that would have been his aspiration, not the wrecked Peugeot that was by now being loaded up for a journey to the breakers, and a photograph of an older woman who had three kids with her: one would have been the game show audience girl, and one was the boy half a pace behind Zed and one would have been the eldest and the owner of a Ducati Monster. He was good at noting what was around him, part of his training, what might be used in evidence in a courtroom when he faced her, had a clear view of the dock where she'd sit with the guards, screened from the public gallery but not from her, and described how he had deceived, betrayed, lied to her, and at the end of it, after she'd been sentenced, left pole-axed by the severity, chances were he'd be called back into the judge's chambers and personally congratulated, and told what a debt he was owed by society – unless the case was waived out. Compromise and entrapment. Deniable. An experienced police officer's relationship with a naive student. Never happened. She might broadcast that she had been seduced by him: about her only chance, but a poor bet . . . The boy waved him down. The big irony: she felt no guilt, in his assessment, of her lies to him, all one-sided. But did not dwell long on it because irony went poorly with a situation such as he faced. He slid his spine on the wall, sank to his haunches. The boy wanted his hands.

Zed aimed the rifle barrel at him.

The weapon might have been with Noah in the Ark. Was the oldest that he had ever seen, certainly more of a museum piece than anything they'd had in the collection at Lympstone. Scratched and scraped and scarred. There were moments when she tilted it and he could see the stock and the evidence of its history . . . Would have expected a modern and unmarked version coming into the courier service. It was almost antique, would have seen service, and the notches on the stock were proof of an enduring effectiveness. He saw the setting of Battle Sight Zero on the rear of the weapon, for close quarters fighting . . . He did not think she would fire.

He held out his hands.

A restraint came from the boy's hip pocket. It went round his wrists, was jerked tight and the boy stepped back. The boy's expression told him that a mistake, big or up the scale to catastrophic, had been made in coming back here, too fast a decision taken, and unable to reverse it. She had gone to the window, had gazed out, then had flattened herself against the wall beside it. He could hear sirens and it would be that time in an operation when the cavalry arrived and would dismount, bivouac, and put a perimeter in place. A mistake to come here because they, the boy and Zed, were now trapped, had nowhere to go, and about all they had as a chip to bargain with was him, the People's Hero, Phil or Norm or Andy, or whoever he had once been before living the lie. He supposed himself a kind of a hostage . . . what would they pay for him? If the question were asked of the Detective Inspector, Gough, or his faithful and foul-tongued bag carrier, then they'd have chorused in unison: 'What, money? Pay for him or give her free passage? Not effing likely. Forget it, sunshine . . .' And, why was he there? Not quite sure, but working on it.

He said nothing, allowed the rant to build. Later he might, not yet.

'Should let you sweat, then hurt you, then fucking kill you – do it like they'd have done with a traitor in Raqqa, Mosul – saw your head off with a blade. Shooting's too good.'

She might do it, shoot him. His judgement might have been mistaken, but he thought she would not. Be a shame if he was wrong, always was the problem for an Undercover, making an error.

He never answered. No response and that angered Zeinab the most.

Neither argued with her nor pleaded but sat on this pit of a room's floor and kept his eyes off her, had not looked her in the face since the boy, Karym, had fastened his wrists together . . . She supposed that was what a druggie dealer always carried, not a handkerchief because he always snivelled, but something easy that disabled an enemy. No denial, no squirming with excuses, and what she shouted at him seemed like shower water running off him. He looked round the room, and at the ceiling, and at the floor, and never at the weapon and never at her face. She went closer.

'To go to bed with me, was that a part of your work? Do you draw a bonus because you screwed me, screwed me and might get some pillow talk? They pay you more for that? You are so hateful which is why it is better that I shoot you, shoot you now.'

She raised the rifle. She stared down the barrel, over the V and the needle, and beyond was the shirt he wore and the loose top over it and she let her finger run from the outside of the trigger guard, inside it, into the trigger itself and her finger nestled on it. There were more sirens outside.

'Shoot you, I should do it, should . . .'

She did not know how much pressure was needed to draw back the trigger. Her finger came off it and she closed fast on him and lashed out with her right foot and kicked his ankle and did it hard. The same foot as she had used to kick the man who had come alongside her, riding his motorcycle, and her on the slow-moving scooter which was pathetic and rusted and stank of fuel fumes. Had hurt herself when she kicked the man, and hurt herself again. Dare not show it, could not . . . he gave no sign. He denied her satisfaction, did not reply, did not cry out, did not snarl, did not show pain, so she kicked him again, and limped away. The kid had an arm around her shoulder.

'Don't hurt him, Zeinab, and don't shoot him. He's all you have. You have nothing except him.'

Which was gasoline on a fire to her. She swung the rifle and aimed for his chin, wanted the weight of the wooden part on the end to strike his jaw and aimed and heaved it and waited, closed eyes, for the impact, and blinked, and saw that his head moved – not far and not fast – and she had missed. She felt the room darkening. Not her imagination, but the girl watching the TV had turned the sound higher and that would have been the response to her shouting, and the audience applause cracked across the bedroom . . .

She screamed, 'Talk to me. Tell me I meant something, was not just more money in your wage packet. Fucking man, who are you?'

The sunset, away over the water from La Castellane was spectacular that evening. From gold to blood-red, and rippling on a disturbed sea, and seeming highlighted by banking clouds that gathered to the west, above Port-Saint-Louis-du-Rhone and Saintes-Maries-de-la-Mer, and the shadows over the Camargue hurried towards the housing estate. It was January when the weather could change fast and was unpredictable. There could be thunder, hail, lightning, and crisp evenings and sunsets that were spectacular over the tower blocks, but the weather in all its vagaries had little effect on trade.

An orderly queue had formed. The queue, a snake of persons of many ages and with varied indications of affluence, was there each night as dusk collapsed over La Castellane. Seven evenings a week, seven nights, and the queue would always be hungry, demanding to be fed. But that night, the stomach of the queue remained empty. The queue was formed and waited patiently. Beyond the queue, restless and growing aggressive, were the look-outs and the escorts and the security for the differing franchises that tried, for profit, to satisfy the market-place. But could not. In stairwells, and in various apartments 'owned' by the dealers who had authority, was an importation of fresh merchandise, touted as being of high quality, but it could not be sold. Between the head of the queue and the kids who lived off the dealers was a cordon of police. No person was permitted to enter, and none to leave. It was a lockdown. Anxiety burdened Hamid. He was responsible. In his brother's apartment was a woman, armed, and a foreign policeman, and while they were there, all routes of entry and exit were blocked – and trade was lost, and trade was profit, what La Castellane thrived on, survived by. Like a tap had been turned off.

'It'll end in tears.'

'When it comes to optimism, you are a bucket full of holes.'

She was back beside Gough and he sensed her mood swing had taken her towards the gallows idea of fun, black stuff and larded with pessimism. She had been led away by a female police officer and they had trekked in the half-light towards some dense cluster of bushes. Himself, he would not have welcomed squatting down there, with the fair to middling chance of lowering a cheek on to an addict's hypodermic. Could in a weak moment have sympathised with her, but not made a habit of it over the years.

'I state the obvious.'

'What I don't see is why? Why did he follow her inside that place?'

'You are so naive.'

'Perhaps, but . . .'

'There's an itch down there in the lower regions. A bitch on heat and a following dog, oldest game in the park. Can't dump her.'

'Vulgar, Pegs, and beneath you.'

They were, both of them, the sort of vagrants that their type of work spewed out. The freaks that populated the corridors of the differing sections of the Counter-Terrorist business. Never home in the evenings, seldom present at breakfast because they were staying away or had already left for the train. Noses to the grindstone because that seemed best proof against a cock-up, the level of failure that sent a man, or a woman, out of a back entrance and fast, so that acute failure did not contaminate. He dreamed of reaching the magic retirement age, and then the chance to live close to his mother in a village between Loch Awe and Inverary, in the west of the Highlands, where no one – not even a passing predator in a salmon pool and listening to a lonely monologue – would know who he had once been, what he had once done. Not even a bloody otter.

'And true – wait till it plays out, and come back to me. No other reason for anyone with an ounce of sanity to go where he has gone.'

'He's a professional and you sell him short.'

'An attractive thought. Be real, Gough. We know nothing of him. He was a present at Christmas from the well-known distant aunt, that sort of thing, and you don't know what you're getting. Might be useless, might be valuable – a waste of space or what makes a complex operation run with well-oiled cogs. In the lap of the Gods. We expect to, and fail to, control him and prod him into the directions that suit us. It's a pipedream. What I said, know nothing about him. No name, no history in his rucksack, only the legend cooked up by the people in his office. No file available, no record for us of what he's achieved before. It is, Gough, a disaster recipe.'

'I always like to imagine a good outcome.'

A young officer offered them wrapped rolls and little mugs of strong coffee, and she'd smiled at him. There was an innocence to her face, and an obvious pleasure with her work that rather captivated Gough. But then, she would not be fielding brickbats, would not face a probing inquiry by those who practised hindsight to an art form, and the bill would be questioned. He had not caught a salmon on that river, tried for one every year and illegally, no licence, since he was a teenager and with a spoon on a fly only water . . . it would be good to get there again, and soon. Would Pegs be sitting on the bank behind him as he cast? Probably not.

She bored on. 'What I'm saying, he's put himself in harm's way. Idiotic and impetuous. What sends a man as a volunteer into that sort of place? Can only be the itch . . . why I say it'll end in tears, and there won't be a ride in a hearse through Royal Wootton Bassett for him: he'll go in the dead of night . . . there'll be tears, but not mine.'

'If you say so, Pegs.'

He heard a peremptory whistle. The Major strode towards them.

With sufficient problems to exercise him, he did not need them. Did not require the presence of two passengers with nothing to contribute.

Major Valery had already asked for his principal captain on the ground, who had the notebook and the pencil, to be briefed on the Undercover and had been brushed away. 'Sorry and all that, not intended as disrespect, we know nothing of him – well, next to nothing. Not inside the loop. Whether he's gone rogue, or is doing the Stockholm bit, can't say . . . Don't know whether he has a wife, a partner, a boyfriend, a caravan full of kids, where he comes from, his experience level, his stress tolerance. No idea, don't know him, cannot help.' He came back to lay down red lines, not to be crossed.

'The situation as I see it . . . First, your man is inside, has been denounced as a covert agent, is in a place of maximum danger through his own actions, but I am obliged to consider his well-being. I have a security perimeter around the project. Second, one of your nationals has purchased an AK-47 rifle, presumably with the intention of smuggling it into the UK, and that is a very small priority for me. Thirdly, we deal with suppliers of narcotics, those in the Class B category and I have no interest in them; if they were not here the economies of places such as La Castellane would collapse. There would be a crime wave of endemic proportions as a substitute for that economy. Last, and important, this is not a Disney theme park. You do not walk around, ask questions, get in the way. I will do my best to get your man into a place of safety. If I am successful, you and your colleague and your agent will be driven at speed to the airport and put on a plane, destination immaterial, and taken off my patch. There are no questions from you, of course. But one from me.'

'Fire it,' the man said and the woman glowered at him.

'The girl in there, how will she be? Can she kill? Without an audience and without cameras, will she shoot him?'

The woman answered, 'Have to wait and see, won't we? Which will make for an interesting evening. My promise, Major, if you fuck up then we'll make double damn certain you field no blame, no recrimination. Just so as we understand each other.'

He thought it would rain soon, and be dark sooner, and the added complications screwed each other in his mind.

December 2018

He came out of the Consulate building, clasping the print-out given him, and began to dance a clumsy jig.

Then collected himself and regained his outward calm, unable to harness his inner elation, only disguise it, and walked across the car park, then went through a gate in the concrete walls deemed necessary to protect any United States of America mission abroad, then weaved through the concrete anti-tank teeth that were another layer of defence for the few American nationals in the recently opened building on the outskirts of his home city, Alexandria. Next was the long walk in the stifling heat to the distant area where visitors – applying for entry visas – were permitted to park.

His cup, brimful and slightly overflowing, contained good news, the best news, and was relayed to him in the dry language of the print-out. As a Christian Egyptian national he was to be awarded refugee status: he and his family were to be welcomed in that distant country. They would go quickly, without fanfare, no farewell parties and no wringing of hands with neighbours. Would pack a few of their choicest possessions, would leave the rest in the apartment – furniture, fittings, unexceptional pictures, out-dated clothing, and the keys would go to a cousin and he would dispose of the remnants of their Egyptian life: if he was lucky there would be work for this harbourmaster's office pilot in a port along the Atlantic seaboard, or on the Great Lakes in the north, and the children would have education and the family could worship on a Sunday morning without fear of death, mutilation, any atrocity weapon detonated by the fanatics of his city. He did not go straight home, nor did he phone his family.

The pilot had other pressing business.

Near to his home on the eastern side of Alexandria was a line of poorly constructed lock-up garages and storerooms. Most were used by men who traded in fruit and vegetables in the open-air markets of the city, but he had one on which his father had long ago taken a lease. He had failed to find the courage to bring the weapon into his own home. The risk of its discovery, or of the children finding it and gossiping to others, was too great. Still in the wrapping in which it had been given him by the navigating officer; he warily took it from the garage and stowed it in his car, under his own seat, and drove away.

He went west. He felt a conspirator and his mind was clouded in guilt and nervousness, because he carried the weapon.

Went out on the international coastal road, followed the signs for Alamein and Marsah Matruh and Sidi Barrani. For his work as a pilot he needed certainty and precision. Professional disciplines. Through the middle of that day, in the glare of the sun and against a backdrop of endless, featureless desert, he drove away from all he knew, and all of the people who knew him. He could not go as far as the Libyan border, five hours' drive, but he went for a clear hour and 40 minutes until he spied the caravan. They were a part of the great Bedouin tribe. They had camels. They had desert tents and cloaked women, and still moved across frontiers in search of grazing. Their world was pressured by Japanese-built pick-up trucks, and by the 'sophistication' of TV, by narcotics, by the bureaucrats who needed them corralled into the authority of the state . . . They moved languidly at the pace the camels wished to go under the burden of their load.

He stopped the car beside the road.

The pilot lifted out the weapon in its packaging. Hopefully, in years to come, inside the safety of the United States, he would remember what he had done and might try to explain to new friends how great had been the fear he'd carried both as a Christian and as a man owning an illegal weapon. One might have brought a lynch mob down on him, the other might have had him climb the scaffold's steps. He covered the rifle with the cloth always in the car which he draped over the windscreen when the vehicle was parked in sunlight. To other drivers on the road, past the battlefield cemetery of the British and their allies, forty minutes out of Alamein, he would have looked like a man hurrying towards a dip in the sand where he could hide and relieve his bowels.

He should never have accepted it, should have refused the gift. It had never been in his house. Now, with his visa granted, there were no circumstances when he might have needed its protection. He would be glad to be rid of it.

Kids came running towards him, might have wanted to see if he carried sweets or would give them coins. His shoes had filled with sand which grated on his socks and if he went farther he would start blisters.

No comment, nothing said, he gave up the package, his burden, let it slide into hands that might not yet have lost an innocence, without explanation, and he waved them away. He stood and watched the swarm of youngsters sprint barefoot back to the line of camels and adults. A cluster of men examined what had been brought them, were now 200 metres from him. An arm was raised, to acknowledge the gift, and shoulders shrugged but the stride of the camels never shortened. He watched them go, the package buried in a beast's load, and soon the heat's haze claimed them. He had lost the thing, and thanked his God for it, and went back to his car. In a few days the caravan would have crossed into Libya, well south of the border crossing.

The pilot shook the grains from his shoes, massaged his feet and took more sand from his socks. He would drive home and in the evening when the children were in their beds he would tell his wife of their new future, show her the print-out from the Consulate . . . he believed that their days of living with terror were almost over, that he had no further requirement for a killing machine, a Kalashnikov.

'What did you want?' It was the motorcycle rider, who had exchanged the money belt for the weapon. He did not answer. 'You came here because you wanted something, what?'

He sensed this was a man who made decisions that affected a cash flow of tens of thousands of euros, who would have – in a limited space – the power of life and the power of death over opponents. He would have snapped instructions and lesser creatures would do his bidding: there had been people at the heart of the courier conspiracy when he was Norm Clarke and busy betraying them who would have had such power. If this man decided him better dead and gone, then it would happen, and he would leave the apartment in a body bag, and it would be hard going for the mortuary people to get him down the stairs. He did not help, no answer given. He would speak when he was ready, not wheedle, give nothing . . . his way.

'The old man, he is a grand figure. He is a legend in the city. He said you were a cop. I did not know, but he did. Why does a cop come here, into our life?'

The evening had come down and outside the cloud had thickened, and the power of the wind had slipped. No lights shone in the bedroom. The man was two feet from him, and his breath stank of chillis, and he still had patience, but it would not last. The boy with the wrecked arm stood in the doorway and had a knife in his hand but seemed more interested in looking across the hallway and into the living area and catching some of the game show. Zed sat on the bed. He thought by now she would have realised she had entered a cul-de-sac, and did not know how to retrace her steps, and the rifle was across her lap . . . Long ago, with an identity now shelved, he had apparently idolised a worn and frayed bear and had carried it through the day, and to nursery, and only released it when he was in the bath, then carried it to bed. She had the rifle, held it that way . . . There would have been weapons instructors at Lympstone who could talk about the way in which a Kalashnikov empowered those whose voices had never been heard before. She might not have known how to break out of the tower block, but she would not have doubted that the rifle was her salvation, a protector.

'I do hashish. I do well with hashish. A cop from abroad does not care about hashish in the north of Marseille. Why?'

He could barely see the dealer's face. But enough light came up from the street lamps for some to fall on her cheeks and nestle over her nose and into the small lines at the side of her mouth, and the caverns in which her eyes were set . . . places where a young man and a young woman could lose themselves, be strangers in a community and not hunted down. Not everyone had to belong and have roots, have a granny in the cemetery, to be accepted on certain terms – live and let live . . . he thought her beautiful, stubborn, but beautiful.

'What can satisfy you?

There were no more sirens outside, but sometimes a vehicle moved and then the blue lights climbed the walls of the block and filtered into the bedroom and shone on the ceiling or slid over the walls, once covering the poster of the rifle; the only other light was the flicker of the technicolour from the TV.

'I understand. You do not have to speak . . . You came for the girl. Yes?'

He did not think he was about to die, but had no complacency. Tiredness would build, and with it would come impatience, exasperation, anger, all of them increasing the danger factor. But he said nothing, was not ready to argue his corner.

'It is not romance, no. It is because you are a cop and she is a fugitive, yes?'

He was offered a cigarette, declined. He had noted that the man addressed only him, ignored the others, as if they had no importance, were worthless . . . might have been a wrong judgement because she had the rifle, was the only one of them equipped to kill, as far as he knew.

'You know what? I understand everything . . . The girl is a fugitive, and the girl has a weapon, an automatic rifle, big deal. I have seven under my control. In this project alone there might be twenty-five. And now, I tell you what you are, you are a nuisance to me. You are an obstruction.'

Zed now hovered close, had not relaxed her grip on the rifle, seemed calmer and more settled as if her mind were made up. Andy watched. The man, Hamid, turned towards her as if at last acknowledging her place in the sun, perhaps her right to be consulted.

'And you, what do you want?'

Wanted what she would not have admitted to. Not shared what she wanted. Almost frightened of what she wanted. Would like to have told Andy, snuggled in bed together, bare-skinned and warm and wet, and him loving her, told him as he slept and the rhythm of his breathing was regular, that she wanted to be known. Have her name shouted.

Nobody outside Savile Town knew the names of the boys, her cousins, who had gone from Dewsbury on the bus, or by train, to go and fight in Syria, or in Iraq. And to die there. Only a few could recall their faces: 'a quiet boy, and very serious . . . always polite, always helpful . . . do anything for anybody'. Forgotten now. It shamed her. She had had to struggle to recall the names of the suicide people, and more often now the faces of her two cousins became blurred and merged and it was harder for her to see two individuals. She did not know if the last two had carried Kalashnikovs similar to the one she now held when they'd gone to detonate themselves, driving an armour-plated vehicle, reinforced sides and an engine covered with tempered steel sheets so that they could manoeuvre through defensive fire and stay in control right to the target area. Had felt that power, and the strength given them by the rifle, peering through a slit in the armour plate and hearing the drumming of rifle fire. She did not know whether the cousins, two names and one face, had been armed with them – or had been asleep in a makeshift barracks, or had been grunting through sex with one of the child girls who went there with the fervent adoration of converts, and a bomb or a missile had struck their building. She thought it would have been a cruel fate to have died at the hand of the enemy and without an AK to hold, as she had, in his hand. The answer to the question? She yearned for a form of recognition.

Never listened to at home. Never really shone at school, except for a minimal pass grade for the entry into the university in Manchester, and a heavy hint, a suggestion put on her lap, that she ticked enough boxes for entrance and that another candidate for the course, cleverer and with better grades, had been elbowed. Never listened to by either Scorpion or by Krait, nor by the men she had met in the park in London. Might have been listened to by Andy, or thought he had listened to her . . . then betrayed.

An image played in her mind. She had walked into the heart of the city where she supposedly studied. No laptop, no notepad and pencil, no textbooks in a bag. Heavy against her body as she went down the long street was the assault rifle . . . the first to be brought down would be the security guard at the checkpoint. One shot in the chest and she would run forward. She would hear, each time she fired, the clamour of screaming and might catch the terror in the faces of those cowering in the corridors, trying to pretend they were helpless and innocent and had no hatred of her. Wonderful to see the terror and the begging. All because she carried the gaunt shape of the weapon. Not to do with her personality, and the power of her spoken message, but because she had it in her hand. She would shoot and shoot again, keep shooting through the first magazine, and spin them over and lock in the second that was taped to the first, and would shoot with that, would keep firing, keep knocking over the dolls and the bears and the mannequins until she heard the click and the trigger no longer fired and then all around her would be quiet. She would walk forward and would step around and through the casualties. She doubted she would hear them approach from behind, their weapons already cocked. She would know nothing when they fired. Her photograph would be in the papers. Her name would be broadcast. That was what she wanted.

She shook her head sharply. 'You have no right to ask what I want – and you would not understand if I told you.'

Nor would she tell him that she would shoot Andy before it was over. Not yet because he must suffer . . . it hurt badly that he did not beg her, show any weakness. No balance – his betrayal of her and her deceit in manipulating him . . . no guilt for her, she alone had grievances, was wronged. She did not know how long there would be until the end played out or in what form. Nor would have answered the question had it been put differently: was she getting there, towards what she wanted? The rain came fast, arrived on a wave of cold wind.

Two gusts following close on each other heralded the opening thrusts of the storm. As if a tap had abruptly been turned on. Spots of rain pattering first, then a single thunderclap, then what seemed the tipping of a myriad of buckets. Dogs howled into the growing darkness. Not a night to be out, not for the old or the young, the uniformed or those in flimsy sweatshirts and jeans, those who worked and those who stood in line and looked to buy.

There was little cover from the elements around the project of La Castellane. A foul night and a dirty night, but many braved it. Police huddled under capes and the rain dripped from their headgear, and their focus was on keeping their weapons dry. Alongside them were those standing in the queues, uneasy as bedfellows who waited to be admitted so they might purchase quality Moroccan, a new shipment and well spoken of. Also soaked were those attempting to return to the project after a day of menial employment in the city, and those waiting to leave so that they could work at bars and clean shopping centres.

And there were the women who had emerged on to the narrow balconies butting off some of the apartment windows. Some wore waterproof hats, some had hitched plastic bags on to their heads, some allowed the rain to wash through their hair. The situation was a stand-off, and from the east-facing windows of La Castellane there was a good view of the bare open space under the walls, and the rocks ahead of them to impede access, then the road and finally the slope of scrub leading up to the shopping centre, where marksmen might gather. If there were marksmen, and the situation came to a blood-spattered head, then it was a fair and reasonable bet *he* would be there Only one star-studded figure attracted the attention of the women of the project. Spectacles were regularly wiped, eyes blinked often to dislodge rainwater . . . they did not know who he was because always he performed the death dance with a balaclava covering his features, and they knew his name only from that of a former executioner, and few of them would have known the significance in their adopted country's history of the Place de la Concorde and the work of Charles-Henri Samson.

Sheltering in a police wagon, along with other marksmen, Samson dozed. The Styr SSG was balanced across his thighs, loaded but not cocked. Partly it was his imagination and some of it was the product of dreams: he was in the Tanzanian park of Serengeti and he seemed to see a family of cheetahs. The big female had come effortlessly down from a *kopje*, a small hillock of stones and bushes, and would have hidden her cubs there while she hunted. He had seen this first on television and now it was implanted in his mind, and he would not forget a frame of it. Led by their mother, the family crossed a flat area of arid grassland and headed for a green-painted long wheelbase Land Rover. The boldest of the cubs was the first to jump and skidded up on to the engine covering and then settled and switched a tail, and the mother came next and climbed on to the roof and lay easily down on the metalwork on which the sun had shone all day, and the others romped under the vehicle and round the wheels. A blonde and tanned woman sat at the wheel and must have sweltered because every window was firmly closed. She was, Samson knew, a prominent British expert on the species, and she had written a piece on the trust, the bond, between herself in her vehicle and this one family, and they came to her if she was close by and climbed on to this one zoologist's roof and bonnet to catch the warmth of the metalwork. The dream or the thought of them gratified him . . . His rifle was clean, dry, and he awaited an order from the Major which might come and might not. He might shoot that evening, or perhaps another of the men close to him would, or perhaps none of them would. He was not restless, would not be concerned if he did not fire, or if he fired and killed . . . it would concern him if he fired and missed. Just before he had started to dream or imagine the advance of the cheetah tribe, Samson had received a text, from his wife: *Drafted in. Getting wet. On the perimeter. First one home puts the supper on. What a happy place! Xxx* He had not replied. It would all be connected, the call out. A weapon exchanged for money, and a clever old-school thug, known by the self-gratification name of Tooth, had noted the presence of the English detective, no doubt good at his work but in a location where 'good' was inadequate, and a girl who was moderately attractive but not in comparison to his own wife and his own daughter, and a mess . . . Most of his work involved mopping up after mistakes and errors of judgement – all similar to situations in the Serengeti where wildebeest or gazelles paid with their lives for mistakes. Some talked in the van but Samson held his peace, was quiet and waited.

* * *

'Happy, Gough?'

'Mildly delirious.'

The rain fell on them, dripped off them, and nothing changed and little moved. Maybe they'd have been better in the customer queue that was building steadily. Too many years since, as a teenager, she'd enjoyed a rebellious joint, Moroccan or other, but a smoke now might have been welcome. Had they been in London, or just in the UK, all would have seemed straightforward, and the weight would have been shared.

'Sorry and all that but it's writhing round my head. You and me, what we achieve. Apologies if out of order but it's bitching me. Start with you. Satisfied you make a difference?'

'Never doubted it.'

'An assessment of where we are?'

'Where we are not wanted, not respected, regarded as an interfering nuisance. The Major regards us as a pain, hardly disguised, our own man has freelanced and is out of control, a runaway cannon, and . . .'

They were alone. They were fed no information and there was no more food or coffee. She could remember the face of the would-be agent, drowned, with the smiling anxiety to please scrubbed from his face, and remember the girl at the heart of Rag and Bone who had seemed an innocent marionette, dancing to others' tunes, and remember the sight of their boy, Andy Knight, hugging and holding the girl at the bridge in Avignon, and turned against Gough and her. And could see a marksman expertly killing a youth in a street. Nothing in her memory gave her satisfaction.

'In this job, Gough, do we ever meet, mingle, cooperate, with decent folk?'

'Never intentionally.'

'Not ever?'

'Only by accident.'

Pegs said, 'I am serious, Gough . . . "making a difference" is about all we have to cling to if we're to keep our peckers up. Otherwise, what the hell are we here for . . . It's never-ending, we're on a treadmill, and the threat is driving it faster. It's the present and it's the future, and I do not see an escape route ... Sorry and all that, but I'm in the dumps.'

He put his arm around her. They were in the shadow of a small tree, the sort that landscapers would have planted in the hope of bringing 'civilisation' to this bleak place, and it would not have been noticed by any but a serious *voyeur*. He was a 'good old boy', Gough was, and needed to be because he was all she had ... and nothing was permanent, in her jaundiced experience of life. It was a strong arm, and welcome.

Gough said, 'Regrets for my gloomy view, but I think the rain has come on heavier.'

It had taken Crab several minutes of kneeing and elbowing to get through the clutch of passengers at the desk, their tempers steadily fraying.

He knew the flight was delayed. The hold-up, he gathered, was indefinite. Other aircraft with other destinations had now climbed above it on the departure board.

Life should run smoothly for a man such as Crab. His money and his heritage and his prestige were supposed to ensure that the stresses of 'ordinary' people were avoided. Around him were passengers off a cruise liner, who had gone in search of a wafer of winter sunshine and had been well doused between the coach and the airport, and irritation had spawned. He wouldn't have looked much himself. God knows why ... but a shortage of taxis, an argument about the fare which had ended with him scooting when threatened with a call to the police, a trek towards the terminal doors and the rain at its heaviest. He was soaked, and his jacket and his trousers and his shoes, and a grip of chill damp was on his skin ... and the fucking flight seemed delayed without word of when he might board along with this crowd in their vacation gear. He did not do holidays. Crab did not do beaches, or cocktails at dusk, and did not do the tourism of traipsing round ruins, and now was going nowhere. What he did do was long-standing friendships, alliances, networking with a few people who were trusted, valuable, who respected him. It was like there was a prop that held up a good piece of his life, and it was like Tooth had got hold of a sledge and had whacked the prop, flattened it, and brought a ceiling down on him.

Always been a street fighter, and knew when to kick and punch to get through a close crowd, and ignored the protests, and was panting, quite breathless, when his stomach barged against the front of the desk where a girl sat, flustered.

A mirror reflected his appearance. He saw himself, saw what she saw. His question must have been garbled, and she looked at him as if she were dealing with an idiot. Something about 'engine trouble', and something about 'malfunction' and she was looking over his shoulder and waiting for the next passenger's query; she had told him fuck all. Did she not know who he was? Not know who Crab used to be? Not know that men's chins used to go slack if they'd annoyed him? He was pushed aside. No apologies and no requests for him to move. Shoved out of the way, like he was old garbage: wet old garbage. All a disaster. The board flickered, the announcement was made.

The flight had a new schedule, would take off in three hours . . . trouble was that nobody knew, any longer, who he used to be.

'You should know what happens . . . When we find a police spy, it is what happens. My brother will do it . . .' Karym hissed at the man who sat on the floor, back against the bedroom wall, and who never met his eye. He felt a growing frustration. Behind him, Zeinab paced, backwards and forwards across the window where the curtains were still not drawn, and there would have been sufficient light from the corridor and the TV for Zeinab to have made a silhouette. He could not tell her, imagined that if he criticised her she would have snarled at him. Wanted so much to help her, and did not know how and it was dark outside and the rain came hard.

'. . . If there is a police spy, and he is identified and taken, then he is dead. His mother can scream and his aunts and his sisters, but they waste their words. His father may send an imam to plead for his life, but my brother will be deaf. And not just Hamid, but any leader in the project will be the same. A police spy is a dead man . . . That will be you.'

His brother had gone. Not hostile but seeming confused. Karym would have liked his brother to go rough on the police spy, beat him and kick him, spill blood, make him cry out. The spy had not replied to any of his brother's statements, which was an astonishing display of contempt and should have been rewarded: real pain, and real injury should have been done to him . . . It annoyed him that the girl – the most extraordinary person he had met in his life, though he had barely spoken to her, and the best looking and far ahead of any teenage kid he knew in La Castellane – paced across the room, but he had not the courage to risk her anger: she should not show herself. Would Samson be there by now? Might be, likely to be. He threatened, in the hope of seeing weakness in the spy. He had no reason to hate or despise him, but it would satisfy.

'We take a car. My brother will send people to find one, then to hotwire it, then to drive it down to the back wall of the school, where the rubbish is stored. The owner may complain, cry that he needs his car for work. He will not be heard. Then fuel. We will have gasoline ready. When my brother is ready, he will send for you. Send boys to bring out the police spy.'

He knew the procedure of the 'barbecue', knew it because several times he had watched it, and the smell of it had stayed with him, in his mind and on his body and over his clothes, for days. He took especial care with his language, spoke slowly and he believed he was clear, so that his threat was understood. She stayed on the move and he wondered if Samson had arrived and had adjusted his sight, followed her each time she crossed the window space, was on Battle Sight Zero. He tried a last time to win a reaction.

'Bound and needing the boys to drag you, and a gag in your mouth, but no cloth across your eyes, and you will see where they take you, then you will smell the fuel. You will be put inside the car, across the back seat, which is already soaked. You will see the flame which is brought to the car. A big crowd watches. The flame is thrown in. It is what my brother arranges for a police spy . . . Do you say nothing? You will burn and nobody will care . . . What do you want of us?'

His voice beat back from the walls and ceiling, he understood the depths of his failure. She walked behind him and carried the weapon, and he heard the game show on the TV and the patter of the rain and the beat of her feet.

He was settling in for a long night. Had few other options. Had to wait and take what he thought the best chance for survival. He studied the bedroom, but it was hard to concentrate because of her restless movement, and the boy nibbled at his resolve, with talk of the 'barbecue'. In the centre of the ceiling, was a single light flex holding a low-wattage bulb and cheap shade, brittle plastic already cracked, with no pattern to relieve its boredom. Parts of it were more stained than others, and they'd have been immediately above where the boy might have sat when he smoked, fags or dope. It needed paint, was shabby and tired.

'Even with the gag you will scream after the fuel is lit. Everyone hears the scream but no one comes to help. If the police have a patrol car going by and hear the scream they will not come into the project. You burn and many will come to watch but no one will weep for you. My brother will organise it.'

On the shelves were volumes on the Kalashnikov rifle . . . he knew about people who were fanatic collectors of libraries detailing the working parts of a firearm, and perhaps they played weekend games with decommissioned weapons, or went on paint-ball manoeuvres, or collected the memorabilia that American companies marketed on the internet: underpants with an AK image printed across the crotch, or mugs and pins, ashtrays and posters that might show North Vietnamese soldiers holding them in a jungle, or Iraqi forces in a desert, or Soviet military exercising in the Arctic, or ISIS people who were bodyguards for an executioner in Raqqa. He did not read such stuff, thought it puerile. He had no requirement to fantasise on a war and rubber-neck from the sidelines . . . He was a paid-up member, had the season ticket for the proper business – as had Norm and Phil. And he saw places where there had been adhesive fastenings on the walls but what they held up had been ripped off, out of date or because of a mood swing, and left behind were the scabs where the plaster had come away, and the blue lights from the street caught those places and highlighted them.

'It is what you want, yes? I tell you, you will get what you want.'

The boy was close enough to him. Could have kicked him, maybe felled him . . . but had no reason to. Only a little voice droning on, and unlikely to affect the outcome. Could have felt sorry for the boy. Was not supposed to have sympathies for either targets or those who strayed into the lines of the cross-hairs – also, was not supposed to take targets to bed, and feel affection for them, nor try to find a way out which left them free, clean, with a future worth living. Much that SC&O10 rule books would have said was outside the limits.

'You will get the fire because you are a spy and because my brother will . . .'

The voice faded. Perhaps, at last, enthusiasm for describing the fate of a police agent had palled, and perhaps he had turned towards Zed for endorsement and she had mouthed – her face in shadow – something like 'shut the fuck up'. The boy buttoned it, and turned away. He thought both of them, the boy and Zed, were close now to the mix of exhaustion and fear, knowing the plot was lost, and looking to the irrational. The psychologists who swarmed like a rash over the Undercovers always predicted that a hostage situation deteriorated rapidly, and then was most dangerous to a trussed prisoner. Likely to be close now, the crisis moment, but he stayed quiet.

He thought Rag and Bone was near the end.

18

He watched the weapon.

Occasionally, if light flickered on it he saw the notches cut. He had tried to count them but the stock was never still for long enough. She had it wedged against her hip and the end of it was firm between her elbow and the curve of her pelvis. Once he had counted seventeen, and for a long time that was the best he'd managed, but more recently he had totted up, off two rows, nineteen. He supposed it a sort of ritual . . . Shoot. Kill. Open a penknife, or detach a bayonet. Scratch. Flick away loose wood. Feel good. Look to kill again, or be killed. Many owners. A colourful history, caused a bucket of tears.

It came very suddenly. He had not predicted that moment, that reaction. His backside hurt from sitting on the linoleum-covered floor. His face itched from stubble forming but he did not want to scratch, move. He was sitting still, quiet . . . She exploded. Not at him, at the boy. Passing each other, him going to sneak a look through the window, from the side and masked by the curtains, and her passing the window and fully exposed and they collided. Ridiculous. Hostage-takers in confusion and walking into each other. Almost laughable. The boy swung his foot and kicked her shin. Her reaction was to club him, a short swing, with the body of the weapon, and the magazine would have clipped his chin. And him going to kick her again, and her looking for space to strike a heavier and more significant blow and both missing and both tumbling. A weapon was underneath them, and she was swearing at him and he at her: English words and French words. They wrestled. She was stronger, but he could fight dirtier. She had him pinioned. Beneath her, he lifted his knee into the pit of her stomach. Her hands were on his throat, her knees on his arms. The boy used his kneecap again and she gasped and freed his throat and her weight shifted off his arms and he was scratching at her face, trying to find her eyes.

He watched. He thought it nearly a good time to make his pitch, not yet but nearly the right moment. They broke apart. Were sheepish. Enough light came in for him to see two faces, and their eyes had dropped and their anger was doused, and she pushed back her hair and coughed, and he was snivelling as if the struggle had loosened the muck down in his lungs. The boy was first on his feet and her legs were entangled in the rifle's barrel, then he bent and helped her up and she used her free hand to push herself from the side of the unmade bed. Light, for a moment, flooded the room. She shrugged away from him, rejected the help. Andy could measure his feelings for her: not lust. Not loving. A degree of pity, something of sympathy. She would not achieve her target as a *jihadi* courier; she was neutered, no longer represented a danger. His feeling for her, he supposed, was affection – would not be less, could be more . . . There would be an inquest, in-house and confidential, and his actions would be picked over and he might try to explain that his emotions had been jumbled by events, were not clear-cut. He would look into the interrogators' pitiless faces, and might just rasp at them, 'But you weren't there. Don't know how it is, was. Your sort, sit in judgement, are never fucking there.' He thought she had started to crack under the pressure.

She had shown weakness. The boy was not supposed to know that she had no plan, had failed in what it was intended she should do. Pretty damn simple . . . play the field with a simple guy who drove lorries. Enmesh him, dangle him, get him to drive to the Mediterranean coast and pick up a package and come back to a ferry port where the sleuths and watchers would wave them through. Nice-looking girl with a bit of cleavage hanging out, and a guy who looked like he'd lapped at the cream bowl, and given a thumbs-up by the Border people and the Customs and the security staff who were supposed to ferret out the *jihadis* coming home, and the weapons they'd need for fighting their bloody war.

She was the star girl, and she would have told people near to her cause and dear to it that she could cope with what was asked . . . Where was she? On the floor, scratching and kicking with a kid from a high-rise block where they dealt in cannabis, and she'd no way out.

He thought she had reason, plenty of cause, to have lost the rag. And, getting near to that moment when self-control was lost and crisis blitzed her. He said nothing.

What he reckoned peculiar was that no link had been established. The kid must have a mobile phone. The girl who watched the game shows, and who sometimes shifted on a noisy chair and sometimes coughed and sometimes moved from the next door room to the bathroom, or opened and closed a fridge door, must have a mobile phone. He would have imagined by now that a hostage negotiator would be in place, busy pouring sweet syrup into Zed's ear, and the boy's. He knew something of the negotiation process: it was smooth talk, dripping reason, quiet and patient, trying to build trust and never accepting deadlines and attempting to bore the guys or girls with the hardware into a state of tired surrender. 'We want cigarettes, or sandwiches, or chocolate, or a passage out . . . want it, or we start shooting.' Which was crap, because he was the only person they could kill and that would mean losing their shield and the one bargaining chip they possessed. And the answer would come back that the one official who could authorise the little luxuries had gone home, would not be back until the morning, and they'd delay, obfuscate. No negotiation had started. Next step was the threat that he, star boy on the scene, would be shot. Simple enough. In fifteen minutes, in ten minutes, in five minutes, maybe in half a minute, he'd be dead . . . Not a good prognosis, because at that point, usually the outer door caved in and the flash-and-bangs rolled down the corridor and the storm squad came calling, and were always trigger happy, and high on adrenaline. The chances were good that he'd stop more than half a dozen rounds. He would have expected by now to hear, very faint, the sounds of a drill's bit eating through the thin walls, usually from the apartment next door, or the ceiling, so that a probe microphone, better if it were a camera, could be shoved through to give the boss a clear indication of what was happening inside. He had strained to hear the drill and had not.

She started up again. It was part because of what he felt for her – a kaleidoscope of emotions – that he was there . . . and part from the desire harboured in his stubborn streak, pure obstinacy, to see the Rag and Bone mission to conclusion. Her bark was close.

'Was it all just deceit, all of it?'

Nothing said, his eyes staying low, finding somewhere on the rug, amongst the boy's clothes, and amongst the food wrappers. Zed shouted,'All false, everything?'

From the start, of course. From when she had walked down the darkened street and the thugs had bounced her, and she had been on the pavement and trying to hold the strap of her bag as it was dragged off her, and attempts made to punch and kick her – and him coming from nowhere, a stranger off the street, and what had seemed a ruthless, selfless effort to protect her . . . all a lie.'The men who attacked me, pretended to, they were your friends? Police? More deceit?'

And Zeinab remembered being in her room, struggling with an outline for the essay she was supposed to write, and cursing her tutor who had made it obvious that she was an unsatisfactory student, without sufficient interest in her subject . . . and her phone ringing, and being told to come down. Him being there, and his flowers. First flowers ever brought her. A trick to delude her.'The flowers were a lie, and the kiss was a lie, and walking with our fingers joined was a lie, and because you were so clever I did not see the lie.'

Anger surged in her. Andy would not look at her.'You think I am the stupid bitch who will lead you to my brothers? Do you think that? That I am the weak link? I tell you a truth, could have told it while you fucked me, could have yelled it at you while you were grunting, sweating, whispering lies to me . . . I am a fighter. I am not afraid. I am a fighter, on the front line, I have no fear . . . My two cousins went to the war. Two streets from me, left their home, went away, were martyred. They fought, knew the beauty of fighting, of the struggle, knew the excitement. My street is filled with small and frightened people who do not know of war. I am learning it . . . You have taught me to be a fighter, from today. I show you.'

Zeinab turned away from him. She brushed past the boy, like he was not there, was an irrelevance. She went to the window, dragged one of the flimsy curtains and half the hooks broken and it sagged loose in her fist. She snatched at the window handle, twisted it, forced it and felt the flush of air on her hands and wrists, on her face, and then the wet of the rain. She fired. Zeinab held the weapon firmly, and pulled the trigger a second time – and some more.

She had no target. She went after shadows. Single shots. And then she released the trigger, let it ride back and the grating sound followed as the cases were ejected and fell sideways from her and bounced, careered on the linoleum, then hit the wall and spun before coming to rest. She thought it a feeling like no other . . . in bed with him was secondary. Her shoulder ached from the impact of the stock. At first she had tried to gaze along the length of the rifle barrel, over the V sight and the needle sight and cut a line to dark outlines of bushes beyond the road where the street-lights still burned. She thought herself adult, disciplined and intelligent because she counted the number of times she pulled on the trigger, counted each time the stock thudded into her shoulder. The air around her, in spite of the open window and the driving rain, reeked of the smell that came from firing. Her ears rang with the sound the weapon made.

And thought of her cousins. Nice boys who teased her and called her a 'swot', and had never told her where they would head, but had gone and had fought and had died, and had no marked grave . . . It was said, whispered among the older kids at her school in Savile Town that the suiciders who came from her district, any of them in the armour-plated cars or walking towards checkpoints where the enemy waited and would do inspections, were told they would go to Paradise if they died fighting against the *kuffar*. If they were men, then a bus load of virgins would await them under an orchard's fruit trees, always well loaded, always ripe. For a girl, there would be only one boy, handsome and loving and faithful and not caring if she wore pebble-lensed spectacles and if she had a brace over her teeth . . . and hoped then that her cousins saw her. Once only, she glanced behind her. The boy lay on the bed and had his hands over his ears and seemed to tremble. She looked at Andy Knight, but he did not meet her eye.

Twice more she fired . . . It was, she thought, a supreme moment in her life: she was now separated from her home, and from her school, and the lecture theatres in Manchester, and from the girls – supercilious and haughty – on her corridor in the Hall of Residence. The quiet fell.

The wind had dropped.

The shots were clear and loud, heard by each and every one of the watchers who huddled or sheltered or endured the strengthening force of the rain. No one stirred, made themselves obvious, drew attention to their position. Some claimed to have seen a shape at a window, and others said they had seen the flashes from the barrel as each round was fired. The pulse of the project beat faster, with growing anticipation. There would be a better show than expected, a performance to be remembered. The balconies were full, the queue held its line, the perimeter cordon remained in place. Some said it was a gesture, and bold. Others said that firing high-velocity rounds without purpose showed growing panic, weakness.

Karym yelled, 'What did you do that for, sister?'

Her answer was spoken without emotion. 'To show them.'

'What do you think you are showing them?'

'That I am a fighter.'

'You try to start a war, you know who you are against?'

'I show them that I am not afraid.'

'You have half Marseille's police out there. You have the best they have. You will have Samson, the executioner.'

'I am not frightened of them.'

'You think they will go away now? Leave you to have a fine sleep, after you start a war? Why, sister?'

'I have new strength, new power. They have no authority over me.'

'Who makes money out of fighting in a war? I don't.'

'What is it to do with money? Nothing to do with money. It is about defiance, about being a soldier.'

'To make money, you trade. Trade is not war. We made a trade, a very small one. I am astonished that my brother was prepared to be involved. Even more astonishing that a legend, the man who is Tooth, was prepared to do the organisation. Fuck, sister, this is nothing – for us – to do with war.'

'You are Arabs, Muslims.'

'No, first we are traders – afterwards there may be time to be Arab, to pray. We buy cargo, break it down, sell it on. We have no interest in war. War would interfere with trade. Sister, did no one tell you?'

'Just then I felt I was a soldier, a true fighter. I had the weapon, had an aim, squeezed on the trigger, saw a mass of enemies, and saw them in flight. It is extraordinary to feel . . . You do not understand.'

'Because I have never fired it . . . Sister, that is what they say. It is fascinating, it is remarkable, and it kills. Does not just kill the person who is aimed at, is a target. It kills the boy who holds it. It can kill you, sister. Here, whether you are a fighter or a soldier, no one in La Castellane gives a fuck. You inconvenience them. They want to trade, make money, want to survive, not fight some fucking war . . . I am sorry. I told you the truth.'

He said that he would get her a glass of water. And looked down at her prisoner and saw the raw swelling at the wrists where the restraints were pulled too tight, but the man – the police spy – had not complained and did not draw attention to himself. He went out of the bedroom. In the living-room his sister slept on the settee and he switched off the TV. Before going to the kitchen he walked up the corridor to the front door. It was steel-lined, had two locks, two bolts and a chain. He had not bothered to use the chain or the bolts, and only one of the locks. He opened it and looked across the lobby and down to the first corner of the stairs and saw small bright eyes. Kids' eyes. If the police had been there he would have seen them and they would have called to him, threatened him. He understood that they stayed back. Why? She interfered with trade, as he had told her. There would be an accommodation, of course. He closed the door, did not activate any of the locks and went to the kitchen to get her water. He thought that the truth he'd told would go hard with her, and believed her incredible, wonderful, but fragile. Every waking moment in his life, inside La Castellane, had been dominated by trade: the only issue, of sole importance. Money flooded from the trade and raised a man's prestige. His brother would not have comprehended her . . . she knew nothing of trade, nothing of money, was – yes – incredible and wonderful.

At last, sympathy was shown them. Two rats, three-quarters drowned, were offered mercy.

Pegs said to Gough that it was not personal them being left in the rain, just that they were irrelevant and probably forgotten. It was the same policewoman who had shown her where the bushes were thickest. Now she made a brusque apology for leaving them without shelter, said that they should join her husband in the dry, with the GIPN team, brought them to the wagon. The door had been pulled open and a fog of cigarette smoke had spewed out, and there was a reluctant shuffling of backsides and room was made for them. They were among men heavily kitted. A pistol in a holster was pressed against Pegs' hip. They were not acknowledged, not greeted, not asked how they were, not offered a stiff gin. Pegs giggled.

'A proper comedy club in here, Goughie.'

Silly to laugh like a schoolgirl. There had been the barrage of shots fired from the upper window as they had stood, close together and damn near sharing body warmth, and these it seemed would be the men who would deal with a problem, a situation. Gough shushed her. A cigarette packet went round but they were not given the chance to accept or decline. A lighter flashed, and the cigarettes glowed in turn.

They all wore balaclavas. Some had gas guns. Others fingered machine pistols. One, at the bulkhead of the vehicle, had a sniper's weapon across his thighs, and his head lolled almost to his shoulder, and his breathing was steady and he had a soft and gentle snore. Obvious to Pegs that the burst of shots fired from the upper window had not woken him, nor had any of his colleagues thought it prudent to alert him. She had the feeling, not based on evidence but on intuition, that this was the marksman who had fired the single shot down the darkened street and achieved a head hit that saved a hostage's life. She allowed her thoughts to cavort off into some ill-defined distance: she and Gough could moan, complain, fret, bicker, and pretend that the weight of the world rested on their shoulders. 'Guilty, m'lud, of minor exaggeration.' These were the heroes of the hour, she reflected, and made no fuss and grabbed sleep where, when, it was available, and were at a sharp end that neither she nor Gough knew of, and pretty much any of the others flicking keyboards at Wyvill Road . . . and in with them, as the cigarette smoke clouded them, she should have placed Andy Knight – whatever the hell his name was – who lived with lies. She let her hand rest on Gough's leg and wondered how to tell him what she thought.

This one man still slept. The voices were low and she thought from her schoolgirl appreciation of French that they talked about the best socks to go inside their combat boots, also about a football game that would be played the coming Sunday, Olympique against Rennes, and both discussions were without passion and were thoughtful. And one might be called upon to kill that night, and one might confront an assault rifle held by a British zealot and might die . . . but for the moment socks and football were top of the list.

She shivered, not from the cold nor the damp, or from hunger, but from the thought of what the next hours might carry, what fate. And wondered which of the men was the policewoman's husband and whether she feared for him . . . the consensus now was that the German socks used by the *Bundesgrenzschutz* were the best and that Olympique Marseille would win by three clear goals, and if it would be the sniper. Pegs was humbled, felt small, inadequate.

In Gough's ear, Pegs whispered, 'Goes against the bloody grain, but I feel a bit of a prayer for our boy is called for.'

Was answered bleakly. 'Already been there, done that.'

Hamid approached the Major.

He had asked who was in charge and had been brought to a control vehicle. The engine ran and fumes belched from the back and inside it was dry and warm, and housed a handful of men and women with computers and phones and radios, and a drop-down desk and a screen with a large street map featuring La Castellane. The Major stood on the top step and the open door flapped behind him.

Difficult to phrase the request. Hamid had rehearsed it many times.

He did not know the Major had not had dealings with him. Rumour spoke of him as being an *incorruptible*, not accepting arrangements of mutual advantage. The old gangster was rumoured to have owned the criminal investigation department at L'Évêché, and made sufficient profits to have paid them off handsomely. He had seen Major Valery when his brother had been a prisoner of their Somali rivals, but not to speak with. Now, he believed accommodation was necessary. He was met at the bottom of the steps and the door behind was closed. The Major set the tone, seemed to switch off his personal radio.

'Thank you, sir, for speaking with me. I am Hamid, I am the brother . . .'

A cold reply. 'I know who you are.'

'We find ourselves, sir, in a difficult situation.'

'Do we?'

'Not a situation that is favourable to the residents of the project.'

'Explain.'

'I pick my words with care. I do not wish to offend.'

'I have many officers here. They would prefer to be in their homes or carrying out useful duties. They are wet, they are tired, they are hungry, but there is a situation I cannot ignore, and at the heart of it is your younger brother.'

'All true, sir . . . and with my younger brother is a woman with a Kalash, and an Englishman who has been denounced as a police spy. He is their prisoner . . . We want your officers to return to their homes and duties.'

'So that the normal and peaceful life enjoyed inside La Castellane may be normalised? Yes?'

'You understand perfectly, sir.'

'There is a red line. It cannot be crossed.'

'Explain it, please.'

'It is not possible, in order to open up the essential trading on which the project survives, for the woman involved to be allowed safe passage into the night. It cannot be done. Also, in the short term there would be consequences for your own involvement in this matter. Consequences are difficult to avoid.'

'I am very frank with you, sir. We have a new delivery for the market of La Castellane. Not just in my hands, but other "traders" in the project are in possession of it. Through the action of my brother – infatuated by this woman – none of us can sell the product, and at a time when it would command the greatest reward, and of course it is already paid for and at a high outlay.'

'I grieve for you in your dilemma.'

'I can suggest a programme, sir, by which our mutual problems may be curtailed.'

'Explain your "solution", explain also your response to "consequences", and appreciate that I do not negotiate – but am pragmatic.'

'I have your word, Major, that you are not wired, and . . .'

Major Valery lifted his arms. Hamid accepted the invitation and patted him down, as a security guard would have done, under the policeman's arms, around his waist and inside his legs, then checked that the radio on the clip below the Major's shoulder was switched off, and stepped back. He then lifted his own arms and was also searched for a bug . . . There would be no record of their accord.

The first proposition dealt with the situation immediately confronting them, and the second of Hamid's solutions offered a response to 'consequences', and what he would subsequently offer. He was listened to, then given the briefest nod of the Major's cap, and a little of the water lodged there came down as spray.

'And now?'

'I want your hand, sir. I am told of you that is a sufficient guarantee.'

A glove was removed. The hand was shaken, a loose grip but not limp.

They went their separate ways, had arrangements to make.

He thought it was time.

'Zed, will you listen to me? You should. Should listen.'

She sat on the bed. The boy had gone to the kitchen. He'd heard plates being moved and the fridge opened, and a tap running. He would try, supposed it was owed.

'Best you can do, Zed, is to chuck it out of the window, and any spare ammunition with it. Get rid of it, and then walk down the stairs and out into the night, and do not try any silly bugger games because they will have eyes on you all the way and image intensifiers which are the lenses that will show you up. Best get it over with, Zed . . . What I have seen of you is enough for me to make a judgement. You are not a true *jihadi*, one wrapped up in the faith and yearning for a trip to Paradise. They are few. The many are those who get roped in at an early stage and offer a bit of commitment. In your case it was because of two charismatic cousins, when you were younger and more impressionable – I do not mean to patronise, Zed – and then you met people who could recognise your usefulness, and you went in deeper. I don't rate you as an extremist, so best now to jack it in.'

He reckoned she was desperate for sleep. Her head rolled, and her eyes blinked, and she tried to fight the exhaustion and he thought she'd fail. Was likely a greater threat to him now than at any time. He stayed very still and his voice was monotonous, quiet, his words were for her only. If the storm squad came for her, and saw the weapon, then they would blast her and she might survive fast surgical intervention, and might not – and it might not be a healthy scene for himself – for whoever he bloody was. Wouldn't be any 'Excuse me, sir, just checking, who are you or should I shoot and then go through your pockets?', or 'Sorry and all that, sir, didn't mean anything personal in emptying half a clip into you – and you who we were tasked to save, to release,', none of that and the boys would not give a flying fuck whether or not he was wasted alongside her.

'You were on the radar, Zed, long before I pitched up. There are ruthless men in the frame, Zed, and they are manipulative and saw you as a fine opportunity . . . I was put on the case. What did you mean to me, Zed? Truth, no lie, you meant plenty. I should not have been to bed with you, it was unprofessional and deceitful and not necessary. I apologise.'

Once he had thought she was about to drop away into unwanted sleep, then she'd jerked up and had almost dropped the weapon but now retained it, knuckles tight and her finger inside the trigger guard, which was a bad place for it to be. The boy came back in, and brought a glass of milk for her. He did a last throw.

'Take the chance offered you, Zed. The weapon out through the window. Maybe find a pillowcase or a towel, something white, and wave it after you've dumped the hardware. Like my Christmas, it doesn't come round on demand. I feel this is a chance while everything out there is calm, quiet. Get it over with, Zed . . . We'll all say it was the "other bastards" who pushed you into this stage of an armed insurrection – not your fault, and that will count for you. Get rid of the rifle, that's the first step, and stay alive – dump it.'

She pushed herself up from the bed. Did not look at him but went towards the window. The wind ruffled what was left of the curtains and the rain blew into her face. She stopped there, seemed to want to think, and the weapon was now looser in her hand and against her leg, and her hair danced in the draught.

January 2019

'You want quality?'

'I just want one – quality or junk.'

'Not quality. Junk would be agreeable?'

'And just one, one only.'

The man who ran the warehouse was cautious. Unusual in those troubled days in Libya – his country, described as a 'basket case' on CNN, and a 'failed state' on BBC World – for him to receive a visitor from Europe. A small squat bearded man had arrived in a pick-up, unannounced, and with a minimal escort, and had seemed confident, not intimidated by Benghazi's reputation, and its marauding gangs. The windows had no glass, the air-conditioning unit was punctured with holes from bullets that had pierced it from the outside. What was new was a safe screwed down to the floor, and an Apple laptop on the desk: they were enough for most businesses to thrive, particularly in valuing weapons, quality or junk.

'So, you come from France, and wish to purchase *one* AK-47, just *one* . . . I could do you a weapon in that sort that belonged to a dictator's son, or a warlord's grandson. Could have gold plate, gold paint, platinum inlay, but you want just one, and it could be junk?'

'One, and it can be junk.'

'I have something that might interest you. I could give it to you and not charge. However, if I make a gift then I believe that is insulting to you. You expect to pay a price and you shall. To you it would be one hundred dollars American and a further fifty dollars American for sufficient ammunition to load two or three magazines, which would come with it. It is agreeable, one hundred and fifty dollars?'

'Most agreeable.'

'You wish to see it – of course you do.'

They left the office. A phalanx of guards formed around them, most belonging to the dealer, not the Frenchman. Their feet crunched over broken glass. The wind lifted sheets of corrugated iron, loosened by a previous barrage of mortar shells. The dealer told his story as they walked. A Bedouin party had come to him. He had been recommended to them. They had brought fresh dates, and camel skins, and communications equipment in good condition from a military vehicle out of fuel and abandoned in the sands, and a rifle that had been given them by an Egyptian on the road between Sidi Barrani and Alexandria. They had firearms of their own, had no need for this vintage weapon, had offloaded it and the whole package was paid for with five $20 bills. Probably they had then gone to other traders to purchase what they might need before returning to the lonely, but perhaps satisfactory, life among the dunes. The weapon itself?

'I would call it "junk". Who would want it? I can see from the serial number that it is Russian and one of the first to come from the new production line at Izhevsk. I think it is 1955 or 1956, so it is old. The working parts are reasonable, and it was test fired by my own nephew. I would not have allowed him near it if I had doubted its reliability. It can still do what it was built for. Sixty-five years and it can kill as well as the day they shipped it off the line. I think, my friend, it has many stories to tell because the stock is well scraped. Perhaps one scrape for every killing, but that is my imagination playing with me. If you do not take it then it will go to make up numbers at the bottom of a crate for central Africa. I think, also, and this may be of some advantage, the history of the weapon is not recorded, it would have no trace.'

The dealer mopped his face with a handkerchief already sweat-stained, but the Frenchman did not seem concerned with perspiration nor with the colonies of flies that followed them. The place had once been a camp for the military of the deposed leader, Gaddafi, the colonel who had become a tyrant and whose overthrow had destroyed the country: the dealer, for one, would have welcomed him back, and the security prisons the old régime had controlled. They entered a former barracks, the roof gone and the rafters open to the skies. Guards rose from chairs. The wide double doors were open. The camp had been thoroughly looted after the dictator's death, and sufficient dislodged panels had been taken from other roofs to make a section of the building weatherproof. They walked past filled crates of weapons: assault rifles, missile and grenade launchers, pistols, machine-guns, sniper rifles . . .

'This time, just the one?'

'We examine a new route. We are not interested in the Serbian highway which is no longer secure, and Bulgaria and Albania are exhausted and the people there would sell you to the spies of the western countries. The next time would be a substantial cargo, and the time after that would be a major opportunity for you – and for me. I have heard much of you and look forward to a satisfactory agreement, for you and for me.'

The dealer, fidgeting incessantly with his set of red sandalwood prayer-beads, led his customer into the shed. It was not difficult to find. It lay alone, ugly, unwanted, but still dangerous.

'That is it.'

The dealer bent and lifted it, careful to cover his fingers with his handkerchief so that his prints would not be left on its barrel. He balanced it across his arms and took his spectacles from his nose and held them for magnification closer to the metalwork and read out the digits of the individual serial number for this particular rifle. . . . *16751*. It was from Izhevsk, a piece of history. If that were what was wanted it would be driven to Misrata, a slightly functioning port city, then shipped on by sea.

'Old, yes? But still lethal. Look at the stock and the marks there, and see how many lives it has taken – and capable of adding to its toll. Not pretty, but it can kill. What else, my friend, do you want from a rifle?'

Reaching home, having stayed too long in a bar and finding no one to reminisce with over a juice drink, Tooth was in poor humour. Which turned for the worse. Out of his car, into the kitchen, making coffee, and the wife of his Corsican minder, approached him. She kept house in the villa and had been making beds, and had found a sock and a used pair of underpants under the one used by Crab: should she wash them and find a bag for them so they might be posted to his friend?

He snapped at her.'Not my fucking friend. No. Burn them.'

The couple were used to his mood swings and no offence at his language was taken. He took his coffee to the terrace. He sat in the rain. Smoked a dismal cigar that was quickly damp and hard to relight. Pondered . . . The man who had been his guest was no longer his friend – had been his friend, but not now. The rain was on his face, on the peak of his small tartan cap, across the tinted lenses of his spectacles. Had never known it before, the moment when it was clear to him that his world had crumbled . . . a bad time to have lost a friend.

He considered . . . any other friends? He was uncertain if there were other friends he could claim. Those he had grown up with, his rivals or allies in the carving up of sectors of interest in Marseille, were now either dead or in care homes. The policemen he had bribed and who had preserved his liberty, kept him outside the walls of Baumettes, would not have taken his call, would have crossed a street so as not to meet him. The hoteliers and restaurant managers who had favoured him with the best suites, the premier tables, would not have given him the time of day. He had never before felt such despair . . . what was he left with? Tooth believed himself reduced to naming as a friend a boy from a project in the north of the city, originating from Tunisia, a small-time dope dealer, who at least bobbed a head in respect to him, and stammered nervously when asked questions, and who he had not yet bothered to pay for his services. Hamid would have to be a friend . . . He lay on the lounger and a puddle formed under his back and he wallowed in self-pity, and the night pressed on.

She lifted the rifle.

Seemed not to feel its weight. Raised it in two hands above the level of the window-sill, and the rain caught at the metalwork, darkened it, gave it a sheen as if she had polished it for a grand occasion, a parade. He would be behind her, watching her. She had been many minutes by the window and did not turn to face him, and both had stayed silent. She felt ready now to give him her answer.

Few lights burned below. The police vehicles were in darkness, and the guns were out of sight, using the bushes on the far side of the road as cover. She did not doubt that many were aimed at her. She felt no fear and she held firmly to the Kalashnikov, could not be hurt while she had hold of it. It would have been the same for her cousins, no fear but an overriding confidence: she wondered then how many of the people who had taken ownership of the rifle in its history had felt the same as her. It would be fast, sudden and without pain, and she would know nothing of it.

She moved slowly, deliberately, had the rifle up and lodged at her shoulder and felt the rough edge of the stock against her skin, and she closed one eye and peered down the barrel and had the V sight and the needle sight in place. A finger on the trigger. Her name would be spoken of in every street in Savile Town, none would dare to criticise what she had done. If her body was returned for burial in the cemetery it would not be done in the dead of night as if people should feel ashamed of her. The finger squeezed. She had no target, but would shoot into the black inkiness of the slope beyond the road and below the shopping centre above it and at the crown of the hill.

And fired, and fired again, and felt her shoulder rock back each time, and . . . and waited . . . and fired again . . . and waited for the fractional image of a flash on the slope and then the pressure blow of being struck. Her whole chest was exposed to the window and her head and her stomach . . . and she waited.

She changed her aim, and fired another shot, near to where the stationary column of wagons had been parked.

Stampeding feet behind her, and the boy's shrill voice. 'What do you do, sister, why that? You want them to kill you? Are you stupid, sister?' But the boy, Karym, did not dare to come close to her and would have run from the kitchen and through the corridor and into his bedroom, but had stopped on the far side of the bed. Aimed, squeezed, felt the recoil shock, and closed her eyes tightly, straining until they were bruised, and held the weapon like it was her talisman but there was no blow on her body and no explosion of sound from a bullet striking the concrete around the window.

'Why?'

She did not face the boy. She ignored Andy who had been her lover.

Zeinab said,'I would be a bird in a cage. I could not fly in the cage. Two flutters of my wings and I am at the cage's edge. I could not sing in the cage. The cage is death. To be in the prison that is the cage is to be in Hell, there until the end of time.'

She fired twice more. There might have been as many as a hundred rifles or machine pistols or handguns that could have shot back at her, and any of them could have – through skill or with luck – hit her, brought it to an end She was ignored. Not worth the expenditure of a single bullet? An alternative was to sit on the bed, and kick off a trainer and manoeuvre the rifle until the barrel tip was inside her mouth and behind her teeth, and wriggle her toe into the trigger guard, and press on it, and keep pressing, not squeezing . . . but not satisfactory because then she would not be spoken of with respect, would not be talked of in the library, in the market, in the schools of her town, not on the walkway beside the Calder river . . . would be dismissed as a coward.

'I will not go into the cage.'

'No, sister,' the boy answered.'Did you get any hits?'

'Don't think so.'

'Did you have any targets?'

'Not that I could see.'

'Then you wasted ammunition, sister, for a gesture. Were you set at Battle Sight Zero when you fired?'

'I don't know, I did not look.'

'You should wait until you have a target, then go to Battle Sight Zero. Sister, what is a "bird in a cage", what does that mean?'

'He would understand, you would not.'

Behind her, from the wall by the door, no response. Two loves in Zeinab's life. One stayed silent, and one stayed strong in her hands. One had died, one had remained alive. The kid said he would pour himself water, and fled the room . . . she saw a bird that fluttered and that beat fragile wings against the cage bars.

Samson saw him and responded.

The Major stood in the wagon's open doorway and had flicked his fingers, had pointed to him, then had beckoned.

He worked his way down the line of knees and held his rifle in one hand and had his rucksack of spare equipment in the other, and walked easily down the steps and others of the GIPN team followed, and all were huge in their vests and combat clothing. He had rested, felt comfortable and at ease, had enjoyed being with the cheetah family. The plan was explained. The English couple strained to see and hear, to read the map they used and to learn what the Major said, but they were outside the loop and of little importance. The shots had woken Samson and he'd anticipated that an end-game would soon follow.

They were told where they should be, what was planned.

The rifle was left on the bed. Surplus to requirements, a time for stealth, fieldcraft, and intelligence. Him to lead and Zed half a pace behind him. Him holding her hand, and not again, any time soon, going to loosen his grip.

Down the steps. A nod of his head to the kids in the stairwell.

Slipping away into darkness and not impeded. Talking to teenagers, *patois* language, and a vehicle pointed out and small agile fingers glorying in the opportunity to show their skills. The car might have been a father's, an uncle's, a brother's, but the chance to boast ability took pride of place.

A couple of kids riding on the front, above the wheels and directing them. No road exit but a place where the thin hedge was replaced by a wide strip of plasterboard, and chuckling laughter because this was an unguarded entry point. A fist bumping a slight palm, an indication to ram the board. The kids gone and he gave them a buoyant wave and Zed was close to him and held his arm. Revved the engine, took the barrier at a charge. The car leaping and bouncing, then making it over a pavement and a kerb, and him swinging hard left.

Going down the street like the dogs of Hades were in pursuit, but they were not. So few seconds, and gone from the tower block, from the place where his girl had lost her freedom, had become the bird in a cage, not gilded. Leaving the great darkened shape on the horizon, La Castellane, behind them, and on an open road going to the west where the rain came from and hosed against the windscreen.

Close, inseparable, they would be hunted, having aroused the full fury of their one-time colleagues. Beyond the airport, and the last of the Marseille complex of factories, and heading towards the spiderweb of little roads and tracks that ran down to the harbours used by pleasure craft and fishermen, below villages where most homes were shuttered and locked for the winter. Dumping the car. No time for a kiss or a hug but running full pelt down a sloping slipway. Loosening a rope, freeing an open boat which an owner might have gloried in describing as his third home, or fourth, no criminal tendency, able to leave possessions unchained, unpadlocked, and know they would be safe and undisturbed.

Little fuel left in an outboard, but banking on enough to get clear of the mooring, to weave among the buoys and ropes trailing in the water, and to break out into the open sea.

The engine cutting within an hour, spluttering smoke and then going quiet. Oars up and into the rowlocks, and him pulling hard and her, and he with the skills and her with none and reduced to crab catching, and the craft starting out on an odyssey and not knowing where tides and currents would take them.

Getting into a shipping lane. Imagining the great ships pulling clear from the cranes in the port and starting journeys towards the north African coast, and the straits south of Gibraltar, and the ocean wilderness of the Atlantic. Sweating and heaving and cursing as the spray came high and over them and sloshed at their feet, and the lights receding behind them.

Then the oars stowed, and her head on his shoulder, and soft talk while they drifted, waited for the bridge of a freighter or a tanker or a bulk carrier to spot them. Talking of where they might go, and what life they could make and a wiping of the past . . . a frightening long climb up a shaky rope ladder.

Standing together, bedraggled, flotsam from the sea but hands held as if each were the other's only possession, in front of a starchly uniformed captain of the watch. Where did they want to go? Anywhere that was possible, that was beyond reach of others.

When they were there, wherever it was they would, together, live the lie. He would be her mentor, the expert at existing with deceit. In a tiny cabin, all previous guilt erased by both, rejected and behind them, and they lay together, exhausted.

The door opened behind him, not one that was watertight, but one for an apartment bedroom . . . just a dream. It had been good and he would have wished it true. It was not, was only an indulgence. She still sat on the bed, clutching the weapon. The boy's face was fraught with fear.

Hamid held a knife with a fine curved and wicked blade and reached down towards him.

19

He glanced up.

Could have said, 'I am Andy Knight – but some people know me better as Norm Clarke, or as Phil, but that's not important – except that Andy Knight is my temporary identity. I am a serving officer in the Metropolitan Police, in a section designated as SC&O10. Hurt me, lay that knife on me and I can guarantee you will sell cannabis only on the corridor of a cell block for the rest of your life, is that understood?' Did not say it, did not believe it necessary.

The knife's blade was rough where it had been sharpened on a grindstone. No finesse had been wasted on it. It would have been worked backwards and forwards until it was razor-fine. Not a knife that a *jihadi* would have wanted for a desert decapitation. It was a weapon for filleting fish or slashing or driving into a body. If he had not read the situation he would have attempted to twist his head away and drop his chin, make it harder for the brother to get the blade close to his throat, windpipe, and blood vessels. He had read it, and saw that the older brother stared balefully at the boy with the withered arm, but never looked at the girl, at Zed. He understood and raised his hands, offered them up and prised them as far apart at the wrists as the restraint would permit. He recognised the smile, droll and fast and then gone. His arm was caught and the blade rested on the plastic and then he was held while the ties were sawn through, a few strokes. His arm was dropped and his hands fell free. He sat against the wall and massaged the weals where the skin and tissue had chafed.

Not his place and not the time to ask for explanations. A finger pointed to the door and he was expected to follow instructions.

He reached out and his hand was caught and he was hauled upright, and his knees creaked with the exertion and there were pains in his ankles and his hips, and his throat was dry and his stomach empty. Most times, in an Undercover's world, it paid dividends to stay quiet, do the obvious. He would not have been one of the best at following that particular page in the rule book, but at this time he did.

He stood. She was still on the bed, the rifle on her thighs. The elevation from the adjustment lever was still set on Battle Sight Zero, close quarters combat, and he had counted the number of shots she had fired, and the accidental discharge on the road when the stinger had been thrown out: he thought she'd at least a dozen bullets in that magazine, and another one taped upside down next to it. Her eyes still had the dullness of a wild creature's. Hard to recognise the girl whose face had been above his, mouth close to his, body against his, sweat merged, and when his sole desire had been to protect her . . . all bullshit, and there was no captain's offer of a cabin, and no answer to a request to be dropped off far away – all bullshit.

He went to her. He reached forward, two hands, held the sides of her face, by her ears that had no decorative studs, and bent and kissed her lips. Felt no response from her. Kissed her, held her, broke from her.

He turned his back on the room and went into the corridor. The TV was now off and the sister slept awkwardly draped across the sofa. Out through the main door and into the hallway. The kids were there. They stepped aside and allowed him passage and seemed, truth to tell, a little in awe of him. Might have expected to hear him yelp in pain on the far side of the door, or might have thought he'd be heaved outside, lifeless, onto the tiled floor. He was a survivor and they'd not have expected it. The time for bluffing was long gone and they might by now have kicked themselves for their stupidity.

Questions were chirruped at him but he did not understand them. The ground-floor lobby was empty. No customers waiting to buy. He was not helped, had no guide, but tried to remember anything that was familiar from the time he had entered La Castellane all those hours before. Where a vandalised tree was snapped off, where a red delivery van was parked, where a supermarket trolley had been dumped on its side, where the big stones were that restricted the entry point. He supposed that he should have had a pounding heart, have started to pant, need to resist an urge to sprint the last strides. He walked past the kids and on to a pavement and across a road that was dark and still and silent. There he stopped, turned and looked behind him and up, and saw a single window wide open, with curtains flapping loose, and the rain blurred his sight and he wondered if she had moved. He heard a sharp whistle. What he finally noticed was that each balcony of the close-set buildings was occupied, like they were an old theatre's boxes, and women leaned on the guard-rails. The quiet seemed heavy, deafening. He walked towards where the whistle had come from.

He was greeted.

'I am Valery, Major Valery. I am what you would call the Gold Commander for this operation. You are well, not hurt?'

'I'm fine.'

'You have no need of medical attention?'

'No need of it.'

'You will be escorted to where your colleagues are, given some coffee – that is all.'

The Major was walking away. He called to his back. 'Do you not want a debrief from me?'

'No, I do not.'

'Wouldn't that help enable you to understand what might happen?'

'I know what will happen.' The Major paused. 'It is arranged what will happen.'

Zeinab noted it.

The elder brother, Hamid, never spoke to her, never seemed to notice her. Just a woman, irrelevant and not worth humouring, of no value. She had craved attention, now was ignored.

They talked together, and sometimes smiled and giggled and were together in that moment and she was not a part of them. Sometimes when they talked, Hamid rubbed his brother's arm as if to reassure him, and there was something that Hamid said that caused Karym's mouth to go wide and his eyes to seem to pop out under their lids, like a kid taken to a cave of sweets, and they were hugging . . . She was trusted, she had come to do a deal, and not her fucking fault that she had been duped by a plain clothes police spy. Nothing was her fault – never was and never would be.

She put her finger inside the trigger guard, squeezed, and neither was looking at her. An explosion of sound. Now both turned to face her.

Neither tried to wrestle the Kalashnikov from her, neither flinched away from her. They went on talking – like she was trouble, and the problem to be resolved was how to placate her long enough to be rid of her, and . . . she stood. She walked the three or four short paces from the end of the bed to the shelves where his books were. She could manage in one hand to collect three or four books at a time in her arms. She threw them.

They went through the window. Above her was a wide hole where plaster had been dislodged by the bullet she had fired into the ceiling. Steadily, she cleared the shelves, and the books went down, pages fluttering as they fell, and were taken by the wind and weighted by the rain and slapped on to the ground. She was not a reader, not a self-abuser, but was an activist, a soldier and a fighter, had known the impact of the stock on her shoulder and imagined that if she had peeled off her clothes, as she had in the room above the little square near to the fruit and vegetable market in the centre of Marseille, she'd have seen bruising by her collar-bone, which would have been like a bright strip of medal ribbon. The last titles to be thrown out were *The Gun: The AK47 and the Evolution of War* and *AK-47: The Story of a Gun* and *AK-47: The Grim Reaper*. The one that emptied the shelf was *AK-47: The Gun that Changed the World*. It went out into the night and had a drop of five storeys.

'Will you not tell me what is going on?'

Karym said, 'Patience, sister. We are going to take you from here, make you free.'

Heavier rain fell, drenching the watchers but not dampening their enthusiasm while they waited.

For those who could see it, the throwing out of the books was one of the few signs that something, *anything*, might be about to happen. And the customers still held their places in the queue, and the dealers moved among them and urged them to continue waiting and said that the rumour mill predicted that there would soon be movement, a change of situation. Another crowd had formed in the open, with no shelter, in the car park of the commercial centre – where the shopping malls were – and they came from many of the neighbouring projects and were brought there by the excited exchanges on the mobile phone networks. Their view was across the car park fence and over the slope at the bottom of which was the outer police cordon and across the street and the line of drenched customers, and the inner cordon, over the rocks at the entrance to La Castellane, and on to – full frontal – the walls and windows of one of the blocks. They had seen the books thrown down.

Worth waiting for, the finish of it, and few would bet on disappointment.

'Unacceptable? We have emphasised that?'

'Have hit it hard, Gough. Unacceptable. They understand.'

'What then is the plan?' They were alone, huddled together in the emptied wagon.

'Not privy, not inside the loop . . . a nuisance, and interfering – that's what we are.'

'Can we demand, Pegs, to be told? Have it explained to us, or beyond our remit?'

'We are on sufferance. Can hardly *demand* a cup of Earl Grey and a shortbread biscuit, let alone be accepted on to the inside track.'

'You reckon we'll be out tonight?'

'Can but kneel and can but pray.'

'It's very near the end. I don't have that feeling it will be pretty.'

Pegs let a hand rest on his arm. There was usually a shake up in Wyvill Road after an operation as protracted as Rag and Bone, and it was predictable they would be found new partners to work with. Man and woman together for each team was considered preferable, and it was known as a shake up of 'bedfellows', and there would be an inquest over this one and the chances of them being together again were slim: one big booze binge off the flight and then desks cleared and comfortable relationships fractured. They were fond of each other and convenient.

'Quite near the end, yes. Pretty? We gave it our best, didn't shirk it, but "best" rarely satisfies. That's not in our jobs, Gough, and not in our lives, pretty endings.'

The Major talked to him.

He listened, did not interrupt. A busy man, and now taking time off from his duties, and it might have been something about respect. He chewed on a sandwich, some spiced up ham and foul tasting, and the coffee given him was tepid. And when? Quite soon. A schedule was fixed. Within half an hour. He had one request, reckoned he would be allowed just one, and it would have no effect on the detail of their planning. He asked it.

Was answered, a shrug from the Major, a junior called forward, an order given. He thanked the Major, shook his hand, went with his escort into the deep darkness. It was arguable whether he had committed another act of insubordination in failing to go in search of the couple who nominally controlled him, but not much now could be done to him, and the protocols seemed of low importance. He could feel her lips on his, would nurture the touch of them for the rest of the night, maybe all the way back to whichever home he could claim to belong in. They went up the hill and had almost left the estate with its tower blocks and the open window. A van without insignia was parked half on the pavement and half in the street, its bonnet and front cab faintly lit by a distant street-lamp. Below, down towards La Castellane, were a few lights that showed up the driving rain. The escort led him to the back of it where the light did not reach. He went down on his haunches and the escort doubled away. Realised immediately that he was not alone, that another man was close to him, hidden from view, and his elbow brushed against a rifle's barrel. He spoke quietly, said who he was and why he was there and where he had been, and what he knew of a target.

Then said, 'I come to ask something of you . . .'

Hamid told Karym that it was a matter of trust.

'Trust in who?'

It was a matter of trust between himself and a police commander, Major Valery, a man with as honest a reputation as any senior officer inside L'Évêché. And he had the Major's promise.

'What is the promise?'

The promise was that the window of opportunity would be open. Only briefly, but open, a one-time chance. It was arranged and would happen, and the girl would be gone and he could drop her and make the excuse, and then the problem was hers, not any more to do with La Castellane.

'Why did they make such an agreement?'

It was a matter of negotiation, Hamid told his kid brother. The Major and himself had agreed the deal. His brother asked, reasonably, why the police would talk, even barter, with a dope dealer, and his answer was plausible. From the police side they had a considerable detachment of officers pulled from other duties to enforce a cordon, and the overtime bill was rapidly mounting and would go to the Heavens if the siege lasted after midnight, and it was an embarrassment and reflected poorly: they wanted the matter closed down. From his own point of view the advantages of kicking the can down the street were several. There was the new shipment in the project, customers waiting in torrential rain. Not just his own customers, but every other franchise inside La Castellane was affected, and already his phone was filled with complaints. It was a matter to be settled and fast.

'And her? What if she refuses?'

An idiot's question. How could she refuse? Here, inside, she could do nothing. There, outside, she was a free agent. Earlier she had been told the bare outlines, now his brother was furnished with detail. She could go with her rifle, run in the hills, scramble in the mountains, go anywhere she wished that was far from the *arrondissement* in which the project existed. That was what he told his brother . . . did not tell him that the price for the deal, and the opening up again of the project, and the evening's trading, was that he would betray Tooth, deliver him through evidence provided to the investigators working to the disciplines and cleanliness of Major Valery . . . did not tell him that his younger brother was so infatuated, mesmerised, by the girl that he would likely have stayed with her and supported and strengthened her and that the siege would then have continued – another day and another night, and more trading lost, and more money missed . . . he said that time was now short.

'It will work, it is genuine?'

Would he lie to his own family, his own blood, would he? Of course he would not. The girl was on the bed, and he did not think that she slept and the weapon was held warily, the finger against the trigger guard. He thought she would fight until they killed her. And he saw the way that Karym, the dreamer and the romancer, gazed at her, was starstruck by her but yet wanted to touch, not her boobs but the Kalashnikov, did not want to put his hands between her legs, but on to the stock and the barrel and the selector lever of the assault rifle . . . He thought that when it was over they might do a discount price for the customers lined up outside, held back by the cordon, patient and waiting and soaked.

He checked his brother's wrist-watch, and kept the best until the last. Flicked him the ignition key to the Ducati 821 Monster, and saw a simple face lighten and a smile crack from ear to ear. He supposed the boy, his brother, with his damaged arm could steer the bike – if only for a short distance. Told him he would see him. When? Soon.

Hamid stole a last glance, at his brother, and then the girl and then the rifle.

January 2019

It was his first day and it was predictable that he was nervous. He was Josef, he was 23 years of age and he had earned a 2nd class degree in Mechanical Engineering at the Izhevsk State Technical University. Still dark around the plant and his elder brother, a doctor of medicine but still in training, dropped him off, and waved to him and he crunched away across the fresh compacted snow. He had never been inside the gates, but tried to mask his hesitation and walk boldly, and remembered that it was where his great-grandfather had worked; there were proudly framed monochrome photographs in his parents' apartment to show him at workers' parades and celebrations in the years after the victory in the Great Patriotic War. Josef, whose principal interest in life was football and the teams playing in the main European leagues, was taken by a receptionist to the mess-room where the foremen were. He introduced himself, and added that his great-grandfather had worked here on an early production line.

'. . . for the AK-47. He was here in the middle nineteen-fifties. Would have seen the great and famous Mikhail Kalashnikov. When the rifle was new, and had such advanced technology. I never met my great-grandfather . . .'

He was interrupted. A foreman from the machine tool shop told him that the factory then had been a dark and miserable and dangerous place in which to work, and the pressure on the labour force to achieve targets had been immense . . . 'The miracle was that the product they produced when materials were short and equipment was crude – at the time the whole nation was seeking to rebuild itself after the catastrophe of the Fascist invasion, and those bastards have not changed – reached such high standards. The design was excellent because of its simplicity. A peasant from the steppes could learn to operate it and fight in extreme conditions and maintain it. Extraordinary. I think, even today, it would be possible in remote or backward corners of the world to find a weapon that your great-grandfather helped manufacture. If you were to find it, there would be a strong chance that it would still do its job. It was the best and will never be matched for its innovation. There are some who say that it changed the face of the world, gave power to downtrodden and third-class citizens, provided them with pride and authority . . . but times have changed. You are now in a modern factory. You will be working with a new generation of combat weapons, those carried into conflict by the men and women of our Special Forces, and they expect only the best, which they get. The new versions of rifle and close quarters weaponry are smoother to operate, lighter, have greater hitting power, but the old principles still stand. For all our progress, the AK-47 your great-grandfather made still lives inside all those innovations, the principles remain. Have you been to the museum? No? You should, Josef. You will find there identical rifles to the ones manufactured in those times . . . and a superior type has never been produced. The old Kalashnikov led the world.'

He thought, from what he knew of the history of the former Soviet Union, that more than half a century before military music would have been played over the high speakers, interspersed with exhortations for harder work, greater productivity, and speeches from Malenkov or Khrushchev or Brezhnev; he heard pop music to soothe the workers.

They had reached a belt line and final checks were being made on a stream of weaponry carried along it. He would start here, where his great-grandfather had been, and would first be an apprentice, but with ambitions to go into junior management. He was introduced to a woman on the line who would show him the procedures, and he thanked the foreman for his time.

'Only one thing to remember, young Josef, never drop one, let it fall to the floor, because that is certain bad luck – if it ever happens – to any person who might use the weapon. Never let it fall, or it is cursed. It may appear undamaged . . . Be very careful.'

The foreman left them.

The woman said, 'He talks shit. It is a machine, does not have a soul. Drop it in a factory or drop it in a combat zone – what is the difference? It is shit.'

The weapons rolled on, were checked, and the firing mechanism tested, and one teetered near the edge of the line but Josef was quick to get a hand on it, move it to safety – though he claimed to her that he believed neither in luck nor a curse.

Zeinab came off the bed.

She put her arms around the boy's neck, but still held the rifle. Not the gesture of a lover but of a friend to whom a wrong had been done.

'I am sorry.'

'Sorry for what?'

'I am sorry that I shouted at you. I should not have.'

'You do not have to be sorry.'

'And am sorry for shooting into your ceiling, for making debris.'

The plaster that had come down from the ceiling was almost a metre square and pieces of it were on the bed, and the dust had hung in the air then floated down and she did not know that her skin had a fine coating of it, which gave her a pallor and her cheeks and hair were the colour of an old woman's.

'My room is a dump. No one would notice.'

'And sorry for barging into your life.'

'And bringing confusion?'

She had thought herself a revolutionary, a soldier in an army and proud of where she marched. She was not in the ranks of masked cohorts and heading towards a battle-front but was holed up in a squalid apartment in Arab France, alongside the crippled younger brother of a second-tier drugs dealer.

'Bringing confusion, yes – and leaving a trail behind me, wreckage.'

'Can I ask you . . .?'

'Ask.'

'What is it like? To fire it, how is it? Is it good, is it . . .?'

'It is wonderful, it is better than good. It is incredible.'

'Better than . . .?' The boy sniggered.

'Better than that. You want to?'

'I want to fire it. I would like to.'

'Another way that I am sorry. For what I did to your books. That was a crime to destroy them, it was as if I had stolen them, or worse, because it was temper and destructive, and I gained nothing from it. I am sorry . . . I hope that after I am gone you can forget me – then, one day, sometime, you will see my picture in a newspaper, across the width of a TV screen, and you will remember me.'

The boy kissed her. Zeinab had thought that the perfect kiss, soft lips on her skin and the rub of rough stubble, was when she had been with Andy Knight, police spy and liar – doubted that now. So hesitant, and treating her as a princess, the daughter of an emir, and in wonderment about being permitted that close. A brush of his lips, and his eyes closed as if he did not dare to gaze on her, that it would show disrespect. They stood a long time together, her stomach against the boy's, her chest against his, and the moisture of his mouth on her cheek, and he stirred, and she wondered if he would then push her back, let her fall, use his weight against her so that she was on the bed, and wondered whether she would then spread her legs and reach for the belt at her waist, and wondered . . . He had broken free from her, and was glancing at his watch, and frowning, anxiety ploughing lines on his forehead.

'We can go?'

'Yes, can go.'

'And we talk no more about "sorry"?'

'No more.'

'Give it me.'

She did. He took it with both hands, then laid it on the crumpled bed. His fingers moved at speed. The magazine detached, the bullets spilled out, counted, all nine replaced, and the second magazine checked, and went back on to the belly of the weapon, then the rest of its working parts. She thought at first it was conceit, to show his knowledge, then was kinder and realised that he tested himself to see how well he had mastered the books that now lay on the sodden ground outside where – because of her – they were, muddied and useless. It went together again and the work was done flawlessly and he betrayed no moment when he might have forgotten what fitted where. He aimed it at the window and checked the sight, adjusted it minutely. She followed the aim and saw only the dark mass of the cloud that carried the rain in off the Mediterranean sea. She could see no target. Perhaps he imagined one, perhaps an enemy stood in front of him, perhaps he was about to be overwhelmed by those hating him. He fired. She saw the trigger freed and come back and the cartridge case flashed, then tinkled on the linoleum. Just two shots and the manhood was in his face and the smile spilled. He handed it back to her.

'For the confusion and the wreckage, I am sorry.'

'For nothing. We go, I take you out.'

'Go how far?'

'Who knows . . . till the gas runs out, then buy some more. I think, sister, you can make a man reckless, forget how to be clever – or partly you and partly the work of the rifle.'

'A last time . . . You have trust in what is told you?'

'Of course, he is my brother.'

'I trusted once.'

'He is my brother. Why would I not trust him?'

On the balconies of La Castellane's tower blocks, after two more shots that had howled across the road and the slope and over the car park of the shopping centre before falling spent, the murmur of the question was waves on pebbles, but went unanswered.

'Have you seen him . . . Has anyone seen him . . . He must be here, he would not stay away, would he . . . He would bring the big rifle, the killing rifle, yes . . . He saved that boy's life, Karym's, would he now take it . . . Saved his life with a master shot, but does anyone think he has emotion . . . He will kill, of course he will, was there ever a man so cold? . . . Has no one seen Samson, we should keep watching for him? Heh, where are you, Samson?'

Words rippling from the balconies, spoken quietly as eyes strained, and many more were asking the same question on the top of the far slope and among the empty bays of the shopping area parking lot. A great expectation that they would not, any of them, be disappointed.

A stranger was by his shoulder, wearing the wrong gear for the weather and soaking up the rain. Samson, the marksman, eased a plastic bag off the rifle, drew it clear of the telescopic sight. Tucked in his sleeve was a small square of thin towelling with which he could wipe the lens, prevent it fogging. He adjusted the sight for the range he expected when the opportunity came. The Major would make the call and had control of the big spotlight sited ten or so metres behind him. He had no qualms about the use of deceit, no hesitations about the use of lies to further political or counter-terrorist necessity . . . Samson would have said that the law of the jungle was writ large when in close proximity to this project or any other: he doubted that a lioness or a cheetah, a tigress or a leopard, a jaguar or a lynx, would quibble at the use of subterfuge. There was a bullet in the breech and a radio piece in his ear, and the stranger was close to him but would not impede. He felt calm, no different to any other evening, the same as when he had been out in the rain and on the pavement and waiting for his daughter to come from late-night music lessons at the school, the Lycée Colbert, in the *7th arrondissement* off Rue Charras: a quiet and respectable neighbourhood and one in which few home-owners spent their evenings lying prone in the wet, dabbing the lenses of a telescopic sight, waiting for a target to come into view. He made no judgements, would have claimed that to be the duty of men and women who lived far above his pay grade. He had the Steyr SSG 69 with the 7.62 × 51 NATO-compatible round, nestled and ready. It was a military weapon and in his mind this was a military operation: achieve an end, or fail to. And he thought the stranger beside him also held his calm well. A bike's engine throbbed into life, far away but clear.

They were at the back of a wagon.

Not often that Gough had the chance to watch a culmination, when he supposed there would be a 'whiff of cordite' in the air.

The Major said, 'You stay here, do not move, and you see nothing, hear nothing and know nothing of what might happen. You are surplus and remember it.'

He was gone.

Pegs gripped Gough's arm. 'That bastard has a good bedside manner. A real comforter.'

'It's a dirty business that we trade in, to the exclusion of pleasantries. We are not the ones that matter at these moments. The men, women, who go the extra yards, go alone, the "uncivilised" men. What Orwell said. *Men can only be highly civilised while other men, inevitably less civilised, are there to guard and feed them.* We owe them much, the uncivilised, and should not forget it.'

'Sort of down to the wire . . . I hear you.'

She removed her arm. He heard the rumble of a motorcycle's engine, fiercer than a smoker's cough, and spitting power . . . and he wondered what the girl, the focus of Rag and Bone, understood of the reality of her life and its future, and saw her in his mind, and almost cared.

He had the bike started.

The noise of it blasted at her ears. Fumes spat from its exhaust and the rain and the wind pushed the smell of it against her where it clung. The boy, Karym, faced her. It was her last throw, not that she had ever rolled dice, but that was a phrase her tutor had used to her face: 'Your last throw, Zeinab, and one where I learn of your commitment to the future.' He had been talking the crap about her course-work, but here – in a wretched estate in a corner of a foreign city – it had a truth.

She lifted her leg, swung it over the pillion, and steadied herself. She put her left arm around his stomach and caught at his top, was inside his coat and then had a handful of clothing and a fold of his stomach skin and felt him stiffen, and he turned to face her, and a grin split open his face.

He shouted, 'I wanted to know how it would be, sister, to work the beast, have it against me and do the trigger squeeze, and have done. Felt the hit of it against my shoulder – wanted that and have had it. Another thing I wanted was to be on the bike. This is a Ducati 821 Monster. It is prime quality. Power output at 112hp. He never let me ride it, my brother. Top speed of 225 kilometres an hour, range 280 klicks on a full tank. We are going places, sister, only caring about *now*, not caring about tomorrow, whether we are clever, or fools. Just for *now*, not any other time. You listening to me, sister?'

And she smiled, private, rueful, and considered what else – before that day – he had not done before, and she squeezed the flesh, pinched it hard, and heard the little yelp he gave. There was a roar beneath her and he eased the bike away and he took it over a sodden area of mud and grass tufts, and past a snapped off tree and a rubbish bin that had overflowed and toppled. Dirt kicked up from the wheels and spattered the kids who watched them go. Never before had he been cheered. A cohort of them ran alongside Zeinab and Karym and had to sprint to keep abreast with him. She thought they called his name . . . an expression flashed into her mind, what she heard girls say on the corridor of the Residence in Manchester: everyone 'famous for fifteen minutes', like the boy would be . . . not her. Her fame would last, sure of it, as long as there was breath in her body, and there would be, not minutes, but days and weeks, months and years. The kids running, heaving and panting with them, wanted to touch the shoulder of Karym, and those who managed it were shaken off.

She was strong. She had the rifle in her right hand, and the palm of her fist was around the pistol grip behind the trigger guard and her index finger was inside and against the trigger itself and she knew the amount of pressure required. They bumped over more rough ground and split a dumped can and slid on a slope and he had to hold the bike from toppling with his outstretched leg . . . Something she remembered, and they were within sight now of the exit point from the estate, where more kids were and the crude blasted rocks that were there for security, and he slowed and was gunning the engine. Remembered an afternoon at home, a wet one and the cloud low over Dewsbury, and her mother gone to a friend, and a neighbour come to sit and watch TV with her father, and an old film that the neighbour wanted to see, monochrome. Could not help herself but recall the memory. A film about a warship that had put into a South American port after an action with the Royal Navy, and the German boat was damaged, but was ordered by the local authorities to leave the harbour. All the quaysides were lined with people watching for drama and certain they'd not go short, and the British boats were waiting out at sea for the single German ship. Remembered it all, and the sight of her father staring at the screen and the neighbour wetting his lips in anxiety. Something tragic and lonely and unequal about it. Going towards a certain . . . and trying to kill the memory. She did not know how it had ended because she had gone to her room to complete her homework, nor had she thought it right for her father and her neighbour to watch a film glorifying the British military, nor had she ever asked what happened – only remembered the film showing the huge crowds and their excitement as the battleship had sailed.

Engine at full throttle. Wiped the memory of it. Darkness plunged around them, the brake was off. She was nearly jerked from the pillion but clung to him.

Everything black ahead except for half a dozen pinprick lights from mobile phones that the look-outs, the *chouffes*, had aimed on the rocks so he would avoid them. All the high street lights were out, as his brother had said they would be. A done deal, and aimed at freeing her. He ploughed through a ring of kids and they staggered back and gave him passage . . . like a warship going to sea and heading for an enemy. Karym might never have ridden the bike but was sure, and astride the technology, and his weakened arm seemed not to matter to him. There was supposed to be a window of opportunity, and she could not recall in her mind whether it lasted for 30 seconds or a full minute, but it gave them time. They were between the rocks, and the wind and rain lashed at her face, and she went with him, down low and sideways as he did, the fast, sharp left turn into the street and ahead of her was another wall of darkness. Barely heard over the sound of the engine, guttural and magnificent, a warrior call – what the engines of the warship would have made – were the shrieks and yells of the kids, but they did not follow. Full power, up the slope and far in the distance, near the summit of the high ground, were house lights and street-lights; around them was darkness.

She understood. A deal had been made and a promise had been kept. The open window, the darkness, would free her.

'You good, sister?'

'I'm good – we go to war, I am happy.'

She thought it incredible that he could hold the bike steady, without being able to see anything in front of him or around him. The darkness covered them, hid them, and she realised that he had wedged his open coat over the dials in front of him, and the headlight had not been switched on. They could not be seen, and the breakout point was close. The police cordon was behind them, and the queue of people who waited in line to buy the filth of cannabis from Morocco, and she had the old rifle and her finger was ready to squeeze on the trigger, tighten on it. The darkness was her friend. Where was Andy? Did she care? And he had her bag with the new nightdress folded away in it, had it in his car, and did it matter to her? Zeinab glanced down but had no light to see the bracelet, and she moved her neck but could not feel the pendant, her two gifts from him. And the speed strained the bike but the window was still open.

The thunder of the engine closed fast on them.

Beside him, the French marksman's head was low over the Steyr rifle and he had one eye against the sight. Andy Knight – not to be his name for many hours more – heard the whispered command spoken into the microphone clipped to the corner of a bulletproof vest.

'Okay . . .'

Just that, nothing more. He saw the shape of the blacked-out motorcycle for a moment as a silhouette against the lights of a tower block behind it. Both of them waited: not long.

The blistering power of the light was switched on. The street ahead was flooded with dazzling illumination. The core point of the light fell directly on to the bike. It was bright enough to clearly see each indent in a tyre, each scuff of dirt on the bodywork, and for the holes in the knees of the front rider, and the rifle that the pillion held. The rider would have been blinded, and swerved, and would have seen nothing ahead . . . the way it had been told him it was all so simple. Andy, or Phil or Norm, did not do morality checks but played by the book as it was, relevant page open, and others deciding whether the action was a good fit inside the code of conduct laid down for the countering of a terror campaign, or an organised crime shipment, and what was acceptable in a boot-on-the-throat business of inconvenience. Very simple . . . It was said that the boy would have been too stubborn, too under the spell of the girl, too stupid, to have abandoned the refuge and come out hands raised. Said that the girl would be dreaming of martyrdom and a sort of fame, want to die in a hail of gunfire, and would not surrender. Said that a siege would linger, perhaps for days, and was not worth the death or injury of a single officer. Said that a trade-off was possible through the 'good offices' of Hamid, small-time dealer and thug, who would deliver up his brother. Said that trading could restart inside the project within half an hour, and that the police operation would be over and overtime rates kept in check. Said also that the elder brother would – in return for immunity to prosecution – provide evidence that would convict an elderly gangster with a history of corrupting officials in the Town Hall and the headquarters of the detective force beside the cathedral. Simple, but complex, and satisfactory to many: a favourable trade-off. The way it had been told, the marksman would go for a knee shot, or the flesh of the thigh, and would avoid the stomach area where the vital organs were, and not aim for the head where the boy's thin hair was spiked by the effect of wind and rain, and the bike's tyres had lost traction and the swerve was becoming a skid.

All simple, and he understood.

Time was not on the marksman's side. If the rider regained control, could steer himself out of the skid and straighten up, and hit the accelerator, then in a scrap of seconds, the bike would be past the light, on an open road, one with a spider's net of tracks and side turnings, and would be away and clear, and she would be free.

The hiss as breath was drawn in, and held. He heard the scream of the tyres as they slid. Would have been aiming for the leg shot.

The explosion beside him. A single shot fired and not the opportunity for double tap. One shot.

He understood. The skid that came from the swerve had screwed it. Should not be criticised, was not a mistake, but not the perfect shot. In the fierce light, he had a clear view of the effect on the rider's skull when hit by the bullet from a Steyr SSG 69. Disintegration. Not pleasant. Like it was tomato puree that had been violently thrown up, with white bits and grey matter, and flying straight back behind the rider's loosening shoulders and splattering the face of the girl . . . The motorcycle careered to the side and was in an uncontrollable skid and it hit a kerb then a low retaining wall beyond a pavement. It was thrown back towards the centre of the street, and he heard her scream. The weight of the bike was mostly over her as it slid the last metres before coming to a stop and turning around, and her leg would have been trapped and the pain rich, and it was likely broken.

First the scream that was shock, then the shout.

'Fuck you, you lying bastards.'

A sharp intake of breath beside him, frustration, irritation at a job not completed with the necessary expertise. He tapped the marksman's shoulder. Another shriek in the night, one of fury. He did not think she would be able to free herself from the weight of the motorcycle. If she fainted. If the guns covered her, and she could no longer deal out harm, then the medics could scurry forward. The syringe would come out. The Kalashnikov would be kicked aside. The morphine would go into her thigh or backside or arm, wherever was best, and the break in the leg would get first response splints, and she would be on her way to the cage.

He wriggled forward on the ground, reached out, felt the rifle's weight, took it. No remark exchanged between them. It was what had been agreed. Both were men of the front line, who worked at the 'sharp end', and were spare with words, and did not need encouragement. The French marksman had edged away, left him with room. He settled, checked the range, at Battle Sight Zero for that distance.

And searched for her.

20

The vivid light showed him the scarlet across her face, still wet and glistening, and the meld of other matter mixed with the blood, and she cried out once more.

He thought it would have hurt her to show pain, the equivalent of weakness. She might have known by now that he would be there, on his stomach or standing, hunched over and letting the rain fall on him and the wind to buffet his jacket – but there.

Much of his life in those moments surged in his mind. What they said about a drowning man: there had been moments out on the ribs when in training for the Marines, and in service, when they had been tipped overboard, wearing life-jackets, and had spent those endlessly long seconds trapped under the bulk of an inflatable, learning not to panic but to be rational and manage the crisis. Easier said. Most of the lads had handled it well. A few had flipped mentally and had failed to hold down the air in their lungs and might have tried to shout while underwater and had filled their throats with water, and had come up coughing, choking, and spluttering, and one had had to be revived by the instructors and had been carted off in an ambulance, breathing but not much else. He'd come back four days and nights later and had been free and easy with the anecdote. 'Yeah, saw the whole lot . . . first row with my dad, first tears with my mum about going away, first shag with a bicycle from the next block who charged a fiver, first runaway when the police came and a gang of us were in a graveyard and being fucking stupid, first interview for this lot and near wetting myself, first time a company sergeant major told me that I might be useless shit but I had shot well on the range . . .' The whole of his life was there, and all his names, and the pain he'd caused the family, and the arrogance with which he'd damn near bad-mouthed the hapless pair of plodders who ran him, and the beauty of being with her, with his Zed. And all the lies told her, and the contempt with which she'd regarded him, the little guy that she could snap her fingers for. And was confused and loved nobody and hated nobody . . . and had no contact with the newspapers' litany of condemnation that would follow any atrocity, anything she planned to do, and had no sympathy with the broadcasters who queued to offer a version of piss-poor poetry in their commentaries on attacks that took the lives of what were called 'the innocents'. A good job, a relief, that he did not do judgements or he would have been there all damn night churning them over in his mind, when there was a job to be done, and time he did it.

He put aside his own life, what he had remembered of it. And pushed away the recall of the sweat and scent of her . . . all gone, and a mind cleared, and thinking back only to the days on the common overlooking the Exe estuary, bracken and gorse and scrub and occasional trees bent by the wind with the leaves torn off. Now an empty street and a bright and vicious light that allowed no hiding place for a target.

He went through his checks and nestled the weapon against his shoulder. Would have liked to have a test firing and gauge the sights he'd be using and how the trigger was set and what pressure it would take, and the weight of it and how steady it would be when he held it in the teeth of the wind and with the rain coming down. But did not have the chance.

He saw her trying desperately to break free of the bike's weight, and had already moved enough to have part of her body, her chest and a shoulder, over the rider, almost as if she protected him . . . he did not reckon that figured in her mind. If she could free her leg then she could crawl left or right and on either side of the cone of light was darkness. Competing moods swarmed over each other, and had neither coherence nor shape – changed fast and had no pattern. A mess: what life was.

Time, as they said, to *piss*, or time, as they said, to get off the *pot*. Fair point, and he did not argue. Allowed himself a last luxury before his finger snaked inside the guard and found the trigger, rested there . . . Saw the bird, pretty and fine-plumed, but trapped in a cage with rusted close-set bars, and prepared himself. The voice alongside him murmured: was he ready?

'Yes, friend, ready.'

She could see so little. Her eyes were covered by a film of what she assumed was blood. But she fired a shot. Her mind worked well, might have been aided by the growing intensity of the pain in her left leg as the numbness wore through. Had no target and was blinded by the spotlight but tried to aim at it, into its brilliance. Which was futile, had no purpose and wasted a shot.

Not possible for Zeinab to shift the weight of the bike, and she lay across the boy. Could not extract herself from that position, enveloping him, what a lover might have done. Could not have said that what remained of his face had already started to cool, nor that the whiteness of death settled on his cheeks, but was aware there was no breathing.

A voice was yelling at her over a megaphone, distorted in the wind, and she'd no idea whether it was English with a foreigner's accent, or French. They would be telling her that 'resistance is hopeless', that she was surrounded and 'you have no escape route available to you', and 'if you are hurt, Zeinab, the ambulance team will give you the very best medical help,' and 'throw aside your firearm, Zeinab, so we can help you'.

She fired again, but the light was constant on her face, and one of the boy's eyes was wide open and was ringed in blood from the scalp wound . . . A party of them had been to a TV studio in Manchester before a filming schedule of a limited view of life in the Hall of Residence for first-year university students. To get to the main studio they had been walked through, like it was a fucking Holy of Holies, the newsroom. Had seen the screens and the little desks with the computer consoles, and the reporters had been pointed out, and where the camera crews waited for action, and the desks of those who would edit and control output into news programmes. Somewhere it would have happened . . . a crisis moment of excitement . . . in Marseille or London, even reaching Leeds, and interruptions in programmes to report a 'developing incident', and soon her name would float in the air and be snatched, caught, introduced to the homes of people she knew. She had felt emboldened to ask why there was not more coverage from the front line around Mosul or near to Raqqa, and had been told the coverage was limited because 'those places are shit, wet shit, and not worth the lives of any of our teams'. When they had her name and her address in the street in Savile Town, and the course she was failing to study at Manchester Metropolitan, they would want to come running. And they'd meet a cordon and might hear shots, hers – the big thump from the Kalash, and they'd be jabbering into their microphones, knowing nothing and seeing less. She fired again, and again missed the light that captured her. With her free hand she stroked his face, where the hair came down to his ear, and saw the acne marks on his face, and remembered his lectures on the virtues of trade. He had been betrayed as she had, had been lied to, had believed them.

And fired again, and fired another time.

Stroked his head and then tried, again to move the bike off her leg and could not shift it.

Darkness was at each side of the street. If she could get out from underneath the bike, then she could crawl either to her right or to her left and it was only a few metres, and she imagined a ditch alongside the road, for flooding rainwater, and she could nestle down in it and then heave herself farther up the hill. There were swathes there of dark strips which meant rough ground, and the chance was good that she could take herself farther from where she now lay, pinioned. She did not think it a delusion. Zeinab looked down, not easy for her to twist her head that far, but caught a glimpse of her leg. Between the handlebar and the curved shape of the fuel tank, and for a moment was confused by what she saw. Her bone was white and had been cleaned of blood when it had broken through the skin of her thigh and then had pierced the material of her jeans, and still did not think it was deluded to believe she might be able to crawl to the darkness and get clear, escape and fight: be a soldier, be a warrior, be a woman whose name was spoken.

First, she believed it necessary to hit the spotlight, bury its eye on her. And fired at it, and fired another time, and writhed on the ground and tried to change her shooting position so that she was better able to fire more bullets at it. And cried in frustration at her failure, and the pain tightened its grip. One more effort to get the bike off her leg. More shouts, from the medical team, she imagined. More shots, at the eye of light. Firing and feeling the impact at her shoulder.

And . . . no more shots. A click when she jerked on the trigger. The V and the needle locked on Battle Sight Zero for close quarters combat, but the magazine was emptied. She had seen him change the magazine, take it out and reposition it, but could not remember what he had done, and was wrestling with it, but could not extract it, and turn it over to use the second magazine that was taped, useless, to the emptied one. Struggled and failed, and howled her anger.

'Are you doing it, are you not doing it?'

He allowed a brief nod of his head.

With a fully armed rifle he had been on the nuclear convoys running from the south of England to the loch in the west of Scotland where the submarine fleet was housed, had ridden shotgun when they took the warheads to be fitted on the missiles. He had been on exercises in the Norwegian tundra, had been on stand-by to fight in Afghanistan but had not made the trip . . . He had never fired, not for real.

He saw her clearly, both images of her were sharp. His Zed – a target and should have been nothing more – summoning all her strength and seemed able to drag the trapped leg away from underneath, and he heard the sharp scrape of metal as it was worked sideways. She pushed aside the corpse under her body, no longer bothered to shelter it. He saw that the rain had diluted the little tributaries of blood that came from the rider's head wound. From the hours he had been with the pair of them, in the boy's bedroom, he might have known them better than any one else.

One was a would-be *jihadi* and one was a drug pusher, and he had no hostility to either, only differing degrees of affection. The boy was dead, killed by an expert marksman, and Zed . . .? She had started to crawl, like some pitiful insect that was damaged and tried only to get to cover.

Her head rose. He saw the bone. She might have been sixty paces from him. Still clung to the weapon and had dropped the taped together magazines that she could not load. The weapon was useless to her but she held it.

'Are you there, Andy, are you?'

He had no reply to make.

'Andy, where are you?'

Again he drew in his breath.

'I am a song bird, Andy, and have a broken wing.'

His lungs were brimful.

'But a broken wing does not kill a song bird. Andy, can you hear me?'

His elbow was tapped, the marksman's finger pointed. At the edge of the light cone the medical team in their high visibility clothing were edging forward and would have an escort in the shadows. He started, very slowly, to let the air hiss away between his teeth.

'They'll put me in a cage, Andy. No key. Please . . .'

He supposed it was owed . . . no such thing as a free lunch, the guys who did the corruption inquiries always said. He saw her coming off the medical evacuation flight and lifted down on a stretcher, and saw her propped up on crutches in the Central Criminal Court, and alongside her would be the goons who had used, manipulated, her. He saw a judge read out the sentence, big years, and do the same condemnation speech that had seemed suitable for the last time round, and would be as apposite for the next terror case he heard, and saw the manacles and the gates closing on her, and saw the bars on a high cell window. Heard the beat of the feathers, but not the song.

She moved slowly. Quite a simple shot for him. In the magnification of the sight he could see the blood smear on her face, where it had dried close to her left ear.

He murmured, 'Let's get this show on the road, Zed.'

Did it well, without snatching. Squeezed and felt the impact against the bone beside his shoulder. Saw her recoil from the impact. Nothing spectacular, not arms thrown up and no squeal, instead something that seemed more like a bullet going into a filled and wet sandbag. Not an heroic passing, but he thought it a decent way to finish their business. No fuss, no drama, and he passed the weapon sideways and it was taken from him. He did not have anything to say . . . the marksman cleared the weapon, and would have clicked the 'safety' into position. He wiped his eyes.

It could have been rainwater in them, or might not have been.

The spotlight was doused. For a few seconds the street was in darkness. Then the coordinated reaction. The street-lights came on. He thought it had been a good shot but twice she had moved, and finally there was a last convulsion . . . Done and over. The medical team were now coming forward, but they'd been given no worthwhile job to do. He stood. Did not know where to put his hands, so dug them deep down in his pockets.

The marksman pushed himself up, used the vehicle's fender to get better traction.

'What do you want to do now, go where?'

'I want to go home.'

'Where is home?'

'Sort of varied, gets to change, maybe it's just where there is a warm beer – and no girls that need killing.'

'Which is a version of "get the hell out", to anywhere?'

They drifted towards the shadows where the street-lights did not reach. His cheeks were wet, but it might have been because it was raining even harder.

On the balconies of the project's tower blocks, any vantage-point overlooking the Boulevard Henri Barnier from La Castellane came the rippling sound of voices, a wind that swept up the remnants of the autumn's dead leaves, in a whisper.

'It was Samson . . . I saw Samson . . . Samson shot the boy, Karym . . . saved his life one night, took his life on another, it was

Samson . . . Preserved him, then destroyed him . . . But there was another man who fired, was slow with it, did a mercy shot . . . Like a dog has been hit by a car, is finished off to end pain . . . Samson never showed "mercy" . . . perhaps the other man is out of love with his work. He was an agent and tracked that girl, but he killed her. Why? . . . It was a good show, as good as any we have had from Samson . . . I saw his face, the other man's face, the stranger's. Samson would not have . . . I think the stranger wept . . .'

Within minutes, ambulances had left with the two bodies, and the Ducati 821 Monster had been recovered and driven off on a flat-bed, and a scenes of crime team was at the point in the road where there were oil stains and spilled blood and they worked quickly, anxious to be finished and gone. Within minutes, the queue for buyers had started to shuffle forward and the entrance to the project was again in the hands of the *chouffes*, who patted them down and then directed them towards the different stairwells where the *charbonneurs* waited to sell to them and take their money. And, except for the tidying up of the dregs of the occasion, the life of La Castellane had returned to its own degree of normality.

Pegs asked, as they were ushered towards a car and told their destination was the airport, 'Did you see him, know where he went, was taken?'

Gough answered her, 'Not had sight nor sound of him.'

'We'll not see any more of him.'

'Not disagreeing. They get to a point, these rather sad individuals, where they're not up to taking any further punishment. Plenty was asked of him.'

'We'll get a bollocking for this, Gough, mark my words. In my water. They'll hang us out in the wind. Throw the book our way.'

'Do you think, Pegs, he went soft on her, or was that just part of the job? Which?'

They took their time in grabbing a last look at the scene, where the rain ran on the street and police hurried to clear away their major incident equipment, and Major Valery paused mid-stride to shake their hands but said nothing, and was gone.

She said, 'I'm not bleeding in a corner for him, Goughie, but I tell you the sad bit. You could say that he was burned out, was running on empty, would want to wash his hands of it all and get back to doing what "ordinary" people do, and knowing who he was. Except that it doesn't apply with the type suited for that work. They can't break the link . . . Don't fucking laugh at me, I mean it. I'm sad for him . . . they don't know another life. It's a man-trap on their ankle, teeth tight . . . As trapped as she was, and nowhere to go.'

They were ushered to a car, heard something about a flight having been delayed, the last of the evening, and they'd catch it.

An hour later . . . He'd asked it enough times. Crab had demanded to know when the plane would eventually take off. Could not wait to get clear. It was a full three-quarters of an hour since the aircraft had been boarded, but the steps were still in place. He saw a man and a woman brought to the base of the steps by a police vehicle, a brisk farewell, nothing to indicate fondness, and they scampered up the steps. Crab did not know them, not from Adam and not from Eve.

He saw a dowdily dressed man, with thin hair plastered down on the scalp, and the rain had been on his shoulders and his ankles were sodden and his shoes looked to have taken in water.

The woman, behind him, hustled him along the aisle. She was well built, had a strong and angular face, a hatchet jaw, and he thought there was an arrogance about her. Her clothing was similarly sodden and her hair was a mess: he wondered how such people, so obviously low in the chain of importance, could be responsible of keeping a plane on the apron all this time. He had a book of crosswords to tide him over, but had forgotten them, and then his seat shook as the woman held it as she lowered herself down behind Crab, and the man was in a seat across the aisle.

They were talking, fastening their belts, and the girl over the speaker system was apologising for the late take-off – as she bloody should. They had started to taxi.

Crab felt a tug at his shoulder.

He turned, irritation rife, would tell any stranger to keep his fucking hands to himself, and the woman's voice purred in his ear.

'Wanted to let you know, sir, that it might have been a mistake to give your name, rank and number – know what I mean – to the check-in. We've forwarded them on. North West Counter Terror Unit will enjoy matching them to records and locations. We take this sort of thing very seriously. Conspiracy to facilitate the importation of firearms, notably an AK-47 assault rifle is an offence that the courts seem to view in poor light. Any liaison with a *jihadi* group, people committed to murder and maim in a crowded place, would – I believe – carry with it a sentence of the utmost severity. I would have to assume that your only motive in this matter was to get your hands on "a nice little earner". You disgust me, sir, and you will disgust the judge who presides on your case. This flight will be met at Manchester. Enjoy your journey, sir, and you might consider calling a solicitor because you'll need one.'

The voice so quiet and so reasonable, died on him. He wondered, as his hands shook, how the girl had made out, pretty little thing, and with balls to her, and she'd run well when in flight. The aircraft lifted and started to bump through the low dense cloud.

A day later . . . They were summoned.

The marching orders were for them to attend Room 308, an inner sanctum, where the angels sang and incense burned. They had arrived at the flat they shared in the small hours, and Pegs had made a cup of tea and Gough had done a load for the washing machine including pretty much all they wore. Then Pegs had made a sandwich, and he'd heaped a pile by the door of all the stuff for the dry cleaners. They had come in late, too knackered to touch each other and had slept like noisy logs, and it might be the last time because the anticipated criticism was liable to be vicious, mostly undeserved, and brutal.

They were awaited. The guy who presided in that room – with his nail bomb scar to declaim his 'sharp end' experience – identified a man by the window. A Chief Superintendent, a God figure from the national HQ of Counter Terrorist Command, and there was a tall and willowy woman, no make-up and no jewellery who was from SC&O10. A silence hung. Always was a silence when a hanging was due, so they said. The wound was alive and he'd likely been scratching it. Three Zero Eight kicked off, delivered the verdict on Rag and Bone . . . Gough was not going to permit a critique lying on the carpet with his feet in the air, and Pegs promised to 'take no shit from them'. A cough and a throat cleared.

'We think it went well. We have a very clear understanding of a mission fraught with difficulty. It did not work out as our planning suggested it would, but that in no way lessens the benefits gained by the operation. You handled a difficult diplomatic *impasse* with skill and sensitivity, and are to be commended. Congratulations, very sincerely meant.'

Pegs had her head forward, as if her hearing was playing up, and Gough stayed inscrutable.

The Chief Superintendent said, 'We expect a considerable level of success, a large trawl and a network emasculated before getting clear of puberty. I believe them to have been a particularly focused and dangerous group, not least the woman at the heart of the smuggling concept. We add our congratulations to both of you, and for your control, in trying circumstances, minimum resources, of your Undercover. First class – and to be added to the list is the excellent cooperation you received from our French colleagues – pretty rare – and that is down to your winning ways. It was a damned good effort.'

The woman said, 'You don't need to know where he is – anything, in fact, about him. The French took him down to Toulon, he spent the night at the airport, had a flight in this morning. I saw him briefly, thought he looked rough. Don't know yet whether he'll call it a day. Plenty try to, few succeed. What I am pleased about is that a ring of dangerous young people, carrying huge burdens of hate will be negated . . . The thought of a flow of automatic assault rifles coming into the UK is too frightful to contemplate . . . It leaves our people scarred, damaged at the end, but that's the price that has to be paid, by them – by that boy – not by us.'

Did they want coffee – did not. Did they want to share anecdotes – again, did not.

Back in the office, within ten minutes, they'd their gear together and would go their separate ways, take a good furlough, might bump into each other again after Human Resources had done their worst with new postings, but might not.

A week later . . . Coordinated arrests were done efficiently and allowed for the two time zones.

At 04.00 Zulu, the sledge cracked open the door of Crab's mansion in the bacon belt area of Altrincham, while a line of unmarked cars and police vans, all with blue lights rotating, ostentatiously filled the tree-lined avenue. A good show put on for the neighbours and an effort to humiliate him, and he was taken out, handcuffed . . . Across the range of the Pennine moors a car was stopped and a man who went by the codename of Krait was spread-eagled on the road under cover of automatic weapons and then dragged away, and another – known as Scorpion – was intercepted on his way to a *poste restante* address . . . and in the capital city, two men were taken into custody – identified because of the tickets that had not been destroyed as the traveller had been instructed, and they indicated where the documents had been purchased, and by whom, for a journey between UK and Marseille.

And, at 05.00 European time, when a middle-ranking officer, a Major, led a team of specifically chosen detectives, up to the gates of a coastal villa, and used an armoured car to break them down, and an old man – who had once been a legend in the undercurrent life of organised crime in Marseille – was snatched from his bed. One photographer only, from *La Provence*, was present to record the arrest . . . Also visited that morning, in the apartments that seemed to belie the meagre pensions paid to former investigators, were men who had done well from association with Tooth, and it was a safe bet that they would soon be in an orderly queue to denounce everyone's actions, not their own, in the hope of leniency . . . And Hamid was taken, in bed with a girl, and no crowd had gathered to impede the police, and a brother due to be buried that day when he would be in the interview room, pleading surprise that a deal had not been honoured.

A terse message would be sent within an hour from the Major at L'Évêché to a senior officer working from an address in Wyvill Road, London, SW8: *Colleagues, A good day for us (and 'Samson' not needed and left in bed), and my appreciation of a fine association. Valery*. All considered satisfactory.

And a month later . . . The mourners were leaving. Not just family but the whole population of the road in which she had lived, and many who had been her contemporaries at school, and a few had journeyed from Manchester Metropolitan to attend. It was unfortunate but inevitable that the procedures for a funeral embodying that faith had been delayed. She should have been buried within a few hours of her death, but there had been many obstacles placed in the way of her parents' wishes. A French magistrate had not hurried, and details had remained vague as to the exact circumstances of death, and the British authorities had been slow to reveal what information they were in possession of . . . but arrests, and charges and initial appearances before magistrates, and trial dates set, had brought matters into the public domain. Bluntly, everyone in that street, in the community of Savile Town, had either seen with their own eyes, or knew of, the repeated visits by detectives of the North West Counter Terrorist Unit to the home address, and it was claimed her bedroom had been systematically ripped to pieces. Her father had said, repeatedly, that he refused to believe the allegations made against her, her mother had said that their only daughter was a 'dutiful and obedient girl, perfect in all ways'. When the body of Zeinab was prepared for burial, having been washed and then bound in white sheets, a shroud, they would have seen the single bullet entry wound, and the exit, in her chest and adjacent to her spine.

Plain clothes police were there, and peeping from behind a stone wall in the dawn gloom was a bright lens catching what light was there. The cemetery area, beyond the precincts of the crematorium, emptied.

A favour was asked of a detective constable, huddled in her overcoat, dying for the first fag of the day. The request was from behind her. She turned.

A single scarlet rose was given her, the petals close and tight. She was asked to take it and place it, and the question was on her tongue: who was he? She saw the gravedigger with his long-handled tool put the first load of earth back into the cavity, and swung on her heel, but he was already walking away and his stride had a purpose, an authority, and she thought his bearing made him one of their own. She did not call out after him, nor did he look back. She shrugged, then went forward.

At the grave, eyed by the workman, she placed the single bloom on the grass surround to the grave, and she wondered how it was that a *jihadi* gunrunner, dangerous and committed and shot dead, should be remembered in such a tender way by a man she thought could be a police officer.

February 2019

A technician said, 'I've never seen one as old as this, surprised it's not going to a museum. Look at it, Pierre, see the age of it. More than sixty years old, and still in working order – what a goddam history it would have to tell. How do I know that? The history? Look at the stock, those marks. I think it had many owners . . . but just a machine and due to be disposed of – and no tears wept . . . but if the story could have been told then its place in a museum case would be assured. Load it up.'

The machine was new, purchased from the United States, and the system was novel in the annexe to the Ballistics and Armoury division of the Marseille police. In the past it would have been done with an acetylene flame cutter, and before that the task of immobilising a firearm would have been consigned to Claude, a giant with muscles to match his bulk, and he would batter the body of a pistol or rifle to bent pulp with a sledgehammer. But the machine had been purchased and should be used. They put on their protective clothing and faceguards.

'What I just noticed, it's last run out was in close quarter fighting, short range. Look at the setting, that's Battle Sight Zero . . . It's an icon, know what I mean?'

There was a procedure almost as formal as that employed when the executioner came with his apparatus to the Baumettes gaol. A photograph was taken of the AK-47, and another of the serial number. The pulveriser was started up. It ground the remnants of its previous job between the blades, and spat them into a bin, and the cutting edges turned. It was to be treated with care and respect.

The machine's teeth snapped on it. The noise was a rasping wail. It had never ceased to astonish the technician and his assistant that a weapon in the process of being torn apart, its life expiring, always seemed to cry out as if in defiance, a last protest. And the pieces that had been manufactured many years before, and had been on many journeys, dropped as scrap into the bin. The parts would be photographed and what was left of the serial number – *260 16751* – for a bureaucratic record. No lingering, and more to follow and its lethal power destroyed.

And a year later . . . it was scheduled as an important meeting, but few in the building knew of it. Coffee and biscuits would be available. The room had been electronically swept before the small group, half a dozen men and women, had gathered there. The base used by that unit was inside the police station dealing with the district of Kirkby, out on the east side of the city of Liverpool. It had a busy car park because it shared with the fire brigade, and ambulance teams often parked up there; a quality location for a covert meeting and visitors came and went and the parking lot was secluded and hidden from the main road.

There was high anticipation.

The team were customers. They had needed to make a case, prove that their need was greater than other teams throughout the country. What the customers looked to achieve did not come cheap, was sought after, and they'd had to show a potential result that would affect the material good of the population at large if the prize was awarded to them. They had never met him. In fact knew little of him, except his name . . .

Their guest was a few minutes late, which annoyed.

They were all senior people and unused to being kept hanging around, expected subordinates to be punctual. All were key personnel in a team that had come together to target a local godfather whose empire prospered from coke, smack, hash and 'phets, and the efforts of east European girls who performed for fierce shifts. To infiltrate such an organisation was regarded as next to impossible for any officer with a background in the city and an accent to match, and offering a legend of childhood in Liverpool. The principals operated from inside a mosaic of links within extended blood and marriage lines. Efforts to recruit from the family, working off the periphery, had bounced back from an inevitable brick wall, a thick one topped with razor wire, even those who were compromised and faced long gaol terms. Truth was, the inner members of the clan exerted more fear and provided greater rewards than the team did, or could. So, they had gone with a begging bowl to London and been hosted by a woman called Prunella, who had given them scant respect, but had – a couple of months back – indicated a possible option.

Not for them to like or dislike.

Not for them to regard the guy as suitable or unsuitable.

And, not in their bailiwick, to suggest how proximity, and trust, from the target family, might be gained.

They did not know where he had been before, what his speciality was – knew fuck all, as the senior man, eyeing his watch, had said four times. But it was agreed there was a pattern with that style of work, and coming off a plot: say 'never again', say it was 'quit time', walk out and not get a medal, nor a gold clock, nor much in the way of thanks, and head off for 'nowhere', somewhere remote and over the horizon, where the big stresses were supposedly absent – and die of boredom, fail to adapt, and come back. What they all did – silly beggars. Safe to assume he'd be no novice. Safe also to assume that he knew of the inherent violence as practised by a typical crime syndicate, made into an art form by this crowd. Nor did they have a file on his previous deployments, successes or failures, nor had they been shown any of the psychologists' reports.

A knock on the door. Conversations died.

An assistant to the boss stood in the open door, pulled a face, let slip a little grin, then stepped aside.

The man was in overalls, with nearly fresh paint stains on them, and patches at the knees where he might have knelt in engine oil. His hair was reasonably neat, short but not clipped. He had shaved, but the day before. His work boots were scuffed. His eyes were clear, decisive, and did not spare any of them . . . It was as if tables were turned and roles reversed, and he checked them to see if they suited him. He had a quiet voice and they needed to strain to hear him. He started with an apology which none of them believed genuine.

'Hello, sorry to be late, traffic was a nightmare, and then parking here was difficult for what I'm driving . . .'

Several of them, a reflex and because they were supposed to react, were at the window and raising the blinds and would have seen a small delivery lorry, what a self-employed builder – 'no job too small' – might have used. A good-looking guy, and with a straightforwardness about him, and an apparent honesty.

'. . . Not that names are important to any of us. Good to be with you . . . for what it's worth, I'm Sam Peters – I think that's who I am. Anyway, learning to be Sam Peters.'

He was smiling. It took them a moment to respond, then all of them were laughing, but hollow, and wondering – puzzled – if there was an ignorance about him, and an innocence, as if he might not have appreciated the risk of going against a crime baron and his tribe. Or perhaps not, perhaps just lived a lie and did it well.